Marked
by
Instinct

To those who are waiting for Hope, remember—
Instinct is the most powerful magic a human can possess.

And Time listens.

Playlist

Check out the official soundtrack for Marked by Instinct!

Author's Note

Please note that this book contains explicit sexual scenes and language, so reader discretion is advised. A content warning is listed at the back of the book for those who want to check them before diving into the story.

PROLOGUE

"You left the front door open again, Hëna."

She looks up at the figure walking barefoot across the silver patio—small purple, blue, and pink flowers grow through the many cracks behind her footsteps. Golden hair is left in waves down her back, vines and flowers woven randomly in between. A light brown shawl is draped across her shoulders, the silk fabric covering most of the intricate design taking up the front of the low-drooping green garb.

Even after becoming a mother, she still hasn't changed. Same deep green eyes, her depths overgrown with love. Same small smile, her soft lips pulled only slightly at the edges in mirth that enhanced rosy cheeks.

She, too, once had rosy cheeks and love-filled eyes.

"Liridoña," Hëna says in greeting before gazing back down at the red-stained world below. Another one is dead. Shot clean through with a blue-tipped arrow. Her heart cracks, pieces thudding onto the cold ground beneath her covered feet in tandem with the cub's body. "I've heard whispers of your own ... strife. Should you not be dealing with your children?"

"Time is still young. He's learning, slow may it be." Liridoña rolls her eyes, waving her hand in the air before sitting beside her friend at the edge. Her gaze drifts to the world below while her bare feet drag across the small lip of dry soil separating the patio's edge from the drop of the floating castle. Small shoots of green roots slither in the wake of her feet's movement, the once dry soil slowly deepening in color as life is kneaded back into it. "And I'm not here to talk about me, my friend."

Hëna hums low in her throat. They have been friends since Creation, since long before they had their children. She knows firsthand that no one can make the Goddess of Nature do something she doesn't want to. If she has decided to leave her booming universe and come help this small one, then she will. Though ... Hëna doesn't know how.

The patio scrapes across her fingers where she grips it tightly. Blood trickles down the dirty silver concrete and onto the dead dirt below. Another stain. Something else to try and scrub clean.

She ignores it.

Does her old friend witness the same death that she does? Does her heart crack and burn the same each time one of her children's blood and disfigured pelt is left to seep, again, into the stained earth?

"Not very talkative today, I see." Liri spares a side glance at her friend, shoulders taut as she uses them to push forward over the edge—a meagre attempt to try and look upon Hëna's pale face.

"Well, I haven't been doing much talking lately." She watches as her husband walks to the young cub and places his hand over its heart. Its bright soul shoots toward the sky, nestling among the rest of the stars. He moves on to the next, his long black cape so deeply stained, the visible red transfers across the grass as he walks. She should be grateful that her friend's husband does not come for her cubs, that she can have them returned to the stars from whence they came. At least that way ... she can still see them.

Can still sit in her agony.

Her punishment.

"Hmm." Liridoña turns her head, looking about her. She wishes her friend wouldn't; she knows how shameful her palace looks right now. The vegetation—a gift from her friend when the castle was first built, risen from the world below—is all dried up, the flowers long buried in the soil. Darkness lines the silver stone, the usual shine always competing with the stars around them, nowhere to be seen. Cracks line the patio and tall pillars, new ones appearing with each sun pass. The curtains are dusted; the gray rubble covers nearly all the furniture. The food has spoiled. The water has dried. Her husband does his best when he is home ... but he is far busier than she is.

No. The shame of this graveyard is Hers and Hers alone.

"You really shouldn't keep the door open like that. What if one of those monsters we were warned against as young Goddesses comes in and kidnaps you?" Liridoña tries to gaze upon her friend once more, bumping their shoulders together. The words are meant to soothe. A jest, followed by a billowed laugh.

Hëna does not hear it that way.

"Then maybe this world will have peace," she whispers, gazing away from the battle. It is over now. The last of the cubs ran deep into the forest to hide. The Others didn't give chase. They were never meant to use the forest to hide, to use their powerful legs to run away in *fear*. This was meant to be a sanctuary—a place for her cubs, her wolves, to have peace and freedom. To run as fast as they could in *joy*.

But an unforeseen change in the creation of one wolf was born. A cub without any wolf instinct in its design. That cub grew and bred, and then its cubs bred and bred and bred and bred ... This new design carried down the line. Faithfully.

Like a blessing.

She didn't intervene. She thought it would be fine.

It wasn't.

Greed replaced the missing instinct. Fear and jealousy took over the new species like a weed.

Like a curse.

Her hope that this new species could live side-by-side with her cubs was very quickly shot through with a blue-tipped arrow.

Any other God would give up. The warring species will all kill themselves anyway. Best to start fresh. Create from the ashes.

Or not create anything at all.

Liridoña reaches out and grabs her hand, face downcast in pity. "Na—"

A sound cuts through the breeze, and they both freeze. Hëna stands, body rocking from the sudden movement after sitting for so long. Neither of them speak. She holds her breath. She knows that sound. She remembers it. Oh, how long it has been.

The impossibility of it slithers through her body, yet a new sensation chases it. This one is green and bright, a startling contrast to the cold, dark despair she has been living in. This one ... she had forgotten it existed. The name of it is on the tip of her tongue ...

Movement beside her overrides her senses, and she turns toward it. Liri is standing now too, her eyes focused like small almonds.

There.

The sound rings out again. It's deep, but warm. Like soil that has been warmed by the sun all day long.

Hëna runs across the lip. Her long dress gets caught underneath her feet and she sways, one hand reaching for the edge of the patio to steady herself while her feet continue onward, trying not to break her stride. Her heart leaps into her throat, her body tensing, twisting to brace for the inevitable impact of the world far below. But she needn't worry. A warm palm settles on her back as soft fingers grip her bicep, steadying her on the lip. Liridoña is beside her, lips pulled thin, and eyes now set firm.

She knows Liri feels it too—the charge in the air.

Something is happening.

Something her magic is reaching for.

It crawls underneath her skin, ricocheting across her heart. Pounding like a drum during a grand feast. Liri nods forward, and they run toward the northern side of the patio, her long hair tangling even more behind her. The light of the moon in the star-filled sky is brightest here. The silver concrete more intact. The patches of grass not as dead as the rest of the once colorful yard. She takes it as a sign. A good omen.

Hope.

She licks her cracked lips, the tangy taste of blood coating her tongue.

She ignores it.

Her chest heaves as her head whips down. Her legs shake, body barely standing upright.

She ignores that, too.

Her wide eyes narrow, focusing on where the sound came from. There, beneath a tree. Two reside, hidden amongst the billowing branches. One is a male cub. He bears the mark of Heir. And the other male ... he's one of the Others. Their arms are wrapped around each other, armor forgotten amongst the grass beside them. Foreheads touching. Eyes gazing.

Laughing.

The sound reaches them. Hëna sucks in a shuddering breath, and Liridoña wraps an arm around her waist, letting her head drop onto Hëna's shoulder.

It was laughter. That harmonious sound—deep and warm and unrestrained.

Her eyes scan the surroundings, locking on a metal crown hanging low on a branch of the tree. It looks like a knight standing guard over their tossed aside weapons. No blood drips down them. No blue can be seen.

No hatred.

Only ...

"Liri, my friend," she says. It has been ages since she heard her voice sound so steady. So determined. She reaches for Liridoña's hand draped across her hip, squeezing it tightly between her trembling fingers. Her heart settles. It beats with warmth once more in rhythm to the love now spilling like tears from her eyes.

Perhaps she does not have to live in a grave any longer. Perhaps Time has finally learned his lesson, gracing her with a blessing of his own.

Perhaps ... there is still hope for her dream of this universe to succeed.

"I believe there is something I must do."

ONE

"Just one more s—"

"No."

"Come on, Fletcher!"

"No, Layla, the whole point is to get drunk at the party, not before." Fletcher places the half-empty bottle on the floor in front of him. Layla huffs, leaning back and crossing her arms over her chest, turning to look out the open car window. As soon as they left Fletcher's house, she grabbed one of the bottles of whiskey they had stolen from the wine cellar and started drinking. Her argument—it's always more fun turning up to a party already a little buzzed.

"We're almost there," Erin says, pushing some of the loose black hair off his forehead and keeping his eyes alert as he speeds over the hill.

The sound of upbeat, remixed pop music grows louder through the open car window as they approach the old cotton factory at the bottom; loud laughter and off-tune singing begin to filter through more noticeably. Multi-colored lights from inside Donny's Warehouse, mixed with light fixtures around the outside, transform the night sky into a rainbow. It makes the whole place feel like one is stepping into a magical land, not a half-renovated factory at the bottom of a hill in a little off-the-map Texan town.

"We might have to walk a bit." Any space Erin sees not occupied by a car is filled with either people or piles of empty beer bottles. Some of them have both. It isn't a surprise—people talk, and social media works quickly. One viral video, a café catch-up with friends from different towns, and boom, Donny's 'secret' is out. Over the past few summers, people from neighboring towns have started driving over to participate in Black Hill's little start-of-summer tradition.

"Dibs not carrying Layla." Fletcher smirks. "She won't make it far in those mile-high heels."

Layla reaches over the back of the seat and slaps Fletcher with her long, blonde ponytail. "At least some of us dress up for a night out instead of jorts and a muscle tee with raggedy sneakers."

"It's called comfort, my dear," Fletcher replies before pointing to Erin beside him. "Erin is wearing the same thing."

"Pretty sure *clean* cowboy boots with a *stylish* pair of blue jeans and a *cool* graphic tee are not the same thing."

"Why do you keep drawing out your words?" Fletcher asks, brown brows raised as he turns around to face Layla. "I am very *clean*, and *stylish*, and *cool*. It was me who taught Erin about fashion back in high school."

"That's not how I remember it," Layla mutters.

"Hey, don't get me involved." Erin finds a spot near the dense forest edge, in between two massive Ford trucks. A perfect hiding spot for his little white hatchback; no need to worry about drunk college students stumbling about and breaking his side mirror. He turns around in his seat and unbuckles. "Besides, I'm pretty sure I was the one who taught you about fashion, Fletch. You've never cared about style unless it had a sportswear label attached to it."

"Dude," Fletcher whispers. He has one hand on the door handle, the other over his mouth, covering his small pout. "Rude. Next time you want to impress the hot lifeguard by the community pool, don't come asking me for Speedos."

"You're the lifeguard for the community pool," Erin deadpans.

"Aw, thanks, Erin! I knew I was smoking, but hearing it from you warms my heart." Fletcher blows a kiss to Erin. "It would never work between us, though, my dear friend. The male appendage is not something I find—"

Layla groans as she opens the car door. "Just thinking about all the apologies I'm going to have to make to your future girlfriend is giving me a headache."

"You sure that's not the whiskey?" Fletcher teases, offering his hand to her and helping her out of the car. She loops her arm through his, sticking her tongue out before reaching back to grab her purse. When Erin rounds the car, she takes his arm too, and together the three of them begin the trek across the dry, crunchy grass.

There are others around, walking toward the warehouse with bottles of alcohol swinging in their hands; Layla's 'on the road' idea seems to have been shared. Everyone is dressed similarly to them, too. Growing up in the humid summer air, one learns to adapt style to temperature. It may not be a fancy nightclub like the ones in big cities, but they were a small town. It was the best they were going to get, even with all the newcomers coming to celebrate. They all knew that.

Except for him.

Erin spots him as soon as they enter the warehouse. It'd be hard for anyone not to; he's all alone, dressed differently from everyone else. It's like he's a deep red wine stain on a white carpet. He's leaning against the back wall in a corner, directly opposite the door, away from the mass of sweaty bodies. Erin's brows pinch tightly. Who comes to a nightclub party alone? A look of boredom masks the man's face, his lone wolf persona strengthened by crossed arms and closed eyes.

Eyes that snap open and lock onto Erin.

They're beautiful, like twin moons reflected in ocean water. Erin feels no sense of shame in being caught openly staring. Instead, something inside him begins to burn. It starts deep in the very pit of his stomach, before spreading up his throat and across his limbs. His heart shudders, and he holds his breath. There's a burn behind his eyes, forcing his throat to close in tandem. The feeling is almost ... nostalgic, mixed with intense desire and longing that is very quickly coursing its way throughout his whole body like a wild jackrabbit. He's seen plenty of good-looking men before, but this ...

He can't look away.

He doesn't want to look away.

The man pushes himself off the wall, arms hanging loosely by his side. His features twist into something sour. Slack lips slam shut, pulling down harshly as a straight nose curls upwards. Shock, into ... disgust?

Erin's heart drops.

He doesn't know this man—he's not from Black Hill nor has he ever been to one of Donny's parties. Erin's been coming since the summer before his last year of high school, four years ago. He'd remember seeing a man as good-looking as that, especially one who looked at him like he was a poison to society.

"I'm going to get some snacks," Layla yells, grabbing their hands as she leans in. "Matt is working the bar. I'll meet you at the spot?"

Erin flinches, tearing his eyes from the mysterious man to Layla.

"Ok," Fletcher yells back, oblivious to Erin's internal strife. "Don't forget the Skittles this time!"

Layla rolls her eyes. She reaches into her purse, taking out her credit card before handing her bag over to Erin. He slings it over his shoulder, nodding, before looking back over to the wall. The man is still there, staring with that complicated look of sour awe and confusion.

"You ok, man?" Fletcher asks, leaning in and raising his voice slightly to be heard over the music. The loud beat travels up their legs, already turning them into loose jelly.

Erin glances toward Fletcher. "Yeah, yeah, all good. Just ... uh ... silk. That guy in our favorite corner is wearing a silk top. Maroon, I think, with dress shoes and jeans. Thought it was a bit different from what people normally wear to these things, you know. Way too fancy. And in this heat? It caught my eye."

Fletcher looks toward the man before looking back at Erin, eyebrows raised. There's a brief silence before he sighs. "Man, do I envy your 20/20 vision, especially with how dark it is in here. Where can I get some golden night-vision eyes from?"

"Hazel, not gold." Erin laughs awkwardly, clapping his hand on Fletcher's back. "And I ate lots of carrots growing up, dude."

"Uh-huh," Fletcher huffs. "Well, considering he's standing in our spot, we best go over and introduce ourselves. Make sure he's not some weird serial killer."

"The way your mind works," Erin laughs.

They weave through the crowd, and Erin's forced to scrunch his nose as the smell of sweat and too many strong perfumes and colognes assault his senses. Thankfully, no matter how full Donny's Warehouse gets, the back steps always tend to remain secluded. Not many people like the old rusty feel of iron steps and wooden cotton barrels, preferring instead the newly renovated black tables with multi-colored cushioned chairs, strobe lights, and glittery stools underneath the cold blue metal bar. It's a blessing in disguise.

Tradition be damned, Erin doubts he'd come back at the start of each summer if that wasn't the case.

However, there's a new scent that stands out among the rest, one Erin has never smelled before. A rich scent that's a mix of old leather and spicy sandalwood. It's a nice combination, one that simultaneously heats his insides and relaxes his limbs. The closer they get to the back steps, the stronger the smell becomes. It must be coming from the mystery newcomer.

Who is still gazing at him.

Erin feels that piercing gaze follow his every step. Somehow, he knows those pale moon eyes never left his face. When they reach their spot, Erin quickly looks the man over. He's taller up close, at least half a head taller than Erin, which must make him at least 6'3". His long legs are covered in fitted black jeans, and his arms are bare besides a silver watch on his right wrist and an antique jeweled ring on his left index finger. The strobe lights make his hair color impossible to discern, but it looks like a dark blonde, slicked back with a fancy side part. And his eyes. Erin sucks in a breath. They're even more piercing up close. He knows those eyes would glow even in the darkest of nights.

"Nice ring." Erin winces internally. Way to start a conversation with a handsome stranger at a secluded section of a crowded midnight party.

"Family heirloom," the man replies. He looks like he's hardly breathing, fingers twitching wildly against his thigh.

"From Black Hill?" Fletcher jumps in, always Erin's savior. "I don't think I've seen you around before."

"Um, no. No. I'm from New York. Bellmore, specifically." The man glances at Fletcher before sliding his eyes to Erin again.

Erin can't tell if the noise in his ears is the loud music or if his heart is about to explode from the intense attention, which is weird. Men have stared at him many times before—he's no stranger to sexual attention—but never with such a complicated look. So then why does this stranger feel ... different? It's like this guy can't decide if he wants to pummel him or fuck him.

He clears his throat and looks toward the bar. Layla is leaning halfway over the metal bar top, her hand raised to cover her lips as she whispers into Matt's ear. Even with his hands full mixing drinks, Matt's cheeky grin is on full display. Whatever it is Layla is promising she'll do for him, Erin only hopes that it is a promise for much later in the night. He really needs a drink.

And maybe those Skittles would do wonders to sweeten this man's sour pout.

Fletcher whistles, brown eyes blown wide. "New York! Long way from home then." He raises his hand. "I'm Fletcher, and this is Erin."

"I'm Victor." The breeze from the ceiling fans makes some of his hair sway as he reaches over and shakes the offered hand. It looks as soft as honey. It also causes his nice cologne to rush over the space. Erin shivers.

He raises his hand toward Victor for a handshake, readjusting Layla's bag on his shoulder. Was the metal chain always this cold? "Nice to meet you, Victor. Welcome to Black Hill."

"Thanks. I haven't seen much of the town yet, but I've always loved the country. I'm sure I'll love it here too." Victor's lips twitch at the sides, his small smile looking more like a grimace before he coughs into his shoulder. "Sorry, so many smells in here," he chuckles, shaking Erin's hand. His palm is warm, slotting into Erin's hand perfectly; a shiver runs like electricity down his spine.

Time stops.

Erin watches as Victor's eyes widen. His breath hitches, lips parting in wonder before curving into a ghost of a smile.

And then, it's gone.

Time resumes.

Victor hardens his gaze and yanks his hand away, long fingers closing into tight fists by his side. He clears his throat and smiles, the corners pinched tight. Erin returns the sentiment as embarrassment crawls up his neck, eyes sliding to Fletcher. What the hell was that? Surely Fletch would have seen ... whatever that was, too?

But Fletcher is smirking, looking between them.

Oh no.

"Well, I'm going to go see what's taking Layla so long getting those Skittles, and get us some Full Moons while I'm at it. I'll be back." Fletcher claps Erin on the shoulder, winking as he leaves. Damn him.

"Full Moons?" Victor tilts his head to the side.

It's cute, like a puppy. Erin licks his lips, stifling a laugh. "I don't know what's in it, but the foam on the top with the dark blue lacquer looks like a full moon in the night sky. We always have a round to start the night, have been ever since we first started coming here."

"Ah." Victor has a gleam in his eyes, like he heard the world's funniest joke that only he understands. "You make it sound like you've been coming here for a while, but you don't look much older than twenty-one."

"I grew up in a small town." Erin shrugs one shoulder. "You tend to get away with a lot more when everyone has your parents' phone number on speed dial. Plus, I have a good reputation."

"Interesting." Victor's nose twitches and his eyes narrow as he leans back against the wall, putting some distance between them. "Are your parents cops then?"

"Is there anything else you find interesting?" Erin asks boldly, ignoring his question and looking straight into Victor's eyes. Searching. That electric feeling finally settles in his stomach, Victor's cologne spreading between them pleasantly. Why does it feel so natural? Feeling drawn to this man and looking into his eyes ... it's like a habit or déjà vu. He doesn't know Victor—doesn't know if he's gay or straight, or if he's interested romantically in people at all—and yet somehow, he knows Victor will respond to his goading. Erin's always been good at spotting flirts in a crowd; hell, he can practically smell it oozing off them. And now, with Victor, his face may look sour and quizzical, but his eyes and scent ... those are sweet.

"Just one thing," Victor responds, voice low. He smiles like a rogue wolf, and Erin's insides light on fire. The distance between them is giving Erin a chance to breathe, and he turns his head to look out at the mass of bodies mere feet from their sheltered corner, the heat rising to his cheeks a clear indication of the effect Victor is having on him. Yet, he can't find it in him to care. When Victor looks at him, it's like he's seeing something more, something deeper.

Something even Erin can't see himself.

It's a bit overwhelming, but Erin doesn't want him to stop. He's enjoying the attention and the way his heart squeezes every time he gets a whiff of that addictive scent.

Maybe the fumes from Layla drinking in the car rubbed off on him. He should've had the window open sooner.

A snickering couple stumbles past them, and Erin takes a step back to avoid the alcohol falling out of the woman's glass. His hands instinctively grab the bag slung over his shoulder to stop it from swinging. Good on them for finding a dark corner to grope each other and make out, but he's not about to pay to get that pink stuff scrubbed off Layla's blue leath—

"Erin." Victor tilts his head, lips twitching as they graze the shell of Erin's ear. Warmth hits his neck, his back, behind his knees. Victor isn't touching him—not physically, his hands still clenched tightly by his side—and yet, Erin's soul is on fire. "You didn't answer my question," he whispers.

"Three Full Moons at your service!" Fletcher places a black tray onto one of the cotton barrels turned tabletop, three packets of colorful Skittles rolling between them. Erin quickly steps away from Victor and grabs one of the glasses.

"Where's Lay?" He clears his throat, swatting at the hair sticking to his forehead before tapping his fingers on the sides of his glass sporadically.

"I did see a blonde ponytail tangled with a panting curly black-haired dog by the 'staff only' door, who I'm assuming was Matt and not an actual dog, obviously." Fletcher holds out the remaining glass to Victor, grin wide on his face. "Bottoms up!"

"Of course." Erin rolls his eyes, and they clink glasses. Fletcher starts chugging straight away. Erin brings the curve of the glass to his mouth, the cool liquid swimming against his lips when he catches Victor's wary eyes. He lowers the glass to his chin and taps the table to get Victor's attention. "Chug it," he mouths around a smirk.

Victor raises a brow but brings the drink to his lips anyway, tipping his head back as he quickly swallows. Erin follows suit, the liquid burning down his throat. He loses to Victor by one gulp.

"Wow, you can certainly hold your alcohol." Fletcher burps and wipes his mouth with the back of his hand, laughing as he places his empty glass back onto the barrel next to them. "You'll give Erin a run for his money."

"Oh?" Victor also places his glass on the barrel, taking Erin's from his hand to do the same. Their fingers almost touch. "You a heavy drinker, Erin?"

"No, no. I just don't get drunk easily." Erin shrugs, shoving his hands into the back pockets of his blue jeans. "Fast metabolism, you know?"

"More like lucky genetics." Fletcher points a thumb at his friend. "Erin's always been top of the class on the physicality rope. He even keeps up with me in the pool, and I've been swimming since before I could walk."

"Oh? A wolf who can swim, then." Victor laughs. The sound is deep, rich, like his voice. It suits him.

"What are you on about?" Erin chuckles, ignoring the butterflies swarming in his gut. Victor juts his chin toward Erin's shirt, a smirk pulling one side of his mouth. Erin follows his gaze and makes sense of the joke. Laughing, his hand comes up reflexively to tap the graphic abstract image of a wolf across his chest. "Well, aren't you funny." He shakes his head, punching Victor's bicep softly.

Victor flinches, a soft wince slipping past his lips.

"Oh, sorry. I—"

"No, old bruise. Not your fault." Victor smiles. "You like wolves then?" he asks, leaning forward and resting his elbows on an empty barrel ... three whole steps away from Erin.

Erin forces his face not to pout and shrugs. "This was a gift from my dad, and I thought it looked cool."

"Please, that's an understatement," Fletcher scoffs, stepping back to take a seat on the steps so he's now eye level with them, nudging Erin's boot as he does. "According to Layla, it's more than *cool*."

"Fashion aside, for the record, I could never actually beat you at swimming. You've been training in that sport as an athlete. It's not all genetics."

Fletcher laughs, raising a hand to salute Erin. But Victor's smile turns downward, the same sour look from earlier twisting his face again. Before he can say anything else, a loud whistle tears through the room, and Erin turns. Between the ocean of bodies, he sees a man waving his hand over his head, gesturing toward them. He's dressed like Victor—fancy fitted jeans and a plain black silk top—with reddish hair and eyes that glow a deep green.

"Wow, that was some whistle," Erin mumbles.

Victor snaps his head to Erin. A deep line appears between his brows as shock contorts his face. "You heard that?"

"Heard what?" Fletcher cups his hands behind his ears to try and echo the sound better.

"Never mind." Victor shakes his head. "My cousin is calling me. I was waiting for him, but he's run exceptionally late. I should go figure out why. Nice to meet you all. Erin." Victor nods as he walks away.

Erin stares after him. Why does he feel so disappointed? Sure, Victor is hot, and he knows with a body like that, the sex would've been mind-blowing. But it's more than that ... this feeling running through his veins. His heart is heavy, a sensation that makes him want to cry. Regret burns along his throat with words unspoken. But ... what words? He's a stranger, so why are his emotions so out of control?

"Dude, what did you hear?" The steps screech as Fletcher shifts, lowering his hands to rest on his knees.

"A whistle," Erin responds.

Victor is talking with his cousin, distress perfectly clear in the hard lines of his face as he waves his arm toward them in the corner. The cousin looks over Victor's shoulder as he continues to speak. His round eyes twitch. It was small, but Erin caught it. The slight widening of his eyes. The way his chest froze, as if his breath stuttered. His nostrils flare, and he frowns, turning to Victor. His lips move rapidly as he speaks; there's no sense of awe hidden behind his forest eyes. Victor flinches in response to whatever is being said, head bowing and fingers clenching so tightly into fists that veins pop along his forearm.

Erin's jaw clenches in tandem with his heart. He can't see Victor's profile anymore, but the tight anger clinging to his broad shoulders speak loud enough.

"Well, they are from New York," Fletcher states. "They probably learned how to taxi-cab whistle before they could say mama."

"Who's from apple town?" Layla asks. She has more drinks on a tray Matt's carrying behind her. Fletcher leans down and takes one, tapping it twice on the barrel before chugging it.

"Nothing." Erin finally looks away from the direction Victor went. He forces a smile with a shake of his head. "Lovely to see you again, Matt. Nice lipstick, really brings out the brown in your eyes."

"Hey," Matt smirks, nodding in greeting. "I'll leave this here. Catch y'all later."

Layla blows him a kiss as he walks away. Erin holds out her bag, which she takes with a quick thanks.

"Erin was trying to bag a hottie from apple town," Fletcher exhales, placing his finished glass on the step below him.

"I wasn't trying to bag him ... ok, maybe just a little. But it wasn't just like that."

"Then what was it like?"

"I ... I don't know."

"Well," Layla drawls, "did you get his number?"

"No." Erin turns back toward Victor, only to find him already looking his way. He's still standing next to his cousin, hands clenched tight by his sides, and his face has twisted once more. Erin doesn't know what to think about him. He looks like he wants to leave, but he hasn't. "No ... I didn't."

"I can't leave you two alone for five minutes." She sighs, taking a sip of Erin's drink before licking her lips. "Ok. Point him out to me, I'll get it for you."

"Wa—"

"Well, if it isn't the Texas Stooges!"

Erin tenses as two strong arms wrap around his shoulders from behind. His hands reach up reflexively to half-hug him back. "Greg, hey. How've you been?"

"Good, good." Greg looks around, nodding to Layla and Fletcher. "Long time no see, team."

Fletcher stands, his hands crossing over his chest. He looks to Layla, whose eyes have darkened from their usual bright blue into deep ocean black.

Shit.

Erin chuckles. "Yeah, last year was crazy. I hardly saw you around campus."

"Please, because taking photos of flowers and sunsets is hard." Greg barks a laugh as he steps back, keeping one arm slung around Erin's shoulders while the other slides thick fingers through oily blonde hair. Layla pinches her lips into a smile, throwing her bag onto the wooden barrel acting as a table for their empty glasses ... right onto a navy-blue stain of ... something that wasn't there before. And Fletcher's no longer smiling.

Double shit.

"Well, you know how it is." Erin turns around, placing his hand on Greg's chest and tapping gently, smiling sweetly up at him. "Not all of us can get into biophysics." The last thing they need is to be involved in a brawl and be forced to do community service when the summer has just started. There's no way in hell his last summer before finishing university is going to be spent in those ugly vests picking up trash off the highway toward the main city center.

Greg smirks, and his squinty blue eyes darken. "And I've never thought less of you for it, baby." He lifts his free hand to Erin's ass, squeezing it gently. Erin forces his grimace into a smirk. The memories of why he dumped Greg's muscle headed ass surfacing like the bile hitting the back of his throat. His heart burns, and not in the same way Victor made it feel only moments before.

Oh, God. Victor. If he's watching all of this ...

"Greg." Erin reaches behind to grab the hand off his ass. "It was so good to see you again, but I'm afraid—"

"Oh, come on, Erin, the night's still young." Greg wraps his arms around Erin completely now, caging him against the barrel. Burnt oil and deli meat drift around them, and Erin clenches his throat to suppress a gag. If he knew how clingy this buffoon was, he never would've slept with him in the first place last year. How did he manage a whole semester dating this guy?

"Greg, you know how tradition works." Fletcher steps forward and grips Greg's shoulder, yanking him back so he's forced to release Erin. "First night at Donny's is Stooges night."

Layla takes the empty place Greg once stood, wrapping her arms around Erin's midsection from beside him. Erin gulps her perfume, letting it slide over him. Wild peony and vanilla—the same fragrance she's worn since they met back in middle school. The year was coming to an end; she had just turned thirteen back in March, while he and Fletcher were already fourteen in the grade above. He remembers how striking the scent was back then, unlike anything he'd smelled before. Especially when he was surrounded by Fletcher's grassy chlorine smell nearly every day. He told her as much, and she hasn't changed perfumes since. It was comforting back then, to smell something so sweet and calming.

Just as it is now.

Greg's narrowed eyes travel from Fletcher's grip to his dark eyes. To his credit, Fletcher doesn't flinch at his hard glare. He keeps his sardonic smirk exactly where it is, posture as loose and friendly as ever. Greg rolls his eyes and shoves Fletcher's hand off him. "Whatever," he mumbles. Huffing, he smooths down his white t-shirt and walks away.

Erin sighs, eyes trailing his path through the dense crowd. It's gotten even more packed since they've been here. Donny's going to have to expand the warehouse at this rate, if that's even possible.

"What a dick," Fletcher sneers, lips curling as he plops back onto the steps. "Yo, Layla, where's your dog scampered off to? I need another drink after that."

"Shut up, Fletcher." She drops her head onto Erin's shoulder. "While I'm glad you dumped him, I wish you never got involved with that prick at all," she whispers, knowing perfectly well Erin can hear her over the music. "Maybe we can get a restraining order against him. That groping was basically harassment in a public place."

Erin hums, watching Greg stumble through the crowd, small eyes roaming for his next victim. He sighs, ready to turn and put the whole fiasco behind him, when bright blue eyes catch his attention.

Victor.

His jaw is clenched, eyes pulled taut. He looks furious. His cousin is holding onto his arm. Like he's trying to hold him back. From what? Coming over to Erin? That would mean he did see the whole thing ... even with how dark it is in here. He was still watching Erin. But if that was the case, there would be nothing to be mad about. From anyone looking in, the whole interaction looked like an old friend saying hi and getting a little too handsy. The only way he would know how uncomfortable Greg made him feel was if he heard the conversation. But ... that's not possible. Not from that far away.

A taxi-cab whistle is one thing, but a whole conversation?

"Erin?" Layla moves her head closer to his ear. "What do you think? Starting off the summer like that? Good omen or bad?"

Erin shakes his head, brows pinched. His thoughts?

"I ..."

"I vote bad omen," Fletcher interrupts, raising his hand, scowl still tight on his lips. Layla ignores him, her face focused solely on Erin. He hates the concern he finds there, because she needn't be. None of them needs to be.

He turns from Victor. God, he's acting like some high-school girl who got turned down by her first crush. Time to snap out of it. Fletcher was right. Tradition is tradition, and night one of summer is always spent with his small pack of friends.

"I vote no omen. Shit like that doesn't exist." He taps Layla on the chin lightly, and she gives him a soft smile. "It was simply an ex being drunk and getting handsy. Nothing I couldn't handle. And it'll probably happen again, truth be known. But it's a good thing I'm a strong man."

"Yeah, yeah," Layla scoffs, patting the biceps he's flexing. "You aren't that strong, your mom just taught you how to fight by hitting someone's pressure points."

"Tomato, potato." Erin shrugs. "Let's not let it ruin the last summer we all have together. I have a great feeling it's going to be a good one."

TWO

E rin hears rain bouncing off the roof. It's dark outside, thunder chasing lightning across the sky. He's lying in bed on his back, staring at the clock above the door in front of him, watching the little red arrows dance in a circle controlled by time.

He turns, lying on his left side. The wind howls, rattling the window frame like it wants to climb straight in. Rain pelts against the glass. He can't see where the drops land.

He glances at the clock again.

It's still dancing.

Erin pushes the covers aside and gets up. Barefoot, he walks to the door. His toes twitch when he steps off the fluffy white rug beside his bed and onto the cold floorboard.

He carefully opens the door inward with his right hand, grimacing as the strong wind hits his face. The door is yanked open completely. His eyes narrow, arms rising instinctively to cover his face from the rain clawing at his skin. The smell of ozone coats the air like a thick fog. It's hard to breathe.

There's a sliver of dense grass in front of him, separating him from the lake of blood and forest beyond. Erin's stomach churns.

The wind howls.

The rain claws.

He spies a creature sitting near the edge of the forest with its back to him, curled into a ball. The creature's white coat stands out like a lighthouse against the darkness of the forest. Erin's brow twitches. He leans forward, head ducking to see the creature better. It's completely soaked—the cold rain must feel like whips on its back.

Lightning strikes the ground.

Erin takes a step forward, his toes squishing into the flooded grass.

The creature turns, facing Erin. Wet earth rushes up his nose, the scent chased by a sweetness he knows. That smell ... What was it again?

Thunder claps across the sky.

The clock stops dancing.

Erin gasps as he jolts up in bed, sweat making his pajamas stick to his skin. His eyes dart around the room, head following suit. Rubbing his tired eyes, he throws the covers off and swings his legs over the side of the bed. The floor is warm, and the hint of sunlight streaming in between the blinds cast his room in a warm glow.

There are no white wolves.

He looks over to the clock above the door in front of him. 10 a.m. Quickly, he runs to the door and flings it open. White walls decorated with wood-framed family photos and childhood art projects line the hallway. The bathroom door on the right is open, a sliver of the yellow painted wall peeking through, as is his parents' room further down to the left. Their bed has been made already, the white comforter stark against the black pillowcases and silk sheets pulled back. Staring at him.

They look nothing like golden eyes.

No storm rages from under the closed linen closet to his right.

There is no lake of blood pooling in the hallway.

There is no white wolf.

Erin groans, the imprint of glowing golden eyes seared into his mind as he shuffles, leaning heavily against the doorframe.

"Erin?" a voice calls from downstairs. His mother. "Are you up? Why are you running around? Your dad made pancakes. Come and eat!"

He sighs heavily and runs both hands down his face and neck, pressing firmly against his collarbone. Grounding himself, he finally registers the smell of maple syrup and cooked batter wafting up the stairs. Spice and vanilla swim alongside it; his mother must have lit a candle already. Sweat clings to his fingers from his neck, and he wipes the remaining moisture onto his sweatpants. He needs a shower. And to find a dream interpretation journal because—

"What the hell was that?"

THREE

"Wolves equal aggression," Layla reads off her phone. She's sitting across from Erin at the corner booth in Café Terra, munching on some fries. Her early morning shift ended fifteen minutes ago, and Erin wasted no time in telling Layla about the weird dreams he'd been having for the past week.

Erin sighs, sticking more fries into his mouth. He licks the salt from the corner of his lips, watching as Layla absentmindedly picks at the coffee grains stuck underneath her nails, her eyes glued to her phone as she reads more nonsense. He should've waited for Fletch to arrive before saying anything. Glancing at the clock above the wooden counter, still damp from being recently wiped, his heart spikes. 12 p.m. Twenty minutes late. Fletch is many things, but he's never late. Plus, his new apartment is within walking distance of campus.

He should have been here by now.

Erin takes a sip of his iced soda. The cool liquid does little to soothe his growing worry.

"Oh, come on, dude. A dream about a giant wolf with glowing gold eyes sitting in the middle of a raging storm? That's so basic." Layla finally drops her phone onto the table and rests her cheeks on her hands to create a more dramatic pout with her red-painted lips. "When you said, 'weird dreams', I thought you meant getting turned into an alien and being fucked under a waterfall or something."

Erin stares at her, frozen, a fry halfway to his mouth as he processes what she just said. All worry surrounding the whereabouts of their late friend now gone. Sometimes, he simply does not get what goes on in her brain. He supposes that's what makes her photography great, though—capturing the weird moments in life, seeing the same image from a different perspective. It makes him very proud to be in the same degree as her.

Even if she does know exactly how to get under his skin.

"They weren't gold." Erin finally composes himself, continuing to eat his fries. The excessive amount of salt is beginning to make his throat dry; not even the ketchup swirled around the edge of the bowl is helping. "They were hazel, like mine, which is why it's weird. Was I imagining myself as a wolf or something?"

"Erin, love," Layla crosses her hands together, sitting up straight like one would when speaking to a child, her sparkly blue eyes full of pity, "your eyes are gold."

Erin rolls said eyes, looking out the giant window at the blooming mountain laurels lining the crosswalk toward the University; the purple petals scattered across the sidewalk twist in the wind of moving feet. Truthfully, his eyes are hazel. It's just that the gold around his iris is so large that the green isn't always seen unless he's standing super close to someone.

Like Victor.

"Sorry ... late."

Erin remembers how close Victor was standing next to him at Donny's Warehouse last Saturday night. How warm his chest was for that brief moment he was pressed against Erin's back.

"...rin."

Or was he the one standing close to Victor?

"... wrong ... dude ..."

Did Victor notice the green in his eyes, even with how dark it was in the back corner?

"Don't ... wolf dre ..."

Erin noticed Victor's eyes, the pale blue overpowering the steel gray around his iris. The complete opposite of Erin's.

"Erin!"

He flinches, looking away from the window. Fletcher is here now, sitting in the booth next to Layla, his hair damp and stringy. They're both staring at him like he just told them he has stage four prostate cancer.

Erin clears his throat, pushing away the last of his fries toward Fletch. The soggy ketchup dripping along the outer edge no longer looks as appetizing. "Sorry, zoned out."

Fletcher squints at him. "Yeah, no shit, dude. You all good?" His hair looks nearly black, like Erin's, instead of its normal light brown color, especially the strands of hair slightly longer along the top of his head and behind his ears. He's wearing one of his Green Lake University swim team jerseys, and he smells like chlorine and salt. Morning swim practice, right, that's why he's late today. Summer is prime practice time, even when a majority of classes aren't in session. Which would also explain the sports bag now beside Erin. He did mention that the other morning.

"Yeah, yeah, I'm good. Just haven't been sleeping well." Erin looks around the cafe. The lunch rush seems to be starting, making it harder to hear Sabrina Carpenter's soft pop music coming through the speakers. Or is it Taylor Swift? Either way, the increased toasted bagels and chicken BLT burgers making their way out of the kitchen doors behind their booth is making Erin's mouth water again.

"Layla filled me in about the dreams." Fletcher leans back in his seat, arms crossing over his chest. He's silent for a moment before a smirk twists his lips, brown eyes turning dark with mischief. "Maybe you just need a good bang."

Layla bursts out laughing, snorts interrupting the breathy sound every few seconds. Erin drops his mouth open in shock.

"I think Mr. Tall, Dark, and Handsome fits the bill. Good bod, intense blue eyes, looks rich, if that ring was anything to go by, and he probably has a big di—"

Erin interrupts him by throwing a handful of fries at his face. Fletcher leans forward, opening his mouth to catch some with a cheeky grin. That just causes Layla to laugh harder. She seems to know exactly who Fletcher is referring to, which means he must have told her more about who they were talking with before Greg arrived at the scene and tried to ruin their night. Traitor.

Erin shakes his head; it's getting harder to keep his lips pressed together in a firm line. He knows his friends mean well. And what's a bit of harmless teasing? "Come on y'all. Let's head to the supply store before I *bang* your heads together."

"Aw, but I wanted a burger," Fletcher mumbles, slinging his sports bag over his shoulder.

"Didn't you eat after practice? Are you still hungry?" Layla replies, horror twisting her soft features.

"How do you think I got these abs, Lay? Something needs to feed them."

"That quite literally makes no sense, moron."

Erin tries to listen to the conversation as they walk to the university office supply shop—they move on from food to exam marks being posted in two weeks, scheduling classes next semester, and which electives to take—but the words aren't fully processing. He feels restless, stressed. On edge.

Like he's forgetting something but doesn't remember what.

Like he needs to go somewhere but doesn't know how.

Like someone's waiting for him but doesn't—

"Ooohh look, Erin, it's a wolf notebook!" Fletcher quickly picks up the notebook, raising it like one would a prized pumpkin. Erin stares at the notebook. The wolf is all white, sitting on a rock with a mountain range behind it. The eyes are black, not hazel or gold.

Or blue.

"Cool." Erin nods before raking his eyes around the supply store. It's practically empty, just a handful of bright-eyed students still on a high from finishing exams maneuvering around the small space, the smell of ink and the sweet candy by the registers filling the air. He doesn't normally get supplies this early. Hell, the next semester is still a good three months away, but Fletcher insists it's better to go now instead of trying to deal with a crowded rush of students a week before school starts. Though Erin supposes that with Green Lake being the only university in the main city, everyone in the surrounding country towns looking for higher education all end up here. It makes sense for the facilities to be in use all year round. Summer term is a thing, and everyone studies differently.

Victor probably studied a lot too. He looked smart. Knowledgeable. Well-read.

Erin shakes his head with a frown, glancing toward a rack of various school caps and hats. He picks up a red cowboy hat, studying his friends through the mirror as they share a look, a silent conversation playing out between them. Fletcher nods toward Erin, raising his thick eyebrows. Layla shrugs, grabbing her ponytail to play with the strands and shaking her head. Fletcher sighs, putting the notebook down and readjusting the thick strap on his shoulder. His eyes squint in worry.

Why does it look like they are treating this much more seriously now than they were at the café?

"Seriously, dude." Fletcher grabs the hat from out of Erin's hands, placing it atop his head before gripping his shoulders and turning him so they're face to face. "What's wrong?"

Erin looks at Fletcher from under the thin leather brim. He sees the concern laced into his sharp features and hears the worry in his voice. He tries to look away, but Layla is there. She's never really shown a lot of expression—something that got her into a lot of trouble growing up—but her bright blue eyes have always made up for it. Most days, you would hardly believe she was a whole year younger; she's always been the more mature of the three of them. Especially once she joined them in high school. It's been their job to protect her since they first met, to make sure she grows up on the right path. Safe. Unafraid. But now, looking into her eyes, Erin sees just how scared she is for him.

His heart breaks.

He gives in with a sigh. "I don't know, honestly." He looks between them both one last time. "Maybe I do need to get banged …?"

They don't buy his diversion attempt. "Or …" Layla drawls, index fingers rubbing over the tops of her thumbs, "maybe you just need a break, like from everything. Greg did kind of put a damper on things during last semester."

"Don't remind me of my past mistakes, Lay," Erin says lowly. "And, in case you haven't noticed, I have been on break. For a week, to be exact." He scrunches his eyebrows as the confusion settles. Summer break started last week. After the party at Donny's, he's done nothing but sit at home and watch TV all day. Peak relaxation.

Fletcher pipes in, finally letting go of Erin's shoulders. "Boys, sex, parties, sex, school prep, sex, photography, sex. Have some quality *you* time."

Layla swings between Fletcher and Erin, smiling as she grabs onto one arm each. "With us still, obviously." Her nose scrunches. "But not the sex part. That you can do without us."

"What, don't want a threesome, Lay?" Fletcher waggles his eyebrows while Erin laughs out loud.

"What happened to you not having a taste for the male appendage?" Erin teases.

"You're right. Having sex with you two would be like having sex with my siblings." Fletch shivers, sticking his tongue out in disgust. "Yuck."

Layla smacks him upside the head as they continue stocking up on supplies, and Erin mulls the conversation over. They do have a point. Part of the reason he's been at home all week is because of his restless sleep. He's been too tired to do much else other than ponder this sudden bloody wolf addiction. Maybe dreaming of thunderstorms and wolves is his subconscious way of saying he needs to spend some time with his friends without overthinking everything. Be wild and free, recharge, and release some pent-up tension left over from last semester.

"Erin, can you grab me a new charger, pretty please?" Layla asks over Fletcher's shoulder. She points to the wall behind him. "A baby pink one!"

"Get her neon orange," Fletcher snickers.

Erin hums, eyes drifting over the electrical section on the wall when they catch on a row of freshly stocked SD cards. An idea sparks in his mind.

He grins.

FOUR

Her husband protested. Said she was being impulsive and foolish. Why intervene now? What good will it do after all that has passed? They won't change their ways.

She ignored him.

She is good at that when her heart beats louder than her mind.

He did not see them—the two below the tree. But she did. Her mind is the clearest it has been since this war started.

She must act now before this moment passes. Before Time takes away his gift.

Before her Hope is found.

Before they are killed.

She treads amongst them, barefoot, with a deep blue shawl over her shoulders and chest to cover her breasts before wrapping around her waist, keeping the long white skirt covering the front and back of her legs in place. No one pays her any mind as she follows the worn trail through the center of the village—not that there are many who still linger. Most of the Pack seems to stand at the center by the raised dais. There is a sculpture there, Hëna remembers, though she cannot see it yet. She wonders if it looks the same.

She wonders if they smashed it in anger.

She would not blame them if they had.

Voices are carried on the wind, rustling the hair flowing freely down her back. Loud anger whispers in her ears. She lifts the back of her shawl to cover her hair and forehead. Though Hëna can hear their prayers every night from the home she shares with her husband, she wants to hear what they have to say before they begin to pray. For sometimes, the singing of the dead is louder than the wailing of those still alive. It becomes hard to hear.

So that is where she must go.

That is where He will be.

The Pack looks the same as she remembers from the last time she visited. Cubs linger around the open clearing, tall trees surrounding them. Protecting them. Many homes are made from animal hide and stretched taut with wood to create high peaks, while the remaining pieces cover the ground and wrap around metals used for cooking. Some of the cubs wear the animal hide around their breasts and waists, the pieces blending with the multicolored fur guarding their shoulders or stomachs. Colorful etched bone, flower, and wood-carved jewelry hang around their bodies and lace with their hair. She knows they each mean something and longs to sit and converse with them. To ask about each etching, each design. To hear the stories between the mated pairs and learn what the matching symbol means. Some of them look intricate; they must have taken an age to create. Delicate hands spent such precious time ...

She continues onward, eyes somber.

Everyone is dressed differently, while some are not dressed at all. She stifles a laugh under her breath as a young cub jumps from one of the homes, shifting form in mid-air before running into the forest. More cubs follow suit, paw prints rustling the short grass as they speed after their friend. She can see why some choose to forgo covering themselves; it would be a waste of material.

Pride swells in her heart. At least some things haven't changed.

Her cubs are continuing their community, passing on their love to their own cubs.

Even if there are more rocks lining the border of the clearing than homes, marking the graves of loved ones who have returned to the stars. Even if the sound of laughter is silent, replaced with wailing sobs and angry mutters. Even if she has yet to see a single smile on any face she has passed.

Even if the metallic smell of blood has seeped into the very essence of the Pack, staining their skin and minds and souls, encompassing the smell of flowers she knows used to grow amongst the homes and hang between dried herbs set above the ground for cooking—

Hëna continues her trek, heading to the center where most are gathered. A man sits on a fur-covered seat in front of the fire pit shared by a few of the homes. The scraping sound of sharp rock pulling over wood fills the air as she passes. An arrow. Deft hands work on the rock, sharpening it to a point before tying a string around it so that the wooden shaft snugly sits underneath the head. It's a marvellous creation. Her heart breaks to think about who it will be pointed toward.

She frowns. *When* it will be pointed toward someone.

She leaves the man to his work.

Closer to the dais, she can make out the sculpture. Her heart swells from her chest, eyes softening as a breath of relief escapes her taut lips. Oh, her foolish, loving cubs. They did not destroy it. Memories rush through her at the sight of it—a giant wooden wolf. Stars are etched across its body, with a giant one sitting in the center of the forehead. It's been painted since; multiple colors cover it like fur that has been bathed in the star's nightly aurora. And a swatch of blue cloth hangs around its neck, a crescent moon carved from bone hanging like a jeweled necklace. Her eyes snag on the cleft in the right ear, and her lips lift. That was her mistake. Woodworking was never her forte. Her husband laughed at her for weeks afterward ... He would have loved the colors now.

Ignoring the pang against her heart, Hëna's gaze slides to the right. There is a man there, facing the crowd. Tall, strong shoulders holding straight a matching muscular, tanned body. His face is firm, thick blonde hair neatly trimmed along his jaw and down his chest. A thread of vines sits low on his forehead, some strands hanging loose by his face while others are braided into the hair resting down his back.

She doesn't recognize the man. But the blue eyes and crown, the mark of a black wolf nestled next to a black moon on the side of his neck, she knows.

He's the Pack's current leader. The Alpha.

"This was not what the Goddess had planned, Alpha Alaric," a man yells from the front of the crowd. Further yelling encourages the words, raising them loudly.

"That is not for us to decide, Kazamir," Alaric responds. His voice is low and stern. Tired. It seems this is not the first time this brooding cub seems to have voiced a different opinion.

"Then who does?" Kazamir yells, taking a step forward. Those around let him pass. The red of his hair is a stark contrast to his tanned skin and deep green eyes. "Are we to sit back and let those pests kill us all off? Let them raise their stone walls and think they are better than us? More worthy of her magic than us? The Goddess made *us* first! *We* are the ones who should be living behind those walls without fear!"

A soft snort breaks his decree. She darts her eyes over the crowd—no one seems to have noticed, too focused on Kazamir and Alaric. But She did. To Alaric's left, closer to the statue, is a cub younger than Alaric. He bears the same features, though he is slightly shorter and leaner in stature. The mark of Pack heir sits proudly between his brows, the bright blue jewel nestled amongst vine thinner than his father's. But oh, does it shine just as bright.

A long sigh escapes her lips. She has found him.

One half of her Hope.

Hëna's brows pinch, her sharp blue eyes narrowing. How does he find humor in this situation? His Pack is in disagreement, yet he stands with his hands in front of him, a long bow slung across his broad shoulders and quiver full at his hips. His gaze is focused on nothing in particular, thick eyebrows raised in nonchalance.

"For how long?" Kazamir yells, louder this time. Despair rings around them, mirrored on his twisted face. All other noise stops. "For how long, Alpha, is this war going to continue? How are we meant to give faith to one who won't answer our prayers? It's been twelve and ten moon cycles now! My cubs, who were born into a world rich with the Mother Goddesses' magic, now have none of it! They are near full-grown now, ready to mate and have cubs of their own. Yet what have the Others ripped from them? From all of us here? There are more dead wolves now than alive ones."

Her skin itches. Someone is looking at her. She has been seen over Kazamir's anguished voice. She looks toward the dais, but all focus is on Kazamir still. On settling the Pack. Her limbs grow heavy. Perhaps she should have waited further away. She takes a step back. The soil seeps between her toes. Perhaps she should not have come down at al—

"Well then, let us ask our Mother Goddess ourselves, then." The heir looks right at her. There's a question in his eyes. A challenge. Just as she had seen him, he had seen her.

Hëna raises her head and scoffs, lips curling up at the edges. She can't help but feel pride at his impertinence. After all, she was the one who chose to come here. He simply saw an opportunity and took it.

An Alpha indeed.

"Tala, what do you mean?" Alaric turns to his son, brows pinched in worry.

Tala tilts his head, eyebrows raised, and nods to the back of the crowd. Eyes slowly follow his gaze to her. Silence finally rings true around them.

Hëna swears she hears her old friend's easy-going laughter billow on the breeze.

She lowers her scarf from around her head, letting the material pool around her back and shoulders. A star sits on her forehead, the sparkling gemstone a deep blue as it connects to a thin chain wrapped around her head. It was a gift from her husband on their wedding day. She has worn it since.

"She has come! Our Moon Goddess has come to save us!" someone yells as gasps sing through the air.

Her magic swells, breathing in their prayers deeply. One by one, those around her kneel, respect given wholeheartedly and without question. Alaric bows deeply at the waist. Tala stares at her. A ghost of a smirk lifts one corner of his lips. He bows his head to her.

Hëna grins, eyebrows raised with wild astonishment. She has chosen a brazen cub.

Good.

He will not show fear in the battle to come.

She moves forward through the crowd and climbs above the dais. "My cubs, it is so good to see you all. I know it has been a while. I … am terribly sorry it took me so long to make my presence known. But this anger, this tumultuous path? It is not the right one. I grieve with you every day, watching you get slaughtered, but also slaughtering in return. I feel it in my soul, in the magic binding me to my great husband, and him to this land. But I did not give you teeth and claws for violence. I gave them for protection. So that you had a means to *survive*. Do not seek the dark, cursed blood, for that is one stain that will never come out of your furs."

Kazamir raises his head first. He hardens his gaze at her. "What do you suppose we do then, Goddess? Have you seen a way forward from your palace above in the stars? Has your husband, in between taking the souls from our fallen?"

"Kazamir!" Alaric chides.

She holds her hand out.

"You are an outspoken cub," Hëna smiles sweetly. "I respect that. I have always wanted my children to be ferocious. But that does not mean you need to be vicious, too. There is a mighty difference." She turns her attention to the rest of the Pack. They are nervous—it brews in the air around them, thick and sour. Many wring fingers tightly together, while other cubs shuffle on their feet. Some, more toward the back, have even shifted into their wolf form. She understands how it would be much more comfortable, much less daunting to be in a form that looks different to the enemy they are facing.

But they cannot live in that fear, trapped in one form forever. She would rather perish than see one half of them caged.

She takes a deep breath and lets her magic seep from her. The effect is instant; shoulders drop, and feet still. Relief sings through the air.

"I have seen the way forward and propose peace. Or at least a truce. For now. We must buy some time. We need to teach them about how wonderful you are. How loyal and kind. How they need not fear you or be envious of your abilities. You can live in harmony with the Others. They are simply uneducated, pushed forward with greed and suspicion nipping at their heels. Do not hate the unknowledgeable. The ignorant have committed no crime."

Mummers fill the crowd. Unease swivels its head. Kazamir snarls, canines elongating, when Tala takes a step forward.

"Our Mother has given us her opinion. I say we listen to it. We have not tried for a truce, nor have we looked at a way to teach the Others. They moved away, many moon cycles ago, and created their own home, their own Pack. When they attacked first, we retaliated. No questions. No communication. Perhaps it is time for a different tact. When a wolf hunts, it hunts as one, looking at all angles above and below where its prey sits. Now we must prove to the Others that we are above this violence and stop running with our tails between our legs. This is our land, our home. It is time we take control and fight for a harmonious relationship. War should be the last path we trail, not the first."

"My heir speaks true." Alaric stands beside his son and ruffles his hair. The gesture is so … delicate, despite the firmness of the words just spoken. Hëna knows what it must be like for him, to see his blood grow into a fine wolf. An Alpha. She, too, feels that warmth swell in her belly when she looks at her cubs.

Her smile dims.

All her cubs … though some of them may be lost right now, no longer viewing her as their Mother Goddess on the other side of those brick walls.

"The sun is passing through now, supper is nearly upon us. Let us stop this discussion here. I have heard your voices and listened to your scents. In the morning, I will decide how this truce will happen." Alaric turns his head to the sky and howls, the deep sound echoing far beyond the trees. The Pack returns the call.

Her eyes close, and her magic sings. Hearing it from above and being in the thick of it … how different the sensation is.

Once the ringing has slowed, the air settling over thick fretfulness once more, the crowd dissipates. Some linger, eagerness clear in their wide eyes and parted lips as they face her. They want to talk with her. She does too. Oh, how her arms tremble in excitement at the thought of holding each one of them tightly, breathing in their scents, and feeling the warmth of their beating hearts.

But that must wait.

She will make her rounds, and she will learn the name of every wolf here.

Afterward.

"Tala," Hëna calls for the young heir.

He stops in his tracks, halfway down the dais, glancing back at her. Alaric looks between them before bowing his head at her. He presses his forehead to his cub once, large hand steady on his neck, and then continues off the stage.

Tala turns to her and asks, "Yes, Mother Goddess? Oh!" He bows his head slowly.

He holds reverence for her; she can hear it in his voice, the low timber respectful and earnest. And she can see it throughout his body—he looks directly at her, not shying away or closing off his scent. In fact, he seems to spread it more. It's an interesting scent … and he does not hide it from her … it seems he is more comfortable talking with her than the others might be. Not as awe-struck. In his eyes, she is just another wolf, a member of his Pack. She is grateful for that. She has never wanted to be anything more to her children than simply a mother. A protector and guide. Someone able to participate in festivities with them, but still hold enough authority to help them, should they need.

Nevertheless, she is beginning to wonder if that damned smirk has been permanently ghosted to his thin lips, or if a mischievous God from another universe visited him when he was still growing in his mother's womb and twisted them before they finished setting. She can only think of one who would ever be imprudent enough to try ...

Speaking of trust.

"You seem against Kazamir's insistence toward violence," Hëna says, brows raised in curiosity.

"Well, you spoke true," Tala says. He licks his lips and strolls to the side of the dais, next to the statue, resting a hand against the wolf's ear. The clefted one. Her eyes narrow. "They were Pack once, and it is my job as future Alpha to protect us. *All* of us. I want to do everything I can to bring them home before we all kill ourselves fighting."

"That's good." Hëna nods. "This fighting has gone on for long enough. Both sides—"

"Did you mean it?" He turns to her, and she sees in his eyes a pain she didn't know was possible for her cubs to possess. The only other time she has seen that look was when she looked at her reflection. And the last time she did that—

"Mean what?"

"For the Others creation? I don't know how this all started, the stories differ at the start. Father says it was a disease in the blood that spread from cub to cub, until there was no wolf instinct left in the blood at all. A 'flaw in design.' Some of the elders, though, they say it was a curse," his eyes pierce through her, "from you. A test. A punishment. They can never decide. But it all seems so pointless now."

"And you?" Hëna asks. She squares her shoulders, mouth set. "What is it you believe, Heir?"

Tala's eyes soften at the edges, the color glazing over as a memory takes control of his sight. A quiet chuckle slips past his parted lips—the sound deep, rich, like his voice—and he quickly looks away to the dense forest. But she saw it. She can imagine who it is he is thinking about, through the trees over on the other side of the vast river.

Which of the Others he truly wants to bring home to his Pack.

"I believe that you have never wanted to have any control over our blood, that goes against our very instinct," he whispers, thumb rubbing back and forth over the statue. From how lax he is standing, Hëna gets the feeling he has done this many times before.

"And?" she probes.

"And I believe you have probably said very strong words to the one we call Fate, for putting us through all this. Words similar to what that old fool Kazamir has said about you."

She laughs, the sound ripping from her before she can stop it. This cub. She tilts her head and crosses the distance between them quickly. Tala is smiling at her too. Patting his head, she presses two fingers into the jewel resting in the middle of his forehead. The color flashes, the jewel warm underneath her touch as her magic resonates with it. So many heirs have worn this jewel ... she still remembers the first she bestowed it to.

"I've never thought of it as a curse," he admits to her quietly.

She hums. "What did you think it was then? Truly?"

"A blessing."

A rueful smile graces her lips.

"I never understood how a blessing could lead to war. Food does not seem logical. This land is abundant, there is more than enough for us to share."

Looking out at the Pack, the smell of cooking meat wafts through the air. The scent of rabbit stands out more than the others, and her stomach rumbles.

"The beginning of a tale often doesn't matter much. I ... cannot even remember anymore what sparked it." A lie. It doesn't burn her tongue as much as she thought it would. She will never forget the smell of that deadly poison as it rained down around them that day, of which cub hit the earth first ... of the sound that ripped from her throat as her magic *bled*. "But, as all great myths go, most wars start because of one emotion. The ruling emotion, one even stronger than Instinct." Her lips quirk. "Than the one you call Fate."

Confusion pinches his brows, but before she can smooth it out, the tension goes lax. His eyes widen, lips pursing as he gulps thickly. He has realized.

She lowers her hands, dragging his from the statue and gripping them instead. She doesn't need to say anything more, doesn't reveal that she has seen. That she knows what he keeps secret from his Pack, who he harbors deep in his heart. She's placed a heavy burden upon their shoulders. And she can see it in his eyes; he realizes that. The force she speaks of, he harbours it within his soul now. He has gathered the true reason she has finally decided to intervene.

For better or worse, Hëna has chosen him—them—to help her.

Guilt gnaws at the magic in her soul.

Has she made a mistake? Has she chosen wrong? Can they win against Fate and Instinct?

Or will those bastards of Creation laugh in her face when it all goes up in flames and her wolves are hunted into the ground, their blood used to water the growing earth?

Pale blue eyes gaze upon her—see *into* her. Steadfast. Like twin moons reflected upon the ocean in the darkest of nights. Tala squeezes her hands back.

He doesn't run away.

FIVE

The sun is starting to set when Erin pulls into the dark-colored drive-way—his father's idea so everyone knew which house was theirs in the neighborhood. Reaching over the center console, he grabs his camera from its case in his backpack and opens his car door, leaning against the frame. A wide mix of burnt yellows and pale pinks hug the sky, filling his camera lens.

Snap ... snap, snap.

He pulls back to study the images. Perfect.

A huff of laughter reaches him, and he suppresses an eye roll. The garage door is open, giving him a view of his mother painting wooden planks. Her long black hair is in a French braid down her back, strands falling out around her neck; the specks of hot pink paint splattered through the ends match her red bandana surprisingly well. She has her work jumpsuit zipped up to her collarbone, the green Storm Landscaping emblem on the old gray long-sleeved material hidden behind various paint stains. Some clearly old, some freshly new. It makes her look like a mosaic sculpture come to life.

She's humming along to soft jazz music, eyes smiling wide. Erin raps his knuckles on the rolled garage door as he passes through. It's filled with the thick smell of acrylic chemicals. But drifting underneath it all is the scent he has forever associated with love and promise. He inhales deeply, focusing on that undercurrent, letting it rush over him. Sharp ozone, like fresh paint left out to dry right before a thunderstorm. Citrusy marmalade, like orange zest on slightly burnt caramel cookies. Sharp but delicate muguet, like a lily deep in a valley that has been washed in soap. And sweet jasmine and rose, like a strong cup of iced tea in the summer that has been set out in a powder room. All tied together with a warm, earthy bow of amber.

He grins.

"Knock, knock."

"Hey, cub." Natalie turns to Erin, the same soft smile as his gracing her full lips as she nods to the sky. "Any good shots?"

"You know it," he says, pulling the garage door down halfway. An act of kindness to save his mother from standing on her tippy-toes and stretching high to grab it herself after a long day of work.

"How was school shopping?"

"Eh." Erin kisses her on the head in greeting, avoiding the paint on the corner of her brow, "Same as it's been the last three summers."

Natalie chuckles, bumping Erin with her hip as he shuffles past. "Well, lucky this was your last time then, huh."

"Mmhm, let's hope. Unless I wake up one morning and decide to change my whole life's trajectory and get a master's degree in, like, psychology or something." Erin opens the door, placing his bag of school supplies on the laundry floor before turning around and sitting on the steps. The cool air from inside hits his back in a welcome greeting.

She chuckles, "Now wouldn't that be a twist of fate?"

"I have a feeling Layla will drag us along with her next summer, though."

Natalie turns back to her project, the paintbrush moving in slow strokes. "She's not too far behind you boys, right? Only, what, one year?"

"Yeah, she'll be going into her third year in August." Erin nods, bending down to undo the laces of his shoes. "So, one left after that."

"I wouldn't be surprised if that girl finishes up before then," Natalie mumbles with a pout.

"You and me both," Erin chuckles. His eyes narrow, chin jutting toward the project she's bent over. "What're you working on anyways?"

Natalie glances at Erin before dipping the paintbrush into the bright pink paint. "Mailbox for Mrs. Jennings."

Erin places his right shoe next to the bottom step before moving on to the left. "Weren't you and Dad fixing that next week?"

"We were," Natalie hums, paintbrush still swishing across the wood, "but we got a really big project offer from a Mrs. Stella Lovelace. They want us to start on Monday."

"What? Monday? It's Friday! That's hardly any preparation time. Who the hell is this lady?" Erin snaps, disgust twisting his face.

Natalie rolls her eyes. "A rich widow from New York, and wipe that look from your face, mister, before I paint it off myself."

Erin pouts. It's like she has eyes on the back of her head sometimes. "What about all the other summer jobs you usually have scheduled? I was going to ask if I could help ..."

"Oh?" Natalie balances the paintbrush across the top of the tin and turns toward her son. Her crystal blue eyes are stern, locking him in place as she crosses her arms over her chest. "You sure you want to spend your last summer before your final year of university helping your parents do some heavy-duty landscaping? Will that be a big enough distraction from whatever it is you need help being distracted from, instead of lounging around the house all day and isolating yourself from your friends and family?"

Erin looks down sheepishly, wishing he hadn't taken his shoes off so that he had something to occupy his hands with. He should've known better than to pretend everything was all fine and dandy. His mother has always been able to tell when something was wrong with him.

Once again, her and those eyes. It's like she can pierce his heart and scrutinize his soul with them.

"I wasn't isolating myself, I was relaxing. There's a difference, Mom," Erin retaliates.

Natalie tilts her head, giving him that universal mother look of raised eyebrows, pulled lips, and a tight jaw. Translation— 'That better not have been sass I just heard, cub.'

Erin sighs. "I'll be fine. Let me help this summer. It may be the last time I get to spend time with you and Dad anyway. I'll be super busy with getting a job and all once I graduate. And I'll make sure to still spend time with Layla and Fletcher, too. Hell, they may even want to help. You know how they love to get involved with whatever it is we're doing."

Natalie's eyes narrow as they flit across his face. Searching. Watching. Then ... they soften and she expels a sigh. "All right then, you can help. We'll need it anyway, from Fletcher and Layla also, should they ever offer. But don't you go inviting them, cub! I love those two, but they aren't as trained as you are in how these things work." She picks up the paintbrush, wagging it at him. "It's a two-month-long project on the old ranch out of town, 'bout fifteen miles. Mrs. Lovelace is visiting from New York and needs the front and back yards completely cleaned and redone for an extended family reunion in August. The fifteenth, I think she said. Your dad and I plan to have it done the week before, and we get a bonus if we can also tidy up back toward the forest line, behind their fence."

"Old ranch?" Erin stands, wiping the back of his jeans as he does. "The one that's been abandoned for nearly thirty years?"

Natalie huffs, her shoulders loosening as she turns back to the wood and continues working. "Don't go worrying about ghosts on me now, not at your age, cub."

"I'm not scared!" he declares, voice raised as he bends to pick up his shoes and place them on the shoe rack by the door. "I just thought they were tearing that place down. Wonder how they got the rights to buy it …"

"Well, how 'bout you ask them, hm? Your dad should be almost finished with dinner, so quickly wash up and help set the table. I'll be in soon enough."

Erin rolls his eyes and closes the door behind him before turning on the light in the laundry. The door leading into the kitchen is closed, but he can still pick up on the faint thumps of heavy rock music seeping underneath it. Shaking his head, he bends over to pick up his school supplies. John refuses to cook dinner without playing hard rock songs. He says the tastiest food is rocked to sleep at night. Whatever that means.

His mother hums jazz while painting flowers, and his father jumps along to rock when cooking.

For the millionth time, Erin wonders exactly how his parents got together. Even the perfume and cologne are exact opposites, minus the ozone and amber wood. Somehow, they both managed to find signature scents with those notes in them.

He thinks it's kind of cute. And one-hundred percent intentional, on his father's part.

John spares a glance as Erin comes inside, hands never stilling as they mash some potatoes. "Hey, Goldy, have fun today with the rascals?"

"Hey Dad, not a bear nor a trespassing little girl, and I don't know what would ever be fun about school supply shopping, but sure. We had fun." Erin smiles sarcastically as he makes his way to the dining room. "Mom said I could help with the Lovelace project, so I'm going to go check out the old files to refresh my memory on the kind of designs the company does."

He doesn't wait for his dad to reply before making his way through the house toward the back, where his parents' office is, dropping his plastic bag off on the glass hallway table on the way. His mood instantly calms when he enters the back room, the black walls a stark contrast compared to the rest of the house. He's never thought of his house as cold or chaotic. Though many colors were constantly being thrown throughout the place, it all felt cozy. A bright yellow cushion here. A neon green throw blanket there. Bookshelves in a library room, lined with books from every genre imaginable. Family and friends, forever immortalized in photos. The fuzzy rug, black except for a silver moon and stars, nestled under a deep brown couch. Not to mention the various types of plants and flowers—potted, hanging, glued onto rocks—as if Mother Nature herself visited through the years and left presents for them to relish in.

It was a home. A place that showed how long his parents had lived there. How much they cared for him.

But the office was different. It felt like he was being transported to a different era. A different ... plane of existence entirely. Maybe it was as simple as this room being the only one with bare, dark-colored walls, nothing dressing them. Or perhaps it was that all the furniture was old-fashioned, antiques that his parents said they fixed up over the years.

Whatever it is, Erin takes a moment to simply ... be. He welcomes the silence. The stillness. Breathing in, the scent of orchids overwhelms his senses, and he feels an itch creep under his skin. That feeling from earlier in the day returns. His mind, searching and searching and searching.

His nose twitches as he flexes his hands and walks straight over to the wooden filing cabinet in the corner, flicking on the large desk lamp beside it. Opening some of the files, he looks at the dates and corresponding projects. He picks up files at random, choosing a lot from within the past five years. With a project as big as the Lovelace Ranch, Erin needs much more variety. He closes the top drawer, making his way down the filing cabinet. He pauses when he reaches the bottom drawer; the last file is dated back twenty-two years ago, the location Bellmore, New York.

Erin draws his eyebrows together in confusion. The last file should've been the first project his parents ever did, and he thought Storm Landscaping was created in Texas twenty-five years ago … Maybe it's been misdated?

He can't help it as his heart swells with pride when he compares the before and after photos. The picture itself is a little grainy—a sign of the camera quality back then—but Erin can still make out its contents. It looks like the job was to build a gazebo into an old, giant wisteria tree sitting in front of a massive Victorian mansion. In the after photo, the gazebo sits among the wisteria, vines wrapping around it like Mother Nature herself had built it.

Erin smiles, lining the photos up to pack away, when something in the corner of the after photo catches his eye. Next to the mansion, along the edge of a forest, are two women standing side by side. Their backs are to the camera, arms locked together like friends do as they gaze toward the mansion. He recognizes one of them as his mother—Natalie's signature braided hair and red bandana more of a dead giveaway than the Storm Landscaping uniform—but the other woman in the deep blue sundress he's never seen before.

The itch returns the longer he stares. It's fiercer this time. Harsher. *Deeper*.

The other woman has long brown hair reaching the middle of her back, and the arm not interlocked with Natalie's is raised above her head to keep a white sunhat from blowing away.

There's a feeling within him, like when a word sits on the tip of your tongue, ready to charge at the wind, but your mind has forgotten how to open your mouth and speak it. The woman's head is turned slightly, making her profile slightly shown. She's smiling, eyes seemingly closed in happiness. Erin raises the photo closer to his eyes like that will somehow make her tiny image more visible.

"Erin! Dinner!" John's voice cuts throughout the house, jolting Erin. Instinctively, he scrunches the corner of the picture. The other woman disappears between the squished folds. Heart racing, he flattens it back out.

"Coming!" Erin's voice cracks as he calls back. He hastily puts the photos back together, closing the file and drawer before making his way down the hall. His parents are already sitting at the table when he rounds the corner. "I think there's an error on one of the first projects you guys did."

"Oh?" John frowns, holding a bowl of salad. The bright red tomatoes mixed inside make Erin's mouth water. "Which project? I betcha it was that treehouse we built for Nancy's kids. I told your mother we needed to switch to a technology-based system, but she insisted we do everything by hand, like old hermits." He shakes his head. "I've been waiting to catch her out in a mistake ev—ow!"

Natalie places grilled steaks on everyone's plate, a playful frown fixed on John while Erin nabs the bowl of salad from his hands.

"The first one, at the bottom of the file. I didn't pay attention to the project name, but it was the one with the gazebo and giant mansion in New York." He takes a bite of the steak. Borderline rare, just how he likes it. "It was dated April of 2003, not January 2000. Unless I'm remembering when you guys started the business wrong? I could've sworn, being born in December and all, you guys have always called me your Christmas miracle baby, blessed to you three years after you decided on a business name."

"You are our miracle blessing, cub, so it must have been a typo," Natalie says with a tight smile, glancing at John. "I'll admit, your father is right. Our record keeping wasn't the best back then. We were just starting out, after all, and so much was changing in the world then."

"Yes, I remember that project, too. It was a big trip. I knew someone who knew someone, and before we knew it, we were traveling to New York." John chuckles under his breath. "One of these days, I'll need to go through all the records and check the dates. Don't want the tax officers coming after me!"

"Please," Erin waves his hand, speaking around a mouth full of ripe tomatoes, "they wouldn't take you to jail over a mistaken date."

The itch sits under his skin all night.

He can't bring himself to ask his parents about the woman. To question the wrong date further. His parents are like hawks when it comes to their records, despite his father's joke. Because that's all it was, a joke. They've never made a mistake before. But the date couldn't have been written wrong on purpose.

It's not like his parents are lying to him.

He shakes his head, swallowing another mouthful of steak before munching on some vinegar-drenched lettuce.

They are starting a big project after the weekend, so they need to focus on that. Focus on that.

Not the fact that Victor said he was from Bellmore, too.

Not the fact that Victor looks about his age.

Not the fact that the itch. Still. Won't. Go. Away.

SIX

The clock dances again.

Erin is standing in front of the entrance to a cream-colored Victorian mansion with deep navy wooden shutters along all the windows. It looks so similar to the one from the photo in his parents' office. There are storm clouds in the distance. The stench of ozone from lightning strikes fills the air, ears twitching at soft thunderclaps in the distance. Heading this way.

This ... way ...

He looks around, his bedroom nowhere to be seen.

There is no river of blood separating him from the rest of the landscape. And the grass is denser, but at the same time drier.

He wants to walk across it, yet something halts his feet.

Erin re-focuses on where he stands. The sun is hot on his skin, the wooden patio stinging his feet. Likely burning them. He can't step off, can't lift his hand to the handrail traveling down the steps, or block out the sun.

The sun's rays gleam, illuminating the dense forest surrounding the mansion. He squints against the glare; the white wolf still lies at the edge of the forest, its golden eyes flashing, the corners damp with shed tears. But not directed at him ...

Erin frowns, heart *burning* in pain. His muscles seize.

He follows the wolf's line of sight. There's a field where the lake of blood once was, now littered with a plant he recognizes from his front yard—monkshood, his parents call it. Wolfsbane. It's their favorite plant; they have it everywhere. He's never said anything, not wanting to dampen their spirits, but he's always secretly hated the smell. It's too ... much. Like a fire set out to rot after a hurricane. He's gotten used to having it around, but that doesn't mean he has to lik—

A wet sneeze.

A low growl.

A high-pitched whine.

Erin's eyes widen. Sitting among the wolfsbane, next to the wisteria gazebo, is a storm-cloud gray wolf with steel-colored eyes, and a honey-brown wolf with eyes as blue as the ocean. Their tails are entangled together, the gray one alternating between resting its head on the brown one's back and lifting it to gaze at the white wolf. Both of their paws are blistered and red—is it ... poisoning them?—their lips curled, not in a snarl, but in a ... smile.

They are smiling at him. At the wolf whining at the edge of the forest, whose nose is high in the sky and twitching as it smells, throat bobbing like it can't get enough of the scent into its lungs.

But why? If the wolfsbane is hurting the two smaller wolves, then wouldn't just the smell of it also hurt the white wolf? What is it he's trying to smell so bad—

Erin's nostrils swell with the scent of citrus and waves. Of orange juice and pool parties.

Of hope.

Of love.

A feeling wells within him, something so familiar he clenches his teeth and squeezes his throat to stop from gulping. Trying everything he can to keep the taste in his mouth, from swallowing it whole.

The brown wolf turns its head to the sky behind it, to the dark storm racing forward. Rain reaches Erin's ears now. Fast. Hard. A howling of a pack of wolves. Calling.

Calling.

Calling.

His body jolts as if lightning has struck his body, unfreezing whatever spell was keeping him frozen on the patio.

He takes a step, reaching out to them.

The white wolf runs.

The clock stops dancing.

Erin jolts awake, tears streaming down his face. He feels any air left in his lungs woosh out as he falls off the bed, arms flailing as he tries to twist in mid-air and brace his fall. It doesn't work. He lands right on his left shoulder and hip. He forgot to close the curtains, and the soft sliver of moonlight enhances the shadows in his room instead of scaring them away. The color being reflected on his white rug looks similar to the gray wolf's eyes.

Erin groans as the pain in his back starts to throb. Slowly, he crawls to his knees, reaching toward his window. He yanks the curtains shut, the metal pole between the frame rattling.

The room is cast into proper darkness.

No more wolf eyes.

His eyes settle. His heart evens into a steady rhythm.

They said it was a misprint. A mistake. Nothing more.

So why does he dream about that place? Why do tears fall from his eyes? Why is it suddenly hard to breathe? Dreaming of one wolf for over a week is entirely different from dreaming about multiple wolves in one night. What would his friends have to say about that?

A grimace slips through his teeth as he staggers back into bed.

No, not going down that route. Not tonight.

The dreams mean nothing.

The dreams will *always* mean nothing.

Anything important will be thought while he's awake. Thinking happens in reality, which is what this is. Reality. Not a magical world where giant wolves roam free and cry over lakes of blood and poisonous wolfsbane.

He presses the heel of his palms deep into his eyes until black spots swim against the ceiling as he stares at it.

The dreams mean *nothing*.

Nothing.

He doesn't go back to sleep.

SEVEN

"D idn't sleep well?" John looks at Erin in the rear-view mirror.

"Hmm, something like that." Erin chuckles before turning his head to look out the window. He can see his reflection against the glass, the dark bags under his eyes making his ivory skin look even more pale and sick. The gray of his work jumpsuit doesn't help his complexion either. He ignores it, letting his head fall against the glass with a thud as his eyes re-focus on the trees zooming past. This far out of town, the trees get thicker and denser every mile. It reminds him of what it must have been like in the past, before humans became civilized ... when the wolves ran wild and free ... which is why not many people live this far out of town unless they deal in the lumber business. And it's probably why the old ranch became abandoned in the first place. Layla's dad said it was something to do with a dying lumberjack and a widow who refused to sell the property, letting the government claim it upon her death.

"You know, cub, you don't have to help. If you're not sleeping well, we can get you some medicine," Natalie says softly. She spares John a glance before turning around in the passenger seat to look at Erin. "We won't be doing much today anyway. Just meeting with—"

"No, no, I want to help, trust me. I'm fine." Erin sits up straighter, desperation bleeding into his voice. He can't spend another day at home doing nothing. Layla is at Café Terra all morning, and Fletcher is at the community pool teaching the younger kids how to swim, with a workout scheduled with his swim team right after. If he sits still, he'll fall asleep out of boredom. And those dreams— "Please, Mom, let me help."

Natalie's eyes flit over Erin, and her gaze softens. "All right," she sighs and looks forward once more as John slowly pushes on the brakes. "Anything to keep those pretty almond eyes of yours from pouting. But you stop if you start to feel dizzy or sick, Erin. I mean it!"

Erin smiles wide, all teeth, as he leans forward and hugs his mom from behind. "Deal!"

Natalie huffs. John reaches over and grabs her hand, squeezing it without looking at her. She clenches it back, her golden wedding ring glinting in the sunlight, just as the ranch comes into view. Erin, letting go of his mom, leans even further over the center console to look out the window. He's beginning to understand why Mrs. Lovelace gave them two months to complete the project. A few people are mulling around the property in raggedy jeans, shorts, and old graphic tees and tank tops. Are they members of the Lovelace family? There is hardly any resemblance between them ... and none of them seems disturbed by the state of the property.

They should be.

It's a massive wreck.

The fence line next to the main road is broken, falling, or completely shattered in some places, like a pack of wild animals ran straight through it. Erin's lips pull tight. He imagines it looks the same along the back of the house, separating the backyard area from the rest of the property and dense forest. The grass that isn't dead and yellow has grown so high around the house that Erin supposes it would reach his hips. A perfect breeding nest for diamondbacks. There are also multiple rocks, some are large and stained with moss, while others are small and jagged. There are no flowers, cute sitting areas, or trails. There doesn't even seem to be any remnants of a work shed or animal pen.

It's as dead as a desert wasteland.

"I know we live in Texas, but damn, not the wild west Texas," Erin mutters. He grabs his camera from his bag, snapping some quick shots from the road. "We're only doing the backyard area and the space enclosing the main house, right? Like from the fence to the front door?"

Natalie nods, face even more grim than the day Erin came home crying, saying he lost his virginity to a dick who was using him to get an A in AP English. "Get ready, boys. By the looks of these fence lines, I'm assuming even that will be massive."

"Nothing we can't handle!" John declares, confidence oozing as they drive through the open gate and along the loose gravel road to the side of the house. Erin spies some metal pillars and old window frames by the gate as they drive through. The grass is, thankfully, shorter the closer they get to the house. All tell-tale signs of a recent interior renovation.

The house itself is massive, the sun making the brown timber wood look like deep mahogany. It's at least four stories high with what looks to be a wrap-around porch on the first level. There are two old wisteria trees on either side of the main door, the tops bending over to merge like a canopy over the entryway. Erin notes that a couple of the windows have balconies on the second and third levels, most likely connecting to bedrooms. He eyes a window on the fourth level, the only one with a balcony. The curtains covering the window are a deep shade of green, like a forest. There are even little potted plants sitting outside, just starting to sprout. The baby leaves sway in the wind.

He suppresses a smile, capturing the moment on film. Cute.

"No time to waste, Erin. Come on, chop-chop, kiddo!" John sings as he closes the car door.

Erin didn't even notice they had parked. He loops the camera strap around his neck before climbing down from the truck, careful of any forgotten beams thrown to the side, and follows his parents to the front door. The back of his neck tingles, and he turns around. There, along one of the broken fences, sits a little girl, legs swinging freely like the breeze twisting around them. She can't be any older than ten, at most. Erin looks around, seeing no one near her; the closest people are about fifty feet away, back toward the first gate entrance. Where are her parents? He gives her a small wave, perplexity twisting his brows. That fence does not look secure, yet she looks as balanced on it as a gymnast on a beam. Still ... the little girl waves back at him, smiling, sharp canines on display.

"Well, that'll have to be changed." Natalie points to the bright red front door, drawing Erin's attention from the small child's unusually sharp teeth. She's holding a clipboard in her other hand, a pen stuck under the clasp, ready to take notes. "No way in hell am I uprooting these gorgeous wisteria trees."

Erin snaps a photo of the door, shivering in cold sweat as he's suddenly reminded of the lake of blood and field of wolfsbane from his dream. His mom is right, the bright red door doesn't match well with the soft purple of the wisteria. And he much prefers the sweet honey-like scent of the wisteria flowers.

The wooden steps creak as John walks to the door and knocks. Nothing but silence around them. Erin glances to the sky as John knocks again, Natalie tap-tap-tapping her sneakered foot on the grass beside him. The sun is still hidden behind dark clouds, the rain from up north predicted in the early Monday morning weather report not yet cracking through the air.

The smell has, though.

And it's getting stronger the longer they wait outside.

Normally, this weather would be perfect to start a landscaping project. The rain is only meant to last for a few days, the sun won't be out, so they won't overheat, and the ground will be nice and wet for any markers they plant. Though knowing his mother, they might do some actual planting today, too.

Regardless, Erin doesn't want to get drenched before the day's work even starts.

Before John can rap on the door again, it's opened by a man wearing gray trackpants, no shirt, and sipping through the straw of a massive jug of water. The man automatically locks eyes with Erin. The straw drops from his slack mouth and the door is slammed closed.

The man was Victor.

Victor, from the party at Donny's Warehouse.

Victor, who Erin is trying not to think about by helping at Storm Landscaping.

Victor, who has wide shoulders, toned muscles, and a small waist with thin hair that leads down t—

The door opens again.

Erin gulps, wiping at his dry lips with the back of his hand before rolling the sleeves of his jumpsuit to his elbows. When did it get so humid?

It's a woman this time with deep red hair. She has half of it pulled up into a ponytail while the rest falls to her shoulders in soft curls, making the frown on her face all the more prominent. "Oh, sorry about that. You all must be Storm Landscaping, correct?" The woman opens the door wider; her freckled cheeks and green eyes are no longer pinching inward after realizing who they are. Instead, her full lips curve into a smile, showing a perfect ratio of white teeth. "I'm Stella Lovelace, the one who contacted you."

Natalie steps forward, the momentary shock of disrespect already forgotten as she holds out her hand, returning the smile. "Yes. Pleasure to meet you. I'm Natalie Storm, and this is my husband, John, and our son, Erin. He'll be helping us out a bit during this project."

"Oh, yes, I'm Stella." She shakes Natalie's hand, and her nose twitches. "Come in, please. Leave your shoes on, we don't mind dirt here." She steps to the side as they all walk into the house. The smell of sweet strawberries dipped in champagne wafts around Erin as he walks past, causing him to wrinkle his nose. You'd think the smell would be pleasant, but it only serves to make his stomach curdle like he's eaten something sour. He lowers his head and wiggles his nose more, softly clearing his throat to rid most of the scent. But that only makes him more aware of all the other smells floating around the narrow entrance space. There are so many of them, all different types of plants and foods, but a similar undertone carries them all.

Oakmoss. Yes, that's what it is.

It reminds him of a wild forest, all the other scents blending around it with their unique twists. Roses, mushrooms, clay, lilies, animal fur ...

It's ... nice ... and somehow, familiar.

Perhaps everyone in this family shops at the same perfume place? And oakmoss is their signature scent. Someone at Green Lake must have worn one of the perfumes in class last semester, or he's walked past the shop without realizing.

What other reason could there be for his heart to calm so much simply by smelling it?

"Sorry if we scared your son before," John laughs while looking around. For such a big house, the actual entrance is quite narrow, with most of the space opening to a wooden spiral staircase. The rooms directly to the right and left are hidden behind barn doors, the wood matching the outside coloring. Further down the hall looks to be an open floor kitchen and dining area, with a white marble island separating those two rooms from each other.

Erin smiles as the cogs behind his father's eyes turn and twist, already developing color schemes to match the modern, farmhouse design. He looks at his mother. Her eyes are fixed on Stella.

"Oh, no, that wasn't my son. I don't know where he's run off to, but the young man from before was Victor, my nephew." As Stella closes the door behind them, footsteps thump quickly down the staircase.

Erin glances to see Victor wearing a black shirt and worn-out blue jeans; his hair looks semi-dry and brushed now, too. He peers over the railing at Erin, a barely there smile on his lips as his pupils dilate. Erin's cheeks grow warm, that same feeling in his gut from last week coming back tenfold.

"Oh, the door slammer!" John announces. Natalie slaps his shoulder, hushing him.

Victor looks down a bit ashamed with a shy smile as he descends the last few steps. He nods his head to Natalie and John as he walks over to stand beside Erin. "I'm sorry about that, I was a bit surprised."

He's standing so close that Erin can smell his cologne mixing with his shampoo. The spiced, sophisticated scent of leather and sandalwood wraps around his throat like a warm necklace. He wonders what it would feel like if Victor placed his hand there. If the scent would be stronger. If his hand would be warmer.

Erin clears his throat. "Did you not know we were coming?"

Victor's eyes snap to Erin. There's a smirk ghosting his lips. "Well, you never did answer my question. I thought the next time I'd see you would be at the police station, not in my house. You caught me off guard."

Erin raises a brow. He opens his mouth to retort when a cold hand lands on his back, pushing him slightly away from Victor. Strawberries sour the air, covering Victor's heady cologne.

"Police! Oh, dear, I believe I am quite lost … Have you met already?" Stella asks, features remorseful from where she stands between them. She cups her hand, the one that was just on Erin's back, with the other, placing it over her lips and nose. "I hope my son hasn't done anything to get you in trouble …"

"No, no," Erin waves his hands widely in front of him, "he's talking about earlier in the month, just over a week ago now. We met at a party, Donny's start-of-summer party over on the other side of town at his warehouse-turned-nightclub. I made a joke about how everyone knew my parents … and then didn't clarify when he asked if that meant they were cops."

"Erin!" Natalie barks. Erin winces, rubbing the back of his neck. John laughs.

"Don't get mad at him, please," Victor asks, voice tight. "We hung out for a bit, but then I was suddenly called away, so it's my fault Erin couldn't clarify what he meant." He steps closer to Natalie and John, holding his hand out to greet them. "Please, I had only arrived earlier that week, so it was my first night out. Erin and his friends' hospitality was great, despite it not being his house or anything. And they even treated me to a round of Full Moons. It was delicious."

Natalie's eyes twinkle, and she takes Victor's outstretched hand, shaking it. "Well then." She glances to John, who is straight-faced once more as he looks Victor over. "I suppose no harm was done. Erin tells us nothing about those summer tradition nights, but Fletcher sure has told me about those drinks. We even tried recreating them once. They certainly are to die for."

Victor smiles wide. "Right? We chugged them, and I even beat Erin, much to Fletcher's surprise."

"Please, Fletch is always surprised at something." Erin crosses his arms over his chest. Victor's closer again, after stepping toward his parents. Don't lean in. Don't lean in. Don't *sniff* him, Erin. "And besides, you barely beat me. It was one gulp."

"Oh?" Victor leans close. "Want a re-match then? Erin?"

Yes. "No," Erin says. He hopes the deep breath he took wasn't too obvious, but he couldn't help it. The sound of his name on Victor's lips was enough to make him lose all the air in his lungs. Sue him that the next batch of air he wanted was lined with Victor's smell. "I wouldn't want to hurt your feelings when I win."

Victor licks his lips, his eyes falling to Erin's mouth. Then lower to his throat, his collarbone.

"Was my son trying to get you drunk, Victor?" Natalie looks between them. Smirking. No, not smirking ... there's no tease in the smile. It's simply pure joy. Like she's been waiting for this moment. God, has he really been that lonely to the point where the first kind and respectable man who shows an interest in him has wedding bells ringing in her head?

Victor chuckles, the deep rumble sending Erin's nerves into overdrive. "Of course not, Mrs. Storm." He leans back but leaves his eyes still fixed on Erin. "I'm quite stubborn. No one makes me do anything I don't want to."

"Oh, well then, all's well that ends well," Stella chuckles, the sound high-pitched like wind chimes. "And now that introductions are over with, Victor dear, why don't you escort our guests to the kitchen so we can talk design." She uses one hand to gesture to the kitchen while the hand that was on Erin's back is now slithering over his arm, locking them together. "This must be fate, our families meeting already. What a blessed omen!"

Victor finally yanks his eyes away and smiles softly at Stella before nodding. He regards Erin again while motioning for Natalie and John to follow him further into the house. Erin takes a step forward with them, when nails dig into his skin, freezing him in place. His parents don't look behind, preoccupied already with more of Victor's pleasantries.

"I don't know who you are or how deeply you know my nephew," Stella is looking straight ahead, lips still curved into that perfect smile while keeping her voice low, "but if you want this business transaction to continue smoothly, then you need to stay far away from him and the rest of the Lovelace family. He is on a set path in life, and that doesn't involve small-town country boys lying, then getting him drunk and into trouble with the law." Stella lets go of Erin's arm, stepping away to stare into his eyes. Her green eyes are dark and cold, a stark contrast to the warmth of her fiery hair. "He doesn't have time to fool around in bed with the first cute boy that walks past. This summer is incredibly important to his business, his career. That translates to 'life goals' in case you hadn't heard the term all the way out here before."

Erin's gut boils, and he can't tell if the fire lighting it is built from confusion or anger. He doesn't know this lady, hell, he hardly even knows Victor, and now he's being, what, threatened? He's not here to steal some precious family jewels or add Victor as a notch on his belt. This goes beyond protective—this is insane. And besides, shouldn't this be something Victor's parents do? In a teasing manner? True, it's not like they've hidden that they were flirting … which isn't professional as his family is here on business, employed by Victor's family … but still, it's not something to get mad over. Victor is an adult. He can make his own decisions.

He forces the anger to subside, to bury back into the sands of his bones as the fresh nail marks on his skin sting in outrage.

New Yorkers are bred differently.

Don't mix personal affairs with business ones.

Be the better man.

Stop thinking about how this aunt all but confirmed that Victor is into guys.

Erin plasters on his best awkward smile and tilts his head. "Look, Mrs. Lovelace, I met Victor at a party over a week ago. We talked for, like, five minutes before he left, and I hadn't heard from or seen him since. Yes, we mutually flirted, but that's neither here nor there. Not that it's your business, but I have no intention to start anything romantic with anyone on this ranch. And I would never do it with one of my parents' clients. I'm only here to help over the summer before school starts again and take some portfolio photos." He raises his camera between them in defense. "That's it."

Stella is silent, narrowed eyes blinking as she scrutinizes him. Whatever she sees must appease her because she pats Erin on the shoulder, the innocent look from earlier back, before wiping her hand on her dress pants and heading toward the kitchen.

Erin sighs deeply, his shoulders sinking. Looks like his idea to get mysterious hot-business-tourist-Vicky-man off his mind by keeping busy with landscaping projects has just gotten a whole lot harder.

EIGHT

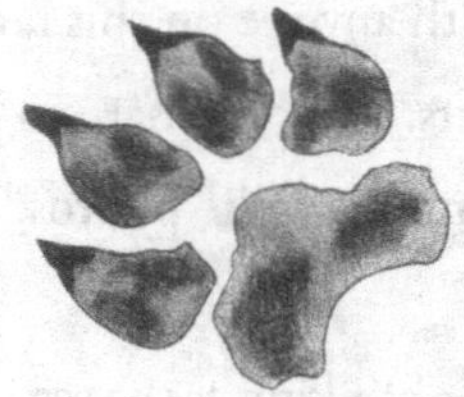

Stella walks into the kitchen with Erin trailing behind her, and Victor's heart *pounds*. He puts his arms behind his back, pinching his wrist. This isn't a dream.

Erin is in his home.

Erin, with the kind hazel eyes that border on gold, and hair as dark as the night sky during a moonless night.

Erin, whose lips pout slightly when he smiles, rising to meet Victor's sassy challenges and flirty remarks.

Erin, who saw Victor practically naked and reeking of sweat, before having a door slammed in his face.

Victor clears his throat as that burnt acid smell wafts into the kitchen behind Erin. That's the one drawback—Erin has this stench of wolfsbane attached to him like a second skin. It was a surprise at first, the smell so strong, so overpowering, that he couldn't keep his lips from curling. But then he saw where it was coming from. *Who* it was coming from. And the smell didn't matter anymore. It was instant, the need to be near him, to study every tiny detail of his features and the way he moves ... like an anchor lifted from the ocean. He's only ever heard that instinct as being described as one thing.

But that wouldn't be possible. Erin's a human.

Isn't he?

Victor's brows pinch tight. How else could he wear that wretched smell otherwise? Smelling it burns his nostrils and throat, making him want to close his eyes against it and gag. Touching him was like standing underneath a scorching shower, the heat burning his skin, but, at the same time, heating his insides in the best way possible. Surprisingly, standing near Erin was the only relief against the onslaught. The closer he was, the clearer Erin's true scent running underneath his skin became. Sweet, like a forest after a thunderstorm. And a pinch of spice that reminded him of the wisteria growing by the front door. Simultaneously calming and rambunctious.

Is that even possible?

Victor studies Erin while he stands beside his parents at the kitchen island. They're explaining to Stella the order of business, how much the full project will cost based on initial impression, what days they will be here working, the hours of those days, and the overall vibe of the project. Design this, design that. That's when they lose him. The money and contract side of things he can understand, but deciding if the fence should be left brown, sanded back to its original color or painted a striking shade of black—"Or a dark green, to blend with the forest," Erin pipes in—his mind shifts, focusing completely on the confusing puzzle piece that is Erin Storm. He's not the son of cops in a backwater country town, but a single child to well-known, respected landscapers, who seem to be the only ones in town, too. He *might* be older than twenty-one, but he's definitely older than eighteen. Studying photography, too, by the camera he keeps expertly fiddling with. And he has a reputation for being a goody-two-shoes, or at least, someone who is kind and caring, to the point where the actual cops of this little town wouldn't care even if he did break the law.

It's weird and confusing. For his standing in the Pack—the role his wolf was cursed into—it's abnormal. It shouldn't be possible.

Does he hate it? Yes. But why does he hate it?

There's only one way to find out.

The first rule in real estate is never to buy a house or sign off on any decision before first inspecting the property.

So, it's time to start the inspection.

Victor walks to the white-washed cabinet and grabs a glass, filling it with water from the fridge. "Here, a clear moon." He slides the glass of water over.

Erin's lips quirk. "Thanks," he whispers. His Adam's apple bobs prominently under his skin as his throat works to swallow the water, and Victor clenches his teeth. Who knew the sight of someone drinking water could be so distracting?

His gaze roams. For working in a landscaping company, Victor notes Erin's skin is unusually pale. But if he squints, he can see a slight dusting of freckles across the bridge of his nose and cheeks. He must not work outside with his parents much, then. His eyes trail down Erin's neck and across his collarbone, ignoring the camera blocking the view of his sternum, before rising to stare at the spot behind his ear. A mark would show up so easily on his skin. Many, many red kiss marks. He wouldn't even have to suck very hard for it to show. And beyond that ... a mate bond.

Beautiful.

The image is so clear in his mind, like a dream painted to life.

Stella raises her arm and pats Victor on the shoulder, causing him to jolt. She isn't looking at him, but her usually sweet scent is turning sour. Was it that obvious he wasn't listening? Wow, he hasn't leaked his pheromones unintendedly since he was in puberty. Feeling guilty, he focuses back in on the conversation, reeling his scent back in, just in case. Erin did say he had a strong sense of smell, perhaps he got it from his parents.

"Natalie or Mrs. Storm. The same goes for my husband, John," Natalie says, voice firm. She looks at him, eyes alight with creativity.

"Of course, Ma'—Mrs. Storm," Victor says. "How long have you been a land-scaper for? You seem very excited to get started. I've worked with various interior designers before on projects where the house needed to be completely gutted, but none of them had the spark that you do."

"Why, thank you, Victor!" Natalie turns to her husband, sweet smile pursing her lips. "See. I have a spark."

"Yes, Love. I never said you didn't," John replies. He kisses Natalie on the hand before turning to Victor. "We started Storm Landscaping here, in Black Hill, back in 2000, so about twenty-five years now. We've been doing this for quite a while," he says, chuckling.

Victor sees Erin twitch out of the corner of his eye. His eyes cloud, a question of confusion and slight betrayal written across his features. By the time Victor fully looks at him, the emotions are gone, replaced instead by bored indifference. His slender fingers are clasped together on the island, his thumbs rubbing over and twiddling with his index fingers.

He stifles a smile. Watching Erin try and mask his emotions when they so clearly want to be seen on his face is incredibly adorable. While he commends the man for trying, a small part of him wonders why he seemed bothered at all. First impressions aside, Natalie and John seem like trustworthy people. Not like those shady businesses back in New York; Victor has had plenty of run-ins with those groups already. They have a certain smell to them, like stale blood and rotten roses that have been left out in the sun for too long. And Erin's parents are not emitting that.

"Well, with a resume such as that, I can see I've chosen a very capable company." Stella's clear laugh rings out, interrupting Victor's train of thought. She straight-ens her back before heading toward the back door. "I'll give you full creative responsibility. Everything we've discussed so far sounds absolutely wonderful, so I'm sure I'll love whatever you come up with. Design isn't my strong suit, but I suppose everyone has that one flaw they can't inject out. Now, why don't I show you around the yard?"

"Oh yes, that'd be great," Natalie responds happily. John quickly finishes the glass of water Victor had given them when they first entered the kitchen, Erin following suit while looking toward Victor. He waits for his father to walk away before moving around the island.

"I didn't think you'd want to see me again," Erin whispers.

"Why'd you say that?"

"Well, given the mean glare you kept sending my way at Donny's—"

"You're on a first name basis with the owner?" Victor's eye twitches. He taps his knuckles on the counter. "I heard he was older, in his fifties."

Erin gives him a flat stare. "I live in a small country town where the main street has one mall, one movie theater, and all the other necessities are spread out along the same road. The next big city is forty minutes away, and even then, Green Lake would look like a bedroom compared to places up in New York. Everyone is on a first name basis around here."

"Ah, yes." Victor licks his lips. It does little to hide his smile. "I can imagine the struggle."

"Are you used to it yet? How long it takes to get from one place to another?"

He hums. "Yeah, in a way. I was never a fan of cramped spaces—"

"You live in New York!" Erin blurts in indignation.

"Outside of, actually," Victor clarifies. He takes a step. Erin tilts his head to keep his gaze fixed on his. "My property is big. So being here is quite similar, except the air is cleaner. It's refreshing. And there's a lot of land between the houses and main street, so it's easy enough to imagine I'm just stuck in early morning traffic."

Erin stifles a laugh. Victor wishes he could hear it more clearly. Even at Donny's, the sound was muted, covered. No part of this man in front of him should be hidden.

"And I don't hate you," he says. "Not at all. I hardly know you."

"That you don't." Erin tilts his head, looking Victor up and down. Searching. "Why the glare then? Did I stink? I had cologne on. It might not have been as fancy and layered as yours, but no one has ever complained before."

Victor smirks, leaning his forearm on the marble island. Further into Erin's space. Closer to his skin. "You think I smell nice?"

"Answer my question first, cowboy," Erin demands. His voice has dropped so low that Victor knows if he weren't a werewolf, he wouldn't have heard it. He suppresses a shiver. All he has to do is twist his wrist, and Erin's hand is right there, grip tight on the glass.

Focus, Victor.

This is an inspection. And honesty between both parties is paramount.

"I was a bit overwhelmed. Your friend, Fletcher, he said you have ... enhanced genetics? I'm somewhat similar. Also, I don't do well in tight spaces."

"Most men like tight spaces."

"I'm not most men."

"No, I'm starting to gather that." Erin quirks a brow, lifting the empty glass to his lips in an attempt to hide his smirk. Victor thinks he's cute for trying.

"You—"

"Yes, to your question from before." Erin lowers the glass and lifts his pointer finger, grazing it against the inside of Victor's wrist. "I like things that are different. They intrigue me."

Victor doesn't hide his shudder as his eyes follow the path Erin's finger is traveling along his wrist. Back and forth. Back ... and ... forth.

He echoes Erin's question back to him, the one he's replayed time and time again since that night in the warehouse. "Anything else you find intriguing?"

Erin takes a step. The tips of his boots touch against Victor's bare toes. "Just one."

"Erin, are you coming?" Stella's voice rings out, one hand holding the door open for him, when Ben wanders into the kitchen. His eyes widen, instantly landing on Erin, flicking to Victor, before locking eyes with his mother.

He recovers quickly, the alluring green eyes he inherited from Stella cooling back into their usual empty, sunless forest.

"Victor, the Harkins have arrived."

"Oh, splendid! Victor, hun, why don't you go and greet them, hm?" Stella lets the massive sliding door close, Natalie and John already waiting on the porch. She has that proud gleam on her face again, the one she wears when Victor does something that benefits the Pack. And welcoming her close friend as soon as he arrives is one sure way to make sure they stay friendly.

Honestly, he wouldn't be surprised if she tried to arrange a marriage between him and one of Alpha Harkin's kids this summer. What does he have again? Three girls and two boys ... all of mating age, too. He knows Miranda well. She's been good friends with Beatrice since they were kids, both girls being the same age, and Alphas. And Abel ... has a crush on Beatrice. Or at least he did four years ago. That leaves three prospects, all of whom are Omegas.

Well, there are worse Packs to choose from, and the Harkins are just as old as they are—one of the original four after the split eons ago. The bloodline runs deep.

And there's no chance that any of them are his mate.

The curse won't affect them.

Maybe it'll even cure it ...

Victor glances toward Erin; he's stepped away, lips downcast and almond eyes squinted at the corners to the point only gold is visible. Erin huffs, shoulders tense. He doesn't meet Victor's eyes as he heads outside.

Victor ignores the pang in his heart.

"Yeah, of course, Stella." He smiles. He could never say no to his aunt. Everything she does is for his benefit.

She beams, sliding the door closed behind her. Victor watches as Erin strolls away, trailing behind the group as Stella leads them off the porch and around the yard. Their voices echo through the glass, Natalie excitedly pointing at plants along the worn fence beside Stella, while John hangs back by Erin. He pats his son on the head, messing with his hair until Erin swats his hand away. Grinning.

Victor clenches his hands into tight fists.

His heart drops to his feet.

He wants Erin to grin at him like that. Open and loving.

"Come on, dude." Ben pulls on Victor's arm, causing him to turn away from the door.

They make their way to the front porch, where there's nothing but dead grass and broken fence lines for at least half a mile in either direction. Even the deep green of the forest in the distance looks sad and depressing underneath the cloudy sky. At least with the sun gone, the air isn't as stale. Erin must have multiple layers of skin to withstand living in this heat all summer long.

Bending to grab his sneakers from the basket by the door, Victor hones his senses to his Pack scattered across the yard. Some are taking a break, sitting piled on top of each other on the grass, while others are carrying camping supplies from their cars parked in the paddock beside the house to the forest behind. He cocks a brow, not surprised in the slightest at the topic of discussion being carried on the breeze to his ears. The Council Meeting has been hot gossip among his family since it was announced at the last one that they could start hosting again.

"Alpha Victor!"

"Why, if it isn't little red!" Victor braces as a flurry of red hair rams into his legs, laughing manically.

"Who's that man? The young one? He waved to me before! What's his name? Is he going to stay? Is he your mate? He's very handsome. But he smells weird. Does he smell weird to you, too?"

"Woah, calm down, Red." Victor kneels so he's eye-level with Rachel. Pushing some of her long red locks out of her face, he squeezes her cheeks until she squeals in a flurry of giggles. "That man is named Erin. He's the son of the people here to do our landscaping for the Council Meeting. You be nice to him now, ok?"

Rachel sucks in her lips and nods feverishly, like a bobble head on a rollercoaster. "What about his smell? I don't like it. The others are saying it smells like the poison plant, the one Healer Haven says to stay far far faaaaaar away from."

"Well," Victor sighs, he'll need to have a word about gossiping while Erin is around. "Humans don't have the same sensitivities as us."

"Sen-sit-iv-it-ies ..." Rachel mutters, sounding the word on against her sharp canines.

"And to answer your question from before, Little Red, no. Erin isn't my mate."

Rachel frowns and looks at her shoes. "Oh, ok. I was hoping ... since he's really nice and all ... I don't know."

"Rachel?" Victor lifts her chin so that they are eye-level once more. She's still young, what does she know about mates anyway? "What do you mean? Hm? You haven't even spoken to him."

"I don't know." She lifts one shoulder in a shrug. "Just a feeling."

Victor licks his lips, mouth open to reply, when a whistle from across the yard calls. Rachel's dad, Jerry. Her ears twitch, and she flicks her head in that direction. Jerry's walking along the outer fence, cigarette lowered by his side, as the blue car door beside him swings open. He nods to Victor, baring his neck to the side.

"Bye, Alpha Victor." Rachel stands on her tippy toes, kissing him on the cheek before bowing her head to the side with a curtsey. "Bye, Ben." She only waves to him.

Ben sighs. "No respect from this new generation of wolves."

Victor watches her run to her father. He snuffs the stick out on the ground before holding his hand high. Little Red jumps, hitting his high-five in mid-air, before she climbs into the car. A tug pulls on Victor's heart. It's not her innocent words in control of the strings, though, but the longing question he knows he'll never get the answer to. Because he'll never be able to ask. His hand stings, the ghost of a high-five with his father splayed across it. What would he say about all this? About Erin? About the possibility of Erin being his mate?

"Do you think a wolf and a human can be fated mates?" Victor whispers, voice small and quiet as they stand in the shade of the wisteria trees covering the front steps. Ever since Victor first laid eyes on Erin, he's been restless. He's had this urge underneath his skin, an itch that's been screaming and howling, mixing with the voice in his head begging him to protect. But protect what? Erin? A human? It's unheard of.

Especially for him.

Specifically for him.

"I mean, the legend goes that The Black Wolf is fated mates with The White Wolf. That they will find each other in each life, regardless of what Pack they belong to." Ben stuffs his hands into the pockets of his jeans, ears twitching slightly as they pick up on a low rumble, unmistakably a truck engine. "Maybe this is just another one of the Moon Goddess' blessings? She might classify humans as packs … I mean, they once were. If legend is to be believed."

"Blessing? Please, you mean another layer to her fucked-up curse," Victor hisses.

"She's a Goddess, Vic. She can do what she wants." Ben side-eyes Victor, face softening before looking straight ahead again. "And who are we to question her judgments, however cruel and abnormal," he mutters.

"I'll question everything she does, especially if it puts someone I care about in danger," Victor growls, twisting the Pack ring on his index finger. He would never tell a wolf to ignore their instincts … but Little Red is still young. She could have heard someone talking and misunderstood it as her own thoughts and opinions. Yes, that's what Stella would have to say about this. And she's never been wrong before. About anything.

Rachel and her dad drive out of the paddock, their car leaving dust in its wake. He makes a mental note to ask Erin and his parents about that, see if there is anything they can do to reduce the dust in the air every time a car drives over the dead grass. It'll do wonders for keeping their lungs clear, since the main garage beside the house doesn't have enough space for all their vehicles.

"You don't even know if he's gay, Victor," Ben says, strained annoyance clear in his tone. "Just because he was flirting—"

"He seemed annoyed when you pulled me away earlier," Victor retorts. "That means that he's at least interested! Or curious. Fuck, I'm curious! And I never have been before, about anyone! I'm still a virgin for crying out loud. Doesn't that mean something, that I want to jump into Erin's pants?"

Ben steps into Victor's line of sight, forcing him to pay attention to him once more. To heed his words again. He takes a deep breath, voice low as he speaks, "As your Beta, cousin, and best friend, I'm telling you to just let it go. For now, please. You've spoken to him twice, that's not enough time to get to know someone. Sexuality beside the point, *your* interest and curiosity beside the point, you don't have time for it. This is the first time the Pack has held a Council Meeting in twenty-two years, and it's your first time hosting an important event as our official Alpha. We must look like a united and strong front, especially since the other Packs gave us an extra year to prepare, at *your* request. It had only been two months since your Alpha acceptance ceremony. They had no right to grant you that. But they did. The other Packs can't see any weakness or think for even a moment that the Bellmores left any gap in leadership."

Victor sighs, shoulders slumping forward. He squeezes his eyes shut. "I know. You're right, I know." He can feel his throat tightening even more. He hates it when Ben throws logic in his face, when he can't say anything else in response without sounding like a child throwing a tantrum. But this time is different. There's more to this. He just needs to figure out what.

"I feel like there's a string pulling us together, and my instincts are going haywire. I need to be close to him so I can smell him and touch him, but also far away to make sure the Pack is safe for him. And then there's that fucking smell. It's like a leech on his skin. I want to rip it off him, to smell the truth underneath his veins." Victor looks to Ben, eyes as wide as the moon. "Am I going crazy, Cousin?"

"No, you aren't." Ben squeezes his cousin's shoulder in reassurance before gently nudging him to start walking. "Look, I'm not saying there's no attraction there. Erin is a good-looking guy, so it may be fun to explore the possibility as a summer fling." Ben holds up his hands in defense as Victor glares at him. "But that could be all it is. Your inner wolf is missing his mate, and you're lonely, though I don't have the faintest idea how with me around." He smirks, mischief rolling across his face.

Victor chuckles, shaking his head as the Harkin Pack parks their fancy cars along the front fence line. On the road. A typical showing, like a flock of peacocks all puffing up their feathers at the same time, refusing to get their precious feet dirty.

For all the love he has for the Harkin Pack, they sure are pretentious bastards. At least the older generation is.

Pack members chilling by the fence perk up, excitement evident by their huge smiles and voices singing greetings to the new arrivals. Victor doubts much more work will get done today now, the bags of camping supplies forgotten already across the lawn.

"All I'm saying is that it's natural. Projecting something onto someone you've just met, who isn't part of your world, is easy. So, don't stress and don't act on it. Focus, remember? Work now, party later." Ben holds his fist out toward Victor as the driveway gravel crunches underneath their sneakers. "We've got three whole months here."

Matt Harkin is getting out of the car, prowling toward them with arms open and a wide grin plastered across his face. Victor can only imagine how the smile is making his already small brown eyes look underneath his block sunglasses. He looks the same as the last time Victor saw him four years ago—short black hair gelled to the side, a neatly trimmed beard, crisp white linen top, sleeves rolled up to his elbows with matching trousers, tan loafers, and his red Pack ring glistening on the index finger of his right hand.

"Yeah. Focus." Victor bumps his fist against Ben before putting his best diplomatic smile on. "Alpha Harkin! Welcome to my new ranch." He holds his hand out to shake, but Matt ignores it, instead going in for a hug.

"Victor! Look how big you've grown!" Matt barks a laugh, clapping Victor on the back before turning his attention to Ben. "And Benjamin, you are the spitting image of your mother."

Ben nods his head, hands clasped behind his back. His smile is tight as he says, "Thank you, Alpha. That is an honor. I hope I can live up to her standards, too. She's a great role model."

Matt chuffs, "Such a respectful Beta you've got here, Victor." He removes his sunglasses, draping them across his top before stuffing his hands into his pockets. "So, I saw some of your Pack carrying what looked like camping supplies on the drive in. Is that for us?"

Victor nods. "Yes, a show of hospitality. It's been so long since we've hosted, after all. I know everyone tends to bring their own supplies, but I wanted to offer a bit more than the usual complimentary blankets. As thanks. Especially to our close-knit allies, such as yourselves. I figured if our Packs are going to spend extra time bonding, then why not do it in comfort?"

"Yes, yes. Good job, son. Well, I am exceptionally early—perks of living in the area already." Matt barks a laugh again, the deep sound somehow louder when it's not right next to Victor's ear. "Unfortunately, we will be staying a few towns over. Green Lake, the city is called. They have such a splendid hotel there, pool included. And oh, the air conditioning is divine." Matt places a hand over his heart as more Harkin Pack members finally shuffle out of the cars. They are all dressed in various shades of white, nearly identical to their Alpha. Victor sees Matilda and Abel, nodding to them with a small grin.

"You'll be staying for the night of the Council Meeting though, yes?" Ben asks. Ever the diligent helper. "That'd probably be for the best, with drinks involved and all."

Matt puffs his lips, looking Ben up and down. "Your father would be proud." He turns to Victor, the same gleam in his deep brown eyes. "Both of your fathers."

Victor pulls his lips into a tight smile and places his hands behind his back. He twists the ring on his finger again. The metal burns. "I would hope so, sir."

"Now," Matt claps his hands, "where's Stella, hm? And your little sister, Ben. Beatrice! Matilda said she wants to check out Green Lake University with her, and not this old wolf."

"Abel's coming with us," a high voice announces. Matilda struts past them toward the house. She's the spitting image of her father—both her and Abel, who's hot on her heels.

Victor nudges his head toward where the Storm Landscaping truck sits parked by the house. "We hired some landscapers to clean up this place. Aunt Stella is showing them around. And B is in her room, most likely. Third floor, Ilda. Or watching the little cubs."

"Oh, going all out, I see. Just what I'd expect from a Lovelace." Matt hums as he looks around at the ranch. "As much as I was looking forward to traveling to New York this year, I am glad I don't have to go too far. But, had I known this place existed, I would have snatched it up sooner. It's practically in my backyard. You didn't keep it from me on purpose, did you, Mr. Relator?"

Victor laughs. "Of course not, sir. I just happened to see it and thought it'd be a good investment. For future meetings, too."

Matt opens his mouth, confusion written on the tip of his tongue. But before he can wrangle them out, Ben takes a step back.

"Why don't we save that surprise for later? I'm sure Mom is nearly done showing the landscapers around. I know she'd love to see you, Alpha Harkin. Like you said, it's been far too long."

"Sure." Matt points toward the house, a wide smile plastered on his face once more as he looks at Victor. "Lead the way, Alpha."

NINE

The meeting happens after four moon passes. Alaric had sent his fastest hawk to the Others, asking for a moment of discussion—one single day of peace. The hawk returned the next day. The Alpha of the Others had agreed, responding with a specified time and place.

It was a miraculous blessing.

It raised the hairs on the back of Hëna's neck.

They stand now, along the great river's bank, a whole day's trek from the Pack. The air is cool, a morning breeze ripping summer flowers across the top of the still water.

There is no place for her cubs to run. For either side to hide.

The Others stand with metal spheres on their forearms, long swords hanging at their sides and across their backs. Some even carry bows and arrows with colorful feathers far more intricate than the ones from her Pack. There are many of them over there, too, with metal covering their heads and parts of their bodies. Much more than she had anticipated. Far more than her wolves.

"There is a scent lingering on the air," Tala whispers from her side with narrowed eyes.

They wait as the Alpha of the Others approaches. King, she's heard him called on the winds, far above, within the walls of her home in the sky. He wears a wide crown, the thick golden ore twisted and curved to look like branches from a tree, covering most of his black curly hair. He flounders off his tall tan steed, footsteps louder on the river's rocky shore than the metal clanking from along his arms, legs, and against his midsection.

She lifts her nose and sniffs. "Fear, Tala. Do not let it become you. Your Pack is strong. This meeting will succeed." It must. For she knows not what to do if it fails.

"I know the scent of fear, Goddess. I grew up surrounded by it. That is not this. And besides ... the scent does not come from us." Tala's expression hardens, a mirror image to the deep rumble of his voice. The Other King has stopped right at the water's edge; he looks at it with disdain. Alaric shuffles forward a few paces, Tala following one step behind. The cold water laps at their bare feet.

Her children stay where they are, spread across the rocks and field. Some fidget their arms and fingers, weight hopping from foot to foot, but most stand as still as the ground beneath them, tense in shoulders and face. She does not know which is better. She does not care which is better. Who is she to judge how they show their strength? Their bravery and loyalty?

They are here. They have come with her.

That is all that matters to her.

With closed eyes, Hëna exhales a deep breath, forcing the tension loose from her limbs. She, though, cannot afford to be stiff. Oh, how she wishes her husband were here. He always knows exactly what to say to ease her racing thoughts.

"Thank you for agreeing to meet with me and my Pack," Alaric shouts, his hand raised in greeting.

The Other King narrows his already small green eyes and licks his lips, moving them slightly, before raising his hand as well. A wry smile pulls his lips back.

Hëna's brows furrow as he looks behind him expectantly. Her ears do not pick up on the words, but theirs do. Tala's resounding scoff and Alaric's clenched fists tell enough of what was said. Her heart cracks into a thousand pieces.

Is this going to fail before it even begins?

Movement behind the Others King draws her gaze. A young Other gracefully dismounts a white mare and strolls forward as if summoned. Golden eyes glimmer, the vibrant green grass from beside the riverbank reflecting across his downward gaze. A blush stains the tops of his cheekbones, stark against his pale skin, light freckles, and black hair as a metal crown, identical to the Others King, though smaller in size, sits on top of his head. He must be their heir, child to the King.

And that crown atop his head … she recognizes it.

Tala sucks in a quick breath, and she licks her lips, suppressing her smile.

Yes. Her other ray of hope.

The young Other stands beside his father, head bowed to hear the words spoken directly into his ear. With lips pulled tight, the young heir nods and faces them. He removes the sword from his back, places it on the warm rocks, and wades into the shallow river.

He is coming toward them.

Tala flinches, taking a step forward. Alaric's arm across his hips stops him.

Hëna's eyes twitch. Does Alaric know? Has he seen his heir and the Other together? She peers at the Alpha, sensing no hostility from him. So why has he not spoken? Why has he not helped his cub?

"Wait," he commands in a hushed whisper. "Patience, cub."

Tala pinches his brows, lips downturned. But he takes the offending step back. The encounter is small, the movement not picked up by anyone else, all eyes too consumed with the water dancing around the Others heir. It is up to his knees now.

Hips.

Stomach.

While the metal around him seems sturdy, the cream-colored material beneath is thin. Already, strong muscles can be seen through it. Surely he is weighed down. Yet he doesn't struggle, each step secure in footing as he continues toward them with his head held high.

He looks at her first when he reaches them and bows his head, slightly showing his neck. Interesting. He knows who she is, and he knows their customs. She glances at Tala, who hasn't let his round eyes wander from him since arriving. She smiles. It does not surprise her that Tala had shared her description with the Others heir, but time changes appearance. For this cub of a King to recognize her based on an age-old description goes to show how quickly his mind works.

Fitting, for an heir. They are a good match.

Alaric's cub has chosen well.

Hëna nods her head to the side, thankful for the respect, and giving her own to him in return. The young heir turns to Alaric, eyes stolid. Her stomach churns. He has not glanced at Tala since breaching their side of the river.

"Hello, I am Nahale. Prince of the humans." Nahale holds his hand out in front of him.

Alaric grins and grips Nahale's forearm, shaking it twice. "Human, that is what the Others call Pack?" he asks. "The name does ring familiar."

Nahale chuckles. "Yes, though we do not refer to ourselves as such. Those related by blood are a family. They harbor a father, a mother, a son, and daughter. Often one, but sometimes two or more."

"And those not?" Tala questions. Though she guesses he already knows the answer. Like a cub begging for attention from its mother, he's transfixed, the heady scent of longing rolling off him in waves. He is not trying very hard to keep his desires hidden, knowing who he stands amongst. Nor is Nahale. The young Prince's lips may not be smiling, and he may not be touching the young Alpha heir in a possessive nature, but his eyes are etched in truth. They ooze want, practically scream it for all to hear.

She huffs. How they have managed to hide it for this long is a magic she has not heard of before.

Nahale gulps, consciously shutting himself off from Tala. He raises his chin. "Those not related by blood are not called anything to each other. They simply are a part of the same race. There is no relation. They mean nothing."

Alaric howls, drawing their attention. Metal squeals on the other side of the river, a glint catching the sun in the corner of her eyes. Swords have been drawn. "Well, I'm sure we will have all night to discuss our different ... cultures. I am hoping that is why your Alpha sent you over here?"

"King. Our leader is called King, Alpha," Nahale corrects with a small smile, voice soft. "But yes, my father asked me to cross the river as the yelling was ... is ... not dignified for one of royal blood."

Alaric raises a brow. "Well, that is another difference we have. I hope I did not offer any disrespect."

"Of course not, Alpha. My father agreed with your demand for peace—this war has gone on long enough. There has been much death on both sides. It is time to end this. Please," Nahale gestures behind him, "my father waits on the other side of the bank. He has a gift he would like to give to you and your son."

"Of course, we will follow you across." Alaric pats Tala on the back, relief evident in his voice. He glances at her. Eyes pleading. She nods softly, following a step behind them as they make their way across.

They have barely left the water on the other side when the human King speaks. "I am King Halian Treebane. My son, Nahale, spoke wisdom to me when I received your letter."

Nahale ducks his head. "It was nothing you weren't already thinking, Father."

"Well, let's get right to it. Swiftness is key with these things. Guards." King Halian puts his hand in the air and clicks his fingers together. A group of the humans step forward in pairs, a massive oak trunk carried between them as they cross the river. One pair stops before them, this trunk more delicate than the others, with a gold sigil matching the crowns of the human royalty etched deeply in the center of the lid alongside another drawing. The rest of the pairs continue into the water, and soon, there are at least twenty of the trunks being held in front of the Pack now. The lid is opened, and while one guard reaches inside to bring out a wooden goblet, the other pulls out a stained-glass bottle.

Hëna can hear the same happening with the crates behind her. Her forehead creases. Whatever thick material is closed over the top of the bottle is stopping the smell from leaking. And she can't make out the color of the swishing liquid inside through the navy tint. She rubs her fingers against her palm, pressing gently.

"This is a peace treaty gift. It's time to end this silly killing nonsense. I grew bored of all the funerals. Though, I suppose you do as well, given we have killed more of your kind. Alas, as my son has reminded me, a just King doesn't abandon his subjects. I should give your breed a chance at civilization."

Her brows furrow. "Is war and death a game to you, King?"

His eye twitches. "Of course not ..."

"You can call me Na." She gathers her skirt in her hand and curtseys, head bowed low. She feels more than sees her cubs tense all around her.

"Oh, Mother Goddess!" a wolf cries softly behind them.

Patience, she pleads to them all, letting her magic spread over the top of the ground in an attempt to soothe. This is for the greater good. She will bow as many times as she needs to protect her children. Bowing won't rid her of magic, won't make her any less of a Goddess. That power ...

That, one is born with.

That, this human cannot steal.

That, this King can never imagine having.

"Na, you must be the Queen?" King Halian flits his eyes over Alaric in ... disappointment? Her nose curls, and she physically presses down on her lips to stop the snarl. "I must say that is a surprise. Women and children should be left at home. I see many of them on your shore." He shakes his head and exhales deeply. "Not to fret, that is something I can teach your kind. Education is a must here."

The humans sneer, making no attempt to hide their cruel eyes behind their big silver spheres. Her jaw clenches.

Patience.

"Now, before we begin, a toast!" A goblet is handed to each of them, and the liquid, which she now sees is a deep purple, is poured heartily into it. King Halian raises his glass high and swings it around as if showing the Pack that it is ok to accept. Surprisingly, no liquid spills. He must be used to moving around with full goblets.

Nahale holds his goblet against his heart. He is gripping the stem so hard that the cup is shaking. He has not looked up since the crates were brought out. There has been no sign of the happy smile she glimpsed from above. It's as if a mask has been tied to his face.

Tala hesitates, sparing his mate one final glance, nose scrunched tightly as he swallows the liquid. Her heart shudders and she frowns, but lifts the goblet to her lips along with everyone else. Nahale's father does seem to hold a unique opinion about them. It must be hard to have a different belief in his presence. No worry. Once they begin speaking, all the humans will learn of her cubs' kindness. Their loyalty. Their differences are what make them so spec—

The wind whines.

"Aunt, take heed!"

Her movements still. The warm voice of her old friend's eldest daughter glides through the air. Her skin crawls. A burnt scent lingers in the air, like a fire of spice.

The effects are instant.

Cubs begin gasping. The ground shakes as they fall to their sides, fingers clawing at throats and stomachs. None can shift. None can move.

A trap.

They are dying.

She raises the cup to her nose and sniffs deeply. Foolish. Foolish! She is a Goddess, one born from Creation itself! They placed her trust in her—she sits above and sees all. Yet she is the most blind of them. Wolfsbane, the potent plant, was mixed into the drink. The spicy acidic notes blended in with the herbal brewed drink, making it undetectable to their sharp noses.

But Tala smelled it.

He knew something was wrong. With the drinks, with the Others.

With Nahale.

And she ignored his instincts.

She cannot hear; it is as if all sound has been blocked from her. Blue-tinged lips part, red throats exposed in agony. Chests rise and fall in quick succession. Tears fall from red, swollen eyes. Eyes that swivel around widely ...

They still live. Whatever is happening, it has simply kept them all from being able to move their limbs.

"NO!"

Tala is hunched over Alaric, hands clenched tight in the fur on his shoulders as he wails like a young cub again, fresh out of the womb. Lips tremble uncontrollably. Moisture from his nose mix with sweat and drool, pooling onto the rocks below. It is guttural, the echoing sound. A pain that blanches his face and runs his throat raw. Alaric's chest is not moving. His eyes are bugging out of his face and clouded over, the pale blue unseeing. Twin moons, forever covered by thick gray clouds. Never to be seen by the ocean again.

He is gone.

Through death, Tala is Alpha now.

And it is all her fault.

TEN

Erin reaches toward his left, grabbing his phone off the bedside table. He squints in response to the bright light as he dismisses the alarm. 6 a.m. A time when the sun's barely over the horizon. When humanity is not meant to be awake.

Groaning, he lies on his back, phone in hand. Relishing in the limited cool air, he pulls down his notification bar—fifty messages from his group chat 'The Three Stooges', six missed calls from LayLay, and one message from Flerbear.

Erin opens the single message from Fletcher first.

FLERBEAR: Call us when you wake from your slumber, Princess.

He should've known better than to send a quick voice message saying he ran into Victor again, and was weirdly threatened by his aunt right before falling asleep. He was still so full of anger over the whole situation, he couldn't wait till morning to voice it. Now though, the anger is non-existent. No simmer. No bubble. Nothing.

He drops his arms to the side, phone flopping onto the mattress as he stares at the ceiling fan whoosh-whoosh-whooshing around. There's a low hum, with a hitch and click every three turns. The motor must be dying, which isn't a surprise. They're technically only month one into summer, but the heat started all the way back in May. His fan has been working overtime since then. And ... it's just old. Time for the thin, black plastic to get replaced.

But before that, today's Tuesday, so Fletcher will be up getting ready for swim practice, and he knows Layla doesn't ever have her phone on silent or 'Do Not Disturb.' His phone will just keep going off all day if he doesn't respond to them now. Better to get it over with before his inhibitions wake up, too.

Erin leans forward in bed, arms stretching wide above his head. He feels a satisfying click and pop as his joints warm after a long night of tossing and turning. There weren't many dreams last night, none that he remembers anyway, but he still had trouble sleeping. All night, he kept feeling like there was something he needed to do. Somewhere he needed to go. It kept him in that limbo state of awake and asleep.

He stumbles into his narrow walk-in closet to get changed, leaning his phone against some shelving as he starts a group video call with Fletcher and Layla. Fletcher answers almost straight away, one hand brushing his teeth while the other holds the phone. He nods his head in greeting before Layla joins the call. She's still in bed with an eye mask on her forehead and hair spread out behind her on the pink silk pillow like a golden halo.

"So, tell us everything!" Layla singsongs, setting the phone on what he can only assume are her bent knees.

"There's not much to tell." Erin strolls back into the frame with the gray Storm Landscaping long-sleeved jumpsuit hugging his body. He's already rolling the sleeves to his elbows. It's going to be a pain in a few weeks when the heat gets even denser and stifling. "The ranch is in need of major, major repair, so I'll be super busy with my parents. Which means I'll be going into fourth year with some mad muscles. You two are more than welcome to join, and that's not me being sarcastic. Like, please help if you are free. I'll pay you in hugs and homemade pancakes. Plus, it just so happens that the owner of the ranch is pretty cute. I might be into him. He might be into me. Either way, you'll get front row seats to the 10 a.m. showing of 'Erin's flirting attempt.' It's a new reality TV show—quite embarrassing."

Fletcher spits into the sink, waving his toothbrush around like a wand. "Now, skip to the part where your new boy toy comes with a built-in family alarm system. That puts a halt on a second season, and you know I'm all about commitment with these things."

Erin rolls his eyes and walks over to his bathroom, which is connected to his closet. "First off, not my boy toy. And second, her name's Stella. She's Victor's aunt, the one who hired us, and I don't know, I guess their family is pretty important in New York. I know they work in real estate, but that's not usually the type of business you see in those mafia movies. I don't think they're like, bad people. I think I just gave off the wrong first impression, which honestly was Victor's fault. He led with the wrong thing. So, it's only natural for her to think some country boy might be aiming for precious family money. I don't agree with her, but I can't fault her for being ... protective."

"That wasn't the word I was thinking of," Layla mutters around the massive pink scrunchie in-between her teeth. She's twisting her hair around her arm, with her eye mask still on her forehead, before tying it into a loose bun at her nape. How the girl manages to keep her thick hair tied up with only one scrunchie is beyond him. Another mystery best left alone.

"Was Victor the only one leading with the wrong thing?" Fletcher teases, a cheeky look dancing across his face as he moseys out of his bathroom. Erin hears the jingle of his many accessories clinking against his keychain and raises his middle finger to the camera, forced grin in place.

"So funny," he mouths. Fletcher blows a kiss back.

"Wait, so we're pivoting then?" Layla asks. "No more 'doing things to keep your mind off the hot newcomer'? Now we want to stay involved with him?" She raises her hands in front of her, eyes wide but brows pinched. "Just to be clear."

"I suppose so." Erin shrugs. He pushes his curtains aside, letting the early morning sun glide across his room. A ringing echoes in the back of his mind as he watches the sun rise higher in the sky, hip pressed against his desk on the other wall.

A warning? Perhaps. Trepidation? Likely.

Excitement?

Most definitely.

"I ... don't really know what I'm doing. I've dated and hooked up with so many people before, but this feels different. More. Victor interests me ... in a way that I haven't ever felt. When he looks at me ... I don't know. I would like to see where it leads. If it can lead anywhere, ya know? With Stella hovering around."

"Ugh, no, but seriously! What a bitch. How you managed to keep your cool yesterday is beyond me." Layla shakes her head as she finally gets out of bed. There's some shuffling as she throws on one of her matching silk gowns—this one is a baby pink, and the two bears on her tank top hold a heart over her chest match the one on the gown—before walking over to her desk. "Ok, give me two hours and I'll have a new plan started for you, Erin." She has that crazy, determined shine in her eyes that she always gets around finals. "I'm not letting anyone ruin your summer of fun relaxation."

"All right then," Erin laughs. "I'll leave it up to you."

"Oh boy," Fletcher groans. "Here we go again."

Leave it to Layla to stick to a deadline. It's just past 8 a.m. when Erin's phone buzzes. A new email sits in his inbox with an attachment of her new plan. He clicks open the document.

Number One—Avoid crazy bitch Aunt Seirra. Don't go in the house. You have a penis, use it to pee behind a tree or something. Lucky bastard. Just don't forget the hand sanitizer. Or wipes. DON'T BE A GRUB, ERIN! I MEAN IT!

Erin smiles softly; he knows Layla remembers her name. But the sentiment is nice.

Number Two—Keep flirting with Vicky-man! You say he's into you? Curiosity may have killed the cat, but satisfaction brought it back. I mean, look at Mr. Wolf! How many times has he wandered off, like legit disappeared, only to come back days later with bird feathers stuck between his teeth? Sir was living his best life. IDULGING. He's probably knocked up a few neighborhood lady cats that we don't know about. Omg … is your cat a hoe? Like father, like son. It's time you do that, too. You've dabbled in the street life, but now it's your time to dive right in. Remember, friend, sex was on that list … multiple times.

He rolls his eyes at that one. Curiosity? Yeah … that's what this feeling invading his senses is.

Number Three—ROLL YOUR TOP DOWN! Men are animals and love to see skin. Take it from a lady, the collarbones. Ooft. Like a Victorian woman showing off her ankles. Let Vicky-man see what he could have. You said it yourself, you are going to gain so many new muscles this summer. Let them alllll out. Shoulders, biceps, abs. BUT NO TOUCHING! We are in the teasing stage. Teasing, Erin! Teasing!!!

He laughs out loud at that one. He tried one summer to convince his parents to create a summer jumpsuit. Perhaps, with Layla's help, he can finally talk his mom into it.

Number Four—Trust your instinct. You've never been wrong before, Erin. I know you won't be now. Love you!

Erin's heart swells. Pride and love ... He sends a silent 'thank you' to any God listening for sending Layla his way. How did he get so lucky with his friends?

Mr. Wolf, who had been lounging in the truck, jumps out and slinks over to sit in the shade of a massive rock. Erin doesn't blame him. He slips his phone into the front pocket of his jumpsuit. Even though the sun has only just risen, the heat is already sweltering; he knew it was going to be a bad one today. As soon as they got to the ranch that morning, they started setting up a momentary shed in the paddock beside the house, opposite from the garage, to keep all their equipment in. Stella explained how they only use this area to park the extra cars in, so a shed won't disrupt anything. So long as they didn't block the gate or road leading toward the main house, she didn't mind where they set up shop.

She also didn't want them knocking on the door every time they showed up. All the family knew they would be working, and while they tended to be early risers too, she thought their work would go smoothly if everyone stuck to their work schedule. No interruptions. No interactions. Natalie and John could do whatever they wanted with the landscaping, Stella already giving them full creative freedom, so there would be no need to interact with the Lovelace family. At all.

That was fine by him.

With a sigh, Erin looks to the shed. It's nothing fancy, simply a few red metal panels held together with nuts and bolts. Easy to put up, easy to take down. John's been using it since he first created Storm Landscaping, back when they took long jobs all over Texas to build a name for themselves. It's great during winter, but dreadful during summer with the metal keeping all the heat inside.

He spies Natalie striding out of it, sweat curling the black hair along her nape as she heads back toward the truck. Layla would be a better negotiator ... but there's no harm in laying the foundation now. No one said he had to follow her plan in order.

"We really should make tanks and shorts with the logo on them, don't you think, Mom? A nice summer jumpsuit." Erin slides up next to his mother, unzipping his jumpsuit and tying the sleeves around his waist. He can feel sweat slinking down underneath his black tank top already.

"Well, if we did that, my boy, then we would end up spending more on aloe vera cream." Natalie pats Erin on the cheek without looking up from her clipboard, a smug twist to her glossed lips. "The sun is far less forgiving than the moon."

Erin puts on his best pout, leaning over the side of the truck's open back. "That's why scientists made sunscreen."

Natalie sighs, putting her hands on her hips. She looks toward John, who shakes his head and continues carrying leftover flowerpots from a previous job into the shed, determination in his steps to not get involved. She gives in. "Fine, I'll look into it."

"Yes!" Erin beams, jumping over and giving his mom a big hug.

Natalie hugs him back. "Help me take measurements around the ranch while your father starts on the lawn. We'll need to build new fences, and I'd like to do that first. Quickly."

"Kay," Erin agrees. He hurries over to the front fence line, the house looming behind him. His eyes drift over his shoulder toward the window from yesterday, the one with green curtains and plants in funny pots. Erin's not surprised to find Victor standing there, leaning against the wooden balcony with his arms resting on the railing. He's surprised, however, to see him wearing red-striped pajama shorts and no shirt. Victor's face is as expressionless as stone as he stares at Erin. He's … closed himself off. Gone is the open flirtatious smirk from yesterday and at Donny's.

Why? What has changed?

Erin can't help but stare back, feeling heat course throughout his body. His limbs electrify, heart screaming in his chest.

For some reason, this time, Victor is letting Erin look.

The first thing Erin notes is the lack of marks; no tattoos, no scars, no bruises. He sees nothing but sandy beige skin marked only by defined muscles. Victor has a sharp jaw and a straight nose, along with deep-set pale blue eyes and thin pink lips. Even though he's not standing straight, Erin can tell Victor mustn't slouch as his wide shoulders look relaxed and loose, with no hump protruding from between them. He has a small waist, which Erin knows widens out again to powerful thighs. With the sun shining toward Victor, Erin feels like he's looking at some kind of God.

Then there's the ring—the same one Victor was wearing at the party. He must never take it off, or he simply puts it on as soon as he wakes up. With the sunlight, Erin can see it better. The blue jewel looks rich and antique. It sits above the silver band around Victor's finger, threadlike vines interwoven across it, similar to how a crown sits atop a king's head.

Similar in color to the eyes of the brown wolf from his dream.

Erin lifts his head, gaze boring into Victor's one last time before turning and walking back over to the shed. He meets Natalie halfway, grabbing her by the arm and turning her in the opposite direction. "Let's start at the back."

"What, why? Your face is red. Are you feeling sick? Or sunburnt? You never get sunburnt." Concerned, Natalie pushes the pen and measuring tape she's holding into her pocket so she can touch Erin's forehead.

"Well, there's a first time for everything," Erin chuckles nervously. "I was facing the sun for too long, and I forgot my hat. It's hot out here, you know? Maybe I'll borrow your red one in the truck." It isn't a lie because he *was* facing the sun. That has to be the reason why his skin feels like it's on fire and why he feels like his heart is beating too fast. Erin's brows pinch together. That's it, classic heatstroke. He forces his thoughts to stop playing hopscotch in his brain.

Erin doesn't look back, continuing to walk arm-in-arm with Natalie to the back of the house. "You know, this is a great example of why we need summer jumpsuits."

"Go get the hat in the backseat, you cowboy."

ELEVEN

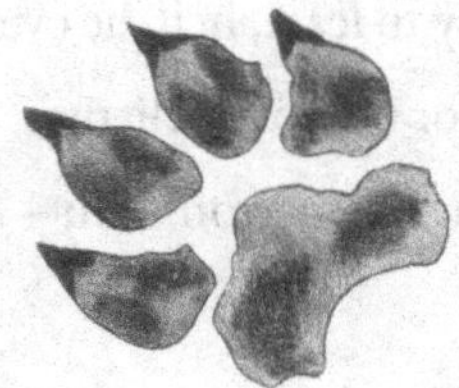

Victor sits in the library at the front of the house, one leg crossed over the other underneath the desk. There's a stack of reports open on the wood—something about new developmental properties on Long Island, but he can't be sure. He had most of his work brought down after the internal renovations were completed at the start of May, and has been successful in fulfilling his duties since he arrived. Even with a Council Meeting to run, he can't afford to fall behind. Businesses won't run themselves. Especially one as old as theirs.

It's only been three years since he took over Lovelace Real Estate, and four since his Alpha acceptance ceremony with the Pack. No one's questioned his ability to call the shots as CEO. He's the Alpha. The Black Wolf. He was born to lead. And Stella has been there every step of the way, guiding him, and showing him tips and tricks in the human world. Being a werewolf when conducting a house inspection does have its perks—and makes the tour run much quicker, being able to smell if the landlord is lying about cleaning the carpet and spying dents on the ceiling—but humans like evidence. They need proof that things aren't up to par.

It was fun to learn how to draw attention to these things naturally and make up reasons for getting itemized lists.

However, learning to adapt to a human society in a highly competitive business was a challenge. But Victor has never been a quitter. He knew this was going to be his career path since he presented at thirteen and rose above the anxiety. Now, his family name is the one advertised on every street corner and high-rise apartment. Properties for sale, rooms ready to lease, hell, he even started a new design project to build houses from scratch for potential clients.

He won't let anyone take that away from him—from his Pack.

And it was running well.

Until recent distractions.

He's re-read the same line for the tenth time, pen clicking absentmindedly in his hand, before finally giving in to the temptation to look out the bay window at the sweet distraction working in the yard.

Said distraction sits on top of a lawnmower—the fancy kind with wheels you drive around—wearing a deep red cowboy hat and round sunglasses to shield his eyes from some of the sun's bright rays. The sleeves of his Storm Landscaping jumpsuit are tied around his waist, except the whole outfit is now dusted green with grass. Victor's eyes soften as he grins, watching the muscles on Erin's back ripple through his sweat-soaked tank top.

He's always been more of a night wolf; the feeling of settling down on the two-seater by the bay window after a long day's work, rum with ice clinking in the silence as it defrosts, and reading late into the night has always been the perfect way to relax. A piece of routine he brought with him to Texas from New York.

But he supposes there are perks to going to bed and waking up early.

So, whether Ben is right or not about Erin being an easy replacement for his missing mate, Victor sure is enjoying the view.

"We've got a problem."

Ben strides into the room, the door closing behind him with a thud. He sits in one of the red armchairs opposite Victor with a pile of paper nearly falling out of his arms. Victor spies the word 'seating chart' on the top and tenses.

"What kind of problem?" Victor tosses his pen onto the desk, praying there hasn't already been a fight between two Packs who are meant to be next to each other during the Council Meeting. He'd much rather deal with Michal, the head chef, being up in arms about how to grill the perfect steak again.

Ben leans back in the chair, left leg bouncing sporadically. "Matt Harkin just told me that the Treelark Pack will be arriving late, practically right as the Council Meeting is meant to begin on the fifteenth." He bites his lip, worry pulling tightly on his brows.

"How did Matt find out that piece of information before we did?" Victor frowns, tapping his fingers on a red book cover to the right of the desk. He remembers the stories Stella used to tell him about the Alpha of the Treelark Pack, Adam Treelark. His name was on the list she always made him write and repeat during Pack history lessons. She never wanted him to forget, saying it was his duty as Alpha to know the names and behaviors of those corrupted by the Moon Goddess, so he could keep an eye on them.

"I don't know," Ben sighs, the hand not holding the papers rubbing against his forehead. "Apparently one of his omegas used to be a Treelark before he married into the Harkin Pack. His little sister didn't follow him into the new Pack, but they still communicate sometimes. Matt heard it from them."

Victor walks to the window, arms crossed over his chest. Erin is sitting atop the lawnmower still, drinking from a water bottle. He's looking toward the red shed Storm Landscaping brought this morning. Natalie and John are there, standing in the open doorway. John is holding some papers—various kinds of mappings of the house—while Natalie is pointing at places in the backyard, two color swatches of blue held in her hand. Victor wonders if they have fans inside the shed. It looks like it would get hot in there, if the sweat dripping down John's temple and the small fan attached to Natalie's hip is anything to go by. Maybe he should buy them some proper portable fans—giant ones with batteries instead of electrical plugs. Or an A/C unit.

"Victor!" Ben yells, throwing his stack of papers on the chair behind him. He stomps over and closes the cream-colored curtains. The room is cast into filtered darkness.

"Hey!" Victor reaches to open the curtains again, but Ben grabs his arm and squeezes tightly.

"This is serious!" Ben barks, the scent of rotted roses oozing out of him like a hurricane. His eyes are wide, pupils shaking. He looks like a man preparing for war.

Victor takes a deep breath, releasing his own pheromones to overpower Ben. "Calm down," he commands.

His cousin blinks a few times before bowing his head and stepping back. His shoulders are still tensed, fingers now tapping his thigh, but he's no longer releasing stressed pheromones. A good sign. Victor turns back to the curtains and opens them. Erin is gone, the lawnmower now deserted. The room is still cast in darkness.

"I'm sorry," Ben says, voice wobbly.

Victor closes the curtains and turns to face Ben. He's always been just a hair's breadth shorter than his older cousin—that's what a six-year age difference will do to you—but now he feels almost a head taller with Ben's shoulders slumped forward and eyes downcast. It's unusual; Ben is normally the calm one in situations like this, while he runs ahead, thinking with his heart first and head second.

"Listen, the Treelark Pack is dangerous, I know that. We all know that, more than anybody." Victor closes the gap between them, touching a hand to Ben's shoulder. "What Adam Treelark helped those traitors do to my parents, to your father, and so many other members of our Pack that night in March will never be forgiven." Victor bows his head, forcing Ben to make eye contact with him before continuing. "It will *never* be forgotten. I vow this to you."

Ben's eyes cloud over, his thoughts burying themselves behind dense foliage before he looks away. Victor has always wondered where he goes in moments like this. Is he thinking about that cool March night? He was old enough to remember bits and pieces. Or is he worrying about ways to protect the Pack? Devising plans to prevent that tragedy from happening again? Either way, it's been happening much more frequently, the absence in his presence when he's with Victor. He should mention it to Stella—she'll know what's going on with her son.

"Adam didn't take part in the killing that occurred that night, Cousin," Ben whispers.

"He did by omission," Victor growls. He sucks his teeth. "He didn't warn us. He chose them by staying silent. And don't tell me he didn't know. They were best friends. He knew. And he said nothing to your dad or Stella at the Council Meeting the year prior."

If Adam had done something, had warned Stella about the attack, then maybe Gray and Stacy could've been stopped earlier. Maybe Stella could've saved them all.

Ben grimaces, lips parting when a sharp knock echoes around the room. Victor waits, eyes glued to Ben. He wants to hear what he has to say. What justification he will try to utter. But Ben's lips seal shut, his words locking away with him.

The anger slides out of Victor, leaving his limbs heavy. "Come in," he calls to the door. A mop of curly brown hair slides inside the room. It's one of the younger cubs, a chef in training by the name of David. He looks nervous, blue eyes blown wide as he stands half behind the open door with one hand still on the handle like he's afraid to come in all the way.

"Sorry to interrupt, but I need some confirmation on the dessert menu from one of you … Michal's pretty insistent it has to be finalized by this afternoon."

Victor's eyes go soft as he smiles. "I'll be right there, David. Just give us ten minutes, okay?"

David nods, a shy smile on his lips as he leaves, closing the door behind him. Ben's now sitting on the armrest of the chair Victor was on before. His head is bowed, hands clasped together on his knees. It almost looks like he's praying; whatever words he was going to speak now being sent to the stars instead.

Victor walks over to the chair and picks up the scattered papers. "I'm grateful you've been handling a lot of the responsibility with the Council Meeting and the temporary move down here with half of the Pack, letting me focus more on the real estate business. And I know buying this property was risky—I know my idea is a gamble. I should be doing more, juggling the two better. But I didn't expect to meet Erin. I don't know why I feel like this, so believe me, I am trying to focus. I'm sorry if it feels like I'm a bit distracted lately," he stands, moving in front of Ben, "but I am listening. I'm planning and keeping all of Stella's training in mind. My instinct as Alpha, and my desire as your blood, is to protect the Pack. And for some reason, Erin makes that instinct stronger. When I look at him, it's like my mind clears. All the black fog lifts, and I can think straight."

Ben's lips quirk. "Maybe Erin is a werewolf in disguise, then. All the signs are there. He might just be a good liar."

Victor sends him a glare, but there's no heat behind it. He holds out the papers, watching as thoughts swarm around like bees in Ben's brain and across his eyes. A couple of seconds pass before he relaxes. Victor sees the moment the determined green glow turns back on in his eyes. A lightbulb with fresh batteries.

Ben slaps his knees and stands, taking a deep breath before grabbing the papers out of Victor's hands. "Well then, Alpha, your orders?"

Victor matches Ben's determined smile. "There's no point trying to contact the Treelark Pack now because most won't be arriving until the start of August anyway. If they have any respect for our kind left, they will notify us within the month. So, for now, let's leave it," he commands. "Extend perimeter checks by five miles and double our numbers on runs. Hell, send the wolves into town if you must. I want no one venturing out alone," the click-click-rumble of the lawnmower starts again, "but no direct action now doesn't mean we won't be ready. Alert the Alphas—the ones we trust who haven't arrived yet, so they can keep an eye out during their journey for any foul play—as well as Alpha Ross

Cooper of the Florida Pack, and Alpha Christian Reed of the Louisiana Pack. They'll be here much earlier than the others since they live so close by. I'm projecting the end of July, so they need to be aware of any potential threats. If I were Adam Treelark planning to set a trap, they'd be the wolves I'd target first."

"Right." Ben nods. "They are two of the biggest Packs out there. Wiping them out reduces the competition against their cause considerably."

"And they're two of the oldest." Like us. Victor doesn't say it, but Ben hears it. His lips thin, jaw clenching tightly.

After the split, wolves separated from each other until each state had their own Pack—names, ring, rules. The whole lot. But those original four Packs, they had valuables, artifacts, passed down through their bloodline, from Alpha to Alpha. No matter how much betrayal they felt toward their once renowned Mother Goddess, they never dared rid themselves of her sacred gifts.

That's magic no wolf wants to deal with.

Victor traces the vine pattern snaking around his index finger. Perhaps it is not just retribution for the Goddess the Treelark Pack is after.

"I'll introduce joint training too with the Harkin Pack, and the Cooper and Reed Packs once they arrive." Ben bumps fists with Victor before leaving, calling out over his shoulder, "Don't forget about the kitchen. You'll upset little David if you keep him waiting."

Victor huffs through his nose. He crosses his arms over his chest as he turns around. Through a slit in the curtain, he can see Erin atop the mower looking even more sweaty than before. As if he could feel Victor's gaze, Erin brakes and turns around in the seat, looking toward the library bay window. Victor reaches out, sliding the curtain aside a bit to wave. The Pack ring on his finger gleams. Erin tilts his cowboy hat in greeting, a small smile on his lips, before he turns back to keep working.

Victor's heart jumps. Ben's joke from before climbs back into his mind, reverberating like ping pong balls on concrete, and setting his nerves on fire. It's plausible and makes much more sense than a wolf and a human being fated mates. It would explain so much …

But that would make Erin The White Wolf.

Pain stabs his heart at the thought.

Not in fear that he may be wrong and Erin really is a human, mated to a wolf—forced to forever be bound to a being in a world he could never truly come to understand—but fear in that he knows it's true. Nothing has sounded more like the truth than that.

One way or another, Erin is a werewolf.

Do Natalie and John know? Is that why they surround themselves with all that wolfsbane? No, don't jump to conclusi—

Was he alone when he first shifted?

Then, a quieter thought. It bites off more of his heart than the last.

Has he even shifted at all?

Victor doesn't remember his first shift, too young to hold onto those feelings. Shifting is something they are all born with the ability to do. Some are late bloomers, not shifting until they are nearly five, but he's heard tales of how early he shifted. Some say he was still a babe, running on all fours before he could even walk on two. Then later, during what the humans call puberty, a wolf will present, their souls ready to finally take on their born role within the Pack. This normally happens around fifteen; the latest he's heard was eighteen.

He was thirteen.

It didn't take long for the awe to transform into fear. Wolves didn't whisper anymore about how strong he was. They didn't congratulate him on being early, on having a soul ready to contribute to Pack life far faster than any other. No, they grumbled about the shame he would bring to their doorstep. They faced the moon, anger breathing down each breath, as they howled, 'Why them? What had they done to deserve even more suffering? Hadn't they given enough already?'

And now Erin.

Sweet, flirty, photo-loving Erin.

Cursed for all eternity.

They'll say the same about him. They'll look at him the same way. He won't have a chance to prove he's more—the clock will have started. It probably already has.

He knows he shouldn't, but he looks toward the sky. The moon hides among the sun, her silver crescent barely visible in the light of day.

"Please, if you hold any ounce of love for us left ... don't let it be him," he whispers to her, eyes closing. The thick curtain is soft against his forehead, where he rests it on the window. "But if it is, if it's him you've punished alongside me, then let this storm pass us quickly."

TWELVE

Nahale was followed.

She wasn't the only one who had seen them. His people had seen him with Tala, too. And they used that against him. They must have. That is the only thing she can think of to explain his behavior. Why else would he betray his love? She does not know how long they have been together, but she knows this ... Love cannot be faked. It is not something one can simply hide behind their gaze.

Nahale loves Tala.

And his King took advantage of that.

Her throat burns with bile, and her heart stings with anger. How despicable.

She didn't consume any of the poison, but she wasn't going to let her children be chained and taken away by themselves. Especially when this was her doing. So she played along, slumping onto the hard rocks. Feeling the sharp edges cut at her bare shoulders and against her soft cheek. Unmoving. The thick metal is harsh on her skin, digging into her pale flesh as they drag her to one of many long carts with the others. Her shawl falls off. Her teeth clank together when they toss her in. Tala follows soon after. His headpiece is missing; it must have fallen off when they dragged him away.

Or they took it.

Broke it.

Left it to be lost in the river.

The cart begins to move, two large black horses snorting as they trot back toward the human settlement. "Tala," she whispers to him. Already, the thick metal chain wrapped around his wrists and ankles stains his skin red. Burning oakmoss fills the space between them, the spice of sandalwood no longer pleasant. The chains have been dipped in wolfsbane.

Her round eyes watered, the odor thick around them, like a forest on fire with a thunderstorm approaching. But the liquid raining down offers no relief, only more acid and pain.

"Tala," she tries again. Either he cannot hear her, or she is being ignored. Either way, Tala lies on his back, eyes squeezed shut and jaw clenched tight. Thick tears roll down his face. It is as if her heart has been clawed from her chest and torched in a flame of poison. Light draws her eyes to the pink-hued sky. A bright blue flame rises toward the stars.

Alaric.

His goblet must have been lined with more poison than the rest of theirs.

A burning sensation builds in her throat, her nostrils flaring.

"Tala, my child, I am here," she says to him. She lets the tears fall. "And I am sorry."

It does not take long for them to reach the human settlement. She is not surprised that the location given to her cubs was close to the kingdom. King Halian did not strike her as one who likes to travel far. The sun moves across the sky as open plains turn to deep forest. Beautiful wild bluebells are trampled over by crates and horses as the dirt trail turns into a stone road. The settlement is big. She can hear many human voices cheering for their king, their prince, over the sides of the crate as they roll through the wood and stone structures. Many new smells assault her nose, but the potent spice of wolfsbane stands out the most.

It is everywhere. She can only imagine how hard her children find it, without magic to ease the sensation. It would not surprise her if some have passed out in the crates that follow behind theirs.

They continue deeper into the settlement, the wide road straight with no bends. Soon, a giant stone structure comes into view. A white flag with the same sigil that was etched beside the drawing of the King's crown on the crates dances freely all around it. She recognizes what it is now, once again reprimanding her stupidity. A bare tree, purple wolfsbane growing along the roots.

How had she not seen it?

They stop, and guards round the cart. She is flung over the shoulder of one of the humans, biting back her groan as his metal shoulder digs harshly into her stomach. Watching from half-shut eyes, they do the same with Tala.

"Take them to the dungeons," King Halian commands. He must have been riding in front of them, leading the way. Victorious. Proud. Slimy bastard.

Oh, how she wants to rip out his throat with her canines.

With a cheerful smile, the King turns on his heel and marches up massive stone steps. The front of his home. The guards do not take them that way. They go around the side of the palace, through a creaky old wooden door, and down, down, down wet steps. Mold sticks to the walls, making her nose wrinkle. She has never liked the smell of damp moss and decaying bark, and now she must sit beside an abundance of it ...

They pass no more humans on the journey.

She is grateful for that. Less humans for her anger to memorize.

There is no light in the dungeon, bar flames licking wood in slots along the wall. But even those quickly disappear as soon as all her wolves are tossed into open rooms, each one separated by thick, purple-tinted metal running from floor to ceiling.

Recoiling, she rubs her burnt fingertips after touching one of the bars. The skin heals over swiftly. So, they have learned how to press the wolfsbane into the metal, then. She frowns. No wonder so many of her wolves would die every time they crossed paths on the battlefield.

A light shines down the hall, the flames dancing with the snarls rumbling from behind the damp stone.

Nahale.

He crouches in front of them, head bowed, golden eyes red and swollen. Even his small nose looks like it's been dusted with the poisonous flower.

Tala is careful as he reaches through the bars, his finger sliding under one of the golden orbs, forcing his head up. "Why do you cry, my Star?" His voice is rough, low, like he has tried to whisper. Though she suspects he could not speak any louder at this time, even had he tried.

Nahale leans into Tala's touch, his bottom lip trembling. The flame he is holding is placed onto the stone beside him, and soon both his hands grip Tala's against his face. "My Star, don't shed tears for me."

Her breath hitches. She lifts a hand to cover her trembling lips. Star? She was so distracted by the pain her Hope was emitting that she had not realized that was what Tala called his mate. Her eyes flutter, her head twisting in agony. Oh, how deep the love runs between them. Deeper than she had seen.

Perhaps ... perhaps her own Star had seen them already. Before she did. He was out amongst them far often than she was. He could have seen the signs. He could have glimpsed them together, underneath that tree, while on his way to gather more souls.

Perhaps that is why he told her not to involve herself.

Perhaps he knew that this would be the outcome.

"I'm sorry. I'm so, so sorry, Little Wolf," Nahale's voice hitches as he whispers, careful not to disturb the others. Not that any of them seem to be paying attention anyway. Most are sleeping off the poison, the others drained of energy after watching their Alpha die in front of them. She knows it is different for those not of the same blood, but the bond between Pack runs deep. They would have felt his death all the same. It would have affected them all, in one way or another.

What a terrible thing to experience.

She understands completely.

Nahale hiccups, "They gave me a terrible choice ... I—help trap the wolves to turn them into slaves for the human kingdom, or die alongside them. And I—"

"You've done nothing wrong." Tala grabs Nahale's hands in his own, rubbing circles across the red, scarred pads. The faint smell of soil drifts into their cell the more Tala rubs at Nahale's fingernails. His face pinches, right eye twitching. His question is silent in the air. Nahale hears it still.

"Your father ... I moved him before they could burn him completely with the poison." Nahale gazes into Tala's hardened eyes. "I gave him a burial, the way you taught me. In the forest. I wasn't able to go as far as I would've liked—he's nowhere near the rest of your Pack ... but I ... I wasn't going to let them throw liquid wolfsbane on him and light him up. He deserves to be amongst his kin in the stars."

Tala pulls Nahale's fingers farther into the cell and drops his head to them. He breathes deeply. "Thank you, Star." Tears stream down his cheeks again, though not as thick as before. And his voice has gotten stronger now. Good.

Nahale cries, any reservations he had broken apart. He tightens his grip on Tala's hands. "I didn't want you to die! I couldn't let you die ... I would be all alone then. In whatever way ... I know this is the worst life you could live—shackled, in pain. But I was selfish. Oh, Goddess! I'm so sorry, my Love. This isn't right. I know ... I knew from the very breath I used to agree. So," golden eyes narrow, fierce strength returning to them, "I'll get you out of here. I swear it. I will find a way. I know this castle like I know my heart."

"No. I don't want you to get hurt." Tala reaches forward, silencing any more words Nahale had opened his mouth to say with a sweet kiss. He wasn't careful of the bars. Sizzling flesh burns around them, but Tala ignores it. Even when Nahale tries to pull away, Tala only grips him tighter and presses him closer. When he finally pulls back to speak, he keeps his lips pressed gently over Nahale's and wraps his hand around the back of his neck. "I would choose to live as a slave to humans for a hundred lifetimes if it meant I could keep you in my sight. My birthright? It doesn't matter. My freedom? I don't care. My instinct?" Tala presses their foreheads together. Her stomach squeezes.

"My instinct is you. To see you. To touch you. To protect you. So long as you live, my instinct, my heart and soul—every breath of air that enters my lungs—is for you. You rule me. From the moment I met you twelve and six moon cycles ago, when we were but cubs, you have been my everything. I did not know then, what that feeling stirring within me meant—what it was called. But I knew it was not something I wanted to let go of. That is something I will never forget, in any lifetime."

Nahale bites his lip as he weeps, the tears plopping onto the stone beneath them louder than the gasps of air he takes. He nuzzles his forehead against his mate. Tala smiles sadly before leaning forward and licking the blood from Nahale's lips.

"I just said not to hurt yourself, Star."

Nahale chuckles. Hëna clenches her hands as her heart rips into a thousand pieces.

"Disgusting traitor," a low growl rips from behind Nahale. Kazamir stands in the cell across theirs, knuckles white from gripping the bars. Despite the blood pooling from the burns on his palms, his grip does not loosen. And neither do the bars bend or break.

"This does not concern you, Kazamir." Tala stands with Nahale, eyes fierce. His fingers twitch as if he wishes he could push his lover behind him to protect him from the disrespectful wolf's wrath.

"Does not concern me?" Kazamir's rough laugh echoes around them, causing more wolves to stir. Their eyes rotate, piecing together what is happening. Many linger on Tala's hands wrapped possessively around Nahale's waist through the bars. The way his fingers grip at the young prince's thick shirt. The lack of armor. The lack of a crown.

"Humans! Bring me your King!" Kazamir shouts. "Humans! Humans! I demand an audience!"

Guards rush in, weapons drawn. More fire brightens the place, the light harsh on her eyes, causing her to squint. Some halted, eyes bugged at seeing their prince standing amongst the enemy, weaponless and unafraid. Nahale makes to move away, but Tala tightens his grip. A hiss slips past his chapped lips at the movement, his arms brushing against the bars. Nahale freezes, hands rising instinctively to place over Tala's arms. As if his touch can heal. As if his touch can erase.

"Prince Nahale, what are you doing here?" King Hailan has entered, disappointment clear in his golden eyes. Until he notices where it is his son stands. Then he boasts apathy. "No matter, I heard a beast was howling for me? What is it? Supper is when I say it is, not when you want it."

"Let me out of here and I'll work as one of your guards." Kazamir grins wide, canines on full display. "I'm one of the Pack's top hunters. I know how to kill."

King Halian takes a step back. "I thought you wolves were meant to be loyal?"

"We are," Kazamir glares at Tala, "to those that are strongest. You killed our Alpha, that makes you stronger than that pathetic wolf who betrayed his trust first." He looks to King Halian again and drops to one knee, neck bared. "I will follow you now, Alpha King."

"Alpha King!" Many wolves stand on their knees and bare their necks, the effects of the poison wearing off now. Howls ring out from within the cells. The chants become louder, drowning out Tala and Nahale's protesting cries.

King Halian smirks. His grin looks more wolfish than any of her children. "Excellent! I am so glad we can see eye to eye! See, Nahale," one of the guards rips him from Tala's grip, thick fingers narrowly missing being bitten off, "throw the pets into the dungeon, and they begin to learn. You were right after all, my son—they are smart beasts."

"Father—"

"Now." King Halian stands in front of Tala, a smirk etched so deep his cheekbones look as if they are about to jump out of his face. "For brainwashing my son, the newly come of age prince of this kingdom, and trying to kidnap him after forcing him to let you out of this cell, you will be sentenced to die."

"No!" Nahale screams as he struggles in the guard's grip. "Please, Father! No! That was not what we agreed!" But he is not strong enough. King Halian waves his hand, and the prince is thrown over the guard's shoulder and dragged away, his cries echoing louder than the heartbeat pounding in her ears. Each one cuts more painfully than the last.

She closes her eyes and turns away.

"Tala, was it?" The King takes a step forward. Tala doesn't flinch, pale blue eyes unwavering as he glares darkly at the smirk, baring his teeth. "Thank you for falling in love with my son."

THIRTEEN

A week has passed since Storm Landscaping was hired to work on the Lovelace ranch. The front yard has been completely cleaned—grass mowed, weeds pulled, rocks moved, and any leftover junk from both the interior re-design and before, tossed in the trash.

Stella seemed surprised when she poked her head out of one of the lower balconies last Friday and saw a clear front yard. Erin may have poured some extra smugness into his grin as they left that afternoon.

Just a bit.

They finished fixing the fence line along the property early this morning, so Erin thought it would be a perfect time to take a stroll and snap some progress photos with his camera for his, and the company's, portfolio. Thankfully, it's a bit cloudy, so even though it's nearly lunchtime, the sun isn't making him sweat his organs out. Mr. Wolf walks beside him on top of the fence, his little claws hardly making a sound on the wood as he keeps pace with Erin. When Erin stops to snap a shot, Wolf will stop, too, and sit with his front paws neatly together, head held high like a regal king in a throne room. It makes Erin snort every time he sees it, unable to stop himself from capturing the moment despite the numerous photos he already has of the same pose.

The spoiled little cat has Erin wrapped around his finger.

Erin rubs between Wolf's ears as he looks through the photos he's taken so far. "So, what do you think, Mr. Wolf? Is the lighting ok, or should I do lower-angled shots?"

Wolf stays silent as he looks at the camera screen before bending backward to gaze at Erin. His heterochromic eyes are wide open, confused and questioning, causing Erin to giggle.

"Lower-angled shots it is, then," he states.

He walks around to the side of the house to stand in the shadow cast by the building, when he spots Victor sitting on the back fence, one earphone in while gazing out at the fields. Erin gulps and raises his camera. With the sun peeking over the house, Victor looks as though he's wearing a halo above his golden locks. Throw in some pretty flowers and vines along the fence, swapping out the gym clothes for a white toga with golden detail, and it would look like Victor had been transported from a different time period.

"Even the universe thinks he's perfect," Erin mutters as he looks at the photo. He looks up to take some more shots of Victor when he sees the man in question's shoulders shaking, his mouth spread in a wide grin. Erin tilts his head in confusion, eyes squinting. He looks at Wolf, wondering what it is Victor could be laughing about, when he realizes the cat is already a few steps ahead on the fence.

Heading toward Victor.

"Hey," Erin calls, letting his camera drop to hang around his neck. Wolf stops and turns around, an exasperated look on his small face. His tail swishes in the wind before he meows once and continues his walk, the cat equivalent of 'hurry up slowpoke, hot Vicky man is waiting for us.'

Erin pouts. Traitor. He raises his camera and faces the direction he came from. He snaps a few shots of the yard with the sun lighting the house—the whole reason he walked over to this spot—before moseying to where Victor now sits patting Wolf's head.

When he's in speaking distance, Victor turns his head to the side and takes out his earphone, stuffing it into the pocket of his shorts, a grin still stretched across his face. "Had some words with the universe this morning, did you?"

"Oh, um, I was talking about Wolf." Erin feels his face tingle with warmth, an embarrassed laugh spilling out of his lungs. "How'd you even hear that? You had your earbud in ..." The night at Donny's flashes across his mind, the memory sharp and quick. Victor seemed to hear the situation with Gary then, too, all the way on the other side of the warehouse with the music blasting around them.

Victor raises one brow, his smile somehow getting even larger and causing his eyes to squint. "I have very good hearing."

"Oh, I guess we have that in common." Erin clears his throat before pointing to Wolf, who is now sitting in Victor's lap. "Wolf has pretty good hearing, too." Wolf's head swivels toward Erin, whiskers twitching. Round eyes innocently asking, 'Who, me?'

Erin's heart races as Victor bursts into laughter. The sound is just as he remembers it being. Deep and rich, but louder, clearer, out in the open air. Erin tilts his camera from where it hangs around his neck, movements slow to not alert Victor, and snaps a shot.

"You have a nice laugh," he blurts as Victor quiets down.

Now it's Victor's turn to look embarrassed. Erin stares as he sees red slowly creep across Victor's high cheekbones.

"Thank you," Victor replies, voice raspy from the laughter. He holds Wolf in one hand as he hops off the fence. Wolf meows in retaliation before going limp in Victor's arms, letting himself be held.

"May I?" Erin raises his camera toward them. There's no way he'd risk taking a bad picture of Wolf—he'd never meow at him again. Victor nods, posing with Wolf for the camera. Erin takes a step back and looks into the lens. Three blue eyes and one yellow eye gaze happily toward him.

"How did it turn out?" Victor asks, walking over to stand slightly behind Erin, lowering his face to get a better look at the camera over Erin's shoulder. Erin blushes when he feels Victor's warm breath fan across the exposed skin at the base of his neck. He's struck once again by how much taller Victor is than him. Usually, Erin is the tallest in the room.

"Perfect," Erin chuckles.

"I'm glad," Victor whispers. Erin turns around to look at Victor, his shoulder bumping into his chest as he does. He opens his mouth to apologize when Wolf starts squirming, tail swatting him in the face as he jumps out of Victor's hands.

"Ooft." Erin reaches up to his nose at the same time Victor reaches forward.

"Are you ok? I'm so sorry." Victor is touching Erin's nose, concern making his voice rise in pitch.

"Yeah, I'm fine." Erin grabs Victor's hands, lowering them from his face. His thumb rubs instinctively across the back of Victor's palm.

Victor relaxes, releasing a shaky breath before stilling. He looks down at his hands being clasped together by Erin. Did he do that? Erin quickly drops Victor's hands while clearing his throat, his arms swinging by his sides as he looks around. With how passive-aggressive Stella was toward him, he wouldn't be surprised if the whole Lovelace family was warned to keep him and Victor apart.

"So, what were you listening to before?" Erin holds onto his camera again, careening back to the fence line with Victor following behind him.

"Murder," Victor replies in a deadpan voice.

Erin freezes.

"A band called Murder," Victor clarifies. Mischief is laughing across his face when Erin sends a glare at him.

"Ha-ha, very funny," Erin says sarcastically.

"Do you like music?" Victor questions.

"Eh, I don't really have a preference." Erin shrugs. "I can't say I like or dislike anything specifically. I can find something interesting in all kinds of music. Layla, though, that girl always has to have something playing. Her and Fletcher have gotten into plenty of fights over songs. Apparently, they have joint playlists for different occasions. My parents are even in some of them."

Victor chuckles. "You seem quite close with your friends. Don't your siblings get mad?"

Erin shakes his head. "It's just me. I was adopted by my parents when I was about four months old. It was a closed adoption. None of us know anything about my birth parents."

Victor hums. His hands are clasped together behind his back as he walks beside Erin. "Does that bother you?"

Erin shrugs, snapping a photo of a bird sitting on one of the balconies with his free hand. "No. I grew up safe with a roof over my head, love in my belly, and two best friends always by my side. They're my siblings at this point. We've known each other since we could walk. Well, Fletcher and I have, at least. We met Layla right at the end of middle school, like the last month. We had a whole summer to bond before we left her to start high school, and then she joined us a year later. What more would I need?" He glances at Victor and sees a sad smile on his face.

His heart drops to his feet. He hates that look on Victor's face. It's not pity—that look he knows like the back of his hand. That's why he doesn't tell many people that he had a closed adoption or that he only has two, true, friends. No, the irritation he feels souring his blood isn't because Victor is getting the wrong idea about how he grew up, like others have in the past ... it's the exact opposite. Victor has understood everything Erin just voiced. He respected all of it. Grasped the situation. So why does he smile with tears clouding his eyes?

Did something happen to Victor's parents? That would explain how protective Stella was last week, and how he has yet to see Victor's parents or hear any mention of them.

Was Victor adopted, too?

Erin faces forward, steering the topic away from parents as his voice takes on a light, airy tone. "And you? What was it like growing up with a cousin? You guys don't look so far apart in age. What's the gap? Did you fight a lot?" Erin nudges Victor's shoulder with his own as a deep chuckle slides past Victor's lips.

"Ben and I are six years apart. He's older, Stella's firstborn. She has a daughter, too. B, we call her. She's just turned twenty-one back in February, and is as sassy as all the other women her age. But Ben, he's always taken care of me like a big brother." Victor looks toward the house, voice quiet as nostalgia takes over his memories. "But oh yeah, we fought all the time. Stella used to pull us apart during our fistfights." He chuckles. "It took us a while to learn to use our voices instead of our fists when we disagreed."

Erin hums, snapping a random shot of the forest beyond the house. "Something tells me it wasn't Ben who didn't realize that."

"That something would be right." Victor bumps Erin's shoulders, gaze dropping to his. "You got quite good instincts, huh?"

Erin holds his stare, heart jumping over boulders in his chest. He can't help but lower his eyes to Victor's lips. They look soft. He wants to photograph them. How do they look quirked into a smirk? He's seen them smile. And frown. A ghost of a smirk, too. What would they look like puckered around—

Erin gulps, looking away and forcing the image out of his mind. "So I've been told."

Did Victor notice his wandering eyes? Would he say anything if he did? Erin kind of wishes he would. Then maybe—

Maybe what? They'd fuck? Here, with a house full of Victor's family and a crazy aunt who literally warned him not to do just that? Where would they go then? His house? Which would be the first place his parents would come looking for him if he suddenly disappeared.

Breathe.

Layla's plan said to flirt. No touching.

Not yet.

Not until they know each other more.

Not until he's sure that's what this burning itch underneath his skin means. If this feeling with Victor really is something different or a lie seeped in testosterone he's spinning.

A breeze cools the heat radiating off his skin, and he notices the scent of Victor's cologne getting stronger—the smell of leather and sandalwood making his insides simultaneously tingle with butterflies and relax in warm pleasure. Safe. The word pops off like sirens in his head. A grand declaration.

"You never told me what brand of cologne you use," Erin says. "I told you last week it was a nice smell, and normally after that, the complimented party reveals the secret."

"Well, what if I want to gate-keep it?" Victor bends, eye-level with Erin, while they stroll.

"That would make me jealous then," Erin chuckles. "I've used the same stuff since I was little—monkshood, I think it's called. It's some off-brand stuff. My parents love the smell and diffuse it into everything. It's very similar to a plant we have growing all around the house, too. I'm not the biggest fan, but," he shrugs, "they're my parents. And they've never let me use anything else, either. I got in trouble once when I forgot to use it in high school."

"Wolfsbane."

Erin stops walking. "What?"

Victor licks his lips, body tense. He walks a few more paces before stilling, hands unclasping to hang in fists by his side. "Monkshood. I've heard of it before. A more common name for it is wolfsbane." He's glaring at Erin with confusion, brows causing lines to appear in his smooth forehead.

"Oh, yeah." Erin mirrors his stance, veins quickly filling with dread. "Does it not smell good? I have a good sense of smell, so I tend to bring it up in conversation, forgetting that not everyone likes to talk about that stuff. I figured, since you said before that you have enhanced genetics, and I told you before no one's ever told me the smell was bad, that you didn't mind. I mean, you've never said anything. But you did cough a lot at Donny's ... I thought maybe it was the stale air and sweat ... Oh God, you hate it, and now I'm rambling nonsen—"

"No!" Victor grabs Erin's hand to hold him in place. "Sorry, I just didn't realize you had on the same cologne. Right now, you smell like the rain, but at Donny's party, you smelled woodsier, more ... acidic. Like a forest right after a fire." Victor squeezes Erin's hand, a tense smile on his face. "Ben always tells me I tend to get quiet and glare when I'm confused. It's a bad habit I'm working on. You don't smell bad. You smell nice. I like your scent. It's soothing. Why would I want you to smell like me when you can smell like you? I smell myself all the time, but I don't smell you all the time, beside me. So, if you smelled like you and like me ..."

Erin's eyes widen, hesitation parting his lips. "That ... surprisingly made perfect sense." He chuckles, shoulders dropping as he looks at his hand clasped in Victor's. They fit together perfectly. Victor's tan fingers fidget with Erin's pale palm, pressing into the skin, almost like a massage. His skin is warm. Erin moves his hand, so his fingers are lined up with Victor's. He raises his gaze. Victor isn't looking at him anymore, his attention focused solely on where their hands touch. His chest rises slowly like he's trying not to breathe.

Erin slides his palm against Victor's. He waits. Victor finally looks at him, and Erin knows that gaze. He doesn't know where he's seen it before. It wasn't from any of the hook-ups he'd had throughout his life, nor was it from his parents or friends. He doesn't know what the word is to describe the emotion he sees on Victor's face, in his eyes, in his lips.

But his soul knows it. His heart recognizes it.

He can practically hear the sound of it ...

Victor follows Erin's lead. He bends his fingers until the pads of his fingertips rest softly on Erin's knuckles. Erin does the same.

Like a lost wolf who hears the call of his Pack and remembers the way home.

The wind breathes, rustling his hair. His mother's laughter rings from the other side of the house, blending in with John's deep chuckles.

Erin takes a step back and clears his throat.

"Is it someone's birthday? I saw Ben walking in from the garage carrying a cake this morning."

"Oh." A small blush covers Victor's cheekbones when he grins. It lights Erin on fire. "Mine."

"WHAT! Why didn't you say anything?" Erin pulls his hands out of Victor's grip, his camera swinging around his neck as he spins. Looking ... looking ... looking ... there. A patch of wild dandelions grows by the fence. Erin runs over and, carefully, picks them from the wet soil. He holds them out to Victor, who followed him to the fence. "Here, I'll get you something else later, but for now ... Happy birthday, Victor."

Victor grabs the flowers with one hand, while the other reclaims Erin's palm. "Thank you." He holds them to his nose, smelling deeply. "They smell wonderful, Erin. You don't have to get me anything else. This is plenty."

Erin rolls his eyes. "Please, you're what, twenty ... I've just realized I don't know how old you are."

"Twenty-four."

"Twenty-four. I'll be twenty-two in December, so you're two years older than me," he mutters.

"Ah, mystery solved," Victor teases, running his thumb over Erin's. "Here I was thinking I was some kind of cradle snatcher."

Erin barks a laugh. "You disappointed, Casanova?"

"Nope." Victor tugs on his hand joined with Erin's, pulling them closer together. Erin can smell mint from Victor's mouth, it's so close to his own. All he'd need to do is lift his head. Three inches. Two inches.

"I need to get you something. You like reading? Do you know Romeo and Juliet?" Erin blurts. He doesn't know where the question came from. He needed something to distract Victor from his racing heart. If his hearing is as good as he says it is, he can probably hear it. And, as much as he would love to kiss Victor right now, he wants to keep hearing Victor talk more than that. The deep timber of his voice. The feel of his palm. He'd say anything to stay in this moment with him right now.

Surprise widens Victor's eyes, and he leans back slightly, putting a few more inches between them. Breathing room. The mint disappears. "The old Shakespeare play?"

Erin nods.

"Yeah, I studied it in English, back in high school. Didn't everyone?"

"Yeah. Yeah, I did. I really liked it. Out of all of his works, it's probably my favorite."

"Oh? A bit of a theater nerd, are you, Erin?"

Erin chuffs. "So, what if I am?"

"Nothing. To answer your question, yes. I do like to read." Victor smiles and taps his hand holding Erin's against his stomach. "So, tell me then, why do you find Romeo and Juliet interesting?"

"It's romantic," Erin replies, voice quiet.

"Romantic?" Victor quips. "It's tragic. Their love killed them. What's romantic about miscommunication and murderous uncles?"

"Nothing ... nothing but ... if you think about it. Did their love *really* kill them? Or did it set them free?"

"Free?" Victor scoffs.

"Yeah, free from the world they were cursed to live in."

Victor's eyes, usually so blue and round, widen even further. He studies Erin like he's just revealed all the secrets of the universe. Like he's found the lady of the moon and danced underneath her magic.

"I—"

CLANG.

Metal screeches, cutting Victor off. The echo rings across them. Erin jolts, yanking his hand from Victor's grip at the same time Victor takes two steps back. Big steps. He closes the hand Erin was holding into a fist, as if he's trying to retain some of the leftover warmth.

Erin does the same.

"I should go see what that sound was, make sure Mr. Wolf hasn't gotten himself into any trouble, and see if my dad is ready to do more work." Erin starts walking backward. "See you, Victor."

Victor nods, brows still slightly pinched together. Erin is halfway back to the side of the house when Victor's voice rings out, "Erin."

Erin pauses and turns around, eyes drifting briefly to Victor's lips as he licks them in hesitation.

"I don't wear any cologne."

FOURTEEN

Erin has officially given up on Layla's plan to seduce Victor, not that he had given it much thought in the first place. Whatever this is simmering between them ... this burning itch, this pull, it's worse than a million mosquito bites in spring.

But more than that, Erin has a feeling he wouldn't be able to resist, even if he tried.

Which he doesn't want to do.

The thought alone causes him to break out in a sweat.

He's decided to take every chance he can to talk to Victor. Get to know him more, beyond the surface stuff like, 'what's your favorite color' and 'do you prefer butter and maple syrup with your pancakes, or just one.' Which, he realized after reading online, are two of the most famous ice-breaker questions he doesn't know the answers to. He knew Greg's favorite, but that's only because he threw a hissy fit the *one* time Erin showed up in black boxers instead of cobalt blue, and then demanded Erin make it up to him by cooking his dad's recipe for homemade pancakes, but butter only. No maple syrup. But that had to come after the sex.

Like a wild animal.

Today was start day.

He knows Victor tends to run along the fence early in the morning, so the plan was 100% guaranteed to work. He was prepped and ready. Muscles loose, script of basic questions memorized in his mind.

Except his mother got involved.

After realizing they couldn't mow the lawn in the backyard due to the abundance of giant rocks, Natalie had a great idea to arrange them into an artistic sculpture in the corner of the yard instead.

"We can create a great backdrop for family photos that can act like an entrance to the trails in the other paddocks," she commented before running off to the shops to bulk order flowers and ornaments. That was nearly six hours ago.

Now Erin is helping load the rocks into the bucket of the bobcat tractor while John drives them to the other side of the yard and dumps them over the fence. It's late afternoon, the sun shining on them like a beacon of warmth. It was nice at first—the heat on his skin making him sweat, while the icy breath of the wind cooled it down—but all it did was remind Erin of the heat he wanted from elsewhere. Of the glimpses he's managed to catch over the past week and a half, but never kept hold of.

Feeling the warmth of Victor's body through his hand. Having those blue eyes constantly looking into his own across a room. Smelling the scent of his warm cologne as it seeps through the air. Because that's what it has to be—he refuses to believe that Victor just naturally smells that good.

And ... beyond that ...

He wants to open the window to the library and peer over the frame, asking Victor what it is he's constantly hunched over every time he takes a peek through the glass. Is it real estate work? Family reunion planning? What about the stack of books sitting on the corner of the desk? Has he read them all? He knows he fancies a long run in the morning over the afternoon, but does he like to read in the morning, too? Or late at night, after everyone has gone to sleep and the house is as quiet as falling snow. He called Erin the theater nerd, yet he's the one sitting in an office with fancy wooden floor-to-ceiling shelves and a jar full of bookmarks on his desk.

It's not natural.

It's borderline obsession.

It's not right.

It's instinct.

Erin doesn't want to fight it anymore; he wants to give in, to see where this attraction will take them. And it clearly is attraction, both physical and emotional. If given the opportunity, he could sit and listen to Victor laugh and ramble on about different kinds of music all day long. That's not something he's ever had with any of his past boyfriends. Hell, even with the casual hook-ups, he didn't feel this *need* to constantly be in touch.

Victor all but confirmed the other day that he feels the same. He still wonders if Victor has ever been with another man. If he's experienced in how this works. He's a damn good flirt, but there's this air of innocence wrapped around him. In the way he flinches from Erin when their arms brush too close, or when he gulps and coughs every time Erin enters the room. His eyes will flit to Ben, who is often one step behind, like he's checking for confirmation or reassurance.

It's kind of cute, actually, and Erin finds himself on most occasions pulling his lips inward or chewing on his cheek to stop from laughing.

He doesn't mind showing Victor how the sex would work—it would be fun. The thought excites him, sharp tension sparking as it slowly rolls across his abdomen. Exploring what each other likes, together. Safely. Wrapped tight in each other's arms. Warm. Protected.

But before that starts, he wants to know if this will be just a summer fling or something more. Something worth spending time questioning how many exes they've each had while snuggled underneath the blankets in bed after multiple rounds.

High-pitched laughter squeals around them. He glances to the back patio, lifting the rim of his hat to see the constant reminder of why he can't explore those moments with Victor sitting right there.

Stella.

With her threat echoing in the back of his mind and the reputation of Storm Landscaping hanging by a thread, Erin knows he can't act on anything. He still hasn't decided if he trusts in her ability to follow through with her threat. He knows the people in Black Hill, and even the surrounding towns, wouldn't believe a word from Stella if she did try and say anything. But ... his parents have been working at this career for nearly twenty-five years. They had opportunities before he came into the picture, and while he knows he wasn't the *sole* reason they've never left the area, he can't help but feel like being *one* of the reasons is bad enough. They deserve the chance to branch out across different states.

He won't risk that chance for them to succeed in their dream.

No matter how loudly his heart screams at him to *screw* the repercussions.

Erin needs to tune it out. He needs to ignore it.

Even if his fingers itch to take a photo of Victor talking to Ben and Stella on the patio, the sun once again perfectly highlighting Victor's golden hair and making his skin glow like he's the God of Sunlight.

Even if the muscles in Victor's shoulders shine as sweat slides down his biceps and over the dip in his collarbone, getting lost in the dark blue material of his shirt.

Even if he feels Stella's dark gaze sliding toward him every couple of minutes, her black polished nails clicking against the coffee cup she's holding. She smiles at Victor and Ben, affectionately patting her son on the head before heading inside.

Even if he sees another woman walk outside and take her place. Her hair is the same dark shade of red as Stella's—they even have it styled in the same shoulder-length, loose curls—but her eyes are a deep shade of brown. Erin stops walking, the wheelbarrow full of boulders still raised in his hands as he openly stares. She's incredibly beautiful. The casual yellow sundress she's wearing is a perfect complement to the tanned freckles on her cheeks and nose.

Victor is smiling. The kind of smile that's all teeth and no eyes. He's laughing, too. Erin could recognize that laugh anywhere at this point, despite him only hearing it a handful of times. He doesn't think he could ever forget it if he tried. A pain tears through his heart like someone has taken the bobcat tractor filled with rocks and dumped them onto his heart all at once.

Victor is happy. And Erin isn't the one who caused it. That woman is.

He forces a smile and quickly strides toward the bobcat to empty the remnants of rocks inside the wheelbarrow. His throat clenches tight, the ground blurring beneath him. He will not cry. There is no reason to cry because he's not surprised. Victor is handsome—very handsome—and he's smart, kind, funny, smells nice, has a good body, and an incredible laugh. Who wouldn't like that?

Of course, he has a stunning girlfriend.

Was it all a lie? No, the attraction was there. He could feel it. He knows Victor felt it too. Then he must be Bi. He was flirting—they both were flirting. So, he's a cheater. An asshole.

A fool.

"Erin, be careful!"

Victor's voice. He's ... scared?

Erin looks up. He notices his dad standing in front of him, back turned, as he drinks some water beside the tractor. Erin lurches to the side, stopping the wheelbarrow from colliding with John as all the heavy rocks fall out. The momentum causes Erin to trip and fall over the bucket on the bobcat, straight onto the other jagged rocks.

"Ow!" Erin hisses. He blinks as the world re-focuses, teeth grinding tight against the pain. His red cowboy hat is gone. There are cuts all over his arms and legs, and his ribs feel like they are on fire. A warmth trickles down his stomach, causing Erin to look down. Ah, that's why—a jagged piece of rock is poking out of his side.

That's going to leave a nasty bruise.

He can already hear the snickers from his friends at his clumsiness.

"Son, what happened?" John drops his water bottle, and the grass greedily drinks up the spilled liquid. "Oh, God—"

"Nothing, I just tripped, Dad."

"Erin, are you ok? Fuck, that looks bad." Victor gently pulls Erin out, careful not to dislodge the rock poking out of his side. His hands hold onto Erin's waist and upper arms like he's made of glass and not 175lbs of fat and muscle. "Can you move your toes, your fingers? Is anything broken?"

"I'm fine," Erin mutters. He takes shallow breaths, watching as Victor runs a stressed hand through his hair. His eyes are blown wide, pupils blacking out the pale blue color. He's shaking. There are at least 350 feet between the fence line and the house. Did he sprint all the way here? Not even the fastest quarterback can make it across the full length of a football field as fast as it took Victor to rush over.

Erin bends, trying to rub away some rubble stuck to his upper thighs, when pain shoots backward toward his spine. He freezes, shoulders flicking back straight away. Yep, his sleep has just gone from restless to insomniac.

Suddenly, comfort washes over Erin in waves. Victor swats away the rubble and small rocks from his jumpsuit. His fingers are delicate the closer he gets to his side. Did he notice Erin try to do it himself? Victor's eyes trail over Erin's body, inspecting it closely for any other injury. Does he think he's important enough to be checked on, to worry for? Erin peers at his father; he's frowning at his phone. Texting his mother that they've raised a stupid son, most likely. But that's fine. He can be stupid and clumsy.

Because Victor cares for him.

Whether it's because Victor likes him romantically or simply because he's just that kind, Erin doesn't care. Both options warm his heart and turn his legs into jelly.

A radical image bursts to life in his mind as he leans into Victor's arms, pressing his nose into the crook of his neck. Later, he'll tell Layla and Fletcher that it was the loss of blood and shock that caused delusions to infiltrate his mind. But for now, knowing Victor's girlfriend is nearby, knowing he still has to ask all his ice-breaker questions, he thinks he's chosen right. Victor would make a kind husband. A caring father. A loving—

Victor's scent skyrockets, growing stronger by the minute. Weird. There's no breeze, so how is his scent getting stronger? He said he doesn't wear cologne, so how come there's such an intense smell of rich sandalwood coming from him right now? And why does it make Erin's insides twist in guilt and shame?

Victor grips Erin's hand. "Keep your hand here," he whispers, placing his hand over Erin's next to the wound. "But don't press too hard."

There's no time to think before Victor is lifting him bridal style. "We should get him inside and disinfect the wounds," Victor declares, speed walking toward the house. The woman from before is gone, but Ben is still there. He's risen from his chair and is standing on the bottom step of the porch. Erin sees worry etched into his face, making him look less like a fairy prince in the forest on a sunny day and more like an old moss-filled statue abandoned in a dark cave.

"We need to get him to the hospital." John is jogging beside Victor in an attempt to keep close to Erin. "Look at all that blood, and what if he has a concussion? Natalie said she'd meet us there."

"One of my distant relatives is a very skilled doctor. She'll meet us inside," Victor answers. He's climbing the porch steps now, the wood creaking under the sudden weight from their hurried steps. "You can tell your wife to come back here. Now."

John's brow twitches, eyes thinning. His steps don't falter, keeping pace with Victor even as he turns to walk sideways through the door Ben is holding open. The cool air conditioning gives immense relief to his stinging skin.

Erin gulps. "I'm fine, really," he says, feeling no jostle in Victor's arms. "And I can walk myself."

"No," Victor grunts, his grip tightening around Erin's legs and lower back.

"Victor, seriously, put me down." Erin starts struggling when he sees people milling around the kitchen and dining areas. They're all wearing various states of workout gear, staring at Erin as Victor carries him past. He hasn't seen Stella since she walked back inside, but who knows how many spies she has lurking around. A joint yoga session would be the perfect melting pot for gossip.

"I'll put you down when the doctor says you can be put down," Victor growls as he turns left past the dining room and heads toward the massive bathroom. He squeezes Erin even closer to him.

Erin spots Ben over Victor's shoulder, following behind John. His hands are clenched, the outline clearly visible through the pockets of his gym shorts, and his lips are pulled into a tight line. He says nothing when he catches Erin's eye. There's no facial twitch, no message flying across his dark eyes.

But Erin knows. He sees it for what it is, loud and clear.

"Damn it," he mutters. He turns his head more into Victor's shoulder to hide his face as they enter the bathroom. "This is embarrassing."

The bathroom itself is spacious, always making Erin startle every time he enters. It must have some sort of optical illusion in play that makes it look bigger inside than from the outside. There's a corner bathtub with steps—green tiles contrasting against the cream walls and floor tiles—as well as an open shower against the whole wall to its left, and a window taking up the top half of the wall to its right. A toilet is nestled into the other corner next to the window, its sill painted brown and lined with funny potted plants, carved wooden wolves, and old-looking artifacts that look like sharp canine teeth. Three green sinks are situated on the wall next to the toilet, opposite the shower wall, while a wall-to-floor wooden cupboard takes the remaining space beside the door.

Yet, even with all the space and people inside right now, it's only once the doctor arrives with her briefcase that the space becomes narrow and cramped. The doctor is an older lady, maybe fifty or sixty, with long brown hair loosely woven down her back in a French braid, and squinty brown eyes that remind Erin of an owl. His relief of her arrival is short-lived when the red-haired woman from before returns as well. She enters the cramped bathroom and stands next to Ben in the shower area, the two of them sharing a look as she crosses her arms over her chest. Ben shakes his head and leans against the wall.

Erin grimaces, narrowly managing to avoid biting his tongue, while Victor places him carefully on the bathtub steps. John takes the space beside him, forcing Victor to sit on the toilet seat instead.

Erin can't help but smile at his small pout.

"Beatrice explained what happened to me on the way." The doctor glides to Erin and holds her hand out. "My name is Dr. Haven. It's a pleasure to meet you." Her voice is raspy but clear, like someone who has experienced all life has to offer and came out stronger because of it. It sounds so familiar to Erin.

Like a voice from a long-forgotten dream.

Must be the blood loss.

"Yeah, you too. I'm Erin." He shakes Dr. Haven's hand. It's much softer than what he was expecting. "Look, everyone is exaggerating. I'm fine, really."

"You have a six-inch piece of rock sticking out of your stomach, Son. You are not fine," John says sternly. "You have blood and cuts all over you. Your mother is on her way back now, and honestly, you're lucky I don't take you off this project right this instant! Do you know how much danger you put yourself and everyone on this ranch in because you had your head up in the stars? I should send you there myself since that's where you want to be so badly. What if you were on the mower again? Or *driving* the damn tractor?"

"I don't think that will be necessary," Dr. Haven interjects as she opens her briefcase and puts on gloves. "The superficial wounds aren't deep at all, so Erin won't need any stitches. They'll heal in no time." She'd been looking Erin over while John talked, checking neither of his ankles or wrists were sprained by rotating them gently, turning his head side to side while shining a light into his eyes, and lifting his tank top to get a closer look at the protruding rock. "As for this one," she dabs the skin around the wound as Erin leans back, loosening the sleeves of his jumpsuit around his hips to give her more access, "it will need a couple of stitches, but it doesn't look like it's hit anything important. Most of the rock is on the outside of his skin."

Without warning, she yanks the rock out, quickly placing a piece of gauze over the wound.

"Son of a—!" Erin hisses, tossing his head back. The tears he was trying to suppress during his father's—albeit justified, though stinging—tirade have no trouble pooling at the inner corners of his eyes. Victor clenches his hands together, the knuckles turning white, as if he can feel the pain Erin is in himself. Erin wishes he were holding Victor's hand instead.

"Hold your top up," Dr. Haven instructs before letting go of the material and reaching for bandages from her briefcase. She sends a skeptical look to Erin as she sprays disinfectant onto the wound before stitching it closed. "I'm using a dissolvable stitch, so don't pick at the wound. You were lucky this time, but be careful in the future. Watch your surroundings. It doesn't take much to kill a man."

A full-body shiver races through Erin's body, and he stiffens, feeling like all the blood in his veins froze with Dr. Haven's words. That was more than just a reprimanding warning. There was fear in her voice.

The doctor stands, sending a beady stare to Victor before leaving the bathroom.

But why would a doctor from New York fear harm coming to Erin? A potential liability case, perhaps?

Ben's voice pulls Erin from his thoughts. "Mr. Storm, why don't we go get Erin some water while Victor takes him upstairs to get some new clothes? He can rest here for the remainder of the day so that you don't fall behind schedule. I know my mom has set a tight one."

John nods before standing. He squeezes Erin's shoulder once and follows Ben.

"Dad."

John halts, hand braced on the doorframe.

"I'm sorry for worrying you. I promise it won't happen again," Erin says.

"Come now, Goldy," John turns, an unsteady smile gracing his lips, "we both know that's not true." He nods to Victor. "Take care of my son."

"Yes, sir," Victor mumbles. Erin notes the woman from before is gone now, too, leaving just him and Victor.

"So, are you going to let me walk myself to your room or are you going to carry me?" he teases.

Victor says nothing, his features tensed and furrowed. There's no huff or grunt accompanied by a smile, not even a ghost of a smirk, before he stands and holds a hand out. Erin takes it, keeping one hand pressed to his side as he shuffles with Victor up to his room. He doesn't pay too much attention to his surroundings as they follow the spiral staircase to the fourth floor, too focused on the warmth spreading up his arm and circulating through his blood from where his hand is connected to Victor's.

Victor lets go of Erin's hand when they reach his room. There's not much inside besides a bed with a black comforter and a side table filled with books. Both are facing the balcony, which is directly opposite the door as they walk in. Victor strolls toward a walk-in closet to the right of the balcony, while Erin sits on the edge of the bed. It's soft, bouncing a little bit under his weight.

"Do you need any Panadol?" Victor stands in front of Erin, a small smile on his face. He's holding a black pair of sweat shorts and a green gym shirt.

"No." Erin stands. A blush creeps from his ears down to his neck. "I didn't peg you as someone who wore gym clothes casually."

"I'm not," Victor takes Erin's spot after Erin heads into the closet, "but I figured you were."

"Oh, what made you think that?" Erin changes clothes slowly, gulping his wince as he lifts his shredded tank over his head. There's a standing mirror in the closet, allowing Erin to finally see all the cuts on his arms and legs as he tears the torn and dirty jumpsuit off his body. The rocks really did a number on him. Despite Dr. Haven's words, some of them will leave scars.

"Instinct," Victor calls.

Erin pauses, the borrowed shirt halfway onto his arms.

Instinct. Yeah, right.

He rolls his eyes as he finishes getting changed. The clothes are a perfect fit.

"I don't think that's the proper way to use that word, Victor."

"Are you sure you're ok?" Victor asks. Erin places the ruined tank top and jumpsuit on the floor by the door and sits next to Victor on the bed, their shoulders touching.

"Yeah. I was just distracted." Erin realizes he's leaning into Victor's shoulder and pulls away. Victor's smell is everywhere in the room, which isn't helping Erin stay alert and on guard. He's supposed to be borrowing Victor's pants, not trying to jump into them.

"About what?" Victor turns sideways on the bed, so he faces Erin, one leg coming up to settle between them. There's concern in his eyes and his voice. Like his very soul is asking what possibly could've distracted Erin enough to get hurt.

Like it was somehow his fault.

Like he's the one who has to take responsibility.

Erin says nothing, looking anywhere but at Victor's face.

"Ah." Victor chuckles all of a sudden. The low sound echoes around the empty room in time with Erin's erratic heart. "Beatrice."

"What?" Erin mirrors Victor's position, their knees clanking together as his brows jump.

"The woman Ben and I were with, her name is Beatrice. I've mentioned her before, remember? She's Ben's little sister. My other cousin," Victor explains. He has a proud glint in his eyes as he smiles. "Stella raised the three of us together."

Erin feels the blush from his neck and ears spread over his face. No wonder she resembled Stella. And Ben. And Victor, now that he has gotten a closer look. They all have the same strong, straight nose. Erin doesn't dwell on the embarrassment he feels when another thought kicks him in the gut. If Beatrice is Stella's daughter, then Stella has definitely told her to keep tabs on him and Victor. But Victor and

Beatrice did seem close. So maybe she won't tell Stella about Erin getting hurt and Victor carrying him inside. Or Erin sitting in Victor's room right now. Distracting him from his duties.

He doesn't know which is worse—Stella hearing about Victor carrying the landscaper's son inside after an injury, or her hearing about Victor and the landscaper's son being alone in a bedroom together. He knows Victor is kind and would help anyone in need, offering up his room to them so they could recuperate. But he gets the feeling Stella won't see it that way.

Especially when it involves the two things she warned Erin against doing.

"You were feeling jealous," Victor tells Erin, unaware of his inner turmoil. "It's perfectly normal for mates to feel that way."

Erin's stills, his mouth still open to protest Victor's declaration that Erin was jealous. The room feels much colder than it did before. Pressure starts to build behind his eyes, causing him to squint, and his breathing becomes labored. It's not from the wound in his side.

"Mates? Like friends?" Erin chuckles, trying to diffuse some of the pressure in the room. "I didn't know New Yorkers used terms like that. Do you have a British friend? Or Australian?"

Victor shakes his head, lowering it closer to Erin before grabbing both of his hands. Erin hates how he flinches at the touch. Hates how his ears slowly start to fill with cotton. How his head leans in to match Victor's, their foreheads almost touching.

"I mean, as in soulmates. Destined ones who'll always find each other, no matter how far apart they are born. Either physically in distance or age." Victor plays with Erin's fingertips, the same way he did the day before. His voice is low, like he's telling a secret only Erin can know. "Ones who have been marked by instinct. Fated by blood and bound by stars."

Erin stares at Victor; his heart is beating so loud he swears Victor can feel it in his fingertips. The pressure in his head is thumping louder, like something is throwing its whole body weight against a door and howling at Erin.

Open.

"Why are you staring at me so confused?" Victor's smug smile slowly morphs until he's frowning. "You're a werewolf, Erin. Didn't you know?"

Open.

Erin yanks his hands out of Victor's. He stands, looking frantically around the room. "Ok. Where are the drugs?"

"What? Erin, come sit down. You'll pull your stitch," Victor stresses. He reaches out to pull Erin back to the bed, but Erin ignores him, heading to Victor's closet instead to continue his search. He's convinced that there must be some hidden compartment in the walls or beneath the floorboards filled with bags of drugs. They do all kinds of this stuff up in New York, right? Erin's never dabbled, personally, but there have been many times at Donny's, and even frat parties, where he's gotten a whiff of the stuff. It's always made his stomach churn, more than the wolfsbane planted around his house ever has.

His heart pounds as he kneels on the floor, frantically knocking against the dark hardwood. He refuses to entertain the idea that Victor is playing some cruel trick on him. Drugs must be the explanation. The only explanation.

But he can't find anything.

Open.

He stands, digging through folded baskets of clothes and yanking thin jackets hung on velvet hangers aside. There are no loose boards, no hollow, hidden shelves. Everything is neat and organized, and even then, there isn't much to rummage through. Victor's closet is as bare as his room.

The. Door.

He rubs his temples. The pounding gets worse. Did he hit his head harder than he thought on the rocks earlier, and now his hearing is messed up? Werewolves? Soulmates? There's no way.

Erin turns to continue his search in the rest of the room, flinching when he sees Victor standing in the doorframe. He corners Erin in the closet. His eyes are dimmed, and not just from the lack of light. He looks drained with his hunched shoulders and loose limbs, like a puppet whose strings have been cut.

Erin straightens his back and juts out his chin. "Move."

Victor says nothing while he stares, expression blank. He makes no attempt to move.

Erin scoffs and turns his head. "What? You going to lock me up in here or something?"

"Do you honestly think I'd do that?" Victor whimpers. His brows are coiled tight. It makes Erin's heart twist the same way. "To you?"

Tingles crawl across his spine. It starts in his toes, before tiptoeing along each vertebra and settling at the crown of his head. "Well, you're clearly high enough to think I'm a werewolf," he whispers.

"We," Victor corrects. There's a sliver of light coming back into his eyes as he clenches his hands into fists at his side. A mix of pride and arrogance colors his features as he steps forward.

"What?" Erin gasps with furrowed brows. He steps back—the clothes hanging on the fancy hooks part around him, some falling soundlessly to the floor—until he hits the wall behind him.

Victor reaches up and brushes a finger over Erin's upper cheek, his fingertip teasing Erin's lower eyelashes, before leaning his hand against the wall. Erin can feel the heat from Victor's hand next to his head; he pinches his thigh tightly to stop himself from nuzzling it.

"We are werewolves. All of us are. The whole Lovelace family is a pack of werewolves. We have been for generations. Eons."

Erin stills as he leans his head against the wall and closes his eyes, taking a deep breath. Victor's scent is everywhere. It invades his nose and makes its way into his blood before engulfing his heart and squeezing it. Tight. Erin hates how the scent helps ease the howling pressure in his head.

"What, do you think I'm from your pack, then? That I'm some lost werewolf who finally found its way home?" Erin opens his eyes and stares at Victor with a calm defiance he most certainly doesn't feel. "Just because I'm an orphan doesn't mean I'm looking for a family. I have a family."

"No, that's not what I mean." Victor shakes his head with a sigh. "Besides, there haven't been any lost or rogue wolves reported in a very long time. You aren't from my Pack."

Erin squints at the hesitance in Victor's voice. Gotcha. Every lie has its flaws. "So, how can I be a werewolf?"

"There's more than just one wolf pack in the world, Erin. You were probably born into one of those before Natalie and John adopted you." Victor huffs a small laugh before gazing at Erin with soft eyes. "Your parents could've hidden the pregnancy from their Pack, which is rare, but not unheard of for high-risk male Omegas. And when they died," he gulps, his eyes flicking down before continuing, "the humans must have found you, them, first. So, if anything, you're probably a member of the Harkin Pack here in Texas."

Open. The Door.

Erin pales, thinking back to the Storm Landscaping file he found and the mismatched dates. No. That has nothing to do with this. His parents said that was simply a clerk's mistake.

There is no connection there.

No link.

"Just think, Erin. You just said it yourself. You were adopted as a baby. You also heal quickly." Victor places his free hand on Erin's side, right above the freshly stitched wound. He presses, and Erin sucks in a quick breath. It's not pain he feels. Pressure builds below his waist as heat rushes through his bloodstream.

Victor keeps his eyes fixed firmly on Erin as he lowers his face mere inches from his lips. His voice is a whisper when he speaks, "Dr. Haven herself confirmed it. No human could've gotten out of that fall with just minor cuts and bruises, let alone just two stitches." He presses harder, and Erin gasps as Victor takes a step forward, his knee resting snugly against him. "Stitches that are already healing over."

Erin remembers Dr. Haven's warning and her beady stare.

His side is itching as a scab forms around the stitches.

"Remember at Donny's, when we first met? You admitted that you don't get drunk easily or at all. I've also seen firsthand how enhanced your senses are, not as strong as the average wolf, I'll agree, but stronger than the average human. These aren't some genetic enhancement jokes. They are all things that point toward you having werewolf genes."

Open the door!

Erin shivers as his mind betrays him. He thinks back to all the times he would get a stuffy nose from the smell of chlorine radiating off Fletcher, or how nauseous he would feel when he would sleep over at Layla's, where her mom would be experimenting with different perfume scents. He thinks about all the times the flu would be going around school, and he would be the only one to never get sick.

Victor finally rests his forehead against Erin's. His brows are clenched tightly together. Erin wants him to rest his head lower. His shoulder. His chest.

"Then there's your scent." Victor's words are more breath than anything. "It's intoxicating, Erin. The best thing I've ever smelled in my life. You said I was high? That I was doing drugs?" Victor's lips curve into a smirk. "Maybe I have been. But can you blame me? You've been spreading your scent everywhere. It's instinctual to want something that you like."

"You're supposed to be lying," Erin pleads in a small voice. He doesn't understand why he feels so much desperation. Victor has to be lying. Erin isn't a werewolf, and Victor isn't his mate. But everything Victor has said makes so much sense. Logically speaking, the evidence is playing like a movie reel in his mind. The attraction. The connection.

The warmth.

The need.

Openopenopenopen the door!

Even now, when Erin knows he should be searching for illegal substances, that he should be fuming with rage, he's not. All he wants to do is lower his hips onto

Victor's leg and close the distance between them completely. He wants to press his lips in-between Victor's eyebrows, kiss away the tension, and smooth out the worry between them.

"Please just say you're lying, Victor."

Victor lifts his hand from Erin's side, grabs one of his hands that hang tense beside them, and places it on his chest. Erin can feel the warmth of Victor's frantic heartbeat vibrating through his fingertips before circulating throughout his whole body. Matching paces. "I wish I were, Love."

Erin looks away. He tries to follow the train tracks in his mind, but all the thoughts lead to a dead end. Just when he's about to give up on any sensible explanation, he catches sight of a pair of black tennis shoes nestled in the corner of a wooden shoe rack by the bed. Fletcher has the same pair of shoes that he wears religiously. Erin can hear new tracks being laid in his brain, the train starting to slide forward, as he remembers the conversation from the café.

The wolf dreams.

Erin chuckles, pressing his head into Victor's, causing him to step back and remove his leg from in-between Erin.

"I understand now."

Victor raises one of his eyebrows. He looks surprised. Relieved. "You do?"

Erin nods sagely. He feels silly for freaking out over nothing when the truth is so obvious. "Honestly, Victor, I'm flattered, really, but you could've just told me you were feeling pent-up. Sexual frustration is nothing to be ashamed of. I mean, I do find you attractive. You're very handsome and kind and funny, and Wolf, my cat, likes you, so there's no reason for me to not like you. All you had to do was ask. I was wanting to get to know you more, on a personal level, before I attempted anything. Still, I would've said yes. This elaborate ruse is very creative, though, so I tip my hat off to you."

The silence that follows Erin's bright declaration starts to make him squirm in discomfort. Victor is frozen stiff. Even the hand still holding Erin's has gone cold like a statue. Erin opens his mouth to say more when Victor barks out a laugh. It's a full-body laugh, one that has him shaking and gasping for breath.

Erin feels his cheeks warm in embarrassment. "So, I was right then?"

"It's cute that you think so," Victor mutters in between laughs, causing Erin to tense once more. "Trust me, Erin, I am very attracted to you. And I want to get to know your deep, dark secrets, too. But this isn't that. It's more. What you're feeling, this unexplained attraction and desire, it's something only mates feel."

"That's—" Erin thinks again about the weird wolf dreams and how they started once he met Victor. No. They had a sex meaning, not a wolf one. They had to. Layla said they did. He didn't entertain the possibility of them meaning anything else.

"We're mates, Erin," Victor declares. His eyes seem to glow in the shadowed closet. He's looking straight at Erin, past all his walls and locked doors, and right into his core. His soul. The pounding in Erin's head is a thunderclap against his skull. As he looks into Victor's eyes, all he can see is a giant black wolf with glowing moons for eyes, long canine teeth visible as it growls at him. But Erin's not scared.

He feels protected.

OPENTHEDOOROPENTHEDOOROPENTHEDO—

Erin gulps the desire down, stuffing it deep into himself to be ignored before wrenching his trembling hand away from Victor's chest. He ducks under Victor's arm and runs out of the room. He exhales.

"Impossible."

FIFTEEN

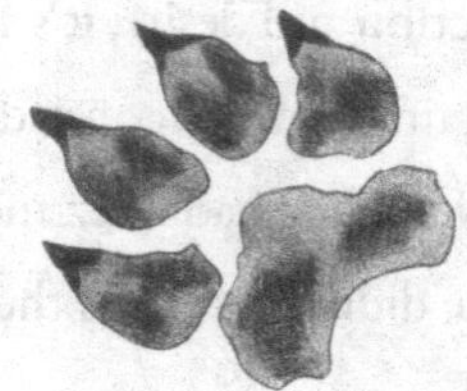

"So, tell me," Ben aims a punch at Victor's right shoulder, "why are we training inside today?"

Victor dodges with a crouch, using the momentum to roll behind Ben. "Because we spent a lot of money renovating this house and buying all this equipment."

Ben drops his arms and turns to face Victor with a deadpan look. Victor doesn't blame him; the excuse is weak. He sighs, letting his arms drop loosely by his side as his shoulders relax. "You're the one always telling me we need to keep our human body in good shape as well as our wolf form."

Ben tilts his head, sweat falling from the short strands around his ears. "Yes, I do tell you that. But it's usually so that I can work on my tan. You know, outside," he waves a gloved hand toward the open window, "on this beautiful, no-eye-around-to-catch-us 5000-acre property. In the sun. Vitamin D."

Victor purses his lips and swats at Ben's hand. "That's a one-way ticket to skin cancer, Cousin."

"For your oh-so-delicate princess skin, maybe," Ben retorts through a teasing smirk. "But I'm a paranormal creature who heals fast. And I use sunscreen." He laughs as he ducks Victor's punch and runs to the other side of the room.

They're the only two in the training room right now, which isn't a surprise. With it being such a nice day, most of the Pack is either outside training in the woods or continuing with preparations for the Council Meeting. Victor can hear them now, various types of laughter and roughhousing drifting throughout the property. There's some clanging from tents being hammered into the ground along the forest, and cars crunching over dry earth, returning after buying more blankets and pillows. The scent of happiness pours through the Pack bond pleasantly, filling him with strength.

This is right.

This is how it's meant to be—to feel.

So why is there still a massive black hole sitting in the corner of his soul?

No, not black.

White.

Victor shakes his head and walks over to the window that takes up most of the wall. With the gym at the front of the house, the early morning sun always warms the room. He used to hate it because the light would get into his eyes, and the heat would cause him to sweat more than usual.

But now he can see Erin.

It's been three days, and Erin still hasn't said a word to him. Every time Victor tries to get close, Erin finds an excuse to keep his distance. He hasn't been subtle about it either, which has drawn Stella's attention. Worry creased her forehead, making wrinkles appear when she asked him if they had gotten into a fight. Victor remembered how wrong it felt to tell her that nothing was amiss. How the guilt crawled up from his stomach and burned his ears. He said the two of them were never really close in the first place; they were simply acquaintances of a similar age who met at a midnight party, flirted and bantered to ease the awkwardness, and then conversed about which plants to have around the house.

Nothing more. Nothing less.

But Victor wants more. He wants so much more.

He knows Erin can sense him staring when his shoulders tense and hands still before becoming aggressive. He's removing weeds from around the newly painted red fence line, red cowboy hat on, but not wearing any gloves, causing his fingernails to turn black.

"With skin as pale as that he'd probably burn, too, werewolf or not," Ben states from beside Victor's shoulder, causing him to flinch. Ben raises a brow while he greedily gulps his water, one glove held tightly beneath his other arm. "I don't remember the last time I spooked you."

"You didn't spook me," Victor growls, yanking one of his gloves off to then snatch Ben's water out of his hands to drink some himself. "And Erin wouldn't burn." Victor wouldn't let him. He'd wrestle the sun out of the sky if it ever tried to leave a mark, and ask the moon to kiss his skin until the pain eased.

Ben says nothing, letting the two of them settle into a comfortable silence. Victor's grateful for it. Ben's never been much of a chatterbox—that was always Beatrice and Victor's role—but silence has never felt silent with him. He was always communicating, whether it be with his scent, his actions, or simply where he was looking. He fills up a space and waits for someone to answer.

Just like now.

Victor can feel Ben's comforting scent spreading around the room, the sweet wildflowers and roses subtle, but questioning, as he sits down and leans his back against the window, peeling his other glove off. He isn't asking what's the matter with Victor because he already knows something is wrong. And he knows it involves Erin. Victor squeezes the water bottle in his hand before sighing. He turns his back to the window as he slides down next to Ben, throwing both his gloves to the other side of the room by the basket of towels.

He knows the situation with Erin is hard to believe, but Ben is his Beta, his best friend, and his family. He's Pack. Sometimes it feels as if Ben understands Victor's instincts better than Victor does himself. Like he has this insight, this wisdom, but purposefully waits, dragging Victor by the hand to the start line so he can run the trail and figure it out himself. Is that what being older does to a person? Makes them an insufferable asshole.

A loving, insufferable asshole whom Victor loves very much.

So, if there's anyone he shouldn't be hesitant with, it's his stoic cousin.

"I've had this thought since last week. I think—No. I know. Erin's The White Wolf."

Ben lurches forward, flicking his head to face Victor. He's wild-eyed and silent as he scans Victor's face. When he's sure Victor is telling the truth, he closes his eyes and furrows his brows together tightly. Wildflowers retreat, leaving the rich fragrance of roses in their wake. Red, red, red—it's so strong Victor has to swallow, momentarily, holding his breath to take a break.

Ben sniffs, his swallow audible as he takes control. "Why?" he asks, voice pained.

Victor opens his mouth to answer and finds no words will come out. Honestly, he doesn't know what he was expecting, but a small part of him was hoping for Ben to dismiss him as he did before. Tell him to focus on what's right in front of him, saying Erin is only a human, not a werewolf. To make a joke of the whole thing.

But he would never do that twice. Ben was the one who said that humans could be considered Pack. Ben was the one who sent Victor on the path to realizing what Erin is.

And Victor was the one who secretly wished his words to be true, despite knowing the anguish it would mean for them all. For Erin.

What kind of mate does that make him?

Bile clings to the back of his throat. This resigned acceptance, like Ben already knew and was biding time for the rest to figure it out, causes Victor's blood to freeze. They all know what history says about The Black Wolf and The White Wolf. They all know what will happen should the two meet. The curse that will finally be spelled across their kind. The calamity. The destruction. The death.

Yet, Ben is saying nothing. How come? His feelings shouldn't be as complicated as Victor's. He shouldn't have personal feelings about this matter. He shouldn't want Victor to have found his mate, knowing what it means. Especially for them, with everything they've gone through. He should be yelling and screaming, reprimanding Victor about how he should be putting the Pack first—that's what Stella would say. It's what she's always said.

'No need to think about mates, Victor.'

'Pay attention, Victor. We need to build allies and strengthen our ties.'

Victor feels his hackles rising, annoyance and doubt seeping into his mind as he replays all the encounters Erin's had with Ben so far. That first party—a glimpse across the dance floor. The day Erin first arrived. The fall on the tractor. He can't pinpoint when Ben might've figured it out. They've never spoken. Not once. It could've been any of those times, though. Ben's always watching.

Victor gulps. He's never been unnerved before about Ben's observant nature, but now ...

He turns to his cousin, ready to throw a barrage of questions at him, when all the fight leaves him at once.

Ben had said nothing because there was nothing to say.

The truth was obvious right from the start.

Victor was just the desperate fool who thought if the heart was ignored, the emotions there would disappear, too.

"Instinct," he whispers. He sees the words as they slide through the air in the training room. He watches them make their way into Ben's head, noticing the way Ben's lip quirks and his hands clench into fists as the words process.

"Instinct," Ben repeats. He shakes his head and sighs, relaxing on the floor while staring at the ceiling. "The go-to excuse for a werewolf, huh."

Victor leans forward, his voice rising in defense, "It's the truth. Do you think I want him to be The White Wolf, to be cursed like I am? My attraction to Erin aside, do you think I want harm to befall us? Again?"

Ben says nothing at Victor's outburst. He doesn't rise to challenge Victor or try to comfort him either. Victor can hear Erin still outside weeding, sounding closer now than he was before. He wonders if that was subconscious or not. Either way, his heart races.

"I told Erin he was my mate. I couldn't keep lying to his face about it anymore or pretending to investigate and get to know him when, honestly, I didn't care. No matter what his response would be when we talked about music and books, I would accept any answer because he was the one giving it to me. Trust me, Ben, please. I tried to deny it. But the fear I felt ... the thought that I could lose him on Wednesday—" Victor swallows around the lump in his throat. "It was like someone had dropped me in a well of wolfsbane, and I couldn't get out. He was right there, and I couldn't swim out."

Ben tilts his head to the side, eyes still closed. The only visible sign he's listening to Victor.

Victor fiddles with the ring on his finger. "He didn't believe me though, not just about being my mate, but about being a werewolf. He thought I was high on drugs." That was one mystery solved. If he doesn't know he's a wolf, then he's never shifted.

Is that really possible?

Ben's eyes snap open, thoughts flicking across his face too quickly for Victor to decipher. "Black and White Wolf aside, if he's your mate, he'd be feeling the same things. And he doesn't suspect he's a werewolf? Doesn't wonder about the itch?"

Victor shakes his head. "He hasn't said anything to me about it." An ant drags a crumb through a sweat puddle in the center of the room from their boxing earlier. He feels like that ant, like he's standing on a cracking beam over a pool of electric eels. Erin stands at one end, while Ben and the rest of his Pack stand at the other. One missed step, and he'll go tumbling down with no one close enough to catch him.

Maybe he deserves to fall and crack his head open on the hard earth.

Ben exhales loudly through his nose before sitting up and facing Victor. "Look, at this rate, you'll spend the rest of the summer either miserably fighting or blissfully pinning." Ben holds up a hand when Victor starts to protest. "Either way, you'll be distracted. So, we may as well make sure you pick the one that'll cause less damage to the Pack. Regardless of whether Erin is truly The White Wolf or not, you need to be the one to make the first step, because Erin sure as hell won't." Ben claps Victor on the knee before standing, his eyes softening at the edges. "And for the record, I do believe you, Vic. About it all. Trust me, I've always been able to see the truth. No Goddess can fool me."

Victor smiles and stands. He looks over his shoulder again at Erin. He's still pointedly avoiding the window, his back facing it while he weeds. But he hasn't moved, solidifying Victor's theory that his actions aren't all subconscious acts. Which means he knows it, too. The fact that he's a werewolf and Victor's mate. The question of if he believes it or not aside, Victor knows Erin can feel the string tying their souls together. He can see it with his golden hazel eyes.

Fighting or pining. He can work with that.

There's no more time to be an idiot in denial. Soon, he'll make Erin believe without a doubt that the string is real, too.

SIXTEEN

Erin closes his car door as slowly as possible to avoid any loud noise before creeping toward the shed to get his camera. He only realized when he was choosing an outfit for his lunch with Layla and Fletcher the next day that his camera bag was empty. Without it, he can't take photos of them as promised.

A small part of him blames Victor for it.

Ever since he started avoiding Victor, Erin's had this pounding migraine. No amount of wet cloths to the forehead or medicine will make it go away. Werewolves and mates. The whole thing is ridiculous. Yet he can't stop thinking about it. It's consuming him. Erin wonders if that was the real reason why Stella had told him to stay away. Rich families always tend to hide away the crazy family member. Maybe whatever it is Victor has is contagious, too.

The only good thing about all this was that Stella glared at Erin less. He found she wasn't stalking their work sites as much, the shining red of her hair no longer in his peripheral vision.

But with Stella gone, his eyes were left to wander freely.

Try as he might to avoid Victor, Erin always knew when he was around. It was the only time the pain stopped, and the world sat in silence. There was no need to try and figure out the why or how. His mom told him once that some flower scents have healing properties, which is a logical explanation as to why Victor's scent affects him so much. Sandalwood can be considered a flower; it's a plant, at least. So, this thing between them is simply a physiological reaction that has nothing to do with werewolves and mates. And who doesn't sigh in relief when they smell rich spices?

So, if Victor was going to use Erin to get off in some twisted paranormal fantasy, then Erin had no problem using Victor to ease his mind, either.

The shed door squeals, and Erin winces. He glances toward the house. With it being nearly midnight, he knows most of the Lovelace family are asleep, but who's to say how light a sleeper any of them is? The last thing he wants is for someone to think there's a trespasser and call the cops.

He jogs over to the pile of redwood they were using for the fence, the last place he remembers placing his camera, making sure to put more weight on his toes to keep his steps light. Except, his camera isn't there. Sweat begins to form on his palms, and his heart races as he looks around the pile. He knows his parents wouldn't have touched it, so maybe it fell. He's never dropped his camera before, but the pile of wood isn't that high. It wouldn't have broken into pieces. Hopefully. But it wasn't in a case …

Fuck.

Erin turns on the flashlight on his phone, looking around the shed wildly.

Shit. Fuck. Shit. Fuck.

It's nowhere.

Despite the cold filling his veins, he's relieved that his camera isn't on the floor. Maybe he did place it in the truck and forgot. People forget things all the time during migraine attacks. His parents wouldn't have said anything if they had seen his camera left on the backseat, thinking Erin had placed it there intentionally. Or maybe they forgot to tell him.

With a deep breath, Erin puts his phone away and turns to leave. He's halfway back to the shed door when the scent of soiled strawberries and stale champagne engulfs him, causing him to stagger. He reaches his hand out to the nearest object, a large white ceramic pot, clutching his head.

Run.

Run *now*.

"Looking for this?"

Erin turns, coming face to face with Stella. She's standing by the pile of redwood he was hovering around before, his camera clasped tightly in her pointed black nails. She has a sneer on her face, her green eyes glinting dangerously in the moon's shadow like a predator. Her vibrant hair hangs loosely around her shoulders, the usually curled ends now straight.

Danger!

The thought comes to him like a punch to the gut, traveling from his brain and into his limbs. He instinctively starts to slouch and lowers his head to look at the floor.

That whole werewolf thing with Victor? Yeah, he can see where he might have started it from.

"Oh, s-sorry," Erin hesitates. He's never stuttered in his life. "I didn't mean to trespass this late at night. I was just looking for my camera." He doesn't know if it's the lack of light or the migraine making black spots dance across his vision, but Stella looks older. The lines on her face he had assumed were caused by smiling, instead now look more like wrinkles caused by frowning.

Stella scoffs, her lips morphing from a sneer into a smirk. She raises her chin to look down at Erin as she steps closer. He lifts his eyes to see her flicking through the photos on the camera.

Excuse me?

Erin frowns, back straightening by an inch. "Thanks for finding my camera for me. I'll get out of your hair now," he affirms, holding out his hand. He knows he shouldn't be here this late, and that he is employed by her, but that doesn't give her the right to invade his privacy.

Stella narrows her eyes at him, thumb halting its movements on the camera before her face scrunches in pity and she laughs. It's high-pitched, the shrill sound full of disbelief. Gone are the windchimes. This is like barbed wire on an iron fence. "You really are an absolute moron, aren't you, kid?"

Erin's hand falls to his side as his lips part in shock.

"Staging a fall and getting hurt to take advantage of my nephew's kindness? Not very creative." Stella doesn't give him a chance to respond before she closes the distance between them and raises the camera to his face. Erin looks at the camera and tenses. He closes his mouth and veils his face as all the blood drains out of it and onto the ground at his feet. On the screen is the photo he had secretly taken of Victor on his birthday, when he was sitting on the fence line laughing.

He should be feeling guilty. He's in trouble. Really big trouble. Stella is holding camera evidence that Erin disobeyed her warning. The voice in his head is howling at him now to run and hide. But he can't help the swell of pride he feels when looking at the picture. Victor is beautiful—smiling and laughing with a wide grin and loose shoulders. He's free. And Erin wasn't just the one who captured the moment. He was the one who caused it.

"I told you to stay away from Victor and to stop confusing him," Stella growls at him. The scent of sour strawberries and champagne hits Erin in constant swells, but he holds his ground and looks at Stella with vacant eyes. He doesn't know how she's spreading her scent like that without re-spraying her perfume, but he refuses to let her see how it's affecting him.

He refuses to let her see him break.

"First you and your parents come onto *my* property, stinking up the place with your poisonous scents, and now you blatantly ignore my warnings? Victor needs to focus on the family business. Real estate is a massive endeavor, one with plenty of competition. Our family name has a reputation to uphold. I won't let anything get in the way of my plans, meaning Victor has no time to fool around with some small-town country *human*," Stella spits in disgust as if saying human—speaking this close to Erin at all—makes her physically sick. She pushes the camera into Erin's hands, leaning to whisper into his ear, "If words didn't work for your deaf ears, then watch closely. Actions speak louder, boy, and money goes a long way around these parts. Unless you want to see the power my family truly holds, I highly suggest you listen to me. Car accidents happen so often on these dirt, country roads. And that's the least of it."

Erin holds the camera to his chest, heart still, as Stella prowls away. As soon as he hears her soft slippers slide along the porch and into the house, he moves. Acting on muscle memory, he walks out of the shed and locks the door behind him. The metal door trembles when he shuts it, and the hinges squeal louder than before, but he doesn't care. A quick snatch and grab. That's what this was meant to be. Not an insane encounter with his employer.

Here he was thinking Victor was the only hidden psycho in the family.

He's almost back to his safe, small, white hatchback when he notices a man walking toward it. He knows it's Victor. The way his long legs carry him purposely toward his destination, his back straight and head held high with confidence. Erin clenches his fists and stomps the rest of the way to his car. He underestimated Victor's intelligence. Normally, when people give you the silent treatment and storm off after a disagreement, you take it as 'leave me alone, you psychopath.' But it looks like Victor's drug-filled brain doesn't understand that.

Erin opens his mouth, words loose on his tongue in preparation to yell at Victor across the lawn, when he catches sight of something in his hand. It looks like a piece of paper. Victor carefully places it on the windshield of Erin's car. When he turns, the ghost of a smile lingers across his lips as he dips his head in greeting, before strolling back toward the house.

Erin jogs the rest of the distance to his car and takes a look at the cream paper. It's a note with his name on it in small red cursive. He hesitates, looking back at the house. Victor is gone, no trace of him left in the scarce moonlight besides the lingering rich smell of new leather dipped in old spice and sandalwood.

Did Stella put him up to this? No, she wouldn't bring to Victor's attention that she's trying to force him away. He says they're werewolves, yet Erin's meant to believe that Victor didn't bump into Stella just then? That, by some luck hidden between the folds of the moon's light, she hadn't seen Victor at all? If this isn't a note from Stella on behalf of Victor asking Erin to stay away, what is it?

He tears the note from under the wiper with a frown and unfolds it.

He hates how he immediately falls in love with Victor's handwriting.

He hates even more how much his soul aches after reading the curling words.

Erin,

I'm sorry for dumping so much information onto you. I know it made you feel uncomfortable and caused you pain. It sounds weird, especially when you aren't a part of this life—this world.

I suppose, once I gave in to my feelings, the only logical explanation I could think of was that you were one of us. I wanted you to be one of us. It would be so much easier for us to go through ~~the curse~~ everything together. Ben and I were talking, and then once this idea was in my head ... I ran with it. Of course you would know you were a werewolf. How could you not? All the evidence was there. You were just scared because this new Pack had come to town, and you were a rogue, not officially a member of the community.

And here I go again ... I'm hung up on it because I want everything you being one of us entails. ~~At least, some of it.~~ But in doing so, I rushed it. I didn't stop to think about how the news would make you feel. If you really had no clue about werewolves being real, obviously I would look like a crazy psychopath to you.

But you haven't left yet. Even though you are ignoring me, you haven't called the local authorities and thrown me into a mental hospital. So now I'm going to run with another idea. You do care for me. Or, at the very least, want to care for me.

I don't expect you to believe me about any of it, and I'm going to stop trying to convince you. So, for now, just look at me as Victor, a real estate entrepreneur from New York. Let's go forward as two humans do. We can take it slow; you set the pace. I'll follow your lead because I know there's something between us—something deep and true—and I know you feel it, too, despite how hard you try to deny it. I'm not giving up on it—on you. So please, all I ask is for you not to give up on it—on me—either.

I want to explore this. Together.

The stars can't keep me from you.

I'll be here until the moon falls from the sky, and the sun shrivels up and dies.

Victor.

Erin delicately refolds the letter.

Never in his life has his heart and head felt so out of sync.

SEVENTEEN

"**D**id you get your exam scores back?"

"Yep, aced them all."

"Of course you did."

"How'd you do?"

"Eh, high credits in everything but chem. Barely passed that one. But! I think it was only because Miss Drummond had the hots for me, and when I didn't reciprocate, she retaliated."

"I'm ... pretty sure that's not how that works."

"Psh. Oh, by the way, have the dreams stopped?" Fletcher asks around a mouthful of popcorn, wide brown eyes never leaving the television screen.

"Hm?" Erin turns to his left, where his best friend is sitting, legs stretched out in front of him on the couch. "Oh, yeah. No more sex-craved wolf dreams from me." He thinks back to yesterday when he was removing the weeds by the fence. He knew Victor was in the front room of the house. He could feel those pale blue eyes on him. It took every ounce of self-control he had to not look at Victor.

Keeping his back turned to focus on the task at hand made his stomach churn in anger and guilt. Like by ignoring him he was doing something inherently wrong.

He definitely didn't go home that night and have a dream where a massive black wolf was lapping up deep purple water from a fancy goblet-like bowl, a stone castle looming behind it.

And he most definitely didn't run to the bathroom after waking, strip out of his sweat-soaked pajamas, and bend over the toilet bowl, naked on the floor, puking his guts up as fear clung to him like a second skin.

"I wasn't the one who said they were about sex." Fletcher squints momentarily before sliding down the couch more. "But that's good then."

"Well, what else could those dreams have been about?" Erin mumbles. If that's what others say the dreams are about, then that's what his subconscious is trying to tell him. He has stopped trying to find reason and meaning after every single dream. What would be the point? He had a wolf dream and thought it was because he saw a hot guy and wanted to have sex. He made an attempt to get to know said hot guy so they could eventually have sex, only to be threatened by his crazy aunt, find out said guy is insane, and for the wolf dreams to not stop.

In fact, they've only gotten worse.

He's not stupid enough to believe Google that these weird dreams have anything to do with sex and desire, but ... what do they mean, then?

The thought that he's missed something vital, something important, or that these are some kind of early warning premonitions makes his skin crawl. Add to that Stella's threats—

No, he would much rather just go along with what everyone else—a.k.a Layla—is saying. Out of sight, out of mind.

Erin crosses his legs underneath him, sniffing in the clean scent of eucalyptus that always sits in the air at Fletcher's house, and turns his attention back to the screen. After their lunch and mini photoshoot with Layla, Fletcher invited Erin to spend the night so they could watch some movies together. Erin accepted, despite his mind still playing cat and mouse with his heart. He figured some good old-fashioned action movies would help distract him.

"So, you seen Victor naked yet?"

Erin chokes, popcorn kernels flying out of his mouth. After coughing and gulping down air, he spins to face Fletcher. "Why the fuck would you ask that?"

"Because I wanted to know if he has balls made from hundred-dollar bills? I don't know, dude, you said the dreams stopped and Layla said they were because you secretly wanted some hot dude to peg you, so why d'ya think?" Fletcher looks at Erin with pursed lips and furrowed brows, like he's confused as to why Erin is surprised by his question.

Erin clicks his tongue and crosses his arms. He does admit that going from pining over someone to suddenly avoiding the topic like the bubonic plague can give someone whiplash.

"Well, that wasn't the reason the dreams stopped, so you can stop thinking about my sex life now," Erin says in a quiet voice.

Fletcher says nothing after that. He simply moves his tub of popcorn to the middle of the couch, grabs one of the various blankets from the cupboard beside the TV, and resumes his position.

Guilt pounds against his heart; Fletcher's shape in his peripheral louder than the clashing swords echoing from the TV. He knows Fletcher was just curious, that he was being a good friend and checking in. But it's hard. It's like he's holding a bottle with a lid. Erin is forcing the lid shut on the bottle, then ignoring the bottle completely, even as it shakes from the pressure. Even as hairline cracks start to fissure, growing larger by the day.

But he won't let go of the bottle, because it's his, he wants it ... just ... not yet. If he ignores the bottle completely and forgets he's holding anything, eventually it'll go away. Until he's ready.

There's no need to address it.

So why does everyone keep doing just that?

Erin sighs. The lead in the movie they're watching resembles Victor. Shaggy dark blonde hair and bright blue eyes. A typical American heartthrob. Fletcher didn't choose this movie on purpose—lots of actors have blonde hair and blue eyes. It's a very common genetic trait across many countries. Like the man who works with Layla at the café, or his old visual arts professor.

Great. Erin pouts, mentally slapping his wrist. Comparing strangers to Victor? He feels the pressure on his shoulders pushing down, causing his chest to tighten. The universe only gives out so many coincidences before deciding to slap you in the face with the truth.

Erin breathes deeply and gathers his courage. "Can you pause this for a bit?"

"Need to take a shit?" Fletcher asks with a smirk as he reaches for the remote on the coffee table in front of them.

"No, I need you to convince me Victor is a bad man who I need to stay away from." Erin keeps his eyes facing forward. Fletcher has always stuck to the extremes—extremely funny and extremely serious. Pair that with a face that sucks at lying, and Erin knows that if he looks into Fletcher's eyes now, he'll see worry and fear so real his soul would be ripped to shreds.

Even if he was good at lying, they've known each other for so long that Fletcher would've figured something was wrong eventually. Best to bite the bullet now and get some advice while he still has time to do so.

"Okay," Fletcher drawls. Erin blesses his patience. Fletcher's ability to go with the flow, take life's punches to the gut and keep swimming, makes him a king among men.

Chlorine swims through the air as Fletcher turns his body toward Erin, legs criss-cross-applesauced. Erin mirrors his position, and suddenly, it's like they are little kids again, sitting underneath the large Oak tree in his backyard and playing Go Fish.

Erin claps his hands together to keep them from flailing around as he says, "So basically, Victor dropped a major bomb on me, figuratively speaking, and now I'm really, really angry at him, but I also feel guilty about being angry at him because I don't want to be angry at him. I do like him ... a lot. He's really attractive and kind. And I've already learned so much about him, and that makes me want to get to know him even more. Emotionally ... and physically. But this man is crazy, Fletch! He thinks his whole family is a pack of werewolves and that I am one too, and that we are mates! The logical conclusion is drugs. I don't know, I didn't find any, so that's still up for debate. So, the only excuse I can think of is that he wants to play out some kind of sex fantasy? But then he apologized! He wrote this sweet note asking me to forgive him and give him another chance. To take things slow ... and I want to. I really, really want to ..."

Erin holds up a hand to Fletcher, signaling for him to wait as he reaches over the side of the couch and grabs his soda can. After taking a couple of big gulps, Erin inhales a deep breath and continues. "And don't even get me started on his psycho aunt. I had to physically lock myself in my car and drive home last night so I didn't chase Victor into his house after he left that note for me because she's always lurking. She even threatened me again! Literally held my camera hostage last night. And then I found that note, which, I still don't know how they didn't run into each other. I know the shed is in the next paddock over, and I parked closer to the front gate than the house. Victor must have come out right after Stella went back inside. They just missed each other! But, if they are werewolves, how would they not realize? It just doesn't make any sense, and I'm so confused. This is a guy. A man. Why am I so stressed over another human being, dude? So, now I need you to tell me that it's a bad idea to want to do the tango with a crazy man whose aunt can successfully murder me and get away with it. Oh, but don't tell me she wouldn't get away with it. They've worked in real estate for, I don't know, eons. And they're rich. Like ... rich rich."

"Blood money rich?" Fletcher asks quietly.

Erin nods, chest heaving. "Blood money rich."

Fletcher blinks rapidly. Erin can all but see his hysterical ramble being decoded in Fletcher's brain, the cogs smoking after the massive information overload. He suddenly wishes he had kept the movie playing in the background. At least then he would have more than his heartbeat playing in his ears.

"This is why you were distracted all day today and messing up?" Fletcher asks in disbelief.

Erin frowns, his shoulders tensing. He doesn't know if he likes that accusatory tone coming from his best friend. "I just told you the man I'm developing real feelings for is crazy with a potentially murderous aunt, a fact that hasn't stopped me from finding him insanely attractive like it should, and the first thing you ask is if this is why I took some bad photos at lunch today?"

Fletcher nods his head slowly, lips thinning into a straight smile. "Uh, yeah."

Erin takes the couch pillow from behind his back and throws it at Fletcher's head.

Fletcher swats the pillow from his face, a laugh cracking his voice. "Oh, come on, Erin, it wasn't just some bad photos, it was basically all of them. You even tripped on air. Air!"

"Fletcher, this is serious!" Erin whines. "I know Stella was being serious. My bones quaked. My bones, Fletch! I just know she's waiting around every corner, waiting to mess up this project and blame it on me. Or my parents. And—"

And that's not something Erin could handle.

Fletcher's laughter quiets down, and he stares at Erin with a small rueful smile. "I know, I know. Listen, forget the aunt for now. What if you meet Victor halfway? It's clear he has a massive presence in your head, so you may as well give him a shot. It takes balls to apologize to someone, so this way you can find out for yourself just how big they are."

"You!" Erin growls, hand reaching to grab the other pillow beside him.

Fletcher raises his hands in surrender, his voice rising when he says, "I don't think he'd let anything happen to you. When you told us about how you fell on Wednesday—which, not cool, man. Waiting three whole days to show me your war wound? Shame on you—you said he freaked the fuck out. He's clearly very protective and has a massive crush on you, too, which may even solve your problem with his conniving aunt."

Erin settles down and nods, thinking back to how panicked Victor was. He felt safe then. Despite the fear radiating off everyone else around him, Erin knew there was nothing to be scared of. His heart swells with gratitude. He didn't have much time to think about how he felt during the fall with Victor's werewolf declaration right after swarming his thoughts, which was one of the reasons why he didn't tell his friends about it until they went out today. He knows what he felt then was true. Victor was there for him. In the chaotic moment before ... hell, even the moment after. He would always be there for him.

Was that enough, though?

Erin knows how influential Stella is in Victor's family. He's seen it firsthand over the past two weeks. Everyone looks to her for approval. He supposes it's only natural; from what he's seen, she is the matriarch.

Fletcher takes Erin's silence as a sign to keep going. "Worst outcome, Victor returns to New York after his family reunion and leases out the ranch to someone else. Best outcome, Layla needs to come up with a plan to stop crazy Aunt Stella from burying you under some trees behind her property without us knowing."

Despite himself, Erin chuckles. Give it to Fletch to have some backward ideology that somehow still makes sense. He wants to believe Victor—something inside him has been stirring ever since they met and is now trying to claw its way out. It's not that Erin is afraid of it; the feeling is warm and secure. He wants to feel that way, and that's what's scaring him. He's afraid that once it's out, he won't ever want it to go away.

He's afraid of losing it.

Erin squeezes his thumb in between his fingers, letting his head drop onto the back of the couch. His mind is made up. "What should I do then?"

"You could ..." Fletcher hums, fingers tapping together in contemplative mischief. "Go on a date?"

EIGHTEEN

E nough is enough.

She doesn't know when the human King will come back for Tala, and she's not going to wait around to find out. Her cubs who decided to follow Kazamir and side with King Halian have already been removed from the dungeon. So be it. She will waste no more time thinking about them.

She watches Tala. He sits against the stone, hidden in the shadows. Stale blood stenches the air, making her nose curl. His flesh is blistering faster than hers, or more accurately, he isn't healing like she is. These chains make it impossible for her to help, too. Her magic is siphoned off. How they managed to do that, she does not know. Perhaps it is simply due to the massive amount of wolfsbane soaked into the iron. Either way ...

She clicks her teeth. This will not do.

"Tala."

He lifts his head. Fire pierces her soul. Two eyes. Fierce. Unyielding. Eyes as pale as the moon yet raging like an inferno on the sun.

The eyes of an Alpha.

There is still time.

"Let us leave this place now, Alpha," she rasps. Ignoring the way he flinches at her words, she lifts her head to the corner of their small enclosure. Right at the top is a slit, too small for even a mouse, but it is enough for her to see. For her to ask.

With shaky fingers, she gently touches the sparkling, deep blue gemstone star on her forehead. It glows. Not brightly. A spark sings louder in the darkness. But it will be enough.

Tala shifts, chains rattling in the quiet space as he stands. Eyes narrow on her, assessing.

"Who are you praying to, Mother Goddess?" he asks.

She can smell his curiosity and grins, lips parting to reply—

"Me."

With a gasp, she turns. Black hair, speckled with gray like the stars in the night sky above, and deep-set brown eyes. They gaze at her, the corners pulled down in sadness. Full lips smiling in pitying sympathy. It swells within her, all the emotion she's held onto since the moment she stepped away from their home. Since the day she sat and saw. No, since even before that. Since the day that human first fired an arrow at her cubs. Her lips pull. She can't hide the grimace. Her shoulders tremble. She can't stop the anger. She attempts to gulp down the sob, but it is too thick and escapes anyway.

She knows Tala is here, watching her break. But she can't find it in her to care. When He is beside her, it is like they are all alone again. He is all that matters in that moment. Just like always. Her guiding Star.

"Oh, Light." Ylli opens his black cloak and steps toward her, wrapping his strong arms around her back. Safe. She is safe now. The pressure where he rubs eases the pain, guiding the sobs through her. His skin is warm under her cheek, and she smiles despite herself. He is always warm, like a ball of fire. Her Starfire.

She twists her head, forehead pressing against the thick hair on his chest right above his heart. The rhythm is steady. Calming. Tightening her fingers around the deep blue shawl around his midsection, she matches her breath to his heartbeat. She notes he's wearing loose, billowing white pants, slits along the sides, while black string tightens the material around his ankles. She sniffs as her tears still. He is matching her. Of course he is.

Hooking a finger under her jaw, he tilts her head up, wiping under her eyes. "I told you it would not be easy, Light."

"You told me not to come at all." She pats down his chest, wiping away the tear stains from his skin.

"And when do you ever listen to me, hm?" He yanks the chains from her wrists, freeing them, and inspects her delicate skin. It is raw. A frown pinches his smooth, pale skin, eyes traveling to her once-white skirt.

"And yet, you answered me. A bright star, come to collect my soul." A shiver runs through her as he chuckles and presses a kiss to each of her red burns.

"Always," he whispers against her lips. "Even if it's just to tell you I told you so."

She giggles, kissing him back with renewed energy. "Undo both our shackles, all of them. Quick, Husband. There is much to be done still."

"Of course this has not deterred you," he sighs, bending to yank the poisonous metal from her ankles. She shakes her limbs in an attempt to wake her magic as her husband turns to face Tala. Her cub is still, shoulders taut as he watches them. Pain clings to his skin, and she knows it is not from the shackles. He is lost in memory.

"Tala." She lifts a hand to his shoulder, and he flinches. She smiles gently. "My husband is going to take your chains off now, and we are going to get out of here."

Tala shakes his head. "Take—" Coughing. It is wet, deep in his chest. "Take the others first." His voice is rough. She fears there may still be poison in his throat. She clicks her tongue. Selfish human King. If Tala is still affected, what is the state of the others? Her eyes roam the cells. From what she can see, those who stayed are still slumped in pain; only a few twist their heads to watch them in worry. They are not as strong as he is. The stupid King will kill off all his *slaves* before he even gets a chance to use them.

Perhaps that is for the best.

It will teach him a lesson.

She can start—

"There is no time, young Alpha. Another trip will need to be arranged." Her husband backs Tala against the stone wall and removes the wolfsbane metal. Tala growls low in his throat as he rubs his wrists, to which her husband simply raises an eyebrow. "Thank you is what most would say."

Tala licks his lips and bows his head. "Thank you, God of the Stars."

"You are welcome." He wraps an arm around her as shadows consume them. As soon as it starts, it ends, and they are outside once more. The night breeze is cool against her skin; she did not realize how hot it was underground until now. It helps rid the negative thoughts from her mind. Breathing deeply, she takes in the surroundings. They are still beside the King's bleak stone home. She can see the flags from before flying through the sparse treetops around them.

"Why did you not take us farther from here, Husband?"

"I have used too much of my energy already, Wife." He is panting heavily, the fingers wrapped around her waist trembling slightly. "Death has been too much recently. I am worn thin."

"I am sorry, my Star." Her heart shatters. She can see how thin his energy is as it travels along his skin. And coming to save them, too, must have taken even more. She takes his hands into hers, rising on the tips of her toes to kiss the underside of his jaw where his stubble grows. "Thank you. Even this much I am grateful for."

"When can we return and get the rest of my Pack?" Tala rounds on them. The clear air seems to have given him more strength as well. "I refuse to leave them behind."

"I told you—"

There is a noise in the trees beside them. Her husband closes his mouth, words lost now as they focus. He steps in front of her as Tala crouches, hands flexing and nails elongating into sharp claws.

Someone is coming toward them. There is no scent. The noise quiet as they move. Only the grass beneath the light weight screams in the empty air around them.

Her heart is beating swiftly in her chest, magic building along her veins. It is slow to return. Too slow.

Ylli holds out his hand, a white glow growing in the palm of his hand.

Tala growls low in his throat. A warning. Their presence is made known.

Whoever is moving halts. A moment passes before the shuffling continues, faster this time.

They are running.

Running.

Running.

Running.

"Light, move farther back!"

Nahale stumbles through the dense trees. His cheek is red and swollen. An outline of a ring sits right underneath his jawline, while a thin silver necklace peeks from beneath the pale orange material he wears. He wears no armor, but on his shoulder, a thick bow is slung, the quiver draped over his hip on the other side. Right beside a long sword. A giant black cloth bag is also on his back, the drawstring tight as it keeps whatever is filling it trapped snugly.

Oh.

They waste no time.

Nahale drops what he's carrying beside him, arms spread wide as Tala runs toward him, sweeping him into his arms. The two say nothing, heads buried deep into each other's necks. Nuzzling. Breathing deeply. She thinks they will leave bruises on each other's backs with how hard they are embracing. Though she cannot blame them. And despite herself, she finds her limbs relaxing at the sight.

Magic ebbs and flows underneath her skin—the desperate need for use no longer rushing its repair.

"Great, another cub," her husband mutters. She swats his arm.

Tala breaks away first, hand brushing over the forming bruise on Nahale's cheek. "Why?" he asks, voice strained.

"I will live as a slave to humans for a hundred lifetimes if it means I can keep you in my sight," Nahale declares. "My birthright? It doesn't matter. My freedom? I don't care. My instinct?" He wraps his hand around the back of Tala's neck and presses their foreheads together. She gasps, squeezing her husband's hand on her waist as Nahale repeats Tala's words from hours ago.

"My instinct is you, my Little Wolf. To see you. To touch you. To protect you. So long as you live, my instinct—my heart and soul—every breath of air that enters my lungs, is for you. You rule me. From the moment I met you twelve and six moon cycles ago, when we were but children, you have been my everything. I knew it was wrong, that I should not associate with you. But I wanted to keep hold of the warm feeling that stirred within me every time my eyes met yours. It was a greed I felt no shame in having. And that is something I will never forget, in any lifetime."

Tala shakes his head, laughter replacing his tears. They both do.

"We are bound, my Little Wolf. Whether you want to be or not."

"I do," Tala agrees, sniffling. "I am."

He grins, and slowly, she feels a stitching sensation in her heart.

Her hopes. Together.

They can still do this.

"We need a plan," she says to the group. Nahale looks to them, his golden eyes widen when they settle on her husband. It seems he has just pieced together how they had managed to escape.

Nahale clears his throat and bends to retrieve his belongings. She spies the small dagger he readjusts in his high boots. Clever. Is that how he got away?

"My father has not captured the rest of the wolves yet. I overheard him discussing with the guards in the throne room, as I was escaping. They plan to leave in two moon passes, as soon as dawn breaks the sky." He glances at her. "He thinks that should they attack during the day, then Mother Hëna, Goddess of the Moon, will not aid them in strength."

She scoffs. Her magic does not cease to exist just because her brother is awake and in command. Besides, she hasn't seen him since before the humans were born, and Liri has not mentioned seeing him for an age as well. Which means he hauled himself off into some corner of Creation's Space and is doing ... something. If he cared what was going on in this world he agreed to create with her, then he would have come back. But he hasn't. Which means he doesn't.

"They will not make it far. The Pack will not let them anywhere near the border," Tala states, grabbing the sack from his mate.

"Kazamir will lead them," Nahale says. "And you know he has a ... way with his words." He looks at Tala. Waiting. Watching as anger twitches along Tala's jaw.

"Like I said," Tala grabs Nahale's hand, "the Pack will not let them anywhere near the border. And if they break through, then we will fight."

"Do you think that is wise?" Her husband interjects. His eyes are narrowed, and his brows are raised. He is judging.

"Doesn't matter. It is right. My Pack will agree." Tala shrugs and begins walking deeper into the forest, Nahale right beside him.

"And if they do not?" Ylli stands tall. She wants to berate him for pushing, for taunting her wolf into a fight. But she knows why he does. If Tala backs out now, if he falls for the trap, if he does not show strength or wisdom, then the Pack has no right to call him Alpha.

"If they do not, then we will do all we can to convince them." Nahale wraps his hand with Tala's, forcing him to turn and wait for them. She sucks her lips to stop them from smiling. His eyes shine even fiercer than Tala's. A wolf in human clothing.

"What was I expecting?" Her husband sighs and rolls his eyes. "They are your children after all," he mutters.

"A Pack's strength lies in their loyalty to each other, not in their numbers," she reminds them, closing the distance to squeeze Nahale's shoulder. "Though numbers do help."

"Let us be quick then." Her husband follows the direction the others have gone. Hopefully, he will have regained enough strength from the night to travel them when the sun rises. The closer they can bridge the gap, the better.

She wraps her hands around Nahale's arm, slowing his stride. Voice low, she asks, "Tell me, Nahale, how long have you known Tala?"

"You do not know?" Nahale questions. "He has not said?"

"I have guessed, but I did not want to pry."

Nahale laughs under his breath. "We met nearly twelve and six moon cycles ago, Goddess. I had run out of the palace, trying to escape my studies, when I met Tala. He was sitting underneath this large tree, purple flowers dangling around it beautifully."

"Wisteria," She clarifies. One of her old friends' favorites.

"Yes," Nahale nods. "I knew what he was as soon as I saw him. Yet still, I kept looking. I stayed."

"Why? You were at war by that stage, you had been for at least twelve and four moon cycles. You knew the consequences that would befall you both, should anyone find out." She gestures back toward the palace, to Tala's wrists and ankles as he limps beside her husband, skin still bleeding from the blisters. "Take a look."

"He was crying, Goddess." The young prince's eyes glaze over as a sweet smell swirls around him. Like a forest after rainfall. "His big, round, pale blue eyes that reminded me of moonlight were crying, and it broke my heart. I asked him what was wrong, and he told me his mother had just died. He held the weapon that took her soul out to me and I ... My mother, the Queen, is still alive, but she may as well be dead. She has always found it hard to show me affection. Love. I resonated with him because of that. I thought, how, perhaps I was the only one who would know what to say to stop him from crying."

"And did he?" She stills. Greed. Selfishness. Human traits. There must be more, something Tala saw that made him want to tie their souls together. "What did you say to him?"

"I started a fire and burned the arrow that killed his mother, and told him that she wasn't going to return because she was dead, and nothing was going to change that, no matter how ugly he cried."

She is not quick enough to hide her shock. Nahale laughs. The sound is sweet, full.

"I know. I know. I was young. But he laughed. And that was it for me. It became my favorite sound, and soon, I found myself traveling out to that tree to meet him. Time passed … he told me about the Pack, and I told him about my subjects. We got closer … in many ways." He looks down shyly. Yes. She can imagine what two, who are freshly of age and in love would do with no one around.

She pats his arm before locking them together, her hand resting on his wrist as they continue to walk. "That is why you are willing to sacrifice it all for Tala? Because you favor his laugh?"

She needs to be sure.

Needs to double-check.

"No. I'm with Tala because I love him. And sacrificing it all, without care of your own self to protect the other, that's what it means to love someone." He smiles wide, eyes looking ahead at Tala and her husband. They are conversing. Awkwardly, if Tala's shuffling feet and constant looking back at them are any indication. "Perhaps, as a human, I can't reach my instinct as readily as a wolf. But it's still in there, I can feel it. And it's pointing me to him."

Instinct?

Her hand tightens on his wrist.

Could it be … can these humans still be Pack?

"I choose to listen to this voice, quiet as a whisper and not a howl it may be," Nahale continues. Narrow golden eyes turn to face her, strength etched along his jaw. "But that just means I need to fight harder at making it seen."

Oh.

For the first time since that moment in her courtyard, up in the sky above, Hëna begins to wonder if maybe ... just maybe ... it was not her who picked them to be Hope. Not her who will save them at the end of all this.

But they picked her.

They, who will save *her*.

NINETEEN

Erin doesn't have Victor's phone number.

At first, he was apprehensive about agreeing with Fletcher's suggestion of a date with Victor. He thought his friend was joking around again before realizing it might be a good idea. He needs closure with Victor, a way to settle things once and for all. Victor told him not to feel any pressure about the whole 'we're all werewolves' thing, thinking that would make it easier for Erin to accept. He still thinks Victor made the whole thing up, so if it means he must use Victor's kindness now to buy him time while he wraps his head around the possibility of everything, so be it.

Victor asked to press the reset button.

This is Erin pressing.

He leans on the shovel in his hands and looks toward the house, picking at the blisters on his palms. His normal shovel was broken when they got to the ranch this morning. Natalie saw red at the sight, and the spilled bags of soil all over the ground, mixing together. Expensive soil, for the temperamental flower hedges she had wanted to plant today along the freshly painted fences barricading the house. Flower hedges that don't like to share their soil.

Surprise, surprise, Stella walked by the shed, shock spilling past her plumped red lips. She blamed it on Mr. Wolf.

Then it was Erin whom John was holding back instead of his wife.

Mr. Wolf would never. He's also not strong enough to knock over bags of soil weighing over eighty pounds. You'd need to be a werewolf or something—

Oh.

Stella left, pity on her lips and a malicious glint in her mascaraed eyes. Erin sneered; he knew Stella was going to try shit. He just didn't know she'd start so soon.

His parents went to the store to buy Erin a new shovel and more soil. They salvaged what they could, but it wasn't going to be enough. Which means Erin's spent all day digging holes and prepping the soil along the fence lines with a brand-new shovel. One that's had no wear and tear on it. So, like a brand-new pair of shoes, his hands are now suffering.

To make matters worse, the whole time, Victor's been in the front room. There are other people in there with him. Lots, actually. The massive windows opened to let the wind whisper in. He sees Victor boxing with Ben's sister, Beatrice, who has on a cute, bright pink sports bra with matching tights, while Victor is shirtless. Again.

The whole time he's been working, not a single person has blocked their view of each other. Erin doesn't know if Victor made up an excuse for the others to not stand in front of the window or if they are simply trying not to block the cool summer breeze. Either way, he's not complaining. Erin's eyes follow a bead of sweat rolling down Victor's jaw before it nosedives onto his collarbone. He can see it tremble and change direction when Victor tenses to block Beatrice's punch, his muscles rippling under his skin. Erin doesn't think there will ever be a breeze cool enough to dry the sweat on Victor's arms.

Laughter from across the lawn causes Erin to swivel his head. Natalie is talking to a man wearing navy blue loafers and a matching linen outfit. Who the hell is that? A guest? Erin gulps, scratches his chin, and gets back to work. He must be one of Victor's relatives. No. He glances back again, his ears picking up on a southern twang as he relays a famous soup recipe to his mom.

"My, your family must love it when you cook dinner, Mr. Harkin," Natalie says, one hand stuffed into the pocket of her jumpsuit while the other holds a tissue with writing on it. The recipe they were just discussing, he assumes.

"They sure do." The man, Mr. Harkin, grins wide. "Stella sings my praises the loudest."

"Yes! That's right, the family reunion." Natalie smacks the tissue against her forehead. "I completely forgot that's what we were here landscaping this ranch for. Pardon my saying, though, but did you marry into the family? I don't see any resemblance."

"No, no, we're not related by blood." Mr. Harkin waves a hand between them before stuffing it back into his pants pocket. He rocks on the heels of his feet. "Let's just say ... we go a long way back, Stella and me. Many times removed, and all that."

So, if he knows Stella ... then that makes him a werewolf from a different Pack.

Frustration rushes into Erin's arms like lightning, and he overthrows the dirt pile, making a mess beside him on the makeshift driveway. He just entertained Victor's werewolf illusion. He took note of Victor's rambling and applied it to a stranger talking to his mother, simply because he doesn't look related to anyone from Victor's family, has a Texan accent, and knows Stella.

How foolish.

Holding the shovel lax out in front of him, Erin stares at the mess he's made. If only cleaning this werewolf dilemma were as simple as moving away all this dirt. Victor's not even the problem anymore at this point.

It's Stella.

However, taking Stella out of the equation is easier said than done. Erin doesn't know anyone else in Victor's family; he doesn't know how many of the people milling around are spies for Stella and how many are simply cousins of cousins. Fletcher's plan was great, but there's no way for Erin to go through with a date if Stella knows. He shivers when he remembers the darkness in her eyes, the way her body seemed to hover over his, even though she's much shorter. At that moment, Stella wasn't just some rich aunt from New York. She was an executioner.

He had the thought before, but he would believe it if she were a werewolf; he can already see the image she'd create on a canvas. Bloodthirsty claws and sharp canines. A giant red wolf sitting in a field of spoiled strawberries, no one able to decipher if the red underneath her belly is the juice from the fruit or the blood of her victims ...

Movement from the road catches his eye as the image fades. He can't help the smile that lightens his features when he sees Ben driving slowly through the gate on a motorcycle. Erin might not know exactly who Stella has in her pocket, but he knows Ben isn't one of them. He can't be, not with the way he hovers around Victor all the time.

Even if he is working with his evil mother, Erin's sure he can get some names written on a list of others involved before Ben figures out what's up.

He drops the shovel and kneels next to the mess. Although everyone has been mostly using the paddock as a parking lot alongside their shed and equipment, some of the smaller motorbikes and vehicles are still being parked inside the four-door garage along the driveway next to the house.

It just so happens that Erin's mess is right in front of the only accessible path to said garage.

He glances around, checking to see if anyone is paying attention to him, scooping small piles of dirt closer to the hole he made as he waits for Ben to get closer. When he hears Ben's bike right in front of him, he looks up and forces his features into one of surprise.

"Oh, sorry," he says. Ben narrows his eyes as Erin stands. His face remains impassive underneath his helmet screen, but Erin can see the question flittering around at the edges. Erin's heart beats like a war drum in his chest. All he can hear in his mind is a mantra of 'please understand, please understand, please understand.'

Erin feels his heart sink to his feet when Ben starts to drive the bike forward. That's it. Operation-kidnap-Victor-and-outsmart-Stella's-spies failed before it could even begin. He'll never be able to get Victor alone now.

Erin huffs and bends down to pick up the shovel when Ben stops in front of him. From this angle, they're blocked. No one from the training room, nor Natalie and the man beside her, can see their faces. Erin thrusts his hands into the pockets of his jumpsuit as Ben lifts his helmet screen. He can feel his nerves tingling like electricity.

"What did you say?" Ben articulates. Each syllable is a shot at the targets in Erin's mind.

Erin takes a step closer on trembling legs. They don't have much time. Ben may be Stella's son, but Erin won't put it past her paranoid ego to question him, too, once she hears of this. In one swift movement, he takes his hand out of his pocket, phone grasped tightly in his fingertips, and leans forward. He loosens his fingers around his phone, letting it drop onto Ben's seat, before raising his now empty hand to his eyes like a shield from the sun. "I said sorry for being in the way."

"Ah, gotcha." Ben keeps his eyes on Erin through it all. His arms are lax and loose on the handlebars, even with Erin's phone unbalanced on the leather seat between his thighs.

God. What a stupid plan. His phone is going to fall off the seat and break; Ben's thighs won't be able to stop it. There goes two grand.

Erin nods and steps back. He turns his back as Ben drops his helmet screen and slowly continues on his way to the garage. Kneeling next to the pile to continue moving it, Erin waits for the sound of cracked glass to reach his ears.

It never does.

Only the clack of a kickstand, the deep splutter of an engine turning off, and the squeal of a garage door rolling down. He peeks to his left. Ben's gone, and Erin breathes a sigh of relief.

Ok, the plan is back in action.

Pinpricks trickle along his neck. Someone's watching him. He looks toward the gym window, instantly catching Victor's eye. He's sitting sideways on the floor with a water bottle in his lap as if he were admiring the view during a break.

Bullshit.

He saw them.

Erin knows he did. He waits for the remorse to trudge through his bloodstream, but it never does. All he feels is hot blood coursing throughout his body. He feels a gust of wind at his back and watches as it travels toward Victor, patting his hair and causing his nostrils to flare.

He's grateful when Victor breaks eye contact and walks away from the window.

Victor wants to play? Then Erin is setting the rules.

On the drive back home, Erin takes his mom's phone out of her bag beside him on the backseat.

Natalie raises an eyebrow. "Lost your phone, cub?"

"Nah, just left it at home. I'm sending myself a reminder for plans I want to do tomorrow, so I can add it into my calendar," Erin replies as he types. "I'll be gone all day, I think."

Natalie scoffs and shakes her head. "Oh, plans. Going to leave your dad and me to do all the work while you go off and enjoy your young life, huh? During the middle of the week, too."

John hums, nodding. He catches Erin's eye in the review mirror and winks.

"You're the one who told me at the start of all this to make sure I'm still hanging out with my friends, Mom." Erin smiles at his mom's sarcastic tone. "I'm just following the rules you set."

Natalie ignores him and continues, "You know, back in my day, we had these things you hung on walls called calendars. You'd write on them, so you knew what your plans were for the month. Oh, and the planner! John, do you remember those archaic devices? We would keep them in our bags and write notes on them for the times when we weren't at home with the wall calendars. Shocking, right?"

"Oh my, what has the world come to? We've gone backward." Erin laughs, playing along.

"Tell Fletcher and Layla I say hello when you see them," Natalie says. He's grateful that's who she assumes he's going to meet. Trying to explain otherwise would simply be too complicated.

Erin glances down at the text message, shining like a lighthouse in the night.

MAMA BEAR: Take Wolf to Botanical Gardens, Tuesday 1st July, 9 a.m.

Victor said in his letter that he spoke with Ben about the ... werewolf illusion, and everyone has seen Mr. Wolf lurking around the property, making himself at home. So hopefully, Ben will see Erin's phone light up with an incoming text, read the message on the screen, can decipher code, and figure out Erin means Victor the human and not his black cat Wolf.

"Will do."

Erin didn't sleep a wink.

The whole night he was thinking about Ben. More specifically, if Ben was going to deliver the message to Victor without telling Stella. Erin, not knowing if Ben will read the message or not, doesn't help the spike of anxiety he feels every time a black motorcycle like the one he's seen Victor ride passes by the parking lot.

He's always enjoyed the walk from the parking lot to the gardens' entrance. The climb up the hill brings forth a lot of fond memories of his friends and family.

He starts to rethink those feelings of joy now that he's alone with his thoughts, worry changing their usual bright colors into muted shades. If Victor doesn't show, he'll never be able to come here again. This place will forever be a haunted memory for him.

Maybe Victor never received his message. Perhaps Ben was acting so nonchalant because he had little sensitivity in his thighs and didn't feel Erin's phone drop in his lap. In front of it? Close enough to it. But Erin definitely didn't see or hear his phone drop as Ben parked his bike. He must have had enough strength to keep the phone balanced on the seat ... right? Ben is Stella's son, but something deep inside Erin is telling him to trust him, not just because Victor does, but because it's the right thing to do.

Ben is on their side.

Erin knows it.

Why else would he provide the perfect blind spot? Or even be willing to listen to Erin in that moment at all? The look in his eyes when he lifted his screen, paired with the slow and purposeful question. Ben was giving Erin a chance to speak without Stella's influence.

Erin huffs a long breath as he reaches the top of the hill, his camera swinging widely around his neck. The sweat dripping down his hair is making his white t-shirt stick to his neck. He wills the fear out of his lungs as he stares at the giant flower gate. He still has half an hour until Victor is meant to arrive. Plenty of time to relax, refresh, and prepare.

"This is a date, but not a romantic one," he mutters as he walks past the empty rainbow-colored benches. "This is for closure. An end to some weird sexual, emotional, all of the above, attraction." Erin tilts his head in contemplation. "Unless he tries extremely hard to act like a normal human being, and not someone high on drugs who wants to use me for sex, and instead actually wants to get to know me more. Then this can be a romantic date."

Erin pauses, his determination already rising from the trenches with a white flag waving high above, when he sees Victor leaning against the dark red brick next to the gate. He has his head down, a woeful look on his face as he kicks a rock across the ground with his black suede shoes. The black jeans with rips around the knees and his light blue t-shirt make his eyes shine even brighter from where they peek behind his hair. His bottom lip is rolled between his teeth, the skin red and torn from where it's been aggressively chewed on.

"You're early," Erin speaks lightly, like one would to a wounded animal, so as not to frighten it.

Victor's head instantly whips to Erin, his teeth releasing their prey to express a look of timid apology. "I wanted to make a good impression."

Erin smiles. He supposes his message was cryptic. Add that to them not being on speaking terms, and it's easy to see how Victor might be scared, thinking he was brought here only to be told to stay away forever. The thought makes his heart ache, but he pushes it aside and refocuses on the here and now.

Which is Victor, standing mere feet away from him, his fancy silver watch glinting in the early sun.

Erin puts his weight on his right foot, jutting his hip out. He catches the way Victor's eyes flit to his side and smirks. These are his 'leave nothing to the imagination' blue jeans and combat boots because this time, Erin's the one letting Victor look.

"Thank you for coming, especially after how I left last time. I needed a model for some summer photos. My friends are busy, plus I have plenty of photos of them already. Portfolios need variety to stand out in college, you know."

Victor relaxes, looking relieved. "So, here I am."

"Yep. We should get a move on. The sun won't stay out forever today." Erin takes the lead as they walk through the gardens, Victor following close behind. He doesn't pay much mind to Victor's presence right behind him in the line until he feels fingers on the small of his back. Victor's fingers. They're warm through his top, like always, and press gently as they walk down his waist.

Erin stills, trying to control his breathing. A family of three pays ahead of them, and the line moves forward. Erin takes a step, Victor's fingers now wrapped around the belt loop of his jeans, keeping him from going too far. Keeping him *close*. Erin presses his lips tightly together, praying Victor can't feel his pulse jumping through his skin as the fingers move past his waist and over his ass.

Pressure digs on his right as Victor's fingers lift open the back pocket and deftly push Erin's phone into the slot. How Victor was able to hold a phone in the palm of his hand while still using his fingers to open the back pocket of Erin's tight jeans, he doesn't want to know. All he knows is that the prospect of having those fingers on his ass, curled around something other than his phone, is not the thought Erin should be having in a public place.

"With the rain forecasted, is that why there aren't many people around?"

Erin shrugs with a small cough. If Victor notices the flush down his neck, he doesn't mention it. "It's a Tuesday, so the families with kids won't start showing till later in the day as a last-ditch attempt to rid them of energy before bedtime. But with the rain supposed to be coming in, they might not." He shows his yearly pass to the lady at the register and holds his card out to buy Victor a day pass when it's snatched from his hand.

"That works out well for us then. Not many people will get in the way of taking photos." Victor smiles, stuffing both his and Erin's credit cards into his leather wallet. Erin raises his eyebrows before striding to their first destination. Well. That was way hotter than it should have been. He's heard how girls swoon when men pay on the first date, but experiencing it first hand ... they never said it was going to be this sexy.

Erin was meant to be the one setting the rules. But this side of Victor, following along silently and doing what Erin wants, but still showing up and taking a stand? He's bending the rules. That's something Erin can get used to. He likes multiplayer games.

With how often he's been here throughout his life, Erin knows the layout like it's his own house. Even the overwhelming smell of various flowers and fertilizer the gardeners use to keep everything from wilting doesn't bother him as much. Victor looks around curiously as they walk, the intense smell not seeming to bother him either. Does he have lots of wildflowers growing by his house in New York? He did say he lives more outside of the city ... Regardless, Erin's grateful for it. Victor poses where Erin tells him to pose without complaint, never once bringing up werewolves or fated mates. After a couple of hours, Erin starts to wish he would, just so the tension can finally dissipate.

He's starting to choke on it; not even the humidity sticking to the air is as thick. Erin sighs, wishing the rain would stop lurking and pour down already as he flicks through the photos he's taken so far. He sits at one of the small wooden tables inside the quaint café, his sore feet resting on the metal bar beneath it, while Victor waits in line to order their food.

Victor hasn't helped much either, though Erin wonders if his lack of conversation is his way of sticking to his promise. The only time Victor spoke was to ask about flower names or to comment on the pretty landscape. He even asked if some things could be incorporated into the ranch design.

Erin could do nothing but answer his questions honestly and nod in agreement. All other times he's faced Victor to talk about anything other than bluebonnets or if the colors red and yellow go well together, his throat has tightened, sealing the words. Looking at him through the camera lens is the only thing able to loosen it so he can breathe.

This was meant to be a way to get out of Stella's reach and give them a chance to talk, to sort out the blossoming feelings growing between them. But it seems to Erin like she's still here, lurking behind Victor's gaze and in his poses.

"One strawberry milkshake with extra whipped cream and two blueberry waffle meals. Such a healthy lunch." Victor places their food on the table, a childish grin taking over his face.

Erin laughs, putting his camera to the side before sipping his drink. "So good," he moans, closing his eyes. When they open, Erin sees Victor staring at a spot, right under his nose. He releases his straw, lips smirking slightly as he licks his lips.

Victor gulps, eyes darting down to his plate. "Did you get any good shots?"

"Of course," he chuckles silently, pushing his drink to the side so he can eat his food while Victor digs into his own. He can feel the awkward tension gripping his neck being replaced with a different kind, one he's more familiar feeling when he's around Victor. It's hotter. Resting in his limbs before traveling lower and settling in his stomach. "I think that'll be all I take today, though. It's already starting to sprinkle."

Victor hums, glancing around them as the raindrops paint the ground, his eyes glazing over. "I've always loved the rain. Stella used to drag me inside during storms. I would've stayed out there all day and made myself sick otherwise."

Erin slows his eating at the mention of Stella. "She seems very protective of you." Just like he'd been ignoring Victor, he'd also been ignoring the angel whispering on his shoulder to be honest about Stella's threats. What good would it do to speak ill of her when she's a Goddess in Victor's eyes? He wouldn't believe it anyway. It's not like Erin's told him about her stealing his camera that night and the other—

Nope.

Not getting involved.

Victor huffs, the sound more like an exhale than laughter. "That's one way to put it. My parents died when I was little, and Stella was the one who took me in. She has raised me ever since as a single mother alongside Ben and Beatrice. Their dad died in the same mu—accident as my parents."

Erin's attention is drawn to Victor's finger, where he fiddles with his blue antique ring. His voice is soft when he speaks, "Did that belong to them?"

Victor glances at the ring. A look of guilt twists his face before anger washes over it. "No. This belonged to the previous Alpha," he spits.

Erin slams his cutlery on the table and rolls his eyes. "Victor—"

"Wait, Erin," Victor interrupts. His voice sounds taut like the string of a bow, while his eyes stay transfixed on Erin, pleading. "When Ben told me you wanted to meet today, I was so ecstatic, I felt like I had just touched an electric fence. You must have read the note and not ripped it to shreds, and my words must have had an impact on you. Then, when I saw you this morning, Erin ... it felt like I could breathe again. You're like the rain, cleansing all the darkness out of me and filling me with light."

Erin turns his gaze to his milkshake, pointedly following a drop of condensation down the cup until it settles over an old coffee stain on the table. Heat sings at Victor's words, staining his cheeks in a deep blush. That's one of the most romantic things a man has said to him.

Victor taps his finger on the fork still gripped in his hand. "I don't want to tiptoe on eggshells around you. Which is why I need to tell you about this. It's been on my mind for days, driving me crazy. I said you don't have to believe me, and that I wouldn't try to convince you to believe me. But I didn't say that I would stop talking about it. This is my reality, and I need to make sure you fully understand before making a decision."

Erin flinches as Victor reaches across the table to grab his hand. The cool metal of the ring pierces his soul.

"Please," he whispers. "I'm more than just a werewolf. I'm a man with a soul. In a way, I'm human, too."

Erin feels all the stubborn energy leave him. He pulls his hands into his lap, rubbing the spot where the ring touched, before finally, slowly, nodding.

"Ok. I'll listen. Tell me your story, Victor."

Victor sighs, relief evident in the way his shoulders drop as he leans back. "I'll start at the beginning, then. Packs ... they work a lot like how you'd think. It's very similar to how wild wolves live. Except, we know how to walk among the humans and make money. My Pack used to be known as the Bellmore Pack of New York, one of the oldest since the split. That's what we call the time when the wolves of old decided to stop being one singular unit. The previous Alpha and his mate of my Pack were called Gray and Stacy. They started a rebellion twenty-one years ago, in March of 2004. I was two at the time. My dad, Stella's older brother, was Gray's Beta, which is the second in command of a Pack. Ben was eight, almost nine, and Beatrice … she was only a few weeks old. We were told later that Gray and Stacy wanted to become the supreme rulers of all werewolf kind. The Moon Goddess, our Patron Deity, is corrupt. Anyone who believes in her and follows her teachings is poisoned, too. Their souls are darkened, corrupted, and twisted. Their wolf instinct possessed. The traitors gave in to her darkness, and a lot of innocent people died that night, including both my parents and Stella's husband. Anyone who didn't believe in Hëna's teachings, Gray and Stacy killed."

Victor pauses, waiting for Erin to interrupt or ask any questions. He doesn't. Taking his petulant stare as a sign, Victor clears his throat and continues. "Our Pack was renamed the Lovelace Pack, since Stella took charge. As the previous Beta's sister and an Alpha herself, no one had an issue with it. At the time, it was the most logical choice. Until I presented, at least."

"Presented?"

Victor nods, crossing his legs under the table. One of his feet bumps into Erin's shin, causing him to shiver. He notices Victor relax slightly at the touch, his hand still resting on the table, flexing. Erin wants to hold his hand, to thread Victor's fingers through his.

But he doesn't.

"Most present at fifteen, that's when a Pack knows what role the individual will have. We all feel it through the bond. The scent changes slightly, deepens, grows. Alpha, Beta, Omega … all are respected, and each has vital roles that support each other and keep the Pack strong. United. When that happened to me, I was thirteen. Not only did I present as an Alpha—someone capable of inheriting the Pack as leader—but we also discovered I was The Black Wolf. It was … eye-opening." Victor chuckles with a sneer. "See, legend goes that before the split, there was a war. It was bloody. The Moon Goddess took part in that war, but in the end, she betrayed us. Many, many innocent wolves died. Some decided to take a stand against her because of that. Our side won, and as such, the split happened. Wolves decided to live differently from each other as they broke apart into four Packs. They left the instinct she had imprinted into us in the dust.

Stomped on it. Growled at it. Over time, these Packs broke apart again and again, until a Pack sat in each state. But no one forgets the original four. They're the ones who hold the Council Meetings every three years."

"And your family is one of those four," Erin notes, interrupting Victor. Goosebumps crawl along his skin. He doesn't think it's from the milkshake.

"Yeah, we are." Pride shines in Victor's eyes. At what? Erin being able to keep up with this nonsensical story? He looks at his half-eaten waffle while Victor continues.

"However, as part of her vengeance for wolf kind standing against her, the Moon Goddess cursed a pair of wolves—lovers, once her strongest allies, her warriors—turning them into what others called The Black Wolf and The White Wolf. They were made stronger and more powerful than any other wolf. There was more death. More pain. More chaos. Until a brave wolf with striking red hair and flaming green eyes managed to put the two down. Now, the saying goes that Fate and Instinct will act as guides for the cursed pair until they find each other once more, forced for eternity to reincarnate. And once that happens, no one can stop the death and destruction that will follow until it is their blood, the two cursed wolves, left pooling in the grave. Just like before. It was never written which Pack these wolves came from originally, and there's been no record of them having been born before me, that is. The elders had always believed it would be one of the four. And magic like that ... no one has ever questioned it. Because, Erin, Goddesses can't die. So neither can their curses."

BOOM.

Erin startles as lightning flashes, the thunder shaking the café before the rain starts violently pouring. He can feel the lid of his bottled emotions starting to shake ferociously as they desperately try to claw out. In his mind, he can see the white wolf from his dreams standing tall. Its golden eyes glare, fur raised along its back, and lips shaped into a growl. Erin knows instantly that those teeth are sharper than any sword or dagger. Yet ... he feels this overbearing sense of desolation fill him.

It takes root.

Following Victor's logic, if Erin is Victor's mate ... wouldn't that make him this cursed White Wolf?

He clenches his teeth.

That sounds ...

A low howl rings through his ears.

A soft smile overtakes Victor's face as he looks out the window at the rain. Erin feels a small stab in his heart—it's the first time Victor has broken eye contact during the whole story. He looks back quickly, though, and when he does, Erin can see the rain reflected in his eyes. They look more silver than blue. "Four years ago was the last Council Meeting, and I had my Alpha acceptance ceremony two months prior, on my twentieth birthday. That's where I was named the next leader, and Stella presented me with the Pack ring. Each Pack has one that's been passed down for generations. I don't know where mine and the others came from, not exactly. There are still many records missing or hard to translate from the time during the initial split." He shrugs. "I never bothered to look too hard, and there was no one I could ask, either. All that knowledge Gray would've known. Not that I cared much either way. Like I said, I was thirteen when I first presented, too scared and caught up in running away into the forest, where I thought no one would find me. But Stella did. She brought me back to the Pack and told me everything was going to be ok. Looking back on it now, she didn't say a lot to reassure me that everyone I loved wasn't going to die ... that I wasn't going to be the cause of it." Victor's smile turned into a full grin. "But she was there. Always. She even stayed on to help lead until I graduated with my business degree and took over the family business as CEO, saying it was what her brother would've wanted for me."

Victor shrugs before leaning forward, his arms crossing in front of him. "She saved me."

Erin sees no lie or desperation as he peers into the pale blue eyes across from him. Victor truly believes what he's saying is true. Whether the whole werewolf thing was created by a child's mind to cope with the death of his family or not, one fact remains as clear as the photos Erin took today.

Victor sees Stella as his savior, as his pseudo-mother.

Erin feels his heart harden in a protectiveness so fierce he nearly gasps. He knows Victor hasn't told him everything. There are gaps, missing puzzle pieces. Things that just don't sound true. He got the short, watered-down version—the lore drop of Victor's life. In a way, it's a blessing. It's made one thing crystal clear: Victor definitely has some childhood trauma, and Stella is at the root of it.

Which means Erin can never tell Victor about Stella's threats. If he ever found out, if he ever believed it to be true, he'd be destroyed.

They waited in the café until the rain stopped before heading back to the parking lot.

Erin feels Victor's shoulder brush against his every couple of steps. "Thank you for helping me today."

Victor twitches when Erin's fingers brush against his. "You're welcome, but I'm the one who should be thanking you."

"Nonsense," Erin chuckles.

They settle into a comfortable silence before Victor turns his head to Erin.

"Don't apologize," Erin says firmly, causing Victor's teeth to clack when he shuts his mouth. He stops and faces Victor, who stills beside him. "I won't pretend I don't think you're crazy, but I will admit you're right. I want to get to know you, the real you, not the 'Alpha' you or anything else you associate with yourself."

With the sun tucked under the horizon, Erin only has the moon and the streetlamps along the path to see Victor. He uses them to watch the way Victor's face morphs from surprise to bliss, and when he tilts his head to the side, all shadows of doubt bleed from his face.

"Deal?" Erin feels his face mirror the same look as he holds out his pinkie.

Victor grins widely before locking his pinkie around Erin's. "Deal." He moves his hand so it's holding Erin's firmly and starts jogging. "Now come on, I saw an ice cream truck on the way here this morning. Let's get some."

"What?" Erin laughs, easily keeping pace with Victor. He can feel the warmth seeping into his fingertips from where they're nestled in-between Victor's. "They probably left during the storm."

"Nonsense, ice cream sailors never abandon ship." True to Victor's word, the ice cream truck is still there at the end of the parking lot, and they order a bowl with two scoops each.

Erin holds out his bowl to Victor. "Want some?"

"Nope," Victor says around a spoonful of mint chocolate.

"Don't you like strawberries?" Erin asks with a raised brow.

Victor shakes his head as he raises his spoon to Erin's lips. Erin laughs out loud at the irony of it all, opening his mouth to let Victor feed him the ice cream.

"Good?" Victor asks.

Erin licks his lips as the ice cream melts down his throat. The mint flavor cools his insides and clears his head. "Delicious. Strawberry is better, though."

"Ugh, you sound like Stella." Victor bumps Erin's shoulder with his.

Erin sours. The thought that he and Stella could have anything in common makes his stomach churn. "She's been good to you."

Victor hums in agreement. "When I was little, Stella would take Ben, Beatrice, and me to the movies and get us ice cream afterward. It was a little tradition, a way to sweeten our lives, she would say."

Erin steals a scoop of ice cream from Victor before mixing it with his strawberry and eating it. "My family used to get fast food. The one who ran to the bathroom less during the movie got to choose which one we went to."

They both laugh as they continue toward their cars. Erin stares in amazement at Victor's bike parked beside his little hatchback. With how hyperaware he was walking up the hill to the gardens, he couldn't believe he hadn't noticed Victor's bike parked next to his already. Out of all the empty spots this morning ... that's the one he chose.

Victor takes the empty ice cream bowls and throws them in the trash can a few paces away from where they're parked. There's still nervous energy inside Erin, a feeling he doesn't know how to name. But after spending the day with Victor, he realizes he doesn't have to name it. Not yet, at least.

"Well." Victor leans against his bike in front of Erin. The parking spaces are small—a corporate decision to allow more customers in a day that makes it a bitch to park during peak season. Now though, with Victor's feet on either side of Erin and his face only a foot away from his own, Erin silently thanks every one of the engineers on the design team.

"Well," Erin repeats.

Victor leans off his bike and into Erin's space.

Is he leaning in for a kiss? Erin feels hesitant, like a kid on Christmas morning who wants to know what presents are hidden in the boxes under the tree but knows once he does, the moment will be gone. He doesn't want this moment with Victor to be over, but he'd be a hypocrite if he stopped it now.

He wants to kiss.

He wants to do more than kiss.

Erin stops thinking, letting his instinct take over. Feeling the truth deep in his bones, he closes his eyes and tilts his chin up.

He has wanted to claim Victor's lips since the moment he laid eyes on him.

The touch of warmth on his nose instead of his lips causes Erin to open his eyes. Victor is smirking, the tip of his nose touching Erin's. He nuzzles it slowly, his breath hitting his cheek in slow waves, the cold scent of mint chocolate and strawberries filling the small space between them.

Victor gazes into Erin's eyes, unblinking. "Be careful. You had a lovebug in your hair, and it's mating season," he purrs against Erin's parted lips.

Erin doesn't move as Victor hooks his leg over his bike, snugly fits his head into his helmet, and drives away. Erin raises his hand to his nose as he gathers himself. He looks in the direction Victor left.

"Lovebug season isn't till September, asshole!" he shouts with a grin.

TWENTY

After their date two days ago, Victor has started walking with Erin and Mr. Wolf along the fence early in the morning to watch the sunrise. Erin needs to take progress photos for Storm Landscaping, and the beautiful scenery on the ranch, as well as Victor's comforting presence beside him, is a bonus.

Erin knew it was risky. This wasn't the botanical gardens. This was Victor's home. Stella's home. If she woke early one day—if anyone did—and looked outside, they would be seen easily. Erin can't find it in him to care, though. Here he is, listening to Victor ramble on about how ice cream should be included as a major food group, the cold morning mist wetting their ankles, and Erin has never felt more warmth seeping from his bones.

It's thrilling.

He still doesn't believe the whole werewolf thing. Victor's confession of how his parents died when he was young makes the whole situation sound like a fantasy world created by a child to explain an unimaginable horror. Trauma does that, according to the internet. He hasn't told his friends about Victor's detailed story yet. It felt ... too personal. Too real, despite Erin's inability to believe it.

There was still something holding him back from getting their opinions on the matter. He doesn't think they would be able to sway him one way or the other, not on this, but … maybe it's because he can't shake the unnatural way his skin itches every time he thinks about the possibility of Victor telling the truth. What it would mean about *him*.

What would they think if they found out their best friend was a werewolf?

It's just not possible. He's twenty-one years old, twenty-two in December … there's no way he wouldn't have known by now.

At least Victor is taking Erin's skepticism in stride after their date and not bringing it up every two sentences. But he isn't hiding from it either. It cools the heat between them, allowing for something sweeter. Something besides just sexual tension. Erin can sense it in the gentle way Victor touches his arm when he's excited to show him something or the way he looks directly at Erin—giving him his whole attention when speaking, like a golden retriever—as if it would physically kill him otherwise.

One thing Erin can believe is that if Victor were to magically shift into a wolf, his tail would be wagging faster than a tornado every time Erin is around.

Even when they aren't walking together in the morning, Victor will simply be around. Erin hasn't said anything about everything Stella had done, but Victor has been surprisingly observant. When he brought Erin some cold water yesterday, he made sure to bring some to Natalie and John as well, so no one thought he was showing favoritism. Erin knows Victor's doing it because he thinks Erin is wary of PDA and doesn't want him to be uncomfortable. But the truth of it is, Erin loves PDA. Not to the extent Victor seems to enjoy, but the occasional hand-holding, arm slung over shoulders, and back hugging make Erin feel warm and tingly inside.

So, the issue isn't the PDA. It's Victor. They aren't dating or anything, so there's no need to act like they are.

"What do you think?" Victor asks, drawing Erin out of his thoughts.

"Hmm?" Erin blinks, looking toward Victor.

Victor chuckles, reaching up to ruffle Erin's hair. "Off with the fairies, are we?"

Erin looks away, coy. His voice lowers, "Maybe I was. What, you jealous?"

Victor's eyes darken. "Yes."

Erin takes a step closer to Victor. "Good," he whispers, smile filled with mirth, while sauntering away. He hears Victor groan out a laugh behind him. "What did you ask, Vic?"

Victor slides behind Erin, pinching both his sides and making him yelp, before turning to walk backward. "I asked if you could take some photos of my Pack, candid ones that I can show at the Council Meeting."

Council Meeting, a.k.a the family reunion, Erin clarifies to himself. He lifts his camera, and Victor pulls a funny face before he snaps a shot. "Are you sure that'll be ok? Normally, a family reunion is just family."

Victor's lips press tightly together, like he's physically trying to keep words from being said. Erin rolls his tongue over his teeth. He can imagine what those words are. His heart jumps into his throat.

"Well, my family hasn't hosted for a while. So, I want to commemorate the moment," Victor smiles. "Something to show the kids later."

Ignoring the way his stomach clenched, Erin lifts himself onto the fence, straddling it to get a better angle of the mist-filled forest beyond. He remembers the little girl with the red hair, and a thought occurs to him. "Where are the kids anyway? I haven't seen many around over the last two and a half weeks."

"I knew there was a lot of work to be done here, so I had most of the kids stay home. Not that they usually would have come anyway." Victor waves a hand through the air, swatting away a fly. "The meetings only involve around fifty wolves from each Pack—the Alpha and their mate, if they have one, the Beta, a healer, and some more reinforcements. The ones in charge of border control, or the CEO of whatever human business that Pack works in. And if members have married into other Packs, they'll all go to catch up. Each Pack chooses differently, though whoever comes always brings their kids with them so that the next generation can get to know each other, keep wolf-kind connected, and all that."

"Ah. That's what all that camping gear is for, then."

Victor hums in agreement. "Some Packs come early, depending on where they are traveling from and how close they are to those hosting that year. And it's the hosting Pack's job to provide blankets. I'm letting them camp in the woods here and giving them extra supplies as a thank you for letting us host again after twenty-two years. And Black Hill is small enough as it is, so I didn't bother with looking into hotel availability."

"You know." Erin turns to face Victor, settling into the fence. "I've seen you in the gym with some of them, the kids, I mean. Teaching them how to throw a punch and do chin-ups. You seem comfortable around them, and they seem to like you in return. It's cute."

"Well, I was a kid once before, Erin."

"Once?" he teases. A worm catches his eye by Victor's sneaker, and Erin lifts his camera, capturing the creature. He rolls his lips between his teeth. "Just make sure Stella knows."

"About? Oh!" Victor tilts his head in confusion. "Ok, but I doubt she'd get mad at you. It's just harmless photos."

Erin sighs deeply, giving Victor a meaningful look.

"Ok, ok," Victor repeats. "I'll let her know you're doing it because I asked."

"For your family reunion," Erin adds.

Victor hesitates briefly before nodding. "For the reunion."

"All those people, and there's no one in your family who does photography?" Erin questions. He lifts his leg over the fence to hop down, but Victor steps toward him. His hands land on Erin's calves, squeezing as he drags his hands up. Hamstring. Knees. Quads. Inner thigh. It's like his legs are a diagram and Victor is in biology class, memorizing his anatomy. His breath hitches when Victor's fingers graze his ass before continuing quickly to his hips. They still. Victor lifts his eyes to Erin with a smirk.

"You going to fondle me all day?" Erin breathes.

Victor's eyes darken. "Don't tempt me," he commands, voice low. Like a growl. Erin smirks. He drops his camera, letting it dangle around his neck, and wraps his arms loosely around Victor's neck, leaning close. Victor responds, tightening his hands on his lower back. "You have golden stars in your eyes, and the freckles on your nose have gotten darker," he says.

Erin snorts. "Are they pretty?" He leans closer. Victor's lips brush his when he nods, and suddenly Erin remembers the almost kiss from their date. "Your eyes look like moons. Guess we were made for each other, hm?"

Victor pulls back with a frown, pain deep in his eyes. Erin doesn't have a chance to question why before Victor lifts him off the fence. As soon as his toes touch the grass, Victor moves away with a shake of his head. He shoves his hands into the back pockets of his shorts.

"No photographers in the family yet. Most of us end up in corporate jobs, like real estate and banking. Not a creative bunch, my family." Victor stares at him, face nonchalant like he didn't just release ten million butterflies into Erin's veins and stomp all over them.

A blush creeps along Victor's neck.

Ok, perhaps not all the butterflies.

"I see." Erin takes a deep breath, letting the moment blow away, and turns back to the forest landscape. A fox is prowling in the tall grass further down the ranch and stops. He crouches to snap a photo from in between the top and middle fence rail. Smiling, he shows the photo to Victor.

"You have an eye for this," Victor says proudly. "See? I chose the right photographer."

Erin lights up with joy. "Thank you."

"Do your friends do photography, too?" Victor inquires as he rests his arms on top of the fence, back facing the house. "Fletcher and Layla?"

Erin leans his back against the fence. "Layla does. She's a year younger than me and Fletch, but very studious. Fletcher, he's a massive pain in my ass," Erin laughs.

"Sounds like Ben." Victor grins, shifting so his left forearm brushes against Erin's shoulder. He can feel the heat of Victor's skin through his jumpsuit.

Erin watches for any sign of movement from the house but doesn't step away. "Fletcher is a swimmer, has been since we were kids. It was obvious he would pursue sports medicine."

"You all sound close, especially if you go to the same university." Victor looks out at the forest with an unreadable expression painting his face.

Erin leans back a bit to get a better look at Victor's face. "We are," he says slowly.

"Mhm. I'm glad you weren't alone." Victor looks at Erin. There's no sign of distress or anger evident in his moon-filled eyes, yet Erin's lungs constrict all the same.

"You said your family is involved in corporate jobs?" Erin asks. "Did Ben go to the same college? He's older, so what does he do?" His heart feels like it's about to explode out of his ribcage. The way Victor gazes at him, with his lips curved at the edges and his eyes narrowed softly in sadness, makes Erin's stomach clench. He knows what that look means; he's seen other people wear it before in movies and at funerals. Never has anyone directed that look toward him.

Erin makes himself decipher it as wistful and lets the look carve out a home in his heart, so he'll never forget it came from a place of love and not jealousy.

"Yeah." Victor goes along with the sudden topic change as he taps his hands against the top of the fence. "I studied business management. You might have guessed, but my family has dealt in real estate for a very long time. Ben did the same, six years earlier."

"His assignments would have been gold then," Erin laughs.

Victor huffs. "You'd think. The university changes the course around every five years or so. I just missed out."

"Aw, had to actually do some homework, did you?" Erin pouts, dramatically wiping a fake tear from his eye. Victor clicks his teeth and laughs, swatting Erin's arm. "Is that how you bought this property? With your family business?" He knows real estate is big in New York. He's heard how rich upper-class families buy multiple properties to pass down through generations, but he didn't think it was big enough to warrant fierce protection of the next heir.

If Stella was worried about Erin stealing all the Lovelace family money, she could make him sign a prenup. There's no need for everything else she's done.

There's more to the story ... something he's not seeing.

Victor wholeheartedly believes the real estate business is a front, a way for him and his family to fit in among the humans. Disappointment slides into Erin's brain. He'll have to figure out another way to find the real reason why Stella is threatening him.

"Yeah, I bought this place for this idea I've had for a while, now." Victor drops his head to hide his smile. "It's a bit silly."

"Tell me."

"I don't know ..."

"Victor, tell me about your silly big boy real estate idea." Erin pushes against Victor's shoulder. "As the landscaper working on this property, I have a right to know. It's the law."

Victor lifts a brow. "Oh, is it now?"

"I'm friends with the law around these parts, remember?" Erin nods, grinning from ear to ear. Victor laughs.

"All right. I ... geez, I wanted a place big enough for all werewolves to meet, not just a select few. Like how it used to be in the beginning, before the split. Wolves existed as one back in those times. United. Strong. I figured if I found a place big enough for that to happen, then no one would run the risk of being corrupted again. We could keep an eye on each other." Victor shrugs, turning to face the house. "I was looking all over the country, and when I saw this place, I just knew it was the right one. And with Storm Landscaping beautifying the place, it'll certainly impress for many generations to come. It'll let me show everyone that I'm ready for what I was born into. That I can protect us all."

Erin swears his heart stops beating.

Werewolf delusion or not, all Victor wants to do is protect the people he cares about.

And he views Erin as one of those people now.

"Well." He gulps. "I think that's a lovely idea, Victor."

"You do?" Victor asks, voice quiet, like he's scared Erin's lying.

"Yeah, I do." Erin pats Victor on the arm before standing straight. "Which means we'd better get a move on beautifying this place for you. Five weeks will go by quickly, and there is still so much to do." He turns and bows to Victor with an impish smirk. "I can't disappoint the Prince of Real Estate. Whatever would become of me?"

"Please," Victor huffs, returning the look as he lowers his head to Erin. "That's King of Real Estate to you, Star."

TWENTY-ONE

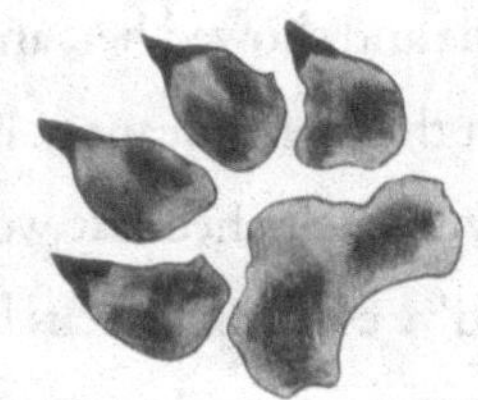

"How have the Storms been, Victor?" Stella asks with a smile at dinner later that night. "I always see you chatting up the young son."

"It's because we're close in age," Victor replies around a mouthful of steak. "He's more approachable and is often not as busy as his parents. In saying that, while they look to be almost done with the front, Erin says there is still much to be done."

"Oh, wonderful!" Stella's eye twitches. "I can't wait to see everything when it's completed. Imagine how the place will look once all the flowers they're planting have grown. It'll be a far cry from those dead trees they had there."

"What do you mean?" Victor asks, confused.

"Oh, Vic, it was earlier this afternoon. You didn't see them?" Her lips part in surprise.

"No." Victor shakes his head. "After my walk this morning, I went straight into the office to work on tying up last month's deals and double-checking the schedules for this month."

"Well, let me tell you!" Stella places her fork down and rolls her eyes. "The two trees at the front gate, the one right by the main road, were dead! They were green yesterday, and then when I went out there to take a photo for Jeremy back in New York, the poor kid has been down in the dumps lately, missing all of us. You know how sensitive he is, still so young, but anyway, the trees were dead! This blackish brown stuff stained the bark on the bottom. I looked it up. Root-rot, the internet is saying. Terrible. I saw Natalie and showed her, and she didn't have a clue what could have caused it! I thought they were meant to be top-notch landscapers, not to mention all the mess I saw in their shed last week, too. Soil everywhere ... I wonder how much that would've cost." She sucks her teeth and takes a sip from her wine. "And their resume was so promising at the start."

Victor frowns. "Erin didn't mention anything about that to me ..."

"He didn't?" Stella clicks her teeth. "I don't blame the boy. Why would he admit to his employer his mistake?"

"Because—"

"We should leave Beatrice here to keep the place tidy when we all return home," Ben says with a lopsided smirk from his spot opposite Victor. Beatrice kicks him under the table.

"Seriously though, Mom, please let me come back when the flowers have all bloomed," Beatrice pleads from her spot next to Ben. "I love it here. Remember when Matilda, Abel, and I checked out Green Lake's university? Mom, it's stunning! She's probably gonna go. Can I go, too? Please?"

Stella chuckles. "I'll consider it, on—" Beatrice squeals, "—ly if your professors give you a good recommendation when we return home. Then I'll look into getting you transferred."

"I'm sure Erin could do it."

Ben's eyes go vacant, any mischief draining the brightness from them. He shares a grim look with Beatrice. Stella smiles slowly.

"If B doesn't end up transferring, Erin could keep watch over the ranch. He'll be in his final year of uni. I'm sure he would love to have a quiet place to take his photos," Victor clarifies.

"You two must have gotten quite close to be able to make that assumption, Honey."

"Yeah," Victor laughs nervously. He's never kept anything from Stella, so it's been hard not talking to her about Erin. He doesn't know why Erin gets nervous whenever she's brought up, but the air always seems to sour slightly. He thinks it's Erin's scent, the one hidden underneath the wolfsbane, but he can't tell. It's like something is blocking it … He glances at Ben to find a pleading look in his eyes. Victor shakes his head. He's done lying. "We have gotten pretty close lately."

"Oh?" Stella continues cutting the steak on her plate. He feels the temperature in the room drop.

"Yeah. Um." Victor puts his utensils down on his plate, turning to face Stella sitting next to him. With his head held high and confidence in his voice, he speaks, "I've developed serious feelings for him. Feelings one would only feel for their mate."

Silence follows the declaration, tension making the hair on Victor's arms stand straight in warning. Victor waits with bated breath for Stella's reaction. He thought she would be happy, already having suspected who Erin was since she was so concerned about them fighting last week. Instead, Stella slams her utensils on the table, leaving a dent in it as the glasses shake. One falls over, the crack on the glass splintering like Victor's heart.

"I think I'm full now," Beatrice whispers. Victor watches as she tosses her napkin onto her plate and scurries out of the room. Ben also places his napkin on the table, eyes lowered, face stolid. He doesn't follow Beatrice. Victor is silently grateful for that.

Stella takes a deep breath, re-centering herself. She plasters a guilty smile on her face, eyes downcast in sorrow. "Sorry, boys. I didn't mean to scare you. You took me by surprise, is all. Make sure you apologize to Beatrice later, Victor."

Victor gulps. "That's all right. I will as soon as we finish talking." He doesn't remember the last time he smelled Stella's scent this rotten. Instinct burns along his stomach, and he gulps down the growl creeping along his throat, lips twitching. Stella is his aunt; she has a blood relation to him. There is no need for him to defend his status against her, even if she is also an Alpha. She's not trying to take over his position. She's just concerned.

"Honey, listen." Stella turns to Victor and places a hand on his cheek. Her voice sounds as somber as her face looks. "Erin is a *human*," she says with such love and care as she moves her hand to Victor's shoulder. He can't help but hesitate. "And you are a werewolf. The Black Wolf. Alpha of the Lovelace Pack. There is no way the two of you are mates."

Victor reaches up and grasps Stella's hand on his shoulder. "But—"

"Remember what happened the last time one of us trusted a human and went against instinct and tradition?" Stella interrupts as a haunted look darkens her eyes.

Victor scowls, looking down at his dinner plate. He refuses to let the tears gather in his eyes when he thinks about who Stella is referring to. The elders say Stacy Bellmore had a best friend—a human—and she was the one who originally corrupted her and convinced her to give in to the Moon Goddess's darkness. Because that is what humans do. That is how they were born in this world. They are selfish creations that only want to destroy.

Stella sighs. "Victor, I say this because I love you. Even if, by some miracle bestowed upon us by ... whatever God that is left up there who cares for us ... or some trial placed in our path that we must overcome to reach our fate of greatness, Erin is your mate, think about what that means. If he's not a human, what does that make him as *your* mate?"

Victor closes his eyes. He can feel the dread climbing up his limbs from his feet, feel the shame suffocating his heart. He knows. If Erin truly is his mate, then that makes him—

"The White Wolf," he whispers grimly.

He was aware of that fact.

The thought was in his mind.

But he thought ... He thought that maybe ...

Stella leans toward Victor and lifts his head by placing a finger under his chin. "That's right. The White Wolf who ...?"

"Who will bring destruction and death to all Packs when bonded to The Black Wolf," Victor finishes, his face wan. Just last week, he was the one repeating those words to Erin. Selfishly, he didn't realize what Erin being The White Wolf meant for everyone else. He was so caught up in the idea of finally finding his mate—that Erin was the soul his was bound to—and trying to convince Erin that werewolves were real, he forgot what being The White Wolf entailed for the rest of the Pack.

No, he did realize. But he thought they could overcome it. That Erin's light could change it. That they could change the curse together.

Stella nods, her full lips pouting before reaching over and crushing Victor in a side hug. She rubs her hand up and down his back. "That's right, sweetie. So, if you care for him at all, you'll leave him alone. Our family has experienced enough hardship. There's no need to get your hopes up. I doubt he's truly your mate anyway. The White Wolf wouldn't have been able to survive without a Pack for so long, the poor thing would've gone mad. I know it's hard without a mate." Stella's voice cracks, and she pauses. Victor can feel wet drops hitting the top of his head as her chipped black nails scratch his back over his shirt.

"Losing my Andrew was the worst day of my life. But you're lucky, Victor." She leans back, tears tracking down her face as she searches Victor's pained eyes. "I know it doesn't feel like it now, but you won't ever have to experience the heartbreak of losing a mate because you'll never have one. You might've been cursed to be The Black Wolf, but even Goddesses make mistakes. If The White Wolf hasn't been born yet, then it won't be born while you're still alive. So, don't fret, hm?"

Victor forces himself to smile at Stella's encouragement while he thinks about all the time he's spent with Erin. Erin's hand slotted into his perfectly, as if the

Moon Goddess tore their souls from the same star. Erin's scent—the rich smell of rain that would lighten the air, ridding it of the stench of a burnt forest as he sweated off the wolfsbane perfume—made him feel relaxed and safe. Like home.

"But ... I'm The Black Wolf ..." Victor fidgets in his seat nervously. He hears Ben's foot tapping against the wood floor and sends him a tense look. "My instinct can't be wrong. The books ... the legend is wrong. Or there's more to it. We can break the curse, and if Erin's parents were rogue, then ... then ... it doesn't matter. There's more to us being foretold to bring death and destruction. The Moon Goddess doesn't have to win. Right?"

Ben says nothing before looking down once more, so Victor looks at Stella.

"Right?" he whimpers.

"I'm so sorry, Honey." She gives him a look full of pity. The warm dining room light casts one side of her face in shadow from where she's turned to him. Her full red lips are a bright stain in the white room. "The stress of the Council Meeting made you misunderstand your instinct, and Erin was in the wrong place at the wrong time. You are simply getting riled up with the incoming influx of wolves. The prospect of a challenge is stirring your instinct, your need to show power and strength by having a mate by your side and Pack at your back. Not that any Alpha would challenge your rule, but even at twenty-four now—oh how you've grown—you're still young. It can be hard to make sense of your instinct now that you are in a position of power."

Victor thinks about this morning, how his pulse was racing when Erin laughed. How free he felt in that moment when they were wrapped around each other. He wanted to be closer, to press his lips against Erin and taste him. His heart felt like it was going to collapse in on itself when Erin smiled at him, the stars in his golden eyes shining brighter than the morning sun. He was radiant. Victor didn't want to look away.

He wants him. Still, even with Stella's words ringing in his ears. He still wants him. It felt right. It is right.

It has to be right.

His heart aches like it's been pierced through with one of the Moon Goddess's misguided arrows.

"Once the Council Meeting is over, you'll see. Anything you feel for him will disappear. He's just a curiosity for you. Nothing more, nothing less." Stella pats his head and rises, gently placing her napkin beside her empty plate. "And if you are curious, Victor, there will be many Omegas arriving soon. Girls and boys. You can satiate your desire with one of them. It might be good to branch out into other Packs and build more solid relations."

Victor's jaw tenses as Stella leaves the room.

Nothing more. Nothing less.

Erin was right all along. The only thing between them is physical attraction. Victor's throat tightens in shame. He practically forced Erin to like him back when none of it was real. Erin probably wouldn't have looked at him had he not pursued him first.

Ben sighs, a conflicted look on his face.

Victor drops his head into his hands.

Fucking shit.

The tears finally fall.

TWENTY-TWO

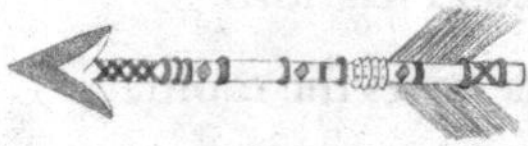

It's been four days, and Ben is stuck. Victor is broken, committed to staying as far away from Erin as possible, and Ben doesn't know how to fix him.

He thought it wouldn't last long. He thought that Victor would spend Friday down in the dumps and ignoring Erin, that the weekend would wash away Stella's cruel words.

It only hardened them instead.

When Erin got to the ranch this morning and began work on the backyard, Victor stayed at the opposite end of the house in the office or training room, doors and windows clamped shut, so he didn't accidentally look at him.

It wasn't enough.

"I can feel Erin in the air. It's like his presence is carved into every nook and cranny of the ranch, and I don't have the strength to change the wood," Victor confides to Ben that night. They sit on the dark roof, gazing at the forest beyond. There are bags under Victor's eyes, darker than Ben ever remembers seeing them during his university days, and earphones blasting music so loud that even Ben is finding it difficult to think. Victor can torture himself by drowning Erin out, ignoring him until he leaves to go back to New York, but that won't stop the longing.

And that doesn't mean everyone else has to be tortured too.

Ben purses his lips and gazes back out to the forest. His room is facing the back of the house and is one of two with a balcony on the fourth floor. Victor had the first pick, being the Alpha, but the rest were first come, first serve. He had to bribe Beatrice with a month's worth of shopping money to get it.

It wasn't the balcony that he wanted—he had hardly used it since being here—but the view of the dark forest beyond tall grassy plains. He knows a river runs far into the dense forest; he can hear it now, if he focuses hard enough. The cool water shining under the moonlight, stones on the bank still warm from the setting sun, the wild crisp in the air ...

It's so similar. If he closes his eyes, it's as if—

"I burn vanilla-scented candles, but that just makes me yearn for his smell instead," Victor says with a shake of his head, hands clenched in front of him. "I mean, burnt wood and rain isn't really a pleasant scent to begin with, but on Erin? I could get drunk on it. I play loud bass music to distract and keep me awake. I don't want to risk falling into too deep a sleep and dreaming of him. But that only reminds me of the childhood memory Erin shared about how Natalie explained that flowers liked singing, too. And when I give in ..."

"When you give in and blow out the candles, turning off the music, it's Stella's voice ringing loud and clear," Ben finishes for him. He can imagine how it would feel, the empty space beside Victor chilling his limbs and freezing his veins. It's not the way it's supposed to be.

It's not the way it was before.

"If Erin is my mate, then that makes him the wolf I've been scared of meeting all my life. The wolf who will corrupt me and destroy everything we've all worked hard to rebuild," Victor mumbles. It makes Ben pinch his brows together. He hates seeing Victor so dejected, especially over something like this. "And I'd let him." Victor laughs, the sardonic sound echoing on the humid breeze around them, as he lies flat against the roof. It's nothing like his deep, rich rumble. "Without a fight, without a second thought, I'd let him ruin us all, Ben."

"Is that why you are trying so hard to stay away?" Ben asks. "Some illusion that if you gave in to your desperation, gave in to your instinct and desire, you'd be handing our Pack over to the Grim Reaper? To the Mother Goddess?"

Victor glances at Ben out of the corner of his eye. "Why do you sound so miserable?" he questions with a frown. At least his desperation has now morphed into something else, directed at some*one* else. Confusion. Or is it anger? Angry confusion?

Either way, Ben finds it better than the pity party Victor's been wallowing in.

Ben brings his knees to his chest and drops his head between them. "No reason," he sighs. A car door slams around the front, the sound of a loud engine sputtering to life before tires move along gravel and dirt. Only once the gate has clicked shut does he lift his head, his nose twitching as he sniffs the air. They're leaving much later today than normal.

"Vic," Ben says in a low voice. "He's gone home."

Victor gulps and casts his eyes down. He pulls the earphones out of his ears and turns off the music before resuming his previous position on the roof. Ben lowers himself flat, his shoulder brushing Victor's.

"The Pack's worried about you," Ben whispers, counting the stars that begin to twinkle awake. You can see them much more easily here than in New York. It makes his heart ache.

"I haven't given them anything to worry about," Victor utters.

"There's this thing called a Pack bond, Victor," Ben scoffs, sitting up and facing Victor. "Nothing to worry about? The Cooper and Foster Packs have arrived, and you didn't greet them."

"I was there when they arrived," Victor replies with narrowed eyes as he scratches his arm.

"Were you?" Ben clicks his teeth before rising and climbing off the roof. He makes it to the closet, running shoes in hand, when Victor drops onto the balcony. He looks offended. Good. They don't have time to play around anymore.

"What is your problem? I was there!" Victor whisper-yells. Stella isn't home. Beatrice and Matilda took her to see a movie out in Green Lake. But that doesn't mean others won't relay what they hear. If she finds out Ben and Victor are fighting ... He shakes his head, tongue running over his cheeks.

"No, you weren't," Ben argues as he sits on the edge of the bed and slips his shoes on. "The whole time you were trembling like a leaf, saying nothing to welcome them as Alpha or thank them for coming. I had to do all of that!"

"What, you want an apology? Thank you, Cousin," Victor spits, bowing mockingly.

Ben clenches his fists on his knees. He keeps his eyes down. Deep breaths. Don't lose control.

"There are rising concerns that you aren't fit to lead this Pack."

Victor stills. His muscles visibly tighten under his skin. "What?"

Ben rises from the bed. He takes a step forward, anger low but crisp in his voice. "I told them you had food poisoning and that you'd be better after a couple of days' rest."

"Well, I'm grateful you did that," Victor says, voice taut like a bowstring. He licks his lips. A muscle jumps in his jaw. The white comforter dips under Victor's weight as he sits.

Ben sighs, all the built-up tension and anger deflating from his limbs. This is much harder than he thought it was going to be. The man he remembers wasn't this stubborn. Impulsive, at times, yes. But he was much calmer then, watchful. Less expressive. Cooler. Though ... his perspective is different this time. That could be the reason he never saw this side of his soul. Age changes much in a person. Among ... other factors.

He plops down next to Victor on the bed. "I know you were distracted before," he ignores the way Victor's lips press tight beside him, "but at least you were still present. Now, it's like you're an empty shell being picked up and placed around for decoration."

Victor rubs his hands against his thighs. Ben waits, which is nothing new. Victor will speak. He simply needs a bit of a push sometimes.

"After meeting Erin, I felt grounded and excited to work. My leadership was the best it's been, like I knew I had to prepare a safe environment for my unmarked mate. Now, though, by trying to ignore Erin—to remember that my instinct is just some weird, misplaced longing—I find I don't care about the Council Meeting at all," Victor admits, rubbing his eyes and taking a deep breath. "It's taking everything I have, Ben."

He doesn't clarify what he means, Ben knows. If he looked in a mirror, Ben knew his eyes would reflect tremendous pain. He understands. He always understands. Erin was Victor's everything. Always has been. And Victor was so caught up in having found him, he forgot what that meant for everyone else, what everyone else *thinks* it would mean.

Not that Ben blames him. Any of them. He can't. Not when he remembers.

Not when Victor doesn't yet.

Ben gently places a hand on his cousin's shoulder. "So, stop."

Victor slowly turns his head to Ben. To say he looked confused would be an understatement. Ben's mind works quickly. He needs to reassure Victor without telling him the truth. As much as he wants them to have their happy ever after, he can't force them. He doesn't know how the magic works, not exactly, but he can't risk it reverting. Not now. All that death will have been for nothing. And then where will they be? Vengeance and justice. Acceptance. Peace. Call it what you want.

It all got so *complicated*.

Deep breaths. He's waited this long. He's *worked* this hard.

He won't let anyone ruin it now. Let alone his mother.

Ben softens his voice, "I know what you feel for Erin is real. A wolf's instinct can't be fooled, especially The Black Wolf. I believe in you and your instinct just as much as I believe in my own. Erin isn't a normal hum—"

Victor stands, laughing in astonishment. "Are you fucking for real right now?"

Ben stands slowly, hands raised in front of him. "Vic—"

"NO!" Victor bellows. He bares his teeth in a snarl, teeth sharpening and nails elongating in a half shift. A warning. He looks like a man whose string is fraying inside him from being pulled too tight. "Ever since we got here, you've had it out for someone. Questioning my authority, telling me to focus." Victor steps close to Ben, jamming his index finger into his chest. "Shouldn't you be happy? Your mother managed to remind me of something you were too weak to do."

Ben's jaw tenses as he swats Victor's hand away. Deep breaths. Ease into the conversation so he can realize for himself. "What if Stella's wrong—"

"Stella's the only one making sense around here!" Victor interrupts. "She's reminded me of my duty, of why I can't have a mate."

Fuck it.

He feels guilty. The blessing isn't meant to be used this way. He knows She would be disappointed.

Oh well. There's only so much he can take. If Victor won't see reason through words, if he keeps helping Stella sit on such a high throne in their Pack, then Ben has no issue using force. After all, he is Stella's son.

"And why is that? Huh, Victor?" Ben shouts back. His eyes have darkened, resembling two tunnels leading to murky, burnt forests. He doesn't move, but strength pools around him, his scent sharp. Gone are the wildflowers; these are the poisonous moss and dead red roses.

Red.

Red.

Red.

He's ready to pounce on his Alpha.

Victor squares his shoulders back in response, letting his scent pool out in warning. Ben flinches but doesn't back down.

"Why is it that Stella's voice is gospel to you? She says one little thing, and you turn tail and run, doubting your instinct, *my* instinct. I mean, do you really think the Moon Goddess has made a mistake before?" Ben tilts his head to the side.

"She turned on us. We can't trust her judgment." Victor's eyes narrow, and he looks to the floor. He's hesitating.

One last push.

"Fuck, Victor, do you think I'd help you with something that'd put us all in danger? By doubting yourself, you are doubting me too." Ben's face is torn apart in strife. He hates that they are fighting like this. It makes bile rise from his stomach when he sees how far Stella has dug her claws into his cousin. He wishes he could drain all the blood from his body so that he doesn't have to share blood with her. With that family line.

"That doesn't matter. It doesn't change the facts." Victor lifts his head, eyes clear and filled with poise as he approaches Ben. "Erin isn't my mate. Stella believes so, too, and her argument is valid. She speaks from experience. From observation." He walks to the door and places a hand on the handle. "I won't deny that since we've been here you've supported me and made me feel better. But you forget what The Black Wolf is, Cousin. Goddesses don't die, remember? If my instinct was able to be fooled by the first cute boy who flirted with me, then it's no wonder yours was too."

Ben's lips part, but he says nothing. Their heavy breathing is the only sound in the room. Unease settles in the air as Ben watches Victor's back. His shoulders are taut, his head facing forward. That's that, then. Pain, rage, and resignation flicker across his features like waves washing across thin sand before he retracts his scent, making it disappear. His eyes glaze over, and his face locks down as if covered by a veil.

Victor's words ring like a gong echoing around them.

Goddesses don't die.

No. No, they don't.

"Don't be fooled, Victor. My loyalty has always been to you, not Stella," he whispers. "You're the Alpha of this Pack. It's my duty to protect you. Not her." Never her. Ben walks to the door, shoving Victor aside to open it. There's no emotion in his voice—no anger, no caution, or conviction. He slams the door behind him, hoping it makes Victor flinch. Hoping Victor's heart dropped in heavy shame.

Damn it all.

Time for plan B.

Ben moves his head from side to side, loosening the muscles as he makes his way to the garage. He's done contemplating why She chose to keep the memories from them, but had him be burdened. If it's his job to protect them, then he will. No matter how or why or when or whatever the case.

He may not be able to reach Victor now, but there is someone who can. Someone who always seems to, one way or the other. Hopefully.

At least he won't have to worry about getting punched or doused in thick, threatening pheromones at his place.

Ben kicks down the stand to his motorcycle and turns off the engine. The stench of wolfsbane makes his nose curl and his stomach curdle. Violently. It's so much stronger here than when they are at the ranch. Which makes sense, as there are rows of the plant along the front of the house, under the windows, and along the side fences. Like a protective barrier spelled by a witch. He almost doesn't want to take off his helmet. But that's poor etiquette.

Especially when he's about to see *them*.

Ben forces his legs to walk casually, stuffing his hands into his pockets, if only to hide his white-knuckled clench. Erin has done nothing wrong. No need to storm in guns blazing. He sees a cat sitting on the windowsill by the door, the long white curtains bunched around its paws as one blue eye and one yellow eye track his movement. Mr. Wolf. Ben's seen him on occasion at the ranch, walking silently along the fence or lounging in the shade on the porch. He's been a big hit among the kids. There was one morning he even followed some of the Pack out to the forest, his prints in the damp soil so much smaller than their large wolf tracks.

He smiles, greeting the cat with a nod. With one fleeting glance behind him, he raises his knuckle to the muted green door and knocks.

The door swings open, and Ben relaxes slightly. Thank the Goddess, it's Erin. He hadn't even stopped to think about what he'd say if one of his parents had answered the door. Or worse, if Erin had gone out for the night.

"Hey," Ben says. He raises one hand, offering a small wave in greeting.

Erin's jaw drops in shock. He's wearing what seems to be pajamas—a loose white t-shirt and shorts, the green logo of Green Lake University stitched into the bottom. Guilt creeps along Ben's throat as the light of the near-full moon shines around them. It burns.

"Wha—"

"We need to talk," Ben interrupts.

Erin's eyes sharpen at his cold words. The door closes slightly, Erin's hand still clamped around the doorknob, when a light voice rings out from behind him.

"Cub, who is at the door?" Natalie doesn't wait for a response, appearing in the hallway behind Erin from further in the house. Her steps don't falter, and her smile doesn't dip. If anything, she quickens her pace to the door, and her smile grows. Only the surprise in her bright blue eyes portrays her worry.

Ben's heart squeezes. He plasters on a smile and dips his head. "Hello, Mrs. Storm. Sorry to bother your family so late at night."

"Oh, not at all. You're Mrs. Lovelace's eldest, yes? Be...?"

"Ben," he clarifies with a smile. She remembered. Of course she did. His stomach does flips. He can feel the heat of a blush creeping along his neck. How childish.

"Ben, short for Benjamin, I assume?" Natalie tilts her head to the side. "What a strong name. Do you want some fresh bread?" She doesn't wait for his reply before calling over her shoulder, eyes still taking in the sight of him, "John, put some of the bread aside! Erin has a friend over."

"Fletcher or Layla?" John calls back. "I need to know how much they want, Love!" He rounds the corner, wiping his hands on the black apron tied around his waist, and freezes when he sees Ben. "Oh."

"It's Ben, Ms. Lovelace's eldest." Natalie's eyes glint as she faces her son. "Cub, what are you doing? Let the man in." She turns to Ben once more with a grin. "It won't take long. Make yourself at home."

"Thank you." Ben nods, crossing into the house once Erin steps to the side. It's cool, the ceiling fan in the living room to the right successfully keeping the humidity from sticking. Unlike Stella's ... thoughtful design, the Storm house is warm. A barrage of color fills the wide space, giving the house a sense that it's been lived in. Memories have been made in this room, in this home. Bright memories. Happy memories. Like what a Pack home is meant to look like.

He tries not to let his eyes linger on the framed photos lining the hallway wall. He recognizes Erin and his parents and wonders who the other two making an appearance in nearly all the more recent photos are. They look slightly familiar, but he can't place their names ... John's words from before echo. Fletcher and Layla. They must be Erin's friends. He remembers now—they were with him that night at the warehouse party. To be shown so frequently, displayed with pride on the family wall for anyone visiting to see ... It reminds Ben of a time long forgotten.

His heart yearns.

"It's homey," he whispers, taking in the multitude of plants around. A quick sniff and he knows there are even more throughout the rest of the house. He didn't know that many shades of green existed. His eye catches on a cluster of crystals in the center of the coffee table, little shoots of green racing to the ceiling. Beatrice would like those ...

"What else did you expect?" Erin is leaning against the skinny glass hallway table by the closed door, hands placed on the edge as he watches Ben. Suspicion is etched in every tense line of his skin.

"Nothing," Ben chuckles under his breath. He forgot about Erin's hearing, even without having manifested. He pauses at the edge of the living room, eyes catching the bright silver moon etched onto a black fuzzy rug. "Oh." He turns to Erin. "Want me to take my shoes off?"

"What are you doing here?" Erin demands, ignoring the question. "How did you know where I live?"

Ben doesn't blame his hostility. He knows his mother hasn't been kind, that much a blind man could see. The weight of it is clear on Erin's shoulders. And Victor's denial over the past few days isn't helping matters. He chucks off his boots, the dark floorboard warm under his socked feet as he walks back to the front door and plops them by the wall.

Up close, Erin looks nothing like a prince. His arms are now crossed over his chest, and he cocks a brow. Waiting. Questions flicker between his golden eyes. Like flames. Ah. Ben bites his lips to stop from smirking as he turns his back on Erin.

The prince may be gone, but The White Wolf remains.

"I found the address on the invoice quote from your mom." A white-faced lie. He's known where Erin has lived since day one. "But that's not important. Victor's in trouble and you're the only one who can save him," Ben states, finally settling into the deep brown couch. It's soft, the pillows instantly relaxing his lower back.

"What?" Erin lowers his arms, stepping over the moon on the rug to stand in front of Ben in a heartbeat. "Has he overdosed? I haven't seen him all day, and last Friday too. I thought he was playing hard to get. But there have also been a lot more of your relatives showing up, so I then assumed he was just busy. Oh, God, please don't tell me he got into a fight with a drug lord. I heard a lot of them live in New York, but I didn't think y'all would be involved with those kinds of people.

Idiot! Have you told Stella? Surely, she could get rid of them after everything she's don—I mean, she seems like she would know how to handle—"

"Wait," Ben interrupts, grabbing one of the bright yellow cushions from beside him and squeezing it over his lap. His sharp eyes narrow even farther into slits. He caught the slip. "What has Stella done to you?"

"That's not important." Erin waves a hand in the air between them.

"Erin," Ben demands. "I'm not telling you jack shit about Victor until you tell me what my mother has done to you. Now."

Erin's shoulders sag. He licks his lips, eyes roaming around the living room before settling back onto Ben. He sighs. "Fine. Stella's been threatening me since the day I showed up at your doorstep to help my parents. At first, I didn't think she was capable of following through, so I didn't put too much thought into it. Just a protective guardian. I mean, we are from different social classes. I get it. But then she stole my camera and threw our soil everywhere, blaming my cat, by the way. Not cool, that's my son. She's also been breaking our equipment, so it's taking us so much longer to do things. I joked at the start of all this that my friends would have to help, but now they might actually need to if we want to have it all done on time. Then there was this afternoon with the tires on my dad's truck—"

"She messed with your vehicle? Why haven't you said anything to us?" Ben fumes. Shit. He didn't think she was that far along. That must have been why they left so late. "Do your parents know about all this?"

"No, they don't. And don't you go telling them!" Erin warns, eyes narrowed so far that Ben swears they flash gold. Ah, there he is. "I'm the one she wants. She can threaten me. She can break my tools. But then what? Kill me? Fine. But I won't let her drag my parents down along with her. My fight is mine, not theirs. And besides, Layla called first dibs on punching Stella, and if my mom knew, she'd go first." Erin shrugs. Ben hears the joke for what it really is. A distraction. Fear.

"I'm sorry she's done that to you, Erin," Ben apologizes. "At least you won't be too surprised when I tell you Stella's the one putting Victor in danger."

"I don't follow ..." Erin stares down at Ben's white knuckles with a quizzical look. "Please, you seem to be the only sensible one. Don't tell me you're on drugs, too."

"Look, Erin." Ben sighs and rakes a hand through his short hair. "Victor told you about us being werewolves, yes?"

Erin rolls his eyes as he places his hands on his hips. His lips part, no doubt ready to complain when he stills. Ben expected this reaction. He was ready for it, argument formulated and memorized on the ride over.

But Erin lowers his hands, takes a seat on the couch next to Ben, and nods with pinched lips instead. Ben relaxes his shoulders and unclenches his shaking hands. He'll take every blessing he can get.

"Good. And you don't believe him yet, right?" Ben doesn't wait for Erin to reply before continuing, rubbing his hands up and down the feathered pillow. "I'm not here on his behalf to try and convince you it's true. The Moon Goddess has a plan, and I'm sure as hell not getting in the way of it. My mother doesn't seem to share that sentiment. She's planning something and I can't let what happened that night in March—"

"Fresh bread at your service!" Natalie sings. The smell of warm butter and herbs gets stronger as she rounds the corner into the room. Napkins are placed next to a flower-printed plate that is filled with sliced bread, steam rising steadily into the air. "Now, I have a container filled with some bread for you to take home, too, Ben. Let me get it."

"Thank you, it smells delicious," Ben says, clearing his throat. Grabbing a napkin, he reaches for a slice. It's as soft as a cloud. Blowing, he takes a small bite that melts instantly on his tongue. There's a subtle peanut butter taste underneath. It's interesting.

"What do you know, Ben?" Erin whispers, nose wrinkled. He can smell it. Shit. He had hoped the bread would cover his rotten scent leaking into the air. Now is not the time to lose control. The sound of Erin's heart racing in his chest sounds like a gong in Ben's ears.

Worry stains his eyes dark, and he glances behind Erin at his parents entering the room. Natalie is worried. He can see it plain as day as she takes a seat on the small couch on the other side of the room. But her husband's dark eyes are mad. He has one arm wrapped around his wife in comfort, while the other arm is tapping the armchair in sporadic movement. He doesn't want Erin involved. Neither of them seems to. And Ben wishes he didn't have to do this either. He wishes Erin could come to their Pack after all the fighting was done. He wishes none of them had to fight in the first place.

But they don't have that luxury anymore.

Time has run out.

"Never mind. I'm sure I'll find out soon enough." Erin sighs deeply. He reaches for a napkin and piece of bread, chewing slowly as he thinks. Leaning close to Ben, he whispers, "Ok, ok ... Um, can you get Victor out of the house at all?"

Ben looks back at Erin and nods. "Yeah. We aren't exactly on speaking terms at the moment, but ..."

"Good. Bring him to the mall this weekend," Erin pleads. "Saturday. Ok? There's only one here in town, and it's not much, but it'll do." His eyes flit to his parents, but they seem to be in their own world, voices hushed.

Ben nods. He knows they are still listening, but he doesn't have to make Erin aware of that. Whatever it is Erin is planning, he doesn't want to get in the way of his relationship with his parents. "Yeah, I'll get him there."

"Awesome." Erin holds out his hand, palm outstretched. His fingers move in a 'gimmie' motion. "Now, hand over your phone."

TWENTY-THREE

She sits on the dais, the smell of roasted meat floating in the air around her. It is dark now, seven moon passes since she first arrived in the wolves' home. The tents are all open, everyone gathered by the fires, eating together. Hands, placed gently on knees. Young cubs, resting on their mother's and father's laps. Some speak in gentle whispers, while others laugh as loudly as they can.

Hëna smiles to herself. This is all she wanted. All she has hoped for. If only the air weren't thick with the promise of war, death mingling in the dancing shadows of the fires.

The Pack was surprised when they arrived a moon pass ago, right as her brother's light rose along the horizon. The strength of its rays was such a vast contrast to her feelings. Her fears. It took them the rest of the night and the whole sun pass to travel from the human palace. Night broke the sky by the time they reached the river. Nahale led them to where he laid Alaric to rest. They paid their respects. Tala's quiet weeping and clenched teeth called to her magic. Nothing could be done. She gripped her husband's hand tightly.

As Tala had said, the Pack knew as soon as her husband's shadows dropped them off in the forest. Weapons were drawn on them instantly, arrows and shifted claws surrounding them. Like they could sense it. Like they were waiting.

Many eyes gawked at their tattered state before they were quickly ushered into a healing tent. Salve was applied to their wounds, and the grime was wiped from their bodies. They were wary of Nahale's presence; she could see it in their narrowed eyes and smell it on their thick skin. One cub in particular seemed more … curious than the rest. A little boy with hair as red as the light that first peeks over the horizon, and eyes even deeper than the forest around them.

He stood on a log by a firepit on his tippytoes, close to the dais. Those eyes trailed after Nahale as he was led away, hand clenched tightly by Tala, before flitting to her husband. Standing to the side, away from them all. Watching. Watching. Her husband quirked a brow at him. The cub's head tilted. Small indents formed on his cheeks as he grinned. The smell of wild roses in freshly turned soil bloomed in the air around them. A man patted his head—an older visage in appearance. The cub raised his arms, and the man lifted him into them before slowly walking away. Muttering. Explaining? Interesting.

The Pack did not attack Nahale.

They did not question his need to stay close to Tala.

He was given food, a wash rag, and new garments to wear alongside them all.

They waited until nightfall for their new Alpha to stand on the dais, face grim and eyes tense. Not even the birds sang while Tala spoke, all ears pointed intently at him to hear of the events that had transpired.

Tears were spilled for Alaric. Claws slashed at the ground for those still trapped. Howls echoed for Kazamir and the other wolves who defected. She watched closely those who shared blood with them—the betrayal in their red eyes tore her heart into pieces. The air was stale with betrayal, like fruit left out to wilt in the heat.

Red.

Red.

Red.

But they stayed. They cheered alongside the rest of the Pack at Tala's call for war. There was no resistance. Even the littlest of cubs wanted to fight. They would prepare once the sun rose, and leave after one more moon pass.

Thorns pricked at her skin when he got to the announcement about Nahale. Tala had turned his head to the side, where the human stood between her and her husband on the green grass, and held out his hand. Nahale had smiled, the corners of his lips barely pulling upward, before stepping onto the dais and placing his hand into Tala's. They stood side by side, hands interlocked tightly.

Tala declared Nahale as his mate. Pack Luna. The one who will forever stand by the Alpha and help make decisions. Help guide. Help *protect*. Help keep their lineage going.

Many eyes swiveled to her, confusion scenting the air. Not because the Pack has not had a male Luna for many years, but because Nahale was Other. He was human. But he is who Tala has chosen. Who is she to get in their way? Nahale is a Prince; it is in his blood to lead. They suit each other, too. From what she has witnessed, Nahale is slow to act, but he listens. He leads with his heart but does not let it rule his thoughts. He values life above duty. Tala, on the other side, is calm. Collected. But impulsive. He lets his heart rule his thoughts. There is balance in them, together. A strength unmatched. She could not have chosen better. But more than that, more than anything, Nahale respects them. And Tala respects Nahale. They care for each other's history, the lives they have lived.

Together, they will make fine leaders.

Ylli had placed his hand on her back, pushing her forward slightly. She lifted her chin, forcing a grin onto her face. It was not as hard as she expected. Her blessing was given. Of course it was. That was the whole reason she came down here.

"Something smells good," Ylli sighs. The dais creaks as he sits beside her, along the edge of the dark wood, drawing her out of her memories. He looks better now, after some sleep. There is more silver color returning to his skin. The night air rejuvenates his magic, as it does with hers.

She passes him her roll of bread. "Are you going to participate in the battle?"

"No," he gulps down a large bite, bigger than she thought he would, and tsks, "and neither should you, Light."

"You know I must. I have come this far, my Star." A squeal draws her eyes to the right. A family sits beside the fire pit. A baby cub has her arms outstretched for balance, her father—an assumption based on the shared deep blue, rounded eyes—behind her as she takes tentative steps toward her other parent. Another male, sitting on fur draped over the log, smiles widely. His hands are clapping as his little cub walks slowly toward him. She must be taking her first steps. "I cannot abandon them now, when they need me most."

"I know," her husband whispers. He reaches over and places his hand on her thigh, squeezing gently. She looks at him, but his gaze is fixed on the family, sadness swimming in his eyes. He loves them, her cubs, perhaps even more than she does. When she proposed the creation of this world, he readily agreed. Coming along with her, letting her shape this world however she wished. Acting as an intermediary when she fought with her brother at the start. Even going so far as to collect their souls for her. Because she cannot bear for them to be alone, trapped in the dark earth. They belong in the sky, free. He exhibits such care toward her cubs.

No.

Their cubs.

She squeezes his hand, and he looks at her. "Thank you, Ylli."

He leans over, kissing her softly. "Don't thank me yet, Hëna," he utters against her ear. His eyes travel above her head, something behind her catching his attention.

She looks back. Tala and Nahale are walking hand in hand toward them. A new mark sits on Tala's neck, the skin slightly red from the needlework. A black wolf nestled next to a black moon. The mark of Alpha. If only he had his father's headpiece as well.

Her husband stands and reaches into his cloak. She gasps at what he pulls out. A thread of vines braided into a circular shape with strands hanging loose by the front and back. The other, a bright blue jewel nestled amongst thin vines. The Pack Alpha and Heir headpieces. She had thought them lost when the humans trapped them, carting them to their settlement.

"How?"

"I grabbed them when I helped the Alpha's soul return to the stars." He holds them out to Tala. "I thought you would need them." He knew. Even then ... he knew she would not give up. That Tala would not give up.

Tears prick her eyes, threatening to spill. Oh, how she loves him.

Tala's eyes shine as he accepts the headpieces. He gulps, glancing at Nahale, before fixing his eyes on her once more. Fierce. Determined.

Her magic squeals along her arms. She stands, meeting his gaze.

"Bind us," Tala says. A command. No. An ask. A want that they wish for her to provide. She swallows down her tears and nods.

"Gather your Pack, Alpha," she says. "If this is to be a binding, then it will be a proper one. Witnessed by all. Accepted by all. That is my condition."

Tala beams, canines on display. "Yes, Mother Moon Goddess." He swivels to Nahale, reaching to grab his hand, but Nahale has beat him to it, latching onto his arm and pulling him away.

"Quickly, quickly," she hears muttered between them as they race through the tents. She giggles to herself. One mighty howl would have alerted them all, yet they choose to do it themselves. How loving.

"I found this, too."

A piece of cloth is draped over her shoulders, the material soft. Dry. Smelling distantly of clean lavender. Hëna turns to face her husband as he lifts her shawl over her head, not enough to cover the gift from him she wears across her forehead, but enough to keep her ears warm and her hair from running widely in the breeze.

"And you only give it to me now?" she questions, a lightness in her voice. A tease in her narrowed eyes. "My shoulders have been freezing, dear husband."

"Please, Wife." Her husband presses his lips to hide his smile. Or tries, at least, for she can see it anyway. "It is the middle of the hot season. There has been no chill in the air for many moon cycles."

"Help me with this binding," she asks him, leaning against his chest. His arms wrap around her back. She feels him nod against the top of her head.

It does not take long for the wolves to begin gathering in front of the dais. She stands in the center, her husband beside her, the wolf sculpture behind them like a guardian. Watching.

Watching.

Watching.

Watching.

The moon is near full, lighting the air. Silence slowly descends around them, eyes lingering. Tala and Nahale stand in front of them, facing each other. Neither carries a weapon of any kind. They wear similar fittings—crisp black cloth draped over black leather around their hips, white thread holding it in place. Over their shoulders are gray pelts of fur. And on their bare chests, arms, and legs are painted markings—reds and blues and greens and yellows. Stars, suns, moons, flowers. Some make sense. Some seem to have been drawn on by the little ones wanting to participate. The only difference between them is the necklace Nahale wears. It is a thin silver chain, a sigil welded out of metal hanging in the center, right above his collarbone. The crown of a King, with a bare tree running through the center of it, purple wolfsbane growing along the roots. An artifact from his people. An identifier of his status as Prince.

This is not the way it is done. It is rushed. There was no grand feast, no flowers tied around tents and braided into a structure for them to stand under. Their markings are sloppy; the paint not yet dried in some places.

She smiles, her heart swelling three sizes too big behind her chest.

This is exactly how it should be done.

Her Hopes have never followed the rules, after all.

Tala drapes the headpiece worn by Pack heir over Nahale's head. "My Star, I promise you, in the presence of Hëna, our Mother Goddess of the Moon and her eternal husband, Ylli, God of the Stars, to find you. To love you. Even if you look different. Even if you smell different. I'll find you. I'll remember you. I'll love you. Always." The blue jewel sparks brightly against his dark brows and golden eyes. Tala's hand lingers on Nahale's cheek, thumb brushing underneath his eye. Love shines brighter than she has ever known possible. "For you are the one I choose to bind to. My love is eternal, just like the moon in the sky."

Nahale's grin is wide as he lifts onto his toes, gently placing the Alpha headpiece over Tala's head. His blonde hair blends in with the thick vines. "My Little Wolf"—Tala huffs at the nickname—"my love. I promise you, in the presence of Hëna, Mother Goddess of the Moon, and her eternal husband, Ylli, God of the Stars, to wait for you. My nose isn't as strong as yours, and my vision isn't as sharp. But my heart *is* just as strong, and my *mind* just as sharp. No matter how lonely. No matter how long it takes. I'll wait for you. I'll love you. And should I find you first, I'll chase your paw prints in the earth. I'll run to your light. For you are the one I choose to bind to. My love is eternal, just like the stars in the sky."

Her husband steps behind him, braiding the strands flowing down his back with the vines from the headpiece. His lips move slowly, whispers spoken into each braid.

A spell.

A blessing.

An old path, newly found.

She laughs, she can't stop it. Tears flow freely now.

Her hand hovers over Tala's heart. "Tala, Alpha of the Wolves, do you vow this love eternal and true?"

"I engrave it on my soul and speak it from my lips," Tala proclaims.

She moves her hand to Nahale's heart. "Nahale Treebane, Prince of the Humans, do you vow this love eternal and true?"

Nahale nods. "My heart knows this sworn oath to be true, so I speak it from my lips as such."

Whispering blessings of her own, she binds them together as mates. She grabs the binding cloth from the wolf statue behind her; the dark blue material is old but kept well. It has been the one used within the Pack for many years. She gently wraps it around their hands and holds it, squeezing tightly before placing her hand against Nahale's lower stomach. She closes her eyes. Magic shivers along her spine. Her skin glows just so. The sweet smell of spellcasting dances in the air. It weaves through the Pack. Noses twitch. Smiles widen. Eyes cry.

She *shines*.

This was why she came down. Love and hope. Strength and power. Loyalty ... Forgiveness.

A wince breaks the air. When she opens her eyes, her gaze instantly locks onto her husband. He is smiling, brighter than she has seen in an age, his skin dimming from a great shine. It held. The bond is set.

Her gaze turns to the two newly mated in front of her. She takes a step back, letting them have their moment. There is hesitation in their eyes, but not from fear. From awe. From disbelief that it worked.

She suppresses an eye roll. Foolish cubs. As if it would not work.

As if she would refuse them.

Tala reaches for Nahale's neck, where a mark now sits. A white wolf nestled amongst white stars. One drop of blood slides down his neck. Tala wipes it away with trembling fingers. A mark to match his own. A symbol of status to the wolves. A promise from his blood to the Pack.

"Alpha Tala and Luna Nahale. I bind a blessing to you, one that shall last for an eternity. In this war of freedom, and for each day that follows. May your love hold fast and true. May it strengthen the Pack and your bloodline."

Tala drops a hand to his mate's waist, pulling him as close as possible with their hands still bound between their bodies. Nahale meets him there, like he always does, a grin splitting his lips as his free hand cups Tala's jaw.

Hope sparks throughout the Pack.

Strength blooms in the air.

It is a gentle kiss, one that pushes lips apart slowly and warms the heart. One a lover gives when the future is uncertain.

"For as long as I live, this spell will hold. And remember, Goddesses do not die. So neither, too, shall my blessing. From now and forever more, you are fated by blood and bound by stars."

Please let this love last longer than the war.

TWENTY-FOUR

"So, tell me, why are we here entertaining these people after what they've done to you?" Layla asks. They're sitting at one of the metal tables in the food court, each nursing a milkshake while a bowl of chocolate-drizzled cinnamon churros sits between them.

"Because Erin's too nice," Fletcher says around blue-tinted lips. His knee bounces underneath the table, making the bench he's sharing with Erin wobble.

"Because Erin *is* too nice," Erin repeats, swatting his friend on the arm, mindful of the shopping bag beside him housing the new glass for his camera lens. "You're meant to say that like it's a compliment, not a dig, asshole. And stop bouncing your leg."

Thankfully, his friends agreed to a shopping afternoon pretty easily. Layla doesn't often work at Café Terra on the weekends, and Fletcher had just mentioned that one of the guys on the swim team was asking about helping out at the community pool for extra cash. So they were both free. Erin doesn't know what he would have done if they weren't. He had panicked when talking with Ben. It felt like if he didn't give Ben a time and place right then and there, that nothing would happen. Even with his phone number neatly tucked away in his contacts, Ben would return home, and they wouldn't be able to discuss it further. Stella would wreak more havoc, and Victor would stay trapped in her troubled claws.

So he gave his friends a quick run-down of why they desperately needed to go to the mall today, the demand for new camera equipment just an added incentive, and bought them food as thanks. After all, he's never needed their help more than he does now.

"Look, I get why you want to hang out with Victor without Stella around, especially after how great the last date you went on with him went, but all I'm asking is, can you *really* trust her son?" Layla fiddles with the strings from the hood of her thin jacket, brown eyes narrowed like a hawk. He tries not to shrink under her gaze. "This was kinda his idea, wasn't it?"

"I chose the mall, and Ben's given me no reason not to trust him," Erin replies, voice quiet. "I know he's not telling me everything, but he seemed sincere. Worried. I couldn't ignore that."

"Friend, he showed up at your house at like 8 p.m. to tell you his mother has been harming Victor, and that's why he hasn't been going on your early morning walks ... Oh, and that was after you explained to him how she's been an evil bitch to you and your parents. And now he wants to put you in even more potential danger?" Fletcher cocks his head. "Not exactly trustworthy to me."

"Exactly my point." Layla points a soggy churro at Fletcher. "Everyone knows to let sleeping bears lie," she says.

That's not exactly how he remembers the conversation with Ben going earlier in the week on Monday. And Stella isn't a sleeping bear ... more like a plundering wolf. Trying to talk to them about everything without going into much more detail about the werewolf situation has been tough. He wants to spill the massive lore drop to them and get their opinions on the matter, but he can't. It's been nearly two weeks since his date with Victor at the gardens, and the story refuses to make it past his sealed lips. He knows it would shed so much light onto his insistence for wanting to help Ben and Victor right now, and yet—

"Guys, trust me." Erin moves his half-drunk shake to the side and grabs each of their hands on the table, the ones they haven't been using to eat the food with because seriously, Fletch? How do you get that much chocolate on your nail? "They've been through a lot together. Ben is different from his mother. Which is exactly why I need to try and help Victor. If what Ben's said is true, then I know firsthand how crazy Stella can be. I don't want to see Victor hurt further because of her territorial trauma, or whatever it is."

Layla sighs, her head dropping between her slouched shoulders. Fletcher is quick to catch her ponytail before it falls into the bowl. "Has she done anything else to you this past week? Any more threats, or broken things which, side note, thanks for telling me about!"

"I did tell you!" Erin argues.

"Yeah, after you told Fletcher at your boy sleepover!"

"Hey, don't bag boy time, Lay," Fletcher says with a pout. "It's a sacred time we use to compare our—"

"DUDE!" Erin yells, yanking his hands from theirs, lips curling in disgust.

"Testosterone! I was going to say testosterone!"

"Ignore him, I do. It does wonders for the skin. Now answer the question, Erin."

"You know, I don't think I like you right now," Fletcher mutters. Layla rolls her eyes, chin plopping heavily onto her hand as she waits for Erin to reply.

He grabs his shake, using the straw to poke around one of the strawberries stuck to the side, while his teeth pull his top lip into his mouth.

Waiting.

Waiting.

Waiting.

The straw clinks against the side of his glass, strawberry forgotten.

"She hit me with her car on Thursday afternoon."

Layla slams the table, the glass straws rattling in their drinks. "That fucking cun—"

"Did your parents take you to the hospital?" Fletcher asks, both voice and face devoid of all sarcasm. He's serious. And angry.

"I didn't tell them," he says. Ignoring the indignation on their faces, and before either could make sense of the other's angry sputtering, he continues, "It was more like a love-tap, to be honest. I was by the porch, taking photos of the sunset, when she pulled out of the garage and hit the side of my legs. I lost my balance, fell onto the gravel, and broke my camera. I had some cuts and a nasty bruise on my elbow all day yesterday, but it's all healed up now! The perks of having good genetics, right?" He elbows Fletcher beside him. His friend doesn't laugh back. He sighs. "I don't want to make a big deal about this. That's what she wants me to do." If the cruel smirk was anything to go by that day.

Someone came to help him, a man with long black hair and striking green eyes. Erin didn't catch his name, but he seemed kind, asking if Erin was injured or wanted help to go see the doctor. Stella had stepped out, face pale and mouth aghast. Blurting apology after apology about how she didn't see him because of the sun glaring in her eyes—she was wearing sunglasses—and how really, he shouldn't have been standing in front of the narrow driveway. It's a makeshift dirt and gravel road that's ten feet wide.

He shrugged the whole thing off. Told Stella not to worry, it was his fault, and thanked the man for helping him stand. Neither of them said anything about the broken glass from his camera slicing his palms.

"That's it, I'm going to punch those fake lips right off her face."

"How do you know they're fake?"

"Does that matter right now?" Layla shrieks.

"No, but—" Fletcher shrugs. He takes the camo baseball cap off his head, running his hands through the thin locks before replacing it back on, backwards. "I'm just saying that some ladies have naturally full lips. And we've never seen the bitch, so who are we to say that they are fake?"

Layla leans back and crosses her arms. "Now I'm starting to think that you're the one Erin needs to worry about, not this Ben guy."

Fletcher frowns. "Ok, now that's too far," he says, voice low and firm.

"Well then, don't act like a fucking dick! She hit our best friend with a fucking *car*! Whose side are you on anyway—" Her eyes lift over his cap, widening at the corners before flitting to Erin and back above Fletcher's head.

He gets the hint.

Erin twists on the bench, wincing at what he sees.

Just as promised, Ben has come to meet them with Victor. He stands tall in black jeans, those same combat boots he was wearing the other day, and a crisp white t-shirt. Victor is wearing a similar outfit, except his top is a sweet baby blue, and he has his white sneakers on. While Ben has his short hair brushed and styled to the side, lips smiling nervously, Victor looks haggard with sunken, dull eyes, shaggy hair, and pale skin. He looks like he spent a month isolated in the Arctic.

"Oh, fancy running into you here!" Fletcher stands from the table, arm raised to shake Victor's hand, which Victor takes. "Victor, was it? We met a few weeks ago at Donny's. And you are?" He looks to Ben.

"Ben, Victor's cousin." Ben laughs nervously. "We figured it was about time we checked out what this little town has to offer. Normally my younger sister does all the shopping."

Smooth.

Erin sighs. "Fletcher, Layla, Ben is Stella's son, the lady who hired my parents to work on the ranch. And you already know Victor."

"Nice! Some men to help carry all my shopping bags," Layla says, voice bright and airy despite what they were just talking about. Kudos to her for being able to brush fights to the side like that. She scrutinizes them, reminding Erin of a headmaster or pageant judge from those early 2000s movies they all used to watch in high school. "You men look strong, too. Perfect! It's so good to finally meet y'all."

Fletcher bends over to Erin, voice low in a whisper, "Should I ignore that very obvious dig at my strength and ability as a man since I've pissed her off and she's now moved on and forgotten about it?"

Erin doesn't take his eyes off Victor. "Yes."

Fletcher nods, chin raised and lips downturned. "All right then." He slaps his knees, standing straight again, just as Layla reaches over the table and grabs Erin's shopping bag from next to him. The motion catches Victor's eyes, and his brows furrow.

"What happened to your camera?" he asks, pointing to the bag. The black and white logo of a camera stares at them all.

"Oh, nothing. I tripped and broke my lens." Erin shrugs. Hearing Victor's voice after so long makes his skin tingle. "No biggie."

"Did this happen at the house?"

"Yea—"

"Was anyone nearby? Did you get hurt?"

"No—"

"Stella was."

Erin glares at Ben. Ben glares back. Victor looks at the ground.

This is not the right way to go about this. How does he even know about that? Did that long-haired man tell him? Regardless, what does Ben think he's doing, bringing up Stella and now making Victor question her intentions when he's already depressed? Isn't Stella the reason they are here at this loud mall anyway?

"Let's save the business talk for later. Come on, boys," Layla interrupts, handing the bag to Ben and pulling his arm away from the table. "Chop, chop! We're burning sunlight!"

Ben looks down, lips pulled tight into his mouth to stop himself from smiling as he lets Layla drag him to whatever clothing store she wants to look at first. Not that their little country town has many to offer, but there can be some fun finds on the days when new stock has just been put out. Fletcher doesn't even attempt to hide his laugh as he follows them.

"She's ... energetic," Victor says. Erin notices some color seems to be returning to Victor's cheeks and smiles. Maybe Victor didn't get what Ben was insinuating.

Maybe the fact that Stella was there when Erin got hurt helped to ease his mind instead of pushing him farther off the edge like Erin thought it would.

"That's one word for it," Erin replies. He stands and holds his hand out toward Victor to take. "Come on, we don't want to be left too far behind. The shops here may not be the fanciest, and there may not be a lot of them, but the ones we do have are quite big. We don't want to get lost."

"No." Victor eyes his hand, an emotion Erin can't place wrestling behind their bright blue color. He lifts his gaze to Erin and takes his hand, threading their fingers. "We don't."

Erin flinches at how cold his hand is. It's never been cold before.

They head in the direction the others went. He's thankful for the strategic split-up. After being apart from Victor for a week and a half, Erin feels much more at ease knowing he's ok. Seeing Victor, smelling his scent, and feeling the warmth of his skin is like drinking water after a three-mile run.

So, he'll pass off a water bottle to Victor, too, in this race they seem to be running in.

"Did my breath smell that bad during our walk the other morning?" Erin asks quietly. "I did brush my teeth."

Victor clenches and unclenches his hand not trapped by Erin's fingers. His nose is scrunched, twitching like a rabbit. "No," he says gruffly, "your breath was fine."

"Oh, that's good then." Erin hears a bang to his right and turns his head. Far across the mall is a group of teenagers laughing together. One of them looks to have dropped their skateboard. When he looks forward again, he catches the pained expression on Ben's face as he wiggles his right ear before they turn the corner of the food court. Erin narrows his eyes. It was loud, but not 'ouch, I'm going to go deaf' loud.

"Do you have something to wear for your fam—Council Meeting?"

Victor begins to shake his head, but then stops and nods instead. "I have something that would look nice."

"Oh? You'll have to show me." He stops just outside the store the others have wandered into, forcing Victor to stop alongside him. Erin watches Layla hold up a tourist shirt against Ben. Fletcher is bent over laughing so hard his cap is falling off. "I'm known around these parts as somewhat of a fashionista. Tons of men come to me for clothing advice."

"They do?" Victor's hand tightens around Erin's, his jaw twitching. Erin smirks.

"Mhm. They sure do ... I would go to their houses, look at their closets, give them ... advice ..."

"Stop acting coy, Erin. It doesn't suit you," Victor grumbles, causing Erin to laugh.

"So, what does?" Erin takes a step closer, pride growing in his chest when Victor flinches. His nostrils flare and his eyes flutter. He coughs, blinking rapidly. With a shake of his head, he takes a step away from Erin, bumping into Ben walking out of the shop.

Who pushes him right back into Erin's space.

Victor sends a glare hotter than the Sahara Desert to Ben, his pale blue eyes dark in betrayal.

"Layla wants to show you guys a dress. She says Fletcher's opinion doesn't matter and mine doesn't count since it's the only one." He shrugs.

"Excellent, lead the way." Erin, ignoring the stab of pain he feels in his withering heart, releases Victor's hand. Ben takes the lead, his head higher than the clothing racks around them as they follow him to where Layla waits, tapping her fingers against Fletcher's arm.

"Oh, good. Erin, look at this!" Layla holds up the dress against her body. It's yellow, the straps thin where her collarbone would be, reaching right above her knee. Her brown eyes pop.

"It's very cute," Erin says. Victor nods, thumbs raised.

"See, that's what I said." Fletcher pouts. Layla ignores him.

"Ok, I'm going to see what other colors they have." She grabs Ben by the arm and drags him toward the back of the store. Fletcher glances between Erin's relaxed demeanour and Victor's tense one. His eyes widen in understanding. "Oh, wait up y'all. I like that style, too."

Erin chuckles under his breath. His friends will never learn the delicate art of subtlety. He walks over to a rack of t-shirts and grabs one. It's black with a picture of a full moon taking up the top half, while cursive writing takes up the bottom.

"Howl at the Haters," Erin reads. He raises the shirt to Victor's chest with pursed lips. "Thoughts? Large too big?"

When Victor doesn't say anything, Erin looks up. His face is impassive, but his eyes are twisted with anger and pain. Erin lowers the shirt and raises a thumb to Victor's eyebrow, following the shape to smooth it down. Victor crumbles, his head tilting into Erin's touch as he takes a step forward. Erin gently places his other hand on Victor's chest, over his heart.

He doesn't understand—things were going so well. They were getting closer, physically … emotionally. And then Victor pulled away. It's been torture. By the time Erin got to the ranch to take his photos with Mr. Wolf, Victor was heading back inside, sweat dripping down his shoulder blades from his morning run. He lingered in the kitchen, refilling the water bottles every few hours to try and bump into Victor. But only the trail of his leather scent remained. Like a ghost.

Erin wishes Victor would haunt him like he used to. Like the way Erin is haunting Victor now.

He took it for granted; he realizes that now. The glances and soft touches they would share. The nicknames. The way Victor's lips would wrap around the nickname. Star. Like it was the most loving word ever created in the human language. Like it was something precious, something irreplaceable. Like Erin was.

It pisses him off that they can't have that anymore. All because of Stella.

Fingers clenching against the side of Victor's face, he whispers into the warm air between them, "What has Stella done to you?"

Victor flinches, pulling his head away from Erin. "Large should be fine," he says quickly as he takes the shirt out of Erin's hand and walks to another section down the rack.

Erin glances toward Ben to find him already looking at them. Erin shrugs with a pout, but Ben shakes his head, raising his eyebrows toward Victor. Erin sighs, walking closer to Victor but still keeping some distance between them as he searches through the rack of clothing.

Now that he thinks about it, Victor and Ben are quite similar. They are related, after all. Maybe it's a genetic Lovelace sensitivity thing.

He thinks about everything he's seen since working at the ranch. Everyone is so hands-on, constantly touching each other, whether it be in greeting or after, when they are lounging around in the sun. Not so much now, but in that first week of working on the ranch, multiple times a day, he would see men and women walking through the grass, their legs slowly disappearing into the long blades as they headed toward the forest beyond the house, camping supplies bundled in their arms. They never showed fear of snakes or wild animals. No, their only worries?

"Do we have enough blankets for the Mayweather Pack. They always complain every year about being cold. In summer!"

"What are David and Chef Michal making for dessert after the Council Meeting? This is the first one in so long, surely it'll be something grand."

"I wonder if I can get Jack to finally teach me that twist and flip move he did last tim—hey, don't laugh! He was a wolf when he did it, and I want to learn, too! Imagine showing that to my mate one day."

"Mary thinks her mate is a Beta from the Foster Pack. She hasn't shut up about it since she went to some real estate convention thing last month in Iowa. One whiff, but then the girl had to run. What a surprise that would be if it's true. Do you think she'd move?"

Council Meetings. Packs. Wolf training. Mates. Stella. Stella. Stella. Stella.

Erin glances between Victor and Ben with a frown. He remembers Ben's warning, and the fear in his eyes when he arrived at his house. The instant smell of rotten roses. The arrival of so many new faces at the ranch the past week, and how the people he's come to associate as Victor's family were the ones with jittery lips and tense eyes. He thought if anyone were to be uneasy from Victor's lack of appearance at the house, it would have been the newcomers, not those he calls ... Pack.

His heart quickens in time with the pressure building in the back of his head. The word runs through his mind easily, with no resistance.

Natural.

Instinctual.

Maybe ... there's more to this whole werewolf thing after all.

"Sorry, I know we just got here, but I need to get going." Ben slides his phone into the pocket of his jeans, drawing Erin and Victor to his side. "There's been a mishap with the dinner menu for the family reunion."

Victor steps forward, his mouth open to say something, when Layla starts speaking. "I'm on dinner duty tonight, so I need to go, too." She smiles sheepishly. "I can drive you?"

"That'd be great, thanks." Ben flashes her a toothy grin before handing Erin the shopping bag holding his camera equipment. "Just to the other side of town, my sister and her friend will meet me there."

Victor frowns, once again breathing in to speak, when Fletcher starts walking backward. "And I need to get in some training before the day is over." He sends a wink at Erin. "These muscles won't grow themselves. See ya!"

"See you at home, Vic." Ben pats Victor on the shoulder before walking away with Layla.

"Come on, Cowboy." Erin bites his lip to stifle his laughter as Victor's look of confusion morphs deeper into frustration. "You're driving me home."

Victor keeps his hands and arms to himself as they walk to the parking lot. Ben did good. Victor drove here in a black Ford pick-up truck and not his motorbike.

While Erin would have loved a ride on the bike, disappointment already smothering the adrenaline pumping through his veins, there wouldn't be much room for talking.

Which isn't an issue since Victor still hasn't said a word. He starts the truck as Erin hops into the passenger seat and plugs his phone into the cord connected to the car so it can charge. Music sings softly from the radio, some pop song Erin doesn't know the name of, but it sounds similar to a song from Alex Warren he remembers Layla begging him to listen to. He takes the initiative and puts his address into the GPS. He wants to believe that Victor already knows where he lives since Ben did. But just in case ...

"You planned this, didn't you," Victor says after the third song by the same male singer finishes playing. He must have a CD in or his Bluetooth is connected to a specific album. "You and Ben."

Erin winces, turning the music down. "Was it that obvious?"

Victor purses his lips, giving Erin a dour look.

"Ben wanted to get you out of the house." Erin glances at Victor. At least they are making eye contact again. And speaking. Victor turns the corner, and the familiar old gas station comes into view. They're almost at his house. If they don't speak now, they never will. "He was worried about you ... said you weren't on speaking terms after a fight."

"We didn't fight. We just had a ... disagreement." Victor tightens his hands on the wheel. "When did you two even speak anyway?" he mutters. The sun has set since they started the drive home, and with the clouds blanketing the moonlight, the streetlamps make his face look harsh and cold. Like a wolf. Shivers play hopscotch up and down Erin's spine.

He takes a deep breath, forcing himself to calm down. He needs a clear, confident head to ask the question that's been plaguing his thoughts for the past few days.

"Why were you avoiding me?" Erin tried to keep the thickness out of his voice, but his throat had other plans.

Victor opens his mouth quickly before changing his mind. His silence causes Erin to furrow his brows and clench his jaw.

"So, I guess the whole mate this was a lie. An elaborate ruse to get into my pants," Erin sneers as he turns to look out the window. "And now that I've caused trouble between you and the glorious Aunt Stella, you want nothing to do with me." He crosses his arms over his chest and digs his fingernails into his biceps, hoping the pain will stop the hot pressure from building behind his eyes. Don't cry, idiot.

Don't cry. Don't cry. Don't *cry*.

"I should've torn your note up and thrown it away as soon as I found it," he mumbles under his breath.

Victor slams his foot on the brakes after turning onto Erin's street, the tires screeching as the truck halts on the side of the road. Burnt rubber assaults the air as he turns the hazard lights on and faces Erin. He looks like someone's ripped his heart out of his chest, torn it apart, and then shoved it back in.

"You know that's not true." His voice is a rasp, low and gentle, but Erin can hear the anger growling underneath it loud and clear. "There's a lot going on, things happening that you don't understand."

"Then tell me!" Erin pleads, throwing his arms up in the air between them. He's tired, exasperated at this push and pull. This goddamned *game* they seem to be playing.

He doesn't want to play anymore.

At least ... not without knowing all the rules.

He focuses on relaxing the muscles in his neck and shoulder blades from the sudden stop instead of the burning tears forming in his eyes. "One minute you're all over me while I'm the one being hesitant, and the next it's all ignorance is bliss with you."

"Erin—"

"You ghosted me," Erin growls, pointing a finger at Victor, whose eyes have widened. Fear pools in them. Good. Let him be scared of losing.

Tears stream down his face, but he can't find it in him to care. His bones ache, his eyes are burning, and his throat feels scratchy. His nose is so stuffy, he can hardly breathe, but his breathing is too erratic for him to take a deep enough breath through his mouth.

Victor takes his hands off the steering wheel and reaches toward Erin. His breathing has quickened, too. "It wasn't like that. Stella—"

"Oh my God. Stella, Stella, Goddess Almighty Stella," Erin taunts with a roll of his eyes. "I bet if she told you to wipe her ass with a hundred-dollar bill, you'd be tripping over your feet to rob a bank and do it."

Victor's face falls, and he stops his advancement, his hands hanging in the air between them like forgotten laundry. Erin closes his eyes and presses his fingers to them, grunting. He hates how mature Victor is acting right now, knowing he's being baited and refusing to bite. Letting Erin vent his anger. Letting him talk shit about his aunt. It's making Erin imagine a life where he can get mad and fall, throwing a tantrum, all the while knowing Victor will be there to catch him after. Knowing Victor won't walk away until they talk about it all.

He can't even yell at him without feeling—

Erin shakes his head and opens his eyes. He can feel Victor's gaze on him; feel the way Victor's whole body, his mind, and soul, are attuned to him only. His skin prickles as it breaks out in goosebumps.

Despite it all, Victor is the one who started this fight. Even if he is letting Erin yell, even if he isn't walking away right now. He still did. He walked away first. He refused to speak first.

Erin's just following his lead now.

"Stella wants me to be happy, Erin," Victor whispers slowly, like he's afraid any quick sounds will cause Erin to run out of the car. "I have a duty, things I need to protect. I can't let my personal feelings get in the way of that. No matter how strong they are."

Victor's words disintegrate in the air around them, the acidic stench causing Erin to pale as nausea slams into him. He hears his heart break like his camera lens did on the ground. But this time, it wasn't Stella's fault. Victor's the one who dropped it, his whispered words having cursed it to stone so it easily explodes on the concrete. But that's not enough for him. No, he steals Erin's breath, too. He feels his oesophagus burn as the intimate words reach inside and tug with all their strength. He feels lighter without his breath and heart, unable to tell where his hands start and his feet end. Maybe his nerves were also destroyed in the removal process.

"Well then." Erin puts on an air of false confidence as he yanks his phone from the cord connecting it to the car and picks up the bag of shopping from the floor by his feet. His throat is scratchy, whether it's from breathing in Victor's scent or licking his salty, tear-coated lips, he doesn't know. "Guess I'm not one of the things you need to protect. I'm not a member of your Pack after all, huh. So much for being mates, right?"

Even though his house is still further down the street, Erin gets out of the car. He can see the lights on through the front window and tries to think of an excuse to tell his parents about his appearance. Anything will work as long as it's not the truth.

He won't tell them about the way he took comfort in Victor's scent even while fighting.

He won't tell them about the tears falling down Victor's face as he told Erin their feelings weren't enough.

He won't tell them about the agony crawling through his legs as he walked away, nor about how every nerve in his body was bellowing at him, demanding him to turn around and run back to Victor.

He won't tell them how his legs gave out when he heard the deep rumbling of Victor's truck drive away, how he sat on the side of the road underneath the broken streetlamp three houses down with no energy left to even cry.

He won't tell them Stella won.

Erin looks at the full moon from in front of his house, the dark clouds finally letting her shine around him. Now she comes out. He laughs bitterly and tilts his head.

"Please," Erin prays. He knows this is foolish, that there's no point in continuing to chase after Victor. But if drugs aren't involved ... if any of what Victor said about his family and their history is true ... then ... then ...

"I don't care if we're cursed, just—" Erin takes a shaky breath and closes his eyes. He thinks about the bottle of emotions he's been ignoring for the past five weeks, since that night at Donny's party, and places his hand atop the lid.

It feels warm.

If they have been marked ... if they are *bound* ...

"Let our instinct be enough."

TWENTY-FIVE

E rin heads straight upstairs to his bedroom after entering the house. He ignores the way John's smile drops after seeing his face, turning off the TV immediately, and the way Natalie calls out his name—his actual name, not his nickname—in alarm as she rises from the couch.

He knows tears are still falling like a thick waterfall out of his eyes, but his face is too numb to feel the trails they make down his skin. He discards his things in front of the bed and notices his hands still trembling. Staring at them, he remembers the delighted feeling he felt intertwining them around Victor's long tan fingers.

The door opens.

Erin clenches his hands together behind his back and whirls around.

"Erin ..." Natalie says in a soft, but stern voice. She hasn't stepped into the room, one hand still on the door handle as John comes up behind her. They both have frowns on their faces and worry in their eyes. Neither of them are breathing. Like statues, they wait for a sign to proceed, too afraid that one wrong step will send Erin tumbling backward off a cliff.

It's too late. Erin stares at them, shaking his head.

He's already fallen.

Erin crumbles. He falls onto the floor, hands clenched in his soaked shirt over his heart. Natalie strides into the room and covers him in a hug.

"Shh ... shh ..." she whispers while rocking them. Erin can't help the wandering thought that this is how the flowers in the garden must feel. Safe and protected with full trust in the person taking care of them. He was foolish to think he'd be able to keep what happened a secret. His parents have always been able to see right through him.

John moves to Erin's desk and switches the lamp on before sitting on the edge of the bed. He takes a deep breath before speaking in a hushed voice, "We know you've had a lot going on lately. That you've been confused."

Erin sniffs, turning his head slightly to peek at his father from inside his mother's embrace. "I thought I was doing a pretty good job at hiding it." His voice is raspy and small, but it makes John chuckle all the same.

Natalie smiles warmly as she pulls away from Erin. She wipes the slow tears from his face and pushes his hair off his sweaty forehead. "It has something to do with Victor, doesn't it, cub?"

Erin nods, his chin all but touching his chest as he averts his eyes. Natalie's question wasn't a question at all, but a statement pointing out the facts. He can't help the spike of fear he feels in his heart. If his parents were able to easily pick up on it, then Stella probably has too.

Natalie and John share a withering look, causing Erin to furrow his brows. "What?" He leans back so he can see both of them. Their lips are pinched, eyes lowered. "What is it? Were you threatened by Stella, too?"

"Threatened?" Natalie flinches. Her eyes flame. "They threatened you!"

"Love, sit down," John pleads as Natalie stands. A hurricane swirls around her as she starts pacing, fingers digging into her hips.

"They threatened our cub, Husband," she growls. Erin shivers, instinctively rolling his shoulders inward. He's never heard his mother speak with such ... rage before. It sounded … generational. He knows it's not directed at him, but he can't help but tense anyway.

"We don't know why they threatened him," John assures her with a pointed look. "It's been how many years now? If it was because of Stacy and Gray, we'd know."

Erin's mind swims. The names roll around his brain in familiarity. Natalie seems to calm down at John's words, exhaling a deep breath through her mouth before plopping down on the bed. She pats the space between her and John, a silent indication for Erin to join them.

Cautiously, he rises from the floor and sits on the bed. "What the hell is going on?" he demands. No more beating around the bush. No more hiding.

Natalie turns sideways with one leg on the bed and grabs Erin's hands, pulling them into her lap. She opens her mouth, then closes it with a huff, glancing at John with pursed lips. John places a hand on Erin's shoulder, but he, too, says nothing.

Why is it so hard for them to speak?

Erin breaks the hesitancy growing in the room. "If this is the part where you tell me I'm adopted, I already know. We had this conversation years ago."

Natalie shakes her head, a nervous smile twitching her lips. "No, this isn't about that." Erin feels his smile drop as she looks at him. He's never seen her blue eyes so dark before. Like she has the weight of a thousand histories buried behind them. "This does have something to do with your birth parents, though," she admits softly.

The photo Erin found last month of his mother and the unfamiliar woman pops into his mind. With everything happening with Victor and his parents' insistence that it was simply a clerical mistake, he had forgotten about it. The emotions were buried deep in the soil of his heart and mind. They return now like a tidal wave, making him clench his fingers around his mother's small hands.

He licks his lips. "What do you mean? You said my birth parents were dead."

Natalie nods, her eyes never leaving Erin's. "They are dead, cub, which I will be eternally sorry for, but they didn't die naturally."

Erin's blood chills, any color in his face bleeding out to strangle his heart. He can't feel it beating. He can't breathe. Can't speak—doesn't trust that he won't yell in a rage of confusion. His brows furrow deeply over his bulging eyes.

"Your mother and I knew each other in New York. I can tell you all about how we met later, it's a much longer story, and I need to apologize first." She smiles sadly. "That photo you found in the records, the one of the gazebo in front of the mansion? Up in Bellmore?" At Erin's nod, she continues, "Your dad and I lied about that. We did work on that project, but it wasn't back in 2000. It was in 2003, around this time of the year, actually. It was the first one we did together as officially licensed landscapers. Stacy was pregnant and wanted something fun done for her Pack before some kind of meeting she was about to host."

Erin stiffens, leaning forward without thought.

"Pack?" he questions, voice low.

"Stacy and Gray Bellmore were werewolves," John clarifies. "As humans, we weren't meant to know, but they entrusted us with that truth anyway. It's a genetic trait; they were paranormal beings, which makes you one, too."

Erin's head pounds, and he looks away from his mother, lips parted. Is he angry that they lied? Yes. But—

The room is spinning, objects blurring together every time he blinks or takes a breath. Maybe Stella planted drugs in their truck, and his parents are high right now.

No.

The answer speaks deep in his creaking bones as he remembers the crying white wolf at the edge of the forest, the bloodied lake of wolfsbane. The blue eyes. The brown eyes. That mighty black wolf and the castle behind it ... All the dreams he's had since meeting Victor.

This isn't Stella's doing at all.

They're telling the truth.

He's a werewolf.

Victor is a werewolf.

Natalie tightens her hands around Erin's, drawing his attention back to her. "We don't know the specifics, or any rules really that your kind must follow. I found out by accident, and Stacy could never really tell me anything more. I asked her if I could tell John, we don't keep secrets from each other, you see—"

"Just from me," Erin interrupts. That anger he was feeling? It's howled for backup, and they've just crawled in and bared their fangs.

Natalie clicks her teeth. "It's not like that, cub. Stacy agreed, and it's a good thing she did, because one night I got a call from her, the only thing I could hear on the other end was you crying with the sound of gushing water in the background. She didn't say anything, which worried me. But it was definitely her phone. I was confused because you were only a few months old, but I knew something serious must've happened."

Erin starts breathing quicker. He licks his lips before parting them in an attempt to funnel the breath out slowly.

Natalie continues, "I woke John up and we headed to the house. Smoke could be seen in the air from a mile away, the red haze of fire made it look like the Devil had climbed up from hell to say hello. We found you bundled in your baby blanket under some rocks along the water. You were soaking wet. It was a miracle you didn't get hypothermia."

"Werewolves don't get hypothermia," he mumbles, slowly shuffling to his desk. He leans on it with one hand, feet tingling from the electric shock of rubbing them on the rug. His ears ring. The sensation isn't enough to distract him.

"You're a shapeshifter, Erin, not a vampire immune to colds," John says. Erin swivels to him. He was pissed off when he heard that the two people he's meant to trust without asking why had lied to him his entire life. He was pissed when he learned that secret-keeping is *their* dealbreaker. But this? Acting like they know more about his genetic make-up after lying about it for nearly twenty-fucking-ing-two years?

No. Way. In. Hell.

Natalie, sensing his wrath, becomes desperate. "We didn't want to keep this from you, but it was the only way we knew how to protect you. Without knowing exactly what had happened, we had to anticipate the worst. And that meant you had to stay hidden. A lone rogue wolf stands out, no matter where they run, so we moved far away and planted monkshood—wolfsbane—everywhere to cover up your scent. I don't know why you've never turned. You never showed signs of being in pain ... Maybe it has something to do with the wolfsbane, or there's a specific ritual that you had to do. We never questioned it. We never researched it. Just let you live."

"We made sure you lived." John rubs his hands over Natalie's hunched back. "We owed at least that much to our friends."

Erin's teeth hurt from clenching his jaw. "Why now? I could've lived the rest of my life not knowing, so why now!" he shouts, whirling on the two.

"Because we see the way you look at each other," John admits. "You and Victor, it's the same way your parents looked at each other." There's no heat in his voice, nor guilt or sorrow. Just a simple spoken observation of the truth. He says it confidently, like no force in the world could change it. Like they've been written in the stars.

Bound by them.

Erin clenches his eyes shut. It's like Victor said, fated mates are destined to find each other. Always.

But that would mean he and Victor are—

"Because Erin, Goddesses can't die. So neither can their curses."

Erin takes a shuddering breath and leans his forearm over the back of his chair, his head dropping between his shoulders as his hands clench and unclench.

Natalie softens. She closes the distance between her and Erin. "Everything we've done has been to keep you safe. We don't know how involved the Lovelace family is, or what their connection is to you, but if your wolf is calling out to Victor, then they must be a pack of werewolves, or at least he is." She places her hands on his shoulders and rubs, a warm smile lighting her face. "We just want you to be happy. Listen to your heart … and your wolf. If your wolf is calling at all, it means something. After all this time, cub, you can't ignore it. Your parents wouldn't have wanted that. Stacy always said a wolf's instinct is never wrong."

The ringing in his ears is louder now, the sound shrill. He breathes deeply through the oncoming headache. This is too much. Everything hurts. He can't think, can hardly breathe …

He's a werewolf.

His parents—his birth parents—were werewolves.

They were friends with the people who raised him … trusted them enough to reveal this secret that apparently must never be known by others.

He squints, turning to look at them now, at the concern coloring their eyes and guilt tensing their muscles. Panic seizes his throat in a lump too hard to swallow. And all at once, the anger vanishes.

They don't know that the Lovelace Pack is the same one Stacy and Gray belonged to because they changed their Pack name. Just because they were friends, just because they worked on their house in New York, doesn't mean they met everyone. She said they found out by accident, then of course Stacy wouldn't have told her Pack about her human friends. If it were him, he would've kept them as far away as possible. Especially with someone like Stella around.

Wait.

He recalls the way Ben acted around his parents. Did he know them? Did he recognize them? Erin knew he seemed to be hiding something when he came over, something more than Victor's fragile state. Maybe he just figured out who they are by looking into who Erin is. Stella hasn't given any indication that she recognizes them, so that must be the case. John's words from earlier sing in his mind. Stella is definitely someone who sticks to the ancient rules. She would threaten—no, they've gone beyond that. She would kill them if she knew their connection to Stacy and Gray, not because they are raising him, but because of who his parents were within the community.

Murderers.

He's the son of murderers.

But how did he survive? Why did they let him live? Who took him out of the house?

Victor said it was a friend of theirs—a human—who convinced them to turn to the Goddess and indulge in her dark beliefs. Was he unknowingly talking about his parents? Natalie and John? But they just said they didn't know anything about wolves … so … how would they have known about the lore?

He grits his teeth and groans at the frustration of it all. Nothing is making any sense! Victor didn't say how Stacy and Gray died, only that they killed a bunch of people, but Natalie has just said that they were the ones who were murdered, yet she doesn't know how or why. Not the other way around. Maybe his mom is lying, but she's never lied—

She has. His whole life has been a lie.

The only one who has never lied to him, no matter how much it hurt or didn't make sense at the time, has been …

Victor.

Erin slams his hands on the desk and lowers his head. "Sorry, I'm tired. I've had a long day, so I'm going to go to bed now."

"Cu—"

"All right," John interrupts Natalie. Wrapping an arm around her waist, he begins to walk them backward. "This is a lot to take in. We'll try our best to answer any questions you have in the morning. Sleep well, Son." He smiles.

Erin returns the gesture with a weak smile of his own. He waits till he hears the creak of the fifth step they've never bothered to fix—a pain back in high school when he and Fletcher would try and sneak out and go to parties at Layla's request in the next town over—and the muffled noise of the TV broadcast fills the background before ripping his t-shirt off.

Breathing comes a bit more easily after that. He opens his window, the cool air on his skin easing the nausea swimming in his stomach. He clenches the shirt in his hand; tears mix with the sweat. He didn't realize he was sweating that much.

Sighing, he flops back onto his bed. The ringing in his ears is louder now, like a bottomless foghorn. He closes his eyes and yanks his pillow over his ears, pressing in the hopes the pressure drowns the noise. It doesn't. If anything, it makes it worse. The deep sound was now like an insistent whine in his head. The kind dogs give when they are tired of being ignored.

No.

Not a dog.

A wolf.

TWENTY-SIX

Morning comes too soon.

The Pack rallies. Unease may swim on the breeze between them all, but not fear. That is something she prides them on. The humans are close; the advance runner telling how they trampled through the river already. Kazamir leads them. Selfish and jealous cub. If only she had come down sooner, then perhaps she could have spoken sense into him, soothed his greed.

No. There is no point dwelling on what could have been.

Only on what can be done.

The humans will be here by the time the sun sits high in the sky. The human's armor slows them down, if only slightly, forcing Kazamir and the other wolves by his side to prowl alongside them.

They will take any advantage they can.

Thick tree bark is held with string over shoulders and wrapped around chests. She does not wear any, besides her shawl. That is all she shall need. The small cubs are ushered deep into the forest, bushes covering the opening underneath a mighty fallen tree. They are told to keep quiet. Not to cry. Wait. The fighting will be over soon, and rabbit will be served with fresh herbs for supper.

Hëna stands in a grassy field, beside the Alpha and Luna, the dry grass tickling her bare shins and feet. The Pack is behind them, shuffling and growling. Her husband left as soon as dawn broke. He most likely stands somewhere near, on higher ground. Waiting. Watching. His job will come after the battle.

She refused the sword that was held out to her before they made their way to the field beyond the forest. The bows and arrows, too. Though she stands with her children, though she came to help them, she will not take a life. Human or Wolf. Not even to protect.

Her magic ... her hands were not created to do that.

And she simply does not wish to.

Does that make her a coward? A fraud? Asking them to fight, to risk their lives, when she cannot do the same.

Perhaps.

But she does not care.

She has done more than most Goddesses would to preserve this world. One flaw in her design is the least they can tribute her with. It is the least they can forgive her for.

The ground shakes. Baying fills the air.

Red.

Red.

Red.

All around, the smell of Pack is smothered as the humans arrive, horses blowing thick steam into the air. Kazamir smirks darkly from beside King Halian. He is dressed like them, full of armor. Though his feet and forearms remain bare, claws extended.

They drip in blue.

Nahale tenses, raising his head with one sharp eyebrow lifted. A challenge to his father. The king snarls. Tala grabs his mate's hand without looking at him and lifts their joined hands into the air.

He roars, "FOR THE MOON! FOR THE STARS! FOR THE WOLVES!"

Her cubs all answer the call of their Alpha, "FOR PACK!"

The battle begins.

Swords clash.

Wolves shift.

Arrows fly.

It is bloody and loud. Her heart splinters more and more with every death she cannot prevent. Her magic depletes quickly; the barrier she holds around each of her cubs is being punctured. Why? Her wolves are strong, yet their presence is dulled, their shifts slowing down … down … down …

There.

King Halain sits above his horse, a flag bearing his sigil flowing in the breeze behind him. At its base is a metal holder. Thick on the bottom, but the top covering it is filled with holes. A mix of blue and purple steam rises from within it. Wolfsbane. They have poisoned the air.

She clenches her hands but doesn't look away. She cannot look away. She did that for far too long.

Not anymore.

Never again.

Lifting her arms, she narrows her eyes on the item. Concentrate. Focus. Sound dulls around her. The air dims. Her limbs glow. Bright. Brighter. BRIGHTEST.

Magic swells and dances. Running at full speed until it sparks against the offence. It struggles to topple over, to be snuffed out. She pushes more, when movement catches her eye. To the left. King Halain reaches behind him at something strapped against his steed. An arrow. A very long arrow.

Her eyes narrow, heart beating strongly in her chest. Too strong. It's going to jump right out.

The bow is brought to him by a human on foot, who scurries back behind those with shields forming a line behind their king.

No. She pushes more magic. The poison wobbles.

His arms stretch, bow tight between them. One eye is shut, the other …

Where is he aiming?

Her eyes flit around the field. There are no wolves close to him, not ones who fight against him at least.

Who is he targeting?

Searching.

Searching.

The King aims higher into the sky.

There—

"TALA!" she screams across the battlefield.

The arrow flies true.

Its target was not the Alpha.

Nahale grunts, steps faltering. She does not know if the loud cry stuffing her ears is her own or Tala's. Her magic rages, and the jar topples over, spilling red coals all over the earth. King Halian's steed startles, trampling the grass and dirt beneath until the embers die out. The poison is gone.

She races to Nahale, weaving across the plain to where he is, sword still in hand, even as his thick blood mixes with that of his enemy at his feet. Her toes slip in the bloody grass; a female wolf catches her on the arm. She does not thank her, righting herself and running faster. She makes it before his knees buckle, his head hitting her hand instead of the harsh earth.

Tala rages from across the battlefield. His howl is guttural, like the arrow pierced his heart instead. It may as well have. The bond between mates is strong, much stronger than that of Pack. What one feels, so too does the other. Many humans are torn apart as he fully shifts. Limbs are ripped and blood sprays in his path as he makes his way to Nahale's father.

She cradles Nahale in her arms, one hand gripping the arrow. It stings; her hand instantly blistering. The humans didn't hold back on coating the weapons with poison.

Nahale holds her burnt hand in his. "Do not ... blame yourself," he wheezes. The sound is wet. Blood is filling his lungs, refusing air into them.

"Shhh," she whispers to him, yanking the arrow out. Blood gushes from the wound, instantly pooling over her hand as she tries to heal the hole. Her husband's presence is behind her. He has come.

But not to comfort.

Nahale grunts, lifting a hand to her cheek. Tears spill down his face. But he is ... smiling. "I had hoped ... for so much. I even had a name picked out, without knowing ..." He laughs, the sound bleeding into a wet cough. His lips paint red. "While I could not live for it all, what I was blessed with ... I am immensely grateful for. You, Mother Goddess ... granted me that."

"FIRE!"

She turns to the human who yelled. A blur of arrows rains toward them. It is so different, looking at them from this angle.

Though the pain feels the same.

A wolf kneels next to her, two shields draped across her back. He must have picked up one from the fallen. His red hair glimmers in the sunlight as arrows burrow into it. Closing her eyes, she imagines it is simply that—rain. Not poison. Not death. Something wet lands on her shoulder, and she turns her head toward the wolf guarding her. He is crying, frown deep and green eyes downturned as he listens to his Luna's words. She recognizes him ... Kzar, she remembers. The grime and sorrow on his face make him look vastly different from the last time she caught a glimpse.

Her knees hurt from kneeling. They tingle, as if the earth is biting at her skin. Her bones. Her heart. The pieces that are left, at least.

She does not think, even if she could find all the pieces once more, it will ever be put back together.

"I do not ... do not regret this war. It needed to happen. For them." Nahale's gaze shifts to the man protecting them from the raining arrows. A smile lifts his lips. She wipes the dripping blood from them. His injury has spread throughout the Pack now. They know their Luna has fallen. They fight even harder. Wails mix into the howls echoing across the field as sadness permeates the air around them. The soil.

Does her old friend feel it, too? Does she want to rip her heart from her chest to not feel it splinter anymore? Does she curse her son for tricking them all into thinking he was on her side? That *Time* had matured. That he had gifted them with a blessing to—

No. What has happened is not the fault of her friend's son.

There is only one to blame for all this. And that is Her.

Hëna. Mother Goddess of the Moon.

She placed this curse on them. She forced her cubs to split, to fight and take each other's blood. She—

"I regret it," she admits to him softly. The tears finally slip past. "I should have acted sooner. I should not have allowed any of this to happen." She does not know if the tremors in her arms are from his body giving into Death's whisperings or her own sobs fighting against the magic begging to be released. To end it all now, across the field, each one of them. Wolf. Human. One spell, that's all she would need to utter. It would be so easy ... so, so easy ...

Yilli kneels on one knee beside her. His face is grim. Sadness is etched into every corner. Ah, he had hoped too. Despite it all ... in the end, he had wanted it too.

"Star," she whimpers. He bites his lip. It does not stop the tears from pooling in his eyes.

"No!" Nahale coughs, the harsh word dislodging more blood from his lungs. "Do not regret this. If you do ... then there is no meaning in it."

"In what?" she asks him. There is blood coated in his headpiece, tangled with his fizzed black hair, and blending with his freckles. She smooths it away.

"In love," Nahale declares. He gazes at her. *Into* her. She has seen that strong look before, on another brazen cub only seven moon passes ago. Her breath sticks in her throat, and she fights the bitter chuckle. Her magic swells. He is resisting her. How similar the pair of them are. Her husband gasps beside her, his hand clenching into a fist on his knee. She ignores him.

"Which is why … I'd do it ov—over and over again. As many times as I needed to, in order to protect my Pack. That is what you taught us, after all, Hëna." His voice is strong. He did not speak loudly, yet the words echoed. It is as if every wolf has heard. As if her old friend had asked her daughter to whisk the words across the battlefield on a wild summer breeze. No wolf has ever dared utter her true name before, not in such a casual manner. Which is why … she cannot help herself. She laughs. It is not a light sound. Or airy. It is deep and sad. Angry. Confused and … hopeful. Of course, it is the human turned wolf who would dare break the unwritten decree her cubs made for themselves.

Not that she cared much for that one order. She has always wished to be called that by one of them.

Which means … her Hope was not misguided after all.

They can co-exist. Together. As one.

With her.

"It seems," she says to him, "that your instinct has been seen after all, my dear cub."

A shrill screech echoes, one louder than any she has heard yet. She turns. Most of the humans lie dead. The green grass is stained red. Wolves litter the space between them all. Weapons are broken. Torn. She thinks her heart sits amongst them, somewhere. Maybe it's the wolf torn in half, its head resting on the chest of a dead female. Purple poison leaks through the arrow in her leg. Or maybe it sits on the edge of the sword held in the human's trembling arms as he points it at three snarling gray wolves. Her eyes continue to trail. The human flag is torn and on the ground. King Halian is lying on it. His crown is bent beside him. Like a mighty wolf has stepped on it.

His eyes are looking skyward. No shine lights them.

He is dead.

They have won.

But the cost ...

"What was the name?" she asks. Nahale turns his head, eyes glazed as they look at Tala. She does not know if he truly sees his mate in his mighty wolf form or not. She imagines that he still can. That Death has not taken the sight of his beloved from him just yet.

Slowly, Nahale's lips part. She lowers her ear to hear the words, her eyes also trained on Tala across the battlefield. Blood seeps from multiple cuts across his body, the purple poison so thick it stains his black fur. Tears fall from his squinted pale blue eyes, not strong enough in number to hide the pride still in them. She swears his lips curl, a beautiful wolfish smirk, as if he could hear the name whispered to her.

She shakes her head as her husband chuckles, the sound finally breaking free from behind his clenched jaw.

Such brazen, *brazen,* cubs.

She will miss them dearly.

"What a wonderful name. Like a strong storm."

She waits until Tala breathes his last breath before slipping her fingers over Nahale's eyes, shutting away the dulled golden light.

For now.

TWENTY-SEVEN

Erin's eyes shoot open. The window is closed, the blinds shutting his room in darkness. There's a sliver of light coming from under his door ... which he didn't shut. The whine is still there. And it's loud. With a grimace, he closes his eyes and strains his hearing, looking for the noise of the Saturday night movie he knows his parents are watching. He can't hear it.

Ah.

He stops straining and looks at the door once more. He's dreaming.

He knows what lies beyond his closed door. He can sense it. But he doesn't want to face it.

"This is my dream, so I can do whatever I want," he mutters, wrapping himself in his bedsheets. The blankets are pulled to his chin, one hand curled underneath his pillow while the other rests over his stomach. The whining gets louder. His neck hurts from clenching his jaw.

"I'm not listening to you!" he shouts to the door. A growl howls through the thin slit separating the door from the hardwood floor. It starts low before rising in pitch. Unflinching. Constant.

Petty.

Erin gets the feeling this creature is even more stubborn than he is. It won't stop until he gets up and sees it.

"ARGH!" Erin throws the sheets off and stomps to the door, flinging it open. The thunder and lightning from previous times are gone, and a glance at the night sky shows no trace of rain in sight. Only a moon glows brightly, its soft rays dancing through the air like the caress of a mother. Just as bright as the sun, if not brighter.

Erin cocks a brow at the sight. Night ... that's new. It didn't cross his mind before, but he's never been here at night. He looks across the field—the blood and wolfsbane have been replaced with short green grass; it looks soft, not prickly like Texan grass normally is in the summertime. The golden-eyed white wolf sits among it, staring right at Erin with a smugness he doesn't think wolves should be allowed to possess.

Erin places his hands on his hips. "Ok, I'm here. Now what?"

The wolf stands, its bright white fur glinting like snow in the moonlight, and begins walking into the forest.

"Where are you going?" Erin shouts. The wolf looks back at him and growls before turning his head forward once more. It wants Erin to follow.

He hesitates, fingers tapping against his thigh. Despite his reluctance before to open the door and face the wolf, his heart pumps wildly with curiosity. What does the wolf want to show him beyond the forest? Perhaps what lies there will explain why it keeps appearing in his dreams.

"Wait!" Erin runs back into his room, feet slipping into old sneakers quickly before running to catch up with the wolf. It stares down at him when he reaches his side. "Ok. Show me."

The wolf's lips curl into what Erin thinks is meant to be a grin before moving forward once more. Its giant paws leave indents in the soft soil as they weave between the dense trees of the forest. It's a warm feeling, having the wolf's presence beside him in the moonlight. It feels familiar … and comforting. Like the memory of a worn trail that's been forgotten but not erased.

They reach a wide clearing filled with tents made from animal hide that's been stretched tight with deep red pieces of wood. Red oak, it looks like. Strong and sturdy—a good choice for housing. Erin's parents have worked with that wood many times. He runs his hand over one of the tents as they walk past; it's smooth to the touch, and the many layers of string tying the wood together at the peak aren't fraying at all. The other houses look the same, with additional animal hide placed like rugs scattered about and covering what looks like wooden seats—short stools, close to the ground—around the open tent flaps. Whoever built these tents spent delicate time working with them, making sure they were sturdy enough to last, regardless of the weather.

It makes Erin feel proud to see them still standing.

Which then confuses him.

He furrows his brows, following the white wolf as they make their way deeper into the ghost settlement. It's eerie. A sense of unease snakes its way down Erin's spine. He jogs to catch up with the wolf, walking beside its massive head.

"This place feels wrong … like something is missing," he whispers, eyes dark as they flick around the space. The wolf grunts, bumping its head softly into Erin's side. It agrees but won't tell him what. It's on the tip of his nose, like a smell that you can taste in the back of your throat.

Cooked rabbit and herbs.

Laughing children.

Warm fur pelts and etched bone jewelry.

Blood and wolfsbane.

Crackling from ahead draws Erin's eyes forward, and he gulps in a deep breath to ease the panic trying to engulf him. They've reached the center where a massive fire rages. It's the only fire pit with dark wood still actively burning instead of lying like dead charcoal. Warmth fans Erin's cheeks when he stops to watch the flames. The wolf licks his arm, and Erin looks down before the wolf continues, leaping onto a giant stage. Dais? It bows to a statue of a giant, colorful, painted wooden wolf, shining like an aurora in the night sky.

He has a sudden thought that his mother would like to see it. She would appreciate the creative art. It's exactly something she would place in her garden. He smirks, eyes trailing over the cleft in the left ear, a mistake most likely, and the blue cloth hanging around its neck that has a crescent moon carved from bone hanging like a jeweled necklace, before reaching the star sitting like a crown in the center of its forehead. It's bigger than the rest and a bright blue color. Like a crown.

Erin's teeth grind.

A feeling spiders down his spine.

Back up again. Whispering between his ears.

Tapping at his neck.

Erin twists his head and rolls his shoulders, cracking the tense muscles.

The wolf howls low, its nose pointed toward the edge of the settlement, and Erin, ignoring the confusion and anger suddenly coursing through him and causing his arms to tremble, follows its gaze. Tombstones. Even from this distance, without the light of day, Erin can see clearly. There are dead buried there. Dead that make tears well in Erin's eyes and his heart lurch like it's been punched. He doesn't know them; he doesn't even know if this place is real. But why does his mind, his soul, his *blood* feel like he does? Why does grief cause his breath to stutter like it's his people, his friends and family, that are buried under cold grass and dirt in those graves?

"What is this place?" he asks softly, voice trembling. He wipes his eyes and looks at the wolf once more, only to find it already looking at him. Its golden eyes are brighter than the sun and wiser than his mothers have ever been. "Why did you bring me here?"

The wolf shakes, his fur shifting as if a strong breeze has run its hands through it, and suddenly, it's not a white wolf with golden eyes standing in front of him.

It's a man.

A man who looks exactly like Erin.

Facial features, body physique ... it's all the same.

He wears nothing over his pale skin, standing nude, except for what looks to be a crown of vines. A bright blue jewel is woven in the center, sitting in-between his dark black eyebrows and golden eyes. The jewel reminds Erin of the ring Victor wears, his family heirloom ... but smaller, if only just, and his skin is unblemished except for the freckles dusting his nose and cheeks, and the scar sitting right over his heart. The skin there is blistered and sharp, reminding Erin of an arrow pulled harshly from delicate skin.

Erin's eyes widen, his mouth snapping shut. Impossible. He notices the tattoo on his neck. A white wolf surrounded by white stars.

He recognizes the mark. His skin burns, like it remembers the momentary flash of pain and the warm pleasure that followed.

"Who ..."

The man smiles gently and lifts his arms. It's only then that Erin notices the jar he's holding. He doesn't know where it came from, how this doppelganger found it, but he knows what's inside it. For the past five weeks, he's been stuffing every feeling connected to Victor into it. Ignoring it. Hiding it.

It looks bigger now, though, and Erin suspects there's more than just his emotions welded within.

"Let go. I will not do it for you." The man's voice is light, but commanding. Erin looks down at the jar held loosely in the man's hands. He's scared. He takes a step back and freezes. A deep howl rings through the air, and the man's head swivels to the left where a giant black wolf has rounded one of the tents. It leaps onto the opposite side of the stage, shifting mid-air into a man.

Erin's heart hammers, the sound so loud he swears his ears are going to pop, making him deaf forever. He holds his breath.

The man is tall, with strong shoulders and a matching muscular, tanned body that is marred with numerous scars. Long blonde hair, neatly trimmed and close to his jaw, also trails down his chest and stomach. He's nude as well, wearing a crown similar to the one worn by the man in front of Erin, except the vines are thicker, allowing the strands framing his face to hang loose, while the rest is braided into the hair along his back. On his neck sits the mark of a black wolf nestled next to a black moon. It's a matching tattoo. Matching but also ... not. Black vs white. Moon vs stars.

A balance.

He looks to Erin, and his smile widens so far that Erin fears his face will split in two. Erin's lips part in shock, a hiccup escaping his mouth. The man's name sits on the tip of his tongue as he stares into those pale blue eyes that remind Erin of the moon.

And behind him ... he's carrying a jar similar to the one being held out to Erin.

His heart freezes and burns at the same time.

"Nahale," the other man says, wolfish grin still in place. His voice is deep, like a wolf's rumble. It makes Erin shiver.

"Tala," the man in front of Erin, Nahale, greets. The men smile at each other. The love is as clear as the moonlight covering the bloodstained earth beneath them.

Erin steps to the edge of the stage, stretching onto his toes to take the jar from the man standing in front of him. Nahale grins. He leans forward, kisses Erin on the forehead softly, then walks away. Tala has a hand stretched out, fingers waiting eagerly for him. When Nahale reaches him, they lace their hands together. The movement is smooth and instinctual, like they've done it a hundred—no, a thousand times before.

Tala bends and kisses Nahale. It's a quick kiss, a simple pressing of lips together. Nothing inherently deep. Nothing dirty or sexual. But it makes Erin's heart pound like an intruder caught in a flashlight's high beam as he watches. The thumb caressing the chin. The soft moan. The fingers squeezing the neck, pulling each other closer like close just isn't enough.

It's intimate and passionate and meaningful, and he shouldn't be watching.

Erin's gaze flits to the man behind Tala. And just like that night, in the shadows of Donny's Warehouse, his sharp gaze finds him. Instantly. And just as before, Erin can't look away. He doesn't want to look away.

The blue jewel from the ring on his index finger glows from across the stage.

Tala pulls back, his free hand caressing Nahale's neck. Over the tattoo mark. Nahale nuzzles into the touch and laughs softly—the sound light, free—before pulling Tala down the stage steps and toward a tent. Neither looks back as they walk, hand-in-hand, inside the tent, leaving them behind.

No, not leaving.

Passing on their mark. Their instinct.

Their hope.

Her Hope.

Smiling, Erin takes a deep breath and drops the jar.

It shatters.

TWENTY-EIGHT

Erin tries to call Victor. He snatches his phone from his bag by the foot of his bed as he walks out of his room, only to pause on the middle of the stairs. He can distantly hear his parents' voices calling for him, asking if he's awake. If he's feeling better now. The sound is like bees buzzing in his ears. He laughs quietly in disbelief.

After all this time, he still doesn't have Victor's phone number.

Some things never change, huh ...

Erin shakes his head and jumps down the rest of the steps. He places his phone on the table by the front door and runs out of the house. He won't need it where he's going. Sprinting down the street, his mind keeps repeating the same word over and over like a broken record. There are other thoughts that beg for attention, other memories screaming to be heard. Trains in his mind screech on worn tracks in an attempt to not crash into each other. It's a jumbled mess. But he ignores it all. Because there's only one thing his heart sings for now, and it's only when he's out of the main suburb does he allow himself to listen.

Shift.

Blood pumps through his veins so fast he thinks the vessels are going to burst.

His breathing quickens, in and out like a hummingbird's wings, before slowing. His breaths become longer, more air able to fill his lungs each time, allowing him more time to savor the tangy taste of chilli powder and lime floating from the houses and clinging in the air.

The wind whooshes past him, faster, faster, faster, cooling his sweaty skin and sweeping his hair back until he can no longer feel the sticky sensation of sweat, the drops seeping from his pores getting lost in his coarse white fur instead.

His vision sharpens, eyes narrowing in shape even more than how they already sit on his face. The shadows around him light up more each time he blinks.

He bends over, his limbs and nails extending to reach the ground.

His nose twitches, elongating. His ears pull, growing.

It's an uncomfortable feeling, shifting into a wolf, like nothing he's ever felt before. It's like a floodgate has been taken apart within him and all the water is gushing throughout his body. A part of him tries to expel it, tries to seal shut the floodgates with a welder like that will stop the creaking of the nuts and bolts. But the other part of him is stronger and faster. Its senses are heightened, letting it grab hold of the weaker side of him—the human side—and pull it in close.

It welcomes the feeling wholeheartedly.

It feels natural.

It feels right.

It feels free.

There's a howling in his head, causing Erin to open his mouth wide and bay back in joy as he runs full speed toward the Lovelace Ranch. The feeling that only hours before was giving him a pounding headache, he knows now was his wolf—his instinct and his past as Nahale combined—trying to break free, to get out of the cage it locked itself in all those years ago when he was a baby, only three months old.

He doesn't dwell on the feelings of abandonment and anger that cling to that cage. He can feel the abundance of love and protection from the Moon Goddess, so he knows there must've been a reason why she built that cage in the first place, and then later—

They will have time to discuss it after, to discuss a lot of things after. But right now ... right now he needs to get to Victor. He needs to tell Victor that he was right and that he's sorry for doubting him.

That he's sorry it took him so long.

Call it what you want—fated pairs, soulmates, destined ones. Mates. The fact of the matter is that they have a string tying them together. They are bound, by blood and by stars. And now that Erin sees it, he won't ever let it fray or tear or break.

Never.

A freshly painted black fence passes him—the starting line for the ranch's property. Erin starts to slow, his mind already trying to figure out how to get Victor's attention without waking the rest of the Pack, when the rich scent of spicy sandalwood and earthy leather drifts toward him. Erin stops, heart thrashing against his ribcage. It smells deeper in this form. Stronger.

Victor is out of breath, standing by the fence, the house dark far behind him. His pupils dilate within his wide blue eyes. Erin can't help but lower his gaze to his bare chest as it rises and falls in quick succession. He ran out in his pajama shorts, with no shoes on. Has he come, prepared to shift and run to Erin, too?

That would mean it really wasn't a dream. Victor was there, beside Tala, in the old village. Erin dips his head so he's at eye level with Victor.

Of course it wasn't a dream. The memories being filled in with color in his mind are proof enough of that.

Tears fall freely down Victor's face, but Erin smells no sadness from him as he raises a shaky hand toward Erin. "My Star ..."

Erin tries to chuckle, the laughter coming out as deep staccato huffs instead. He doesn't know how they are meant to communicate; he was born as a human before, not a wolf. Though he remembers hearing something about ...

'Hi, my Little Wolf,' he thinks toward Victor, focusing on the vibrant red thread binding them and sending the words down it like a zipline. His vocal cords feel different, tighter, and larger than he is used to.

Victor breaks out in a grin; his deep laugh is loud, like a sob that's welled and changed course midway up his throat. He tilts his head and closes the distance between them. Erin feels static run where Victor's hand trails along his snout and jaw. He can hear Victor's heart beating, the sound so calming to Erin that his own heart slows to match its pace.

Oh, how long it's been since he's felt that beat underneath his ear.

He's missed it.

"I felt it when you shifted. You were calling me." Victor rests his head on the space between Erin's brows. "The only thing I could think was *run*, quick. I'll run to you ... so run to me, too," he whispers so softly, Erin wonders if he's even speaking at all or thinking directly into Erin's mind.

Erin whines as more tears start forming in Victor's eyes, nosing them away. "I'm sorry. I should've trusted my instinct more. I should've trusted you more and not let other people get in my head. I shouldn't have driven away earlier in the night, after dropping you off. Why did I do that? I'm such a—"

Erin cuts Victor off with a lick across his face. Victor blinks at him before bending over in more wet laughter. Not even the moon can shine as brightly as the love and adoration glimmering in Victor's eyes right now.

Mate.

He has found his mate.

Erin pushes Victor with his snout, laughing along with him until Victor settles down. With a cheeky smirk, Victor takes a step back and starts to strip. Erin's breath gets caught in his throat, his eyes instantly dropping past Victor's face and down deeply etched muscle and a trail of blonde hair. Victor hangs his shorts over the fence beside them, and Erin's eyes continue seeking past hips and prominent veins poking above bright red boxer briefs. His stomach lurches, and his eyes widen. Victor's hard. *Very* hard.

And huge.

That won't fit. No matter how much stretching he does.

How did it fit before?

Victor smirks, his canines flashing like the wolf he is. His fingers play with the waistband of his boxer briefs. "Wanna look?"

Erin shakes his head.

"Are you sure?" Victor drawls, teasing the band by flicking it against his skin. Erin flinches.

No.

'Yes', he thinks down the bond. He huffs through his nose and turns his head to look at the forest. Victor chuckles lowly beside him, the noise not loud enough to cover the sound of cloth moving against skin.

"Come on," Victor sighs beside him. "You've seen it before."

That was a lifetime ago.

Erin rolls his eyes, ready to turn back to his mate and tell him to stop being a tease when the air shifts. A warm breeze runs through his fur, Victor's presence beside him growing. His scent gets stronger, too, the smell engulfing Erin whole. He closes his eyes, relishing in the sensation of being beside his mate in his wolf form once again, when he feels something cold touch his ear. When he opens them, the first thing he notices is Victor's eyes. Pride streaks across his heart at the knowledge that he was right about them—they do shine just as bright in the dark. The pale blue moons are clear, the silver around his iris acting like a crown for his large eyes, as they gaze into Erin's golden hazel maze.

Victor nuzzles Erin. 'Follow me, Star.'

Erin hears the words ring in his head. The voice is deeper and rougher than he's used to hearing from Victor, but it's Victor's all the same. He turns, leaps over the fence, and starts running into the forest, his black fur blending in under the density of the trees.

Erin follows, clearing the fence easily when the wind shifts. Strawberries float through the air. He skids to a halt, nose held high as he sniffs the air in alert. A flash of red hair among a cluster of trees catches his eye.

'Erin,' Victor whines from the forest. Even though Victor's massive black coat is darker than the shadows around them, Erin can still see him. He feels a stab of guilt at the nervous question in Victor's eyes, like he thinks Erin might be second-guessing something.

Erin looks back toward the trees. Camping bags and wide tents, closed to the night air, are the only things staring back at him. He sees nothing else. The smell of strawberries is also gone. Like a ghost. Paranoia laughs in his mind. Kazamir is dead. And Stella …

Shaking his head free of all anxious thoughts, he bounds after Victor, licking his snout in apology. They race into the forest.

It's more than just being able to see Victor, Erin realizes as he looks to his mate, keeping pace beside him. He can feel him in the air, sense him in his bones. His very instinct is taking over his thoughts, only letting information through that he can use to protect. This is a much deeper connection than they had before. No, not deeper. Clearer. It will take some getting used to, the disconnect of familiarity he feels.

Erin pushes against Victor as he overtakes him, joy melting off his body in waves as Victor nips playfully at his feet. He can hear water rushing in the distance and gets an idea. A memory tugs playfully in his mind.

Erin takes a breath and thinks again of the string binding them. Mimicking the sensation, he imagines his vocal cords relaxing. 'Last one to the waterfall has to jump in!'

Victor's laughing howl behind him is all the confirmation he needs to know this isn't another dream. This is reality.

Victor overtakes Erin quickly, leading him through the forest along a worn trail. This must be the path the Lovelace Pack normally takes while on runs. The tell-tale signs of recent movement are visible in the trodden grass and broken tree branches.

Erin feels giddy every time he looks at Victor. His heart swells to the point he believes it has swallowed all his other organs. He knows Victor doesn't care about getting to the lake first, but he also knows he's not one to give up on a challenge. He never has been. So, they play around while running, nipping at legs and jumping over backs—anything to slow the other down.

Finally, they break through the trees to the sight of a beautiful lake. There's a field of bluebells growing around it, encircling it like a fairy ring. The tall, long-leaf trees peer over the lake's edge at their reflection, some of their leaves coating the lake like icing sugar on a cake. It's beautiful, untouched by human hands.

Victor walks over to one of the trees that has three claw marks scratched deeply across it and shifts back into a human. While he rummages through the hollow hole by the roots, Erin trots over and attempts to shift back, too. He thinks back to all the times he saw Victor shift in their old life, the explanation he got through soft chuckles when he asked, wide-eyed, how it was done. Imagine the body shrinking. The claws softening. The blood thinning. The instinct remains, the heart strong in its beat. But contained. Controlled.

Human.

It takes longer, more than the blink of an eye it took for Victor to shift. But it works. Erin shivers at the lack of insulation over his skin and rolls his shoulder with a cough as cool, fresh air hits his lungs much sooner than before. Everything feels heightened, more intense than ever before. His tongue feels heavy in his mouth, rolling it over his sharpened teeth and against the roof of his mouth, before smacking his lips.

"It tastes different."

Victor hums as he wraps a blanket around Erin's shoulders, pulling them flush together. He has a matching one tied low around his hips, the bottom swishing against the long grass. "You'll get used to it," he says, rubbing circles into Erin's shoulder blades.

Erin smiles, moaning low in the back of his throat as the tension lessens. He doesn't feel it now, but he knows tomorrow the muscles will be sore from his first shift. He heard plenty of stories from Tala about how restless the young cubs were, only to sleep for many days after.

Victor quickly kisses his head before crouching beside the hole. He pulls out a plastic trash bag and opens it, drawing out two pairs of shorts and a thick quilted blanket.

"We won't be needing those," Erin says.

Victor freezes. Slowly, he looks over his shoulder at Erin. "Need what?" His eyes are as dark as his voice.

"The shorts," Erin clarifies, jutting his chin to the clothing Victor's still holding. He lowers the blanket from his shoulders, letting it hang loosely across his abdomen and legs. He's still covered, but Victor's eyes follow the movement all the same. A muscle in his neck twitches, causing Erin's stomach to flip. He takes a step back, the grass tickling his ankles.

"Do you expect to sit out all night naked? It's July, but the air is still cool by the water. The trees don't let much heat into this area during the day." Victor drops the shorts back over the trash bag and stands. The lines of his muscles are tense, rigid, as he takes a step toward Erin.

"Of course not." Erin raises a brow and takes another step back. "I'll be way too sweaty, all hot and bothered, to feel any cold. In fact, the breeze will be welcomed, I'm sure."

"Oh? Is that so?" Victor continues to follow Erin's prowling, a smirk teasing his thin lips. Erin's sharp eyes catch movement underneath the blanket tied to Victor's waist. A twitch. If he wasn't hard before, he is now. The thought makes Erin's blood run south as heat spikes along his veins. Encouraging. Demanding attention.

"Why do you run, Star?"

"Me? Run? Come, Little Wolf. Never." Erin drops the blanket completely. "But hide? Well ..." He turns and takes off, running to the lake. Victor is fast and instantly wraps his arms around Erin from behind before he can make it three steps. Erin screams, the laugh ripping from him as Victor spins him in the air before he's gently lowered onto the soft grass. Victor's knees slightly dig into Erin's outer thighs as he hovers above him. His blanket is gone, disregarded in the grass behind them alongside its counterpart.

Erin hums, wrapping his arms around Victor's neck to pull him in close. His fingers stroke the short hair, massaging gently. Victor's head tilts back slightly, a small smile curving his lips. His skin is warm. It always has been, and Erin suspects it always will, no matter which life they are in.

"You found me," he whispers against his mate's neck, lips pressing softly on the skin. It's not there anymore, but Erin remembers exactly how much space the dark mark took. He draws the form with his lips. Victor shivers.

"Well, you're pretty hard to miss." Victor laughs; the movement presses them even closer together. He drags his thumb under Erin's eye gently before sliding to his neck. He stops where Erin's matching white mark used to sit. "I swore it, didn't I? Etched it on my heart, my soul. Did you doubt me?"

"Never." Erin tangles his fingers into Victor's soft hair and yanks him down to press their mouths together. He's waited long enough.

His lips part instantly, and Victor's tongue dives in to claim him like a man starved. He forgot how addicting kissing Tala is, how sparks fly across his mind like fireworks. No, more like bombs. Encompassing. All-consuming. They briefly fight for dominance, Erin loving the little growl Victor makes deep in his throat at his unwillingness to submit.

Victor pulls back, his tongue taking its time to detangle from Erin's, before moving to nip at his bottom lip. A warning. Erin smirks. He can't believe he made it this long without giving in, without pushing his lips against Victor's. Ever since that first night at Donny's ... Goddess above, he should've dragged Victor by his fancy shirt color behind those creaky wooden steps and made out with him then.

Screw the repercussions. If anything, it might have jump-started their memories sooner.

"Come on." Erin wraps his legs around Victor's waist and grinds against him, pressing his heels into the top of Victor's ass for better friction. He bites his lip, holding back his moan as Victor lowers onto one forearm, pressing his forehead into the juncture between Erin's shoulder and neck. The groan from Victor's lips only spurs him on. He uses the position to his advantage and grazes his mouth along Victor's ear. "Play with me."

"Trust me, Star, I would love to." Victor licks along Erin's neck before biting his collarbone. Erin shudders, his hands loosening their grip slightly as Victor crawls down. "But I'm a young wolf who has found his mate. Who, I might add, has been right in front of me for weeks, walking around unclaimed and spreading his scent all over the place. I'm afraid I'm incapable of playing right now." He stops at Erin's chest, tugging at one of his nipples harshly with his teeth while his hand slowly rubs at the other. Erin doesn't know whether to arch into the feeling or slink away from it. "I want to make this enjoyable, but it's taking every ounce of control I have not to turn you over and take you, thrusting into you mindlessly until you pass out, filled with my knot spilling endlessly inside you," he grumbles.

A million shockwaves electrify in Erin's stomach and across his skin. They travel along his legs and arms. Ransacking his heart and lungs. Taking control. Commanding his lust. It's been so long since he's had Victor touch him. Caresses him.

Claim him.

"Are you going to mark me?" Erin pants, small gaps puffing into the air as Victor nibbles his thigh, fingers digging into Victor's shoulder blades so hard the skin is forming a yellow-white hue. He's so close to where Erin wants him. He presses his legs open wider in invitation, fingers digging harder into Victor's back until his nails begin to curl over the skin. He smells blood, the metallic odor whispering around them mockingly. He's broken skin. Worry spikes sharply in his stomach as he yanks his hands away, holding them in the space above Victor's head. His nails are elongated slightly, the sharp claws stained with thin blood. Tears fill his eyes at what he's done. Guilt laughs in his ears.

He has left scratches before, sure; Tala always loved it when he would dig his fingers across his lower back, reprimanding him every time his hands would fall away and clump the grass or dirt underneath their old tree instead. It was the only way he was able to mark him, without the ability to form an official mate bond before the Goddess blessed them. But this ... he's never hurt Tala before. Never drawn his blood before.

Because he wasn't a wolf before.

Erin clenches his hands, the claws pricking his palm harshly as the calloused skin begins to tear. If he can't even control himself when he's happy, being pleasured and trying to give pleasure, too, then how is he going to control himself when he's mad or sad? What if he hurts someone? What if—

Victor seizes his hands and presses their palms flush together. His fingers press down into the space between Erin's knuckles. Their blood is trapped between them. Staining them. If he feels any pain at the blood dripping from the wounds down his back, any anger at Erin breaking skin, he doesn't let on; his lips instead too consumed with leaving open-mouthed kisses on the skin around Erin's shaft. It grounds Erin. He takes a deep breath and refocuses on the moment, on the pressure building in his stomach. On the small puffs of air escaping from Victor's thin lips that cause his dick to twitch. Erin wipes the tears from his cheeks with his wrist before letting Victor's hands fall from his and grabbing onto his shoulders once more, careful now about his claws. There will be plenty of time later to figure out his new life as a wolf. Right now ...

Right now, he wants to be fucked by his mate.

"No, I'm not going to mark you," Victor grunts, fingers digging into the muscle along his thighs before slowly moving lower to where Erin desperately wants him. He lifts Erin's ass off the ground and swirls around the edge of his rim. Teasing.

"What?" Erin lifts onto his elbows and peers down at Victor. Confusion colors his eyes, gradually replacing the lust. The conversation he started seconds ago swims back into focus. "Why not?"

"Because." Victor uses his thumb to press against his rim, and Erin moans deeply, his head dropping between his shoulders, back arching. His knees instinctively close, legs trembling, but Victor pushes them back open.

"You just—wow." Erin gulps, licking his dry lips. "You only pressed on me, and I nearly came. I've never felt like this before during sex."

"That's because you weren't a wolf—an Omega—before, Star." Victor sucks two fingers into his mouth, dragging them slowly against his tongue while Erin watches, round-eyed and transfixed, before pressing into him. He uses one finger first, slowly using the moisture to work him open, stretching the muscles. It's been a while since Erin last had sex with someone, but that doesn't mean he's an amateur. And some of the guys he's been with, they were much rougher than any wolf's instinct. Victor may be the biggest he's taken, but he said it himself.

This isn't the first time they've done this together.

So he doesn't need to be sluggish like the fucking tease that he is.

"Little Wolf," Erin whines, lips parting to ask again why his mate won't mark him, when Victor begins to pump his finger faster, before gently adding another. He takes his sweet time pushing in and out with two fingers. First knuckle. Second knuckle. First knuckle again. Greedily, Erin moves his hips to meet him as moisture slowly pools, dripping down his thighs. Victor's fingers must be coated with it as he continues to work him, pumping at that agonizingly ... slow ... pace.

He's ready. He's been ready since they got to the lake, but Victor is just ...

"Stop, ah! Victor!" Erin cries, chest heaving as Victor's lips wrap around the crown of his dick, swallowing him whole. His mouth is warm, his tongue swirling over his sensitive spots. Erin grits his teeth and grasps the back of Victor's head with one hand, jerking his mouth off him. "Stop ... distracting me ... and answer the question."

"Your parents," Victor deadpans, eyes dark. Briefly, Erin wonders if it's a hunger darkening their normal pale shade or, instead, anger at being stopped. Not that it matters. Either way, he shivers at the yearning underlying both options being directed at him.

"My parents? Why are you bringing them up?" The memory comes back quickly, like a shooting star across his mind. That's what his thoughts were about before he shifted, back near his house. "Oh," Erin realizes with dread. "Right."

Of course. Marking would raise a lot of questions he doesn't feel like answering right now. Honestly, the whole topic of conversation makes his head swim in a pool of anxiety.

"Yes, 'oh, right'," Victor mumbles, his mouth already wrapped around Erin's dick once again. Dragging his bottom lip between his teeth, Erin slumps back onto the ground as Victor works his length, dragging his tongue over every inch of him. He whines when Victor removes his fingers, and through hooded eyes, he watches his mate lick his lips, using the wetness coating his fingers to pump his own throbbing dick.

"Now, I for one would much rather discuss the confusion surrounding your parents after I fuck you. What do you say? Do you want to keep talking about them now, or would you rather we continue?" One of Victor's hands is thumbing his tip languidly, while the other is pressing hard on Erin's inner thigh. It's going to leave a mark beside all the kiss marks already darkening his skin.

The thought makes him quiver. He imagines how Victor would look with pink and red kiss marks painting his skin. They could never leave any in the past. At least not visible ones. Not until that last night. The Pack would recognize what it meant and raise too many questions.

For a moment, as Erin gazes at Victor on his knees above him through lidded eyes, his image changes. His hair becomes longer, thicker, and there is more muscle around his shoulders and chest. Light scars pepper his skin, stark against his tanned skin and the dark black mark on his neck.

Erin blinks, and it's Victor once more. The Victor he has come to know in this period. Lust has still deepened his eyes, and desire has claimed his scent. His hair is ruffled from Erin tugging at it, and his chest is moving fast in tandem with his beating heart. Erin briefly wonders which image Victor sees—the human Prince Nahale, or the dishevelled, newly shifted, once human Erin.

He huffs. What does he care? Just because they grew up differently doesn't make them any different inside. They fell in love regardless, didn't they?

"Continue," Erin pleads, voice breathy. And Victor does. He grips Erin's hips tight and slides in deeply. Slowly. Waiting for Erin to adjust until one more push, and they're joined completely. Erin doesn't know whether the sound that lifts from his lungs is a gasp or a cry. A mix of both, perhaps. His eyes squeeze shut as Victor's breath fans across his chest.

Victor tries to pull out and grunts. "Relax," he demands. "Star, relax."

Erin breathes out through his nose. Voice strained, he says, "You try doing this then."

"I don't think that would be pleasurable for either of us, my love." Victor chuckles, pressing soft kisses along Erin's neck and jaw in encouragement. Teeth tugging at his ear, sucking it gently. It works, and Victor wastes no time. Erin wraps his arms tight around Victor's neck as all his sensitive spots are hit. Sparks travel up and down his legs and arms and chest. Everywhere. Every inch. Every thrust. It's like that damned lightning from his dreams has struck the ground underneath them, its shockwaves traveling into him with every push.

"Victor," he moans. Sweat coats them both, the grass they lie on flattened from their rocking. His stomach tightens. He's close.

"I know," Victor pants. "Me too." He lowers so Erin's dick rubs between them, offering him satisfying friction, before leaning forward and kissing Erin again. And again. And again. His pace quickens, and Erin lifts his ass higher to meet his thrusts each time. Urging him to go faster. Harder. One of Victor's hands moves to cup his ass, kneading the toned flesh and allowing him better leverage. He gives Erin what he wants.

What they both need.

Crave.

Desire.

They chase it together, moving as one. Tears spill from the corners of his eyes, and Victor kisses those, too. Licks them away before nuzzling his nose against Erin's.

Erin squeezes his eyes shut, his head dropping back onto the ground—

"Look at me, Star," Victor commands. "I want to see you when I come. When I *make* you come."

Erin listens. Victor's growl is the final push that sends him crashing over the edge from that high cliff they've been dancing on. The fall is liberating, and it doesn't hurt when he reaches the bottom. His lips part, and he cries out as thick warmth spatters between them, coating his and Victor's lower chests. Not long after, Victor growls, his movement stuttering, jackhammering, the reach not as deep inside him as before, until finally slowing.

"I'm a wolf now," Erin whispers between shallow pants, stroking the hair off Victor's forehead as he stills completely. "You should've pulled out."

"I held back from knotting tonight, but no way in hell was I not scenting you." Victor winks, pulling out and lying next to Erin. His hand digs into the tight muscle on Erin's stomach, not caring about the residue left there. "I want every wolf within a five-mile radius to know who you belong to."

"Hmm." Erin turns to his side and tangles his fingers with Victor's, his heart jumping. Just when he thought he was coming down from the high, he climbs right back to the top. "And who would that be?"

"Me, Star. Alpha Victor Lovelace of the New York Pack," he declares. Commands. "You belong to me."

Erin hooks a leg over Victor's waist before pulling him close and nuzzling his neck. Victor grasps Erin's leg, kneading the space between his ass and thigh as Erin goes to work. He starts small, leaving soft pecks above Victor's collarbone before moving to that spot Tala always melted at. Right behind the lobe of his ear. That spot he licks and nips with his newly sharp teeth. Victor squeezes his ass so tight it's almost painful, his dick hard again where it digs into Erin's thigh.

Erin shifts his weight, hiking his leg higher until Victor is lined close against his entrance. Reaching back, his hand acting as guide, he pushes back, filled to the brim once more. Victor moans low, the sound so instinctual it has Erin smirking, a moan of his own claiming his throat. He presses his forehead against Victor's skin, nosing the spot where Victor's mark used to sit, and rocks his hips slowly. Victor closes his eyes, and Erin, mindful of his canines, bites down, causing Victor to shudder. Erin sucks, rolling the skin between his teeth until it's a deep shade of red.

Bright enough for everyone to see.

Long enough to last.

"It goes both ways, Little Wolf," he replies, a low growl seeping past his full lips. Nahale had to fight for it to be seen. But this time, he can reach it. His instinct prowls along the surface of his skin, of his heart, of his soul. It's ready—full of energy and free will.

And it's angry at being locked away.

TWENTY-NINE

E rin's body cries out in pain.

He wakes to the sun shining in his face and Victor's arm wrapped around his waist. Cringing, he slowly turns around and snuggles closer to his mate, taking a deep breath. The woodsy smell of sandalwood that coats his scent is stronger now where it blends in with the spicy leather undertones, swirling around him. Inside him. Fresh bark from a cedar forest and warm musk ... and underneath it all, oakmoss. The smell of Pack.

A scent he didn't know he was missing until it reached him again.

Erin snickers under his breath, the comfort of Tala's warm scent welcoming. Wait. No. Erin frowns. Victor. His name's Victor. Not Tala.

This is going to take some time getting used to.

He was able to ignore all the memories and thoughts last night. It was chaotic, easier to live in the bliss of a first shift and connecting with a mate, especially after they were a couple rounds in. But after sleeping, the thoughts have settled and grown. They've taken root. The gaps have been filled.

He can't ignore them now. The questions, the confusion. He understands so much more now, but new questions grow in their place. Darker. More jagged and dipped in dread.

How did everything get so twisted over time?

Why did his parents never tell him the truth? Of any of it?

What will Victor do when he learns?

Erin pulls back, turning so he's leaning on his elbows with his stomach flat on the ground. There's a spike behind his eyes, a pressure that builds and curves around his mind. He has a sinking feeling that this headache won't be going away any time soon.

The wind ruffles some of Victor's thick hair across his eyes. Erin reaches over and gently pushes it aside when something shiny glints, catching his gaze. He looks to the side at Victor's arm stretched across his chest and sees the antique blue ring securely on his index finger.

He didn't take it off.

The thought ... irks him, slightly. Not the connection the ring symbolizes to the Pack, but the way it slithers around his finger like a shackle, reminding him of the thick chains in the dungeon.

Except this time, it's not his father who holds the key to unlock the chains.

It's Stella.

Leaning his head on one hand, Erin caresses the ring. It's the same jewel from Tala's Alpha headpiece. That would be how he's able to still wear it even when he shifts—the Moon Goddess's magic still resides within it. Even after all this time ... They hate her now, yet still wear her gift to them. Do they have the jewel from his headpiece? He hopes so, stored away in some special bulletproof case and locked in a safe in New York. One of the artifacts Victor talked about that the original four Packs kept. It was intended for the next heir. For Näy—

"You should take a photo, Mr. Photographer, it'll last longer." Victor's morning voice is raspy, deeper, and rougher than usual. It makes Erin's stomach swoop at the sound of it.

"I will later, don't you worry, Little Wolf." A coy smile pulls gently at his lips, and he lifts his hand to pinch one of Victor's smirking cheeks. "There's just ... a lot of memories I'm trying to make sense of. I have a lot of questions."

"Hmm," Victor's fingers twitch against Erin's ribs, "I bet you do." He reaches across Erin's back, pulling them closer until Erin can comfortably rest his head over Victor's beating heart. His favorite spot. "However, perhaps we should have this discussion clean. What'd ya think?"

Erin crosses his ankles, only then noticing the wetness still coating his thighs and ass, his stomach, and Victor's. It's only half dry. "I didn't realize. I must be used to waking up naked in men's arms, covered in sweat."

"It's not just sweat, Star," Victor says lowly. The muscle under his right eye twitches, smooth skin rippling. "And what men are you referring to?"

Erin laughs, grabbing some of the hair coating Victor's chest and twisting. Victor yelps playfully, smacking Erin's ass in retaliation before leaning forward onto his elbows. He grabs Erin from under the arms, lifting him as he stands until they are pressed chest-to-chest, Erin's arms around Victor's neck and legs locked around his waist. Victor keeps his hands placed firmly on the curve of Erin's ass as he walks toward the lake, kneading the tight muscles gently. Just for that, Erin falls in love with him even more.

The water is cold; goosebumps popping along his skin as Victor carefully walks them into its crystal-clear depths. He was right, with how high the sun is in the sky, it's probably closer to noon, and yet there still isn't much warmth in the air.

"It's stunning here," Erin sighs, content as Victor slowly rubs circles into his skin under the water. His muscles relax instantly, the soreness from having multiple rounds of sex with Victor last night, as well as shifting for the first time, finally rearing its ugly head. He knew it was going to be rough, but he thought he'd have time to at least bathe and change into comfortable clothes, snuggling under Victor's bedsheets before the tight pain pulled at him. He remembers how soft those sheets looked the last time they were in his room.

"It's not like our old tree, but ..." Victor shrugs, nostalgia coating his gaze. He tightens his grip on Erin like he's scared that if he lets go, he'll disappear.

"It's perfect." Erin leans back to glance at Victor's face. The playful smirk drops when a thought comes to him. How many times has Victor run out here since summer started? Was he sitting in the water, praying to the Goddess—who he grew up believing was evil—that Erin wasn't his mate, if only to spare him the pain of a curse he believed them to be under? Or did he lie in the grass, feet dangling over the lake's edge? Alone. Without him. Praying that Erin was his mate, despite the promise of chaos and death, just so that they could spend five minutes together, connected as one.

Erin drops his voice, "I can't believe it, Victor."

"Believe what?" Victor rumbles, the crisp sound echoing around the clearing. Water sloshes as he raises his hand and fiddles with Erin's earlobe.

"That she'd curse us."

"Well, she did," Victor seethes, lowering his hand. The ring catches his eye again. It glints strongly on the water's surface, the light refracting it all around them, making him squint. Perhaps this conversation would be better had in the safety of Victor's room ... or even Erin's.

No. There are too many eyes, too many ears. People will want answers to questions he doesn't even know are *questions* yet. It's early, and he doesn't want to ruin the serenity around them, but he doesn't want to keep any secrets from Victor either. Not after they've finally gotten together.

Waiting. White lies. Family secrets.

That's what ruined them last time.

It's what killed them.

So if this is their chance to try again, he'll take it. He'll do things right this time. No matter how confusing. No matter how perilous. He's a wolf now; stronger, faster.

If push comes to shove, he'll fight ... over and over and over and over again.

But before fists are thrown, words need to be spoken.

Try for peace, that's what She would do.

Erin detangles himself from Victor. The rocks pocking through dirt and sand grind into his flat feet. They ground him.

"Why?" Erin frowns, looking off to the other side of the lake. The sun sparkles across the still water. There's no breeze now, which means there are no dancing trees whooshing to a silent beat. He huffs at the realization that the birds and forest critters have all fallen silent. Even the bluebells around the lake now seem dull and lifeless, like they, too, could hear the seriousness in his voice.

"I don't know, Erin. I died, too!" Victor yells. He expels a long breath, running a hand through his hair, the strands sticking together, now wet.

Erin cocks a brow, taking a step back from Victor. "Mind repeating that sentence?" he suggests, voice cold.

"I'm sorry." Victor looks to the side, pale blue eyes narrowed into slits and shoulders tense. "I just ... I didn't realize our walk down memory lane was going to be so serious."

Erin pinches his lips before inhaling deeply. He counts to three, then releases it, licking his dry lips, forcing them to move. To speak. "I know, my love. But ... things aren't as I remember, and you know more about how much this world's history has changed than I do. I'll need more than a quick lore drop to understand why Hëna and Ylli did what they did."

Victor pokes the inside of his cheek with his tongue and looks down. Erin counts to five before Victor looks up again. His eyes are still narrowed, anger simmering in the corners. But, he's smiling.

"Come on, Star, let's not have this discussion in the lake. You'll catch a chill." He places his hand on Erin's back, leading them to the water's edge. The cold band of the ring sears into his skin through the water. "Unfortunately, we're going to need those shorts now," he grumbles.

"Oh no," Erin taunts.

Victor side-eyes him while climbing out of the water, growling low. A warning. Erin bites his smirk. Victor heads back to the hidden hole by the tree roots, where the trash bag from last night still sits on the ground. By the time Erin climbs out, Victor is standing beside him once more, black shorts held out toward him.

Erin takes them, sliding them over his legs while jutting his chin to the bag Victor is rummaging through. "What else is in there?" he asks.

"Anything a shifter would need," Victor answers, with identical black shorts sitting low on his hips. "Towels, shorts, boxers, soap, pillows—"

"Pillows? Why would a werewolf care or need a pillow?"

"Comfort! Why else?" Victor turns a quizzical brow to Erin. "Besides, who doesn't love a feather pillow when sleeping? We're wild animals, not vampires. Geez."

"Right." Erin rolls his eyes and rakes his fingers along his scalp. A crumpled bluebell falls onto the ground, the tips of his fingers stained blue from the water still sliding along his skin. Blue-tipped arrows. Red blood spilling from torn limbs. He suppresses a shiver, pushing the memories aside and sitting cross-legged on the grass. "Why do you keep that stuff out here?"

"All Packs have hiding holes of necessities around their territory for situations just like this," Victor explains, plopping down next to Erin.

"Oh?" Erin raises a brow. "Are impromptu races in the middle of the night after finding a mate common? I thought I was special."

"You are special, Star." He reaches into the bag and pulls out a small towel. "Which is why I'm not going to let you sit out all day wet and naked. Turn around." He moves his hand in a circular motion.

"We used to sit out in the sun naked all the time," he mutters, moving so he's sitting comfortably in front of Victor as he starts to dry the water from his skin.

"Times have changed, Star." Victor bends, pressing a kiss to the dip in Erin's shoulder before continuing to dry around his hips and stomach. "And last night was your first shift. I tried to massage what I could, but it won't do much, honestly. By tonight, you'll feel like you've been run over by a ten-ton truck."

"I thought that was just the effect of having your huge dick up my ass," Erin teases.

Victor laughs, winking. "Well, there's that too." He continues to pull the soft towel against Erin's chest, neck, and arms. When he's completely dry, Victor turns the towel onto his own skin. Once he's done, Victor pulls Erin toward his chest, and Erin grabs his arms, wrapping them across his stomach. The rumble of laughter in Victor's chest is soothing as Erin tilts his head back into the crook of his mate's neck.

Nervous energy tingles between them.

They can't drag this out anymore.

"Tell me who started this false legend of the curse," Erin asks.

Victor shrugs, the movement jostling Erin. "I don't know. I'd have to check the records again, but it's been spoken for as long as I can remember. Generations, at least."

Erin leans forward. He pulls his knees to his chest and crosses his arms at his ankles. A gust of wind blows across the clearing, carrying the scent of baked food from the distance. The Pack must have the windows open while they cook. He thinks back to what Victor's told him, and what he remembers from his life before. Sometime after they died in the war, wolves split into four Packs, then into fifty-two. But the humans also grew in society, overpowering the wolves. They came out on top while the wolves were forced to hide. To blend in.

But ... what if one of those original four Packs were those from Kazamir's side? Or more wolves who defected afterward? Could they have spun this tale, calling their Goddess a traitor because She forced them into a war? Anger often speaks cold tales in the dark.

There are still gaps missing, pieces of history that must have been lost in translation. By accident? Or on purpose ...

Erin's head spins. He can't believe that Hëna and her husband would turn on them, not after everything. The way she cried for him—the way her husband did—those weren't the eyes of people wanting to spread chaos and destruction.

She came down to save them.

She chose them to help her.

And in return, she *blessed* them, not *cursed* them. She gave them a chance to have it all. So then—

"How long would it take you to go through all the records?" he asks.

"I don't know, a while," Victor sighs. "It'll be hard to look into it from here. All the records are back home, and since these Council Meetings started as a way to make sure all treaties are kept, including wolf kind being kept secret from humans, my brain has been filled with disputes about rules and regulations for weeks. On top of my normal workload." He groans. "I don't know how much more information it can stuff and sort through without exploding. You know, like when you stuff a Mentos into a soda bottle?"

Erin laughs at the image. "Could Ben help?"

Victor stiffens. "He could."

Erin turns around slightly, his left knee lifting to rest on top of Victor's thigh. His mate is looking away, gaze cloudy as he looks out over the water. Erin narrows his eyes.

"You don't want him to help."

"It's not that I don't want him to help, I just—" Victor starts, clicking his teeth together and sighing deeply.

"Just ..." Erin probes.

"I just don't know if I believe that the legend is wrong." Victor steadies his gaze on Erin. "And lately, Ben has been pretty vocal about hinting that maybe the Goddess isn't evil. I know that if I ask him to look into it with us, he'll spend the whole time trying to convince me of that instead. But I just can't shake this feeling that she is, that *someone* is standing against us. Trying to keep us apart. Who else could that be? Maybe they got mad that we died, or maybe something else happened afterward, and we were just the unlucky fools stuck in the way ... I don't know, but someone cursed us. I mean ... we've come back. If that's not a curse, then what is it?"

"A blessing," Erin says, voice strained. "Victor, can't it be a blessing?" Victor rolls his head and parts his lips, but Erin continues, "We've been given a second chance. Born again into a world freer than the last—"

"What, like some Romeo and Juliet fanfiction?" Victor scoffs. "Their death freed their love and all that bullshit you spouted before."

"Victor!" Erin chides. Hurt pushes against his heart. "Seriously?"

Victor tightens his lips. He pulls Erin over his thigh completely, so he sits in between his legs, and rests his head on Erin's shoulder.

"I had dreams about you after we met," Victor admits quietly, breaking the gathering silence.

"You did?" Erin sighs, throwing him the bone. At least he's still talking. At least he hasn't run.

Victor nods. "I was in my room back in New York. When I looked outside my window, I saw a massive golden-eyed wolf at the edge of the forest. I knew the Moon Goddess was showing me you. My mate. The White Wolf." He chuffs. "I was angry at first, really angry. I thought she was mocking me, dangling you in front of my eyes like a carrot. She knew I could never have you, could never *want* to have you. Not with what it would mean for the rest of wolf kind." His voice lowers, one hand rubbing up and down Erin's leg. "The White Wolf, my calamity. Who I now remember has two more names. Nahale, my beloved Star."

Erin's gut tightens into knots. "I was having wolf dreams, too ..." He looks down shyly. "My friends thought it might be some crazy subconscious way of saying I was pent up. Sexually."

"Well," Victor, never breaking eye contact, lowers his voice to a whisper, "not all of my dreams involved you as a wolf."

Erin clenches his hands where they've fallen to rest against Victor's sternum. "Why are you feeling this need to blame The Goddess, Victor?"

Victor flinches.

Erin waits.

"Because I don't want to believe that my Alpha would willingly murder his own family otherwise," he admits. "If Hëna didn't have a hand in twisting their souls, in darkening their minds, then that means they woke up one morning and betrayed the people we are instinctually born not wanting to betray," Victor says, voice tight and strained. "It would mean that what happened with Kazamir happened again."

Erin opens his mouth but closes it again.

What does he say to that?

"Little Wolf." Erin turns around, the breeze flying across the lake cool against his face. He runs his hands up and down his lovers' arms. "Those were two very separate situations."

"Are they?" Victor croaks.

Erin nods. Discontent rumbles through his gut because Victor hasn't realized yet.

He hasn't put the pieces together about who Erin is.

But how would he?

Throughout each piece of history Victor has shared with him, not once has it been mentioned that Stacy and Gray had a child. It makes sense now, Erin realizes, thinking back to the stares he's gotten over the past month. The whispering that would stop as soon as he entered the house to grab some water or use the bathroom. It wasn't because he was a human. It wasn't because he was flirting with Victor. Hell, it wasn't even because Stella had spies watching his every finger twitch.

It was because they knew who he was—some of them, at least. No child ever looks completely like their parents, but there's always some resemblance. And these are wolves. They have sharp eyes. Even sharper noses.

There's only one person he could think of that would wipe his existence from the Pack. One person who would want to keep him away from Victor, not because she knew he was The White Wolf—Victor said wolves don't present until they are at least fifteen, and he hadn't even *shifted* yet—but because she knew the challenge his blood could hold down the line. The challenge to *her* reign. That must be what she wants, to rule over them all. And what better way to get it than through Victor? She has him wrapped tightly around her hand like a leash with no give.

An evil legend with a magical curse that forces the one with the most power to forever be alone lest he kill them all, his soul too kind, too righteous to want that?

Stella sure did hit the jackpot.

It brings a sardonic twist to Erin's lips now. In this life, he's the Pack heir, and Stella's the one who tried to steal his crown.

He twists the ring on Victor's finger as a feeling rumbles under his skin.

Stella must have had a hand in that night. It wasn't a rebellion—it was a coup d'état.

But how?

His temple throbs, and he sags against Victor. He's going to crush all hope of ever trying to convince Victor that the Mother Moon Goddess has always been on their side, because the sad part is, he can't find an argument to defend his parents—either pair. Why would Hëna let Stacy and Gray kill wolves? Did Natalie and John really not know about what was going on?

What *happened* that night?

"There's something else we need to talk about," Erin says quietly.

Victor tilts his head. Listening. Waiting.

Erin takes a deep breath, dislodging the dread from his throat, and sets his face on Victor. "The reason I shifted last night, the trigger that put me in that dream with you, was because Natalie and John told me who my birth parents were."

"Yeah," Victor nods. "At least that's one good thing they've done. You weren't going to believe me about it any time soon."

"That's not what I mean," Erin says. "They told me because they wanted me not to give up on you, on us. They thought it would help me to trust in the connection between us. They didn't mention anything about the coup d'état, though. They didn't seem to know anything about werewolf life at all ..."

"Coup d'état?" Victor crosses his brows. "Okay, I'm missing something here. What happened twenty-one years ago was a rebellion. A mass murder spree. I've explained this to you. Why are you calling it a coup? And why does it matter to you?"

Erin sniffles and licks his lips. He was right when he woke up; that pressure building in his skull is louder now, like a gong continuously being rung with a heavy mallet. He takes a deep breath, willing away the tears lining his eyes that Victor keeps staring at.

"Erin?" Victor bends his head to look into Erin's eyes, lacing their hands together. "You look like you're about to cry, Star."

Erin shakes his head, nose twitching violently in an attempt to keep from running. He stares with blurry vision at the wet spots dripping onto his shorts.

"Erin?" Victor repeats. There's an air of command in his voice, but all Erin hears is the confusion and panic underlining it. "Erin, look at me," Victor demands, louder, fingers gripping his hips hard.

Erin raises his head. When he locks his eyes on Victor, the words stumble over themselves in a rush to get out. "Natalie and John lived in New York before moving down here with me. They lived in Bellmore and were friends with a pair of werewolves. My birth parents weren't some rogue wolves, and they didn't have some secret pregnancy. They were Stacy and Gray Bellmore, Victor."

Victor stills, his face going slack in surprise. Erin squeezes Victor's cold hand, voice hitching as he clarifies, "You said it yourself, back at the gardens, that the elders believed the cursed lovers would be guided by Fate and Instinct into one of the four Packs from the split, that chaos would follow them. But then tell me, what's the chance of all this being a coincidence? Three months after I was born, a coup was thrown, yet we both lived, and I was taken away, raised by our allies. If this were some revenge plot, hidden magic forcing events to play out scene by scene, then why has it taken this long for us to find each other? Why hasn't any other wolf been 'corrupted' after that night?"

"Allies ..." Victor mutters, looking down. He doesn't move for a while, Erin counting the passing seconds with the rapid beating of his heart. When he does finally move, he squeezes Erin's hand firmly, once, before shuffling to the edge of the rock to dip his feet in. Erin's eyes follow the glint of the ring across the grass from Victor twisting it around his finger, the only sign he hasn't frozen into a statue from shock.

He wants to hug Victor from behind. Tell him it will all be ok. Reassure him that whatever blood runs through Erin's veins doesn't change who he is.

Except it does.

Victor lost his parents in this life, just like the last ... all because of him. Because of the people he shares blood with. Because of the people who raised him. Erin caused him pain, forced him to be alone, to bear the responsibility of Alpha.

Again.

Finally, Victor stands and turns to face Erin. The sun over the lake makes him look like a forest God that has just woken from a deep slumber at the bottom of the lake. "Come on, let's head back. I want you to meet everyone, properly this time. As a member of the Pack."

Erin stands quickly, reaching to hold Victor's outstretched hand. He notices it's his left, the one without the Pack ring on it. "Are you ok?"

Victor nods and gathers the towel he used to dry them off with, slinging it over his shoulder as they begin walking back through the dense trees. Sparing a glance at Erin, he chuckles at the disbelief he finds there.

"Ben told me once that the Moon Goddess doesn't make mistakes," he ruffles Erin's thick, short hair, "and while I'm reluctant to agree with him ... I guess, in a way, he was right. She saved you. I can at least thank her for that."

"Even if she only did it so that we could later enact her revenge on all of wolf kind?"

Victor laughs through his nose. "Yeah, even if that's why. I don't understand why she would curse us, but it's like you said, what are the chances of this being a coincidence? If she wanted to destroy us all, why hide you away?" He averts his gaze, fingers twitching against his thigh. "Maybe ... and this is a big maybe ... there is more to this old legend than I know."

Erin wipes his eyes and smiles, his body relaxing at the acceptance in Victor's words. "Now, that wasn't very hard to admit, was it?"

"Why you." Victor drops the towel, and Erin shrieks as he runs away. The act is familiar, a game of tag they used to tease each other with in their past life. They were still kids then, yet the stench of blood and wolfsbane was so familiar to them.

The sounds of the forest flow back as they run around, like it, too, knows the solemn discussion is over. The worst has passed. The breeze carries their laughter across the lake, through the leaves of the flowers, and under the roots of the trees as the sun continues its trek across the horizon. Erin feels a stab of guilt at the trampled bluebells, his twist away from Victor not fast enough. He's wrapped in strong arms and twirled around playfully before being turned. He's face-to-face with his love. His Little Wolf. Victor lifts his hand to Erin, his thumb rubbing over his cheeks lovingly.

"We were always meant to be together, and I won't let anything or anyone tear us apart. We'll settle the rest later and repeat our vows. We'll reforge our marks. So, for now, let's only focus on the present. Deal?"

Erin holds onto Victor's wrists tightly. He's right. They're soulmates, destined ones fated to always find each other. There is still so much left unsaid between them. So much confusion about how this curse that binds them was started—it's so different from what he remembers. The way people talk about the Goddess is so vile now, rage tainting her image distastefully. And her husband is nowhere to be heard from either, which isn't unusual. Erin remembers how he stuck to the shadows, doing his work quietly and diligently. Large brown eyes protecting Her. But He was at least there—the wolves all knew who he was. Even his Father King knew the existence of the God of the Stars. So, how'd he disappear from current werewolf society completely?

Did They have a say in when they were born again? Was it truly a coincidence or not that they were born into the same Pack? They could've lived a life together from their first run, their first steps, their first crawl. Victor would've been there while he was growing in his mother's womb. A comfort, before he even knew what the word meant.

No.

He steels his racing heart. He'll find a way. He'll find the cure.

The true enemy?

He knows exactly who she is.

"Deal." Erin smiles brighter than the sun shining in the sky. There's no magic in any universe that can break the string tying them together. He'll make sure of it this time.

THIRTY

Quite a few people are milling around outside when they get back to the ranch. Erin supposes that's only natural for a pack of wolves on a nice Sunday afternoon ... which he's about to ruin.

How will they react? Will they accept him? Maybe if he were just a rogue wolf. But he's not. He can never be ... not as Victor's mate. Not with Bellmore blood pumping through his veins.

"Oh, no," Erin drawls, pulling on Victor's hand so they stop walking. "I am going to be in so much trouble."

"What? What is it?" Victor cups his cheeks with both palms, eyes wide in worry.

"I left my phone at home ..."

Victor blinks. "Ok."

"Victor," Erin places his hands on his wrists, "I left my phone at home and ran out of the house right after being told that I was a supernatural giant werewolf, proceeded to stay out all night, and now I'm assuming, won't be home until much later this afternoon. It's the weekend. They don't work on the weekends! My parents are going to kill me!"

Victor laughs loudly at the seriousness in Erin's voice, drawing Ben's attention from where he sits with Beatrice on the back porch. They both smile widely at them.

"Stop it! They're going to kill you, too!" Erin shrieks.

"Natalie and John aren't going to kill you, Star."

"How do you know? They used to yell at me all the time when I snuck out with Fletcher."

Victor drops his hands and continues to the house, Erin hot on his heels. "They've probably guessed you've come to see me."

"Still," Erin mumbles, claiming Victor's arm once more as they walk across the grass. Rattling sounds off to his right—a diamondback. He can't see it fully, its scales doing their job of hiding it in the grass. He instinctively growls low, through clenched teeth. The rattling stops. Ah, that's why he constantly saw people walking to the forest without boots on, or any kind of worry about the critters slithering through the soil.

There's nothing bigger than a wolf out here.

"Star." They stop at the edge of the fence line, Victor placing one hand on the warm wood as Ben rises from his seat, leisurely strolling toward them. "You've had almost twenty-two years with them, let me have at least twenty-two minutes with you. Hm?"

"It's been longer than twenty-two minutes ..." he grumbles. Victor gives him a flat stare. "Fine, ok. I'll trust your judgment on this. But at least let me borrow your phone so that they know I'll be home late. Ok?"

"Now that's how you negotiate." Victor peppers his lips with kisses when the sound of clapping reaches them. Ben's standing on the other side of the fence, a proud glint shining in his eyes.

"Oh, what do we have here? Men who have finally stopped being blind, deaf, and all-round hopeless morons?"

"You're hilarious. Now gather everyone out front," Victor instructs, holding out the dirty towel for Ben to take before leaping over the fence. He holds out a hand for Erin, but Erin ignores it with a raised brow. He leaps over the fence quickly, keenly aware of Victor's eyes on him as he does. Victor beams with pride at the display of agility.

Erin shrugs with mock obliviousness. "I'm a photographer, climbing into hard positions is a needed skill."

"Oh, I'm sure," Victor agrees. Ben sighs.

"I'm going to go gather everyone now, while you two ..." Ben gestures between Erin and Victor with the dirty towel held between two dainty fingers, "fantasize about things I don't want to think about. And maybe run a bar of soap over yourselves beforehand. You reek of cum."

"That was kind of the point. How else am I meant to scent him?" Victor rolls his eyes.

"By rubbing his skin like a normal person, you idiot," Ben grits through clenched teeth.

"Oh, we rubbed skin all right." Victor winks. Ben blanches. Erin laughs under his breath. He grabs Victor's hand, freezing when the back door creaks open. Ben isn't that fast of a walker, even if he is a werewolf, and Beatrice hasn't moved from her seat.

"Victor, honey, what's going on?" Stella's hair is pulled into a messy bun, the thin strands barely being held together with a black scrunchy. She's smiling uncertainly, her loud voice ringing out across the ranch and drawing the attention of everyone near them. He senses an underlying note of caution tinting her voice and shuffles closer to Victor instinctively. The way her squinty green eyes bore into him reminds him so much of Kazamir.

Erin feels like he's a type of new species being inspected under a microscope as every pair of eyes swivel toward him. They know. They can smell it. A part of him wonders who they see reflected in his eyes first—his mother or his father?

Anxiety flickers across his soul, but it's not his. He focuses on it. Pulls at it with his teeth. Inspects it.

The Pack bond.

It's been so long since he's felt any semblance of this connection with others.

But, it's different than before. The bond the Goddess placed on him was just that—one given. One accepted in return. This, though, he was born into. These people ... he can't ignore them now.

And they can't ignore him.

"Head to the front and I'll explain," Victor commands, ignoring her question with a grin as he pulls Erin across the yard and into the house.

Beatrice stands as they pass her, nodding to them. "Congrats, Alpha. Erin."

"Oh, thanks," Erin says. That's the first time they've spoken; her voice exactly what he was expecting. Delicate and soft. Polite, with an undercurrent of tease. She may have called Victor her Alpha, but she was congratulating him as family. He wants to speak to her more, pick her brain on the kind of man his mate was growing up. But said mate pulls him away.

The kitchen and dining room are already devoid of people. Ben works quickly. He must have snuck inside when Stella came out and quickly gathered everyone toward the front.

Victor gets them some water from the fridge, and Erin looks out the giant kitchen window. The white lace curtain is already raised, the corner crumpled like someone was standing there, watching ... waiting ... Wolves exchange curious glances as they make their way around the side of the house, noses raised high. Sniffing. He dares a glance at Stella and sees her standing rigid next to Beatrice, a worried scowl marring her face like a nasty scar. Beatrice places her hands on her mother's shoulder and turns her around, soft smile reassuring, before following the others.

Frowning, Erin turns and heads to the island where Victor is, chugging the water at a concerning speed.

"Ready for the new and improved werewolf house tour?" Victor wipes his mouth and points to the second glass of water on the benchtop. Erin takes it, relishing in the feeling of ice water cooling his throat, and nods. Hopefully it won't take too long. As much as he wants to relish this moment and get to know each wolf here, his blinks are getting slower, and his eyelids are getting heavier. It's becoming harder to keep his head up high and his legs walking straight.

"Excellent!" Victor takes both glasses and places them in the sink. He rushes back over and laces his fingers through Erin's. "This way."

Erin laughs as Victor shows him around everywhere. He's familiar with a lot of the rooms on the first level, having seen them upon arrival five weeks ago, and some he glimpsed briefly when he was taken to Victor's room to change after his fall, but the rest of the rooms are spectacular. There's the training room, as Victor calls it, opposite the office at the front of the house, where Erin has caught Victor spending most of his time working and planning. There's also a gathering room beside the training room with a massive TV taking up one whole wall, a complete bar with shelves of what smells like very expensive alcohol opposite it, and even a popcorn maker with candy baskets beside it. That makes Erin gasp, his jaw dropping and lips parting in shock.

"So, next movie night at the Lovelace Ranch then," he utters. Victor laughs beside him. "I'm serious, Little Wolf. Fletcher and Layla would shit themselves if they saw this."

"Your friends are always welcome in our home, Star." Victor kisses Erin's hand. *Our home.*

He shows Erin the healers' room next, the massive room taking up most of the second floor—they must have knocked some walls down to make that possible—with tons of herbs and flowers releasing an aroma Erin can identify as medicinal. A second open kitchen sits in the room beside it, with a view of what looks like a kids' game room, the space littered with toys and electrical cords. Victor calls it the 'Young Den' where the teens usually congregate, depending on the time of the day.

And, of course, there are the bedrooms. Lots and lots of bedrooms litter the halls from the second to the fourth floors. Erin knew there were quite a few people in Victor's Pack, and not even the whole Pack is here, but seeing the evidence right in front of him is a bit overwhelming. At least fifty people are gathering outside right now to listen to Victor explain how Erin is his mate, and that's not including any of the Packs that have arrived early and are lurking around, camping in the woods. Fifty people whom Erin will be responsible for now, whom he has to impress and befriend, alongside Victor.

And he can't even control his claws from elongating during sex.

His stomach churns, nausea making his dry mouth drier.

"Now, you already know this room," Victor whispers next to Erin's ear, the brush of his lips making him shiver, forcing him out of his stumbling thoughts. Once his eyes adjust, he rolls them dramatically and leans his hip against the doorframe. The room where everything started. The bed looks as soft as he remembers.

"What do you feel like wearing?" Victor walks to the closet.

"I'm not picky," Erin replies. He spies Victor's phone on his desk. Grabbing it, he types in his mom's phone number to quickly send her a text. Only when the phone dings, signaling his apologetic message was sent successfully, does he relax. He doesn't wait to see if she replies, instead placing the phone back down and walking to the balcony, sliding the dark green curtain aside slightly to peek through the crack.

A lot of wolves mingle. He recognizes most. Matt Harkin is there, the wolf who was talking about food recipes with his mom. But he can't seem to remember the other dark-skinned older man standing close to Stella, nor the blonde man with the round glasses. Who are they? They look mean, lips thin and tight, eyes harsh and narrowed. Alphas from the Packs that came early, maybe? If they're gossiping through clenched teeth with Stella …

Two pairs of eyes swivel toward him. Emerald. Pale green. They flash.

"Erin?"

He drops the curtain. Victor is dressed in fresh clothes, his hair smooth now like he ran a comb through it, and a pair of white slides on his feet. A new pair of jeans and green t-shirt are being held out toward him expectantly, black Crocs ready by the door.

"Oh, thanks." Erin dresses quickly while Victor runs out of the room. He returns a moment later with a wet washcloth, wasting no time to run it over Erin's face, using his now damp fingers to smooth back his hair.

"There. Ready," Victor beams. Erin gulps, forcing a smile as he laces his fingers with Victor's. They walk downstairs and out the front door together.

"Everyone!" Victor's deep voice booms out across the yard before the door has a chance to swing shut. "Thank you all for joining me out here so suddenly."

Erin shivers. *Alpha*, a voice whispers across his mind. He remembers hearing it as Nahale before the main battle. It had such a visceral response on him then, just as it does now. Without a shred of doubt, he'd do anything Victor asked if that voice was used. The power in the tone alone leaves no room for disrespect.

"I know you all must be confused, especially with Erin standing here beside me, on a weekend no less." Victor raises their clasped hands with chuckles. "I won't mince my words. Erin is my mate, The White Wolf."

Silence.

Erin counts at least ten people who are holding their breaths, their faces confused on whether they should turn red at the lack of oxygen or pale at the prospect of what Erin's identity means. And they haven't even gotten to the part about him being a Bellmore.

"I know what finding my mate entails, and I'm glad none of you hide your scent from me." Victor looks at each wolf in the eye. "It's ok to be scared. To be angry. But trust me when I say that I *understand*. I tried to deny it. But, I could no longer. It was painful, for both me and Erin. Whatever happens next, I know that we can get through it together. We are Pack. We are the Lovelace Pack. One of the strongest across the country. We didn't break before, and we won't break now."

Stella takes a step forward, arms open wide. "Oh, congratulations, Honey." She engulfs Victor in a hug, squeezing his shoulders gently. Pride glimmers across her eyes and in her smile. "Everyone!" She turns to face the crowd. "Everyone, please. Your doubt is strong through the bond, as is your fear about what this will mean.

Like our Alpha has said, we all know the legend, what the elders have written. But we have trusted in Victor so far. Look at how much good he has done for our Pack, only four years into leading us as Alpha." She turns back to Victor, to Erin, reaching out to grab both of their hands.

He clenches his teeth when her nails prick his skin.

"We must take this as a good omen!" she announces to them all. "The Black Wolf and The White Wolf have found each other. It took a while for Fate and Instinct to guide them together, so let us trust in them. That the length of their time apart was a showing of their strength to fight against Her evil magic. Let us believe that our Alpha, and now, our Luna, will find a way to break this eons long curse. TO ALPHA VICTOR AND ERIN!"

"TO ALPHA VICTOR AND LUNA ERIN!"

Cheers ring around them as wolves run to give them hugs.

"Welcome, Erin!"

"Congrats, Erin."

"He's going to be the death of us all ..."

"Shhh, he can hear you! He's wolf."

"I always knew you smelled a bit off. That must've been the Moon Goddess's magic! She was trying to hide you. But our Alpha has a great sense of smell. No one can hide from him for long, that's why he always wins when we play hide-and-seek."

"Glad you found your way to us."

"God, those eyes."

"I know. So much like his fath—"

"The spitting image of her, though."

"Welcome home, Luna Erin."

Erin looks down, brows flinching. A little girl stands in front of him, her bright red hair braided back. He remembers her—the one from the first day he arrived at the ranch. Victor bends down, scooping her into his arms.

"Little Red, you be good to my mate now, you hear?" He glances at him, jostling the girl in his arms and making her squeal. The little girl nods, tapping Victor's shoulder as she leans down to whisper into his ear.

"I told you I had a feeling about him." She grins wide, patting Victor's hair.

Victor bites his smile. "Yes, good job, Red." He laughs, placing her back onto the ground. Erin watches, eyes soft as she bounds away.

He wanted to be scared, to be anxious of what all this would mean for them as a Pack. His arrival would give Stella the perfect excuse in case anything went bad later down the track. A justification. An 'I told you so' from the very beginning. If the Pack didn't accept him now, it would hurt less later when they rejected him. But they have accepted him, even without knowing the whole truth. Even being scared of the potential he holds. He's never felt so light-hearted and happy before.

Then Stella pulls them to the side.

Erin lifts his head, inner guard raised high. Despite himself, nervous energy flutters in his stomach. Victor engulfs Stella in a hug once again, and she smiles lovingly, but Erin can see the tightness in her lips and the calculating glint in her eyes. He gulps.

Oh, she's livid.

Stella holds her arms out to Erin, too, hugging him so tightly his joints pop. "Erin, dear, will you need help moving your stuff, or will you be selling most of it? New York is quite far. Oh, I know a bunch of people at the universities, too. We will need to start now on the transfer, with summer halfway over. Do you have a portfolio?" Her thick lashes flutter as she blinks, waiting for him to respond.

Erin's brows furrow, but he forces himself to smile. "What do you mean?"

Stella flinches, shocked. "Why, you can't expect to live away from Victor, Erin. You're mates! I know in human society partners can often live apart, but we are wolves. Separate living is not of our way."

"That's not—"

"We can sort Erin's stuff out later. No point in bringing any of it to the ranch when we'll be gone again soon," Victor jumps in, cutting him off.

Erin presses his lips together, rolling his tongue over his teeth. "You know, I can't just abandon my family and my life in Texas," he whispers into Victor's ear.

"We can talk more about it later. Add it to the list of everything else. No need to rush anything now." Victor laughs, raising Erin's knuckles to his lips to give it a quick peck.

Erin forces a smile, ignoring the sense of rising dread in his stomach. "Yeah, ok."

Deep breath, he reminds himself as Victor reaches over to give him a side hug. He doesn't want to squash Victor's high. This is something he's been worrying about since he was thirteen, so now is not the time to cause a scene. That's probably what Stella wants anyway.

Looking at her, nodding toward him with a smug smile, he knows it's true. She's wants him to freak out, to mess up, to act human in a pack of wolves so that she can make an example of him.

He raises his chin, forces a smile at her, wraps his arm around Victor's waist, and pulls him close.

Some might find it difficult to wrap their heads around, a life suddenly being turned upside down like this. One second, he was a normal university student, taking photos of pretty sunsets, hanging out with his friends, partying, and helping his parents with their landscaping business during the week. The next, he's able to transform into a white wolf at free will. The pressure and status of Luna thrust onto his shoulders.

His neck hurts, but not from the whiplash. His shoulders stand straight and strong.

Prince to Luna.

Human to Wolf.

They are not so vastly different at all.

He has watched these games unfold before; he was forced to take part in them. He was too weak then, despite his status, to speak up. To make his one play on the game field. He had learned the etiquette of high society before pivoting, learning of Pack, back when it was one. However, he was not given the chance to find his footing until it was too late.

So this? This is easy.

Stella's nose twitches, her lips trying oh-so hard not to snarl with Victor so close by.

Wherever She is now, whatever Her intention was, Erin finds he doesn't care in this moment because his memories as Nahale might have just given him what he needs to beat Stella at this age-old game.

He smirks.

Checkmate, bitch.

THIRTY-ONE

Natalie and John never replied to Erin's text message from Victor's phone. Erin was glad for it.

When Victor dropped him home after a long night of feasting and mingling with his new family, the house was quiet. Dark. Asleep. Fear took control of him, instead leading him to tiptoe to the fridge, pour a glass of fresh iced tea, and scurry into his room. He was far too scared, and drained, to wake them and face their judgment.

He didn't know what to say to them. He still doesn't. Does he jump right in, revealing all he knows about the curse the wolves think their Patrion Goddess cast on them? Does he tell them about the coup d'état twenty-one years ago, about his assumption of Stella's involvement?

Erin rolls over in bed, ignoring his friends' questions about why he ghosted them on going to the movies yesterday, and sends Victor a text message.

> **STAR:** I'm skipping morning walk. Figured I should talk with my parents … I can't ignore them forever. Maybe I can get more answers too?

His phone vibrates on his chest. Victor didn't take long to respond.

> **LITTLE WOLF:** Good luck.

Erin smiles at the frowning smiley face emoji and glowing white heart. Who knew the human body could experience so much affection and devotion from another person and still have room to send the same back?

Feeling as light as a feather, Erin walks downstairs to find his parents already eating breakfast at the small round dining table. When they see Erin, they freeze. John slowly lowers his coffee mug to the table as Natalie rises from her seat.

"Well?" she asks, brows pinched inward.

Erin lowers his head, hiding his impish grin from his mother's probing eyes. The tile is cold when he walks into the kitchen, meaning the air conditioner must already be on. Today will be a scorcher if his parents are trying to cool down the house this early. Or maybe that's what they're used to ... living up north in New York. He can only imagine how long it took them to get used to the dry heat in Texas.

"Oh, Erin," Natalie sighs sadly. He catches them exchanging sympathetic glances, mistaking his shaking shoulders for crying instead of laughing.

"I'm okay." Erin grabs a plate and croissant, taking his time spreading butter and Nutella on it before turning to face his parents. "I shifted into a giant white wolf and met with Victor. We're together now. Like, officially. Boyfriends. Mates. We're dating." He doesn't try to hide his happiness.

Natalie gasps, nearly tripping over her feet as she rushes to squeeze him in a bear hug, while John jumps from his seat with a whoop.

"Oh, I am so happy for you, cub!" Natalie sighs in relief. Tears well in the corners of her light eyes, causing Erin's lips to pull down in guilt. He knows how much it means to her—to both of them—that Victor found him. That he found Victor. It wasn't on purpose, separating him from the rest of his Pack. They did everything they could to protect him. To keep him safe.

Waiting.

Waiting.

Waiting.

"Ah-ha!" John strides over, gathering the two of them in his arms and lifting, spinning in a quick circle. "I knew it! See, Wife, I told you! True love always wins, even for the wolves!"

"Yes, I never said I didn't believe you," Natalie laughs, wiping away her tears as she gazes at her son. "I have eyes, too, you know."

"Mom, Dad ..." Ein's voice is thick. He grabs hold of both their hands. There's so much he wants to say to them. These people gave up so much for him, moving halfway across America and to a small country town, no less. Raising a baby is a lot for even expecting parents to handle. So, the fact that they took him so suddenly with no hesitation and kept him safe all this time ...

No. They were already mixed up in this world. From the very beginning. Even then ... even before.

He could never be more proud and grateful to call them his mom and dad.

Which is why he can't tell them.

They can't know he remembers a life from before this—a life as a human prince and a gory war that ended with immense pain on both sides—because he wasn't ever meant to remember. Neither he nor Victor was. He realizes it now, looking at both of them. The relief that pours, sweet like the biscuits fresh from the oven. The reason they didn't mention the curse, the reason they didn't say anything about how or why the coup d'état started, is because they don't know. They,

Natalie and John, the human landscapers who accidentally befriended a werewolf Alpha, don't know what goes on in this ancient werewolf world.

Ok.

It's like a secret his soul is whispering as Nahale's soft golden eyes fill his mind.

Hëna's tears roll thickly down blood-stained cheeks as the sun sets behind Ylli, who is kneeling to her left. The pain they were in. He can't put his parents through that. He doesn't *want* to put them through that.

"Thank you," he whispers to them. "For everything … just …" He shakes his head. "Thank you."

John grins widely and nods, while Natalie smiles softly. "Stacy and Gray would be so proud of you," she announces with pride.

"Heh." Erin blinks, stepping away from the two of them.

If that is how She wishes to participate, the role He wants to play in this game, then he will respect it. They choose to stand back and watch this time, so he will let them. The past is best left in the past. He will follow their guidance and find out what went wrong. They have never led him astray before. So why would they now?

"I'll get dressed and then we can head off to the ranch. There's still lots of work to be done before the contract ends." Erin reaches for his breakfast when a knock rings out.

"I'll get it," John says. He hands a tissue to Natalie before walking to the door. Erin leans against the counter and peels a piece of his croissant off to eat when his heart starts beating wildly. Sandalwood and leather waft into the house.

"Look who I found," John sings as he walks into the kitchen with a blushing Victor.

"Hi, sorry to intrude …" Victor's voice is rough as he rubs the back of his neck, shoulders raised high, and one hand holding his bike helmet. He gazes at Erin expectantly. Questioningly. Erin shakes his head, and Victor's shoulders drop. "I was wondering if I could borrow Erin for the day."

"Oh, absolutely!" Natalie all but shouts. She gathers up the dirty dishes and places them in the sink while John grabs his car keys off the ceramic bowl beside Erin. "You two can hang out here for the day, it'll be quieter than the ranch. I know better than to separate newly mated werewolves."

"What? Wait, first, we haven't mated yet, like officially." Erin tears his eyes away from Victor, pinning them on his mother. He doesn't know how much Stacy would have told Natalie about how mates work, but regardless, that is not a conversation he wants to get into with the woman who raised him. "But what about work?"

"Don't mind that." John claps Victor on the back, making him stumble a bit before heading to the front door. "I'll call Fletcher to come over and help. I'm sure if he's free he'll like the workout. And there'll still be plenty of time for you to make up for it. Like removing all this monkswood from around the house. I suppose we won't be needing that anymore, now that you've shifted. Finally. There's no need to hide when we have big, scary wolves around to protect you!"

Natalie swats him on the arm, big green tote bag slung over her shoulder as she walks out of the house. "Have fun!" she calls, tying her red bandana over the top of her head. John winks before closing the door behind him.

Erin waits until he hears the rumble of the garage door close as their old truck drives down the smooth street.

"You're wearing the shirt," he says to Victor.

"Hm?" Victor looks down as he places his helmet on the table, the words 'Howl at the Haters' staring up at him in amusement. "Ah, yes. Well, you picked it out. I went back this morning and bought it."

Erin snorts, stuffing more of his croissant into his mouth. "You hungry?"

"Famished," Victor answers with a sassy sigh.

Erin rolls his eyes and opens the pantry door. "We have cereal, croissants, fruit ... What do you feel like?"

"Is Erin Storm on the menu?" Victor leans against the counter and crosses his arms. Mischief itself clings to him like a second skin.

"Hold your horses, cowboy Loki. I just woke up." Erin closes the pantry door with a thud and glares at Victor. There's hardly any heat behind it, though, as his body warms in other areas against his will.

Victor snickers in victory. Erin suppresses his groan. Of course Victor can smell it in the air.

"I actually came here on official Pack business." Reaching over, Victor grabs Erin's croissant and takes a massive bite.

"Oh?" Not breaking eye contact, Erin leans forward, taking a bite of the croissant still captured in Victor's lips. He relishes the way Victor's blush darkens from embarrassment into desire when he uses his thumb to push some Nutella into his mouth.

"Yeah," Victor's voice cracks. He clears his throat and gulps before speaking again with a clearer voice. "I thought, with your parents being gone, we could get a head start on this whole curse business."

Erin's stomach swoops. That's right, they can still access their records in the office without involving them further.

"I thought you wanted to wait until later, after the Council Meeting, for all that?"

"I did." Victor nods. He steps back, crossing his ankles as he leans back against one of the dining chairs. "I was talking to Stella about it last night, about why Natalie and John told you now—"

"You told her!"

"Not everything!" Victor raises his hands, fingers splayed out wide in defense against Erin's frown. "I just told her how they told you they adopted you in New York and thought you were a werewolf based on your ... genetic enhancements ... and how that pushed you into accepting what I've been trying to tell you for the past, what, month now? I didn't say anything about Stacy and Gray."

"Victor," Erin sighs, a hand rising to rub at his temples.

Victor rolls his eyes. "I couldn't not say anything, Star."

Yes, you could've.

"She's my aunt, she's on our side."

Yep. Sure.

"She's looking out for us and trying to help us figure all this out too, in the best way she knows how."

That's totally what she's doing.

"Anyway, Stella said that it was suspicious that Natalie and John chose now to reveal new information to you. She thinks they were compelled by the Goddess's magic." Victor gives him a look at that, one that's full of amusement, saying, 'if only she knew the truth.' "And I'm inclined to agree with her. So," he slaps his thighs and stands straight, snatching the rest of Erin's Nutella croissant off its plate, "let's rummage through your parents' office. Shall we?"

"All right." Erin sucks on his cheek. "But first, can we do something else?"

Victor's big blue eyes sparkle. "What do you have in mind, Star?" he whispers into Erin's hair. Erin relaxes into the hug as he wraps his arms around Victor's broad shoulders. He didn't realize how much he missed Victor until he saw him walk into the kitchen. It was only one night; there had been countless before then. Years. But one night apart after letting his wolf out of its cage was all it took for him to understand how hard it is to be apart.

Victor noses along his chin, pressing soft kisses along his skin. When he reaches Erin's lips, he parts them, allowing Victor to explore his mouth the way he wants. He tastes like mint and Nutella.

And promise.

Victor takes a step, trapping Erin against the counter. Erin tangles his hands in the front of his mate's shirt as Victor plays with the skin along his spine, right above the waistband of his pants. He tilts his head, giving Victor deeper access, his back arching off the counter when—

ACHOO.

Erin laughs. He grabs a tissue, wiping at Victor's nose. "How about we start by removing all this poison around the house, like my dad said."

"Ah." Victor rubs at his nose. "Yes, good idea. Where are the gloves kept?"

THIRTY-TWO

"There's nothing here," Victor sighs, leaning back in the large, thick desk chair.

The day's almost over, a good chunk of the morning spent carefully riding the property of wolfsbane. He knows his dad was only kidding; had they left it, his parents would have done it themselves. But he didn't want them to suffer any longer. Just having to sleep with the pungent stench of the flowers burning his nose for one night was enough to make him feel sick. He couldn't even spray his usual cologne without sneezing and feeling his skin tingle.

His parents have been living with that for over two decades?

Enough was enough.

It was time he gave back to them.

"We could ask Ben," Erin suggests, for the millionth time. He's on the floor of the office, flipping through old books from the small bookcase by the door. There are only two more left from the 854 that were scattered about—the ones from the library room included—he has to go through. And they are no closer to figuring out who started the twisted curse of their wolves than they were when the day started.

Erin's starting to think that's a good thing. It means Hëna and her husband didn't have anything to do with the legend starting. A wolf from one of the Packs must have spread the word. They *aren't* cursed.

Victor thinks it's proof that they are.

It's starting to annoy Erin.

"Nope, not doing that," Victor sings. He's still at the desk, scrolling through the files on the desktop, despite just saying there's nothing to be found.

Scratch that. It's starting to piss him off.

Erin closes the book with a thud, tossing it onto the stack by his feet. It misses, hitting the edge and causing the whole pile to fall across the dark hardwood floor. He groans, falling back against the floor, his arms spread out beside him. At least the mystery of why this room, why the artifacts inside, always felt so familiar to him has been solved.

"I don't know why you'd think there'd be anything on there to begin with. My dad's the least tech-savvy person I know."

"You're the one who said to be thorough in our search, Star."

"Which is why I'm saying we should ask for Ben's help."

"Oh my, are we having our first fight?" Victor rolls to the side of the desk, long fingers covering his mouth in shock.

Erin's face flushes, and he stands. "I'm going to shower. I smell like ancient dust mites."

Victor stands. "Oh, good idea. I'll joi—"

"No. You don't want help, then you're going to stay here like a good Alpha and put everything back where it belongs so that my parents don't know we were in here. Alone." Erin points to Victor, then to the pile of books and old landscaping files from the wooden filing cabinet strewn across the floor.

Victor opens his mouth to speak, then shuts it again just as quick. His mouth pulls inward, cheeks puffing like a blowfish as he contemplates Erin's command.

Looking at the large window to his right, the black curtains pulled across, his eyes widen. Ponting to them, no, the darkening sky filling its frame, with smug lips, he shrugs. Erin lowers his head. He points to the lamp by the filing cabinet, miming pulling the string to turn it on.

"Fine." Victor plops back down onto the chair, deflated. "You're lucky you're cute when you boss me around. I wouldn't let you do it otherwise."

"Really," Erin scoffs. He begins to walk out of the office when he changes his mind, heading to where Victor sits. He leans down, kissing the top of Victor's head with a smile. "I highly doubt that, Little Wolf."

Victor grumbles, smacking Erin's ass as he jogs away. Just as he reaches the second floor, his phone rings. A picture of three human shadows, two of them holding up peace signs, stares back at him. He smiles, accepting the video call.

"Mind telling me why I spent all day helping your parents dig holes, plant flowers, and lay stones, my good sir?" Fletcher asks. His fake posh British accent makes Erin laugh. He flicks on his bedroom light.

"I stayed home today."

A gasp. "Mr. Lovelace tis there? Ravishing you under the bedsheets! The mother was right!" Fletcher flops back onto his mattress, the towel around his head from his shower sliding off. He lifts his neck to fix it. "Scandalous."

"Yeah, well ..." Erin lifts a brow. Fletcher smirks, lips parted to speak when Layla joins the call.

"I do wonder if it's healthy to constantly be glued to your phone, boys," she teases. Her face shakes on the screen as she tries to balance her phone on the arm of the couch. "What are we talking about?"

"Erin's sex life, apparently."

"Again? Isn't there anything else interesting to watch?"

"I'm hanging up." Erin flips them both off before fixing his phone against the wall on one of the shelves in his closet.

"No, you're not," Fletcher sings, eyes crinkling. "You're going to tell us all about the fact that you're now dating Victor."

"ERIN!" Layla squeals.

"I want to see a ring!" Fletcher declares. "Show me your hands, cowboy!"

Erin howls in laughter, the sound bubbling from deep in his belly as he gathers his pajamas. "What the fuck? I'm not engaged." He tilts his head to the side in mischievous contemplation. "Yet."

Layla squeals again while Fletcher sits up. Leaning back, he balances his phone on his knees before clapping slowly with a look of deep respect.

"But yes, Victor and I are dating," Erin clarifies quickly before they can voice any more wild ideas.

"Oh, my Lord, I am so happy for you, Erin!" Layla says breathlessly.

Fletcher hums in agreement. "Yeah man, seriously, jokes aside, congrats. You deserve it."

Erin raises his shoulders, embarrassment creeping in as he moves down the hall to the bright, yellow-painted bathroom. He feels his lungs loosen as he inhales deeply. He didn't realize how important his friends, his family—his *Pack*—opinion was to him until he saw the overjoyed smiles on their faces and heard the pride in their voices.

He wants to tell them about the wolves. He wants to show them what he looks like, his white coat and golden eyes. Let them feel his wet nose as he pokes at their arms and legs. Swim with Fletcher in the lake. Model for Layla's photographs. Talk with them about what the dreams meant. How he finally, *finally*, found Victor again.

Later.

"Thank you," Erin says between giggles. "I owe it all to you two, really."

"Aw, Fletcher, look," Layla coos, playing with some strands of hair falling over her shoulder. "He got a man on his arm and now he's all mushy and cute."

"Wait, incoming thought. How's that going to work?" Fletcher suddenly asks. Erin places his phone on the countertop, next to the potted fern.

"What do you mean, how's it going to work?" Erin asks, tilting his head. "You've had girlfriends before. You know how dating works."

"I think he means, like, how long is this going to go on for?" Layla explains. "Victor is from New York and here for the summer. Only the summer."

"I don't like how you've emphasized 'only,' Lay." Erin throws his clothes on the toilet seat.

"So, after that, is he going to stay here and live with you, or are you going to drop out and follow him?" She shrugs her shoulders. "What's going to happen next?"

Later. Later.

Erin crosses his arms with a frown. His tongue peeks out, licking along his lips as he takes a deep breath. "Does where anyone is going to live matter right now? We literally just started dating yesterday, all that stuff can be figured out later."

"Transferring mid-year—fuck, transferring right before your final year will be tough, dude." Fletcher shrugs the towel off his head, swatting his fingers through his stringy locks before leaning against his metal headboard.

Stella's high-pitched voice laughs along Erin's neck.

"You think my grades aren't good enough to get me into a university in New York?"

Fletcher's brows crease. Shock. Hurt. "That's not what I said ..."

"We're just asking you to consider how serious you are about this relationship," Layla clarifies. Her blue eyes are hard.

"I'm a twenty-one-year-old male!" Erin cries, throwing his hands up in the air and rolling his eyes. His fingers curl. "So what if I want to fuck around with my ma—a hot CEO? Isn't that on like, some bucket list? 101 things to do before you kick it over or something?"

"Yeah, you're twenty-one and an adult in your final summer before your final year at university," Layla says firmly. She stops playing with her hair. "You'll be twenty-two in a few months. Then twenty-five. And twenty-seven. Thirty. You need to be thinking long-term."

"Who says I'm not?"

"You! Dickwad, that's what we're asking!"

"You sound like a mother, Layla."

"Whoa—"

"Good! Where is yours? What has she had to say about this?"

"Ok, guys—"

"She actually approves of Victor and me. Why do you think she left him alone with me all day?"

Layla huffs. "She tell you where the condoms are left, too?"

"Why are you making this out to be a summer fling?" he snarls.

"Because that's all you've ever had. Toxic boyfriend after toxic boyfriend."

"Both of yo—"

"So what, that automatically makes this one, too?"

"Well, is it?" she demands.

"Victor's not like that. I was going to explain it all to you before you jumped down my throat, asking all these irrelevant quest—"

"They aren't irrelevant, and ignoring them won't make them go away, Erin!" Layla yells. "This is reality, not some fantasy novel."

"ENOUGH!"

Fletcher's face is twisted in a complicated waltz of pain and rage. His chest moves rapidly, at the bottom of the screen. "What has gotten into—"

Erin growls loudly, his lips curled back over his bared teeth. They elongate, just slightly. His friends flinch, and he relishes the satisfaction coursing through his mind. The power. The authority. The tears that pool in Layla's deep brown eyes. The panic set firmly in the line of Fletcher's lips.

"Why can't you just be fucking happy for me? You're always telling me to let go and live in the moment and get laid and all that. So now that I actually have found someone I want to spend my forever with, who yes, I'd transfer universities for, no matter how difficult, you change your minds and tell me to return to the sad, gloomy, lost man I once was."

"Erin—" Fletcher starts.

"No." He hangs up.

Later. Later. Later.

"VICTOR!"

First it was Stella doing a complete 180 and assuming he was going to abandon his life in Texas to become a member of the Lovelace Pack, and now his supposed best friends, his family, are assuming he's going to abandon Victor the second summer is over. Or that Victor would abandon him.

Is that what they think about their love? Is it so trivial to them?

Do they not have any faith in him?

Waiting.

Waiting.

Waiting.

Erin throws his phone onto his bed before stomping down the stairs.

"Star?" Victor is waiting at the bottom of the steps. "What's wrong?"

"I have a headache."

"Not enough water," he suggests slowly, eyes careful as they track him across the kitchen.

Yeah, that, or in-between looking for an alternative reason why his birth parents decided to go on a murder spree, and Victor filling his head with an abundance of werewolf knowledge, he's just been yelled at by the people who mean the most to him.

Shit, did Victor hear any of it?

"Maybe. Is the office clean?"

Waiting. Waiting. Waiting. He's been waiting for so long and didn't even realize it. There's no way he's giving up this life now. This freedom. This gift.

Victor nods. "You didn't shower." It's not a question, but Erin hears it as one. Another. Fucking. Question.

They've had all day to talk about future plans. To ask questions. Instead of showing off the tiny scar on his pinkie from the time he and Ben managed to sew a sheep costume in under fifteen minutes for Alpha Reed's son to wear, bleating across the lawn at one of the meetings, they could've been talking about what's going to happen after the Council Meeting at the end of summer.

"Nope. I want to go to the ranch. I'll shower there if you think I smell so bad."

A muscle jumps in Victor's jaw.

Yes, they only just started dating in the eyes of the humans, so it's not like he's expecting a proposal. But they're mates, they're fated. *Bound*. They're going to be together forever. Is it that unusual for Erin to want to live his life happily doing what he loves while being surrounded by the people he loves?

Why is everyone doubting and ignoring him?

"Your parents aren't back yet."

"Don't care." Erin grabs Victor's helmet from where it's still placed on the kitchen table, pushing it into Victor's chest. He stumbles.

"Star. How about I stay here instead ... I'm sure they won't mind."

"No. I want to get out." It's too cramped here. Too many memories. As much as he would love for Victor to spend the night, he knows Stella would take notice. That's one fire he doesn't want to go near. Not yet. "Let's go."

He can't be here, can't see the photos on the wall. Looking at their faces. The sleepover forts on the couches in the living room. Layla burning her hand on the stove when John was teaching them how to make soup. Playing cops and robbers in the backyard.

His first boyfriend. What he gave that guy. The tears he shed after, and the ice cream they brought over.

Rinse. Repeat.

Fletcher's girlfriend. Trying to explain to him why she broke up with him after two weeks. Laughing that he didn't understand. Frowning when he finally did and cried.

Rinse. Repeat.

Layla's declaration as she stood in the kitchen, proclaiming that when the time was right, her knight in shining armor would appear, so they hadn't fear. They never did.

Victor stays silent as Erin slips his socked feet into a pair of sneakers. Erin opens the door, not waiting for Victor to put his shoes on or grab his keys before he's striding down the driveway and hooking a leg over the sleek black bike. Keys are tucked safely into the front pocket of his jeans. His house keys. Gently, Victor's helmet is placed over Erin's head.

Victor leans his forehead against the closed screen of the helmet. "Hold onto my chest tightly and pinch my thighs if you need anything. Even with my hearing, it'll still be hard to hear you. Let me know first."

Erin nods. Good. He doesn't want to speak—to think. About anything. Layla was right, this is reality. His reality. And he's not letting anyone take it from him. Not again.

Erin groans and blinks blearily, the bright sunlight hurting his eyes.

"Awake?" Victor asks as he walks into the room with a mug of coffee.

"No," Erin mumbles, turning over in bed. The soft fabric of cotton shorts swishes against his legs between silk bedsheets. They're just as nice as Erin imagined they'd be. "What time is it?"

"Nearly midday," Victor chuckles. He waits for Erin to sit up straight before handing him the mug. The bed dips when he sits on the edge.

"Thanks." Erin takes a whiff, the sweet steam climbing up his sinuses and clearing his head. "Smells delicious."

"Good." Victor reaches an arm over Erin's legs, leaning on his fingertips lightly, and looks at Erin. His eyes are piercing. "You going to tell me what last night was all about?"

Erin looks down as he sips the coffee. "Do I have to?"

Victor purses his lips, giving Erin an unimpressed look as he leans more heavily on his hand. Caging him in.

With a sigh, Erin lowers the coffee to his lap. He rubs his thumb and forefinger against the gray mug handle. "Layla and Fletcher called me, and honestly, I ... I was triggered all of a sudden. People had been asking me questions all day, and the day before, everyone was whispering about me. They know Victor. They know I'm Stacy's son. Then it was just all ... red. Red. Red. Red as this wave of fury crashed into me. I had never felt anything that heavy before. So I didn't even try swimming to shore." He glances at Victor and finds an unreadable expression on his face. His brows are furrowed, and his lips are pulled tightly into a straight line.

"I just let it take me," Erin admits with a lowered head. "I'm sorry."

Victor places his right hand on Erin's leg and squeezes. "There's nothing to apologize for. Your friends were just looking out for you, and it's hard because they don't know a lot of the context. But we can figure out the rest later, ok? Who's moving where and everything else people are whispering about. There's no need to rush. We have plenty of time."

Later. Later.

Plenty of time.

Later.

That's what they thought last time, too.

"As for the Pack, well, they were bound to find out sooner or later, so let that one go. Completely. I'll organize a meeting and set the record straight about it all. Maybe even Stella can say something?" Victor suggests. He looks at Erin expectedly.

Erin forces himself to nod. Gratitude seeps into his scent, and Victor smiles in victory. He is grateful his mate is taking his side and calming him instead of forcing him to have all the answers right now or even get mad at his ... admitted overreaction. Victor is right. There's no need to worry about anything. They are mates. They'll stay together forever. Stewing on what caused his out-of-character mini breakdown won't do anyone any good. Besides, it was probably just a hormonal reaction—it's only been two days since his first shift. That's not going to just take a physical toll, but a mental one, too. Unfortunately, his friends poked the starved bear as soon as it woke from hibernation. Or wolf ... in this case.

Victor pats his leg and stands, drawing him out of his thoughts. "Why don't you take the rest of the day off?" he suggests. "I already told your parents you were here."

Erin smiles and takes another sip of coffee. "Did my dad try and tear your head off for kidnapping me on a work night?"

"Oh yeah." Victor pecks Erin's forehead. "Even though I was the one kidnapped, it was still terrifying," he admits, voice quiet. Leaning forward, he kisses Erin over each of his brows.

"I bet." Erin watches as Victor walks toward the door. He can still feel the imprint of Victor's lips where he kissed him, the warmth flowing throughout his whole body. He looks out the open window when he hears a roar of laughter followed by shouts of 'catch him' and 'don't let him reach the top.'

The sound should be bothersome, but instead, Erin feels content. Knowing there are kids running around happily brings him peace deep in his heart. He thought it would be easier to forget his past life. He and Victor *promised* to put it behind them. To focus on the here and now. Wolf and human society are vastly different from what it was, so what use are those lives to them today? Most of those final days were covered in blood and death anyway. Who would want to remember that?

The smell of barbecue and fresh bread fills the air, making Erin's stomach growl. For a second, he wishes it were rabbit—the one he had in the past was delicious. Though he supposes it was in part because of the love he felt coming from the wolf who had made it.

Which is why he does.

He wants to remember.

His stomach flutters, and he squeezes the handle of the mug. He doesn't want to forget the lives they lived before. For as much heartache as it brought, there was also so much love. So much happiness. Especially that last night.

Why would Tala—Victor—not want to remember that?

Layla and Fletcher would want to remember it had they been in his shoes. The good and the bad. The mating, the life of a wolf. The jewelry and the food. How it felt to swim in the river, free and unafraid, as the cool water rushed over their heads. How it felt to stand in the hot sun, armor stinging arms and chest as soldiers were burned on pyres and buried in the ground.

They used to spend so much time outdoors when they were little, tracking mud inside and scraping their hands while climbing trees. Like a pack of wolves, though he didn't even know it yet. They would have fit right in.

He needs to tell them.

How can he not?

Erin quickly gulps the coffee and places the empty mug on Victor's bedside table before sliding out of bed. He spies one of his old backpacks by the closet; his parents must've brought it with them this morning. Did they assume again that he would've gone home with Victor? Finding his phone in one of the front pockets, he walks out to the wooden balcony. The breeze is hot and dry, causing his pores to open and sweat instantly.

There aren't any text messages from Fletcher or Layla, which means they are pissed. The impact of his actions makes his heart drop in sliced pieces into his stomach. One piece for making assumptions. Another for fighting back and not listening to their points. And the last for snarling at them.

Even if they do forgive him, he doesn't know if he ever will for that one.

It's fair, them not having contacted him to see if he is ok. The way he acted was uncalled for. He would be pissed off, also.

The justification only makes the pain hurt more.

He opens their group chat and taps on the speech button to send a voice message. The tears blurring his vision would make it too hard to type.

"I'm sorry. I behaved like a little kid last night. Hanging up and yelling at you guys was wrong of me. There's just ... Victor's family is ... different, so it's taking a while to get used to. My mind is a jumbled mess. There are things I don't want to think of—that I shouldn't be thinking of—and right when I think I've moved past it all, I remember and … it's just a lot. Victor is great! He's trying to stay in the moment, and he's been lovely, and I know that isn't an excuse for how I acted, but he's … I'm …" Erin lets the message run on as he sighs. Praying his voice can still be heard over the unforgiving wind, he whispers, "I'll tell you more as soon as I can but, please, I need you. Both of you. If I'm to make it through this relationship in one piece, I need my siblings beside me."

He can't put Fletcher and Layla in danger. Victor said humans can't ever know about the werewolf world. He didn't clarify what would happen if they ever did find out, but with Stella's threats looming, Erin could only guess how severe the repercussions would be.

Until he knows they're safe, they have to stay in the dark.

A smirk twists his lips. Unless they figure it out for themselves. Layla loves a challenge, and Fletcher is more observant than people give him credit for, though his mind sometimes moves at a snail's pace to connect the dots his eyes see first.

He can't let them go. Won't let them go. Even if he does end up moving to Bellmore. They're family. Pack. Natalie said she found out by accident, and he doesn't know if the rest of the Bellmore Pack knew … but she's still alive. No one tried to harm her. Erin doesn't know what lengths his birth mother went to keep her and John safe, but he's willing to do the same.

He looks down when his phone buzzes twice. On the lock screen, he sees two text messages. The one from Fletcher is an emoji of a wolf followed by a blue heart and a monkey. His eyes skim Layla's message.

> **LAYLAY:** Hang up on me again and I'll teepee your house, slash your tires, and tie-dye all your clothes pink and orange. Love you xx.

Erin laughs in relief and sends a long string of blue and pink hearts with a cowboy emoji and a wolf in response. They'll be holding this against him for a long while. But that's ok; it means they'll still be in each other's lives.

"Now, onto the next pair," he mutters.

Quickly showering—and falling in love with the smell of Victor's shampoo and the pressure of the showerhead as it falls along his head and shoulders—Erin grabs a pair of underwear from his backpack and then dresses in a pair of Victor's shorts and top. 'Howl at the Haters' stares at him from the foggy bathroom mirror. His heart lifts, the tension easing. Hopefully, his parents will find this funny, too.

As he trudges to the shed, Erin makes a mental note to buy a gift thanking Fletcher for his help.

With the backyard and frontyard completely cleaned—all the fences fixed and repainted a nice black, the lawns mowed, any sunbaking snakes relocated, and the grass fertilized—the remaining four weeks of their contract can be used to plant the final fresh flowers and trees, as well as complete any cosmetic placements like deck chairs, tables, barbecues, and fire pits. Despite everything else going on, they're managing to stay on schedule.

"And who might be entering my shed?" Natalie doesn't look up from where she's writing notes on their stock. "Not my son, obviously, because my son doesn't leave the house without his phone nor tell his mother, forcing his mate to call her in the morning and apologize on his behalf."

John glides over to them with dusty hands. "Oh, that sounds like my son."

"John!" Natalie glares at him disapprovingly.

"What?" John holds his hands in surrender, shoulders shrugging. "He's young and going through a lot, cut him some slack. We both knew where he had gone, there was only one place realistically. Victor's call was more like a formality. And it's not like he would let anything happen to him."

"You weren't this mad three days ago," Erin speaks before his parents start arguing for real. "I thought that would've been worse. At least this time I didn't run out and shift in the streets."

"No, you had Victor drive you." Natalie turns on him, her stock book held tightly against her side as she crosses her arms. "And don't tell me if I should be angry or not, cub. Once is different to doing it twice."

"You're right. I'm sorry." Erin bites his lip to keep from smiling. "I shouldn't have stormed off like that, not when you guys weren't home yet, and especially without leaving a note. And I shouldn't have shifted so close to the suburbs the other day either. After all the care you put into keeping me safe, I put both of you in danger."

Natalie sticks the pencil behind her ear as she scrutinizes him for any tell of a lie. Anger still clings to her scent, lips tense and eyes narrowed. She must see the regret in Erin's eyes, because she sighs deeply. "It's ok. I'm not really mad." She drops her notebook onto a stack of fertilizer and opens her arms. Erin rushes into the hug, nuzzling his head into the crook of her neck while she pats the back of his head. Love and promise swirl around him. "I'm just worried about you being involved with these people, is all. Victor is great, and that young man Ben, but Stella ... she gives off some bad mojo. Call it mother's instinct, but there's something off about her."

Erin stiffens at the mention of Stella. Natalie never drops formalities when referring to people, especially their employers. He clears his throat in an attempt to cover the growl sneaking from deep in his throat, the sound low as he pulls out of the hug. If his mother has also been instinctively wary of Stella, then his apprehension toward her must be true. It's not all in his head.

His doubts ... His theories ... They mean something.

"Anyway, since you'll be joining the Lovelace family, you get a personal stake in this here ranch." John swings an arm around Erin's shoulder and drags him to stand by the shed doors. "Is there anything you want to add to the designs before we go out and finish stocking up? Any specific flowers or colors you're dying to see?"

Erin pushes Stella from his thoughts as he looks at the backyard. He takes a look at the landscape around them; all the hard work they've done as a family to make it look presentable and livable. He gets it now, why they accepted this offer in the first place, even though it put their identities in danger. Put him in danger.

They took a risk.

A risk fueled by hope.

He probably grumbled about it. She had most likely already accepted by the time he was told.

Erin smiles softly. It's good to think about how some people don't change.

The cluster of rocks still congregated on the other side of the fence catches his eye. An idea pops into his head. They were planning on arranging the rocks last anyway, as it's a bigger job and Stella will be too preoccupied in the coming weeks with the Council Meeting and his transition into the Pack as the Alpha's mate to stop them.

"See something?" Natalie asks. Erin takes her pencil and notepad from her hands, smiling brightly.

"There's just one teeny tiny thing I'd like to add. You'll both love it."

THIRTY-THREE

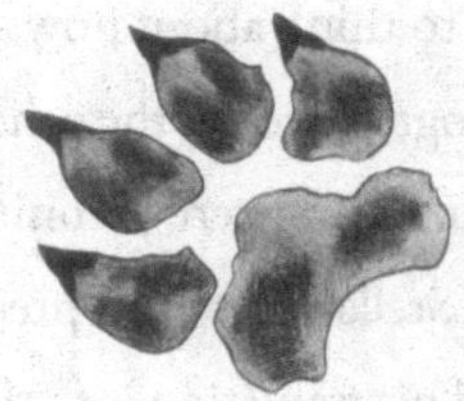

The Lovelace Pack has taken to Erin like how a wolf howls at the full moon, and not a day has gone by this past week where Victor hasn't been seen smiling like an idiot because of it.

His heart flutters in the mornings, watching wolves exchange greetings with Erin. No more silent nodding or blatant ignoring.

Around lunch, he'll smell homemade meals and snacks being prepared and peek over the stairs to see Michal, trying to feed Erin multiple meals at once while David stands there giggling. Wolves expend so much more energy than the average human, and now that Erin has shifted—and will continue to shift—he'll need more nutrients to sustain his form.

Then, in the afternoons, he hears the snickers, teasing coos, and kissing noises from a few of the little cubs when he hugs Erin goodbye. That part, he could go a couple of days without.

Erin is good with the cubs. When Victor watches him turn, eyes crossed and tongue lolling out as his nails sharpen and a playful growl rips past his lips, his heart breaks. Tiny cracks that grow larger later in the night, once Erin has driven away with his parents and the little cubs have run back inside, squealing. Not only is his mate leaving his side, but the memories that get kicked up like the dust in the trucks' wake are not ones he wants to think about. He promised Erin he would forget, put the past behind them. They are living new lives now—better lives, without the threat of war or violence. They won't have to bury anyone else.

There is no more time for what ifs or how old or names that sound strong like a raging storm—

He shakes his head.

Even the weird whispering Erin mentioned had stopped, not that Victor ever heard them to begin with. Still, his mate was uncomfortable, so he gathered the Pack and had a word with them. Questioning eyes and trailing faces? Those weren't going to stop, and he didn't want to draw any more attention to Erin being a Bellmore than necessary. But the doubt? Any fear of what their relationship meant? That he could lay to rest, because curse or no curse, no one was going to treat his mate with disrespect.

It was quite easy, too, with Stella's help.

He really does owe it all to his aunt.

Walking toward the back fence near the corner where Erin kneels next to a pile of rocks, he supposes that if he had to choose between hiding a relationship with Erin or putting up with his family teasing him, he would take the teasing any day.

"I need a break, which means you need a break," Victor announces to Erin as he pulls himself onto the top fence rail. He feels his heart flutter when Erin looks at him and smiles. It's like all the light in the air was sucked out and pulled into that smile, forcing him to look at it.

Erin takes his gloves off and leans his back against the fence next to Victor. His voice is laboured when he speaks, "Do you need a break or are you just procrastinating from dealing with the Council Meeting?"

"Well, it sounds like *you* need a break," Victor retorts, ignoring the pointed question. Erin slaps him lightly on the thigh, his breath falling past his lips in quick staccato huffs as he laughs.

Victor waits until he can hear Erin's heartbeat slow to a normal pace before speaking again. Another perk of everyone knowing about him and Erin is that they can take longer and more frequent breaks. Together. Out in the open.

They don't have to hide.

"So, how are you finding Pack life?"

"It feels the same." Erin taps his fingers where they still rest on Victor's thigh. "I remember how loving Pack can be. Everyone knows everyone's business, but in a good way. There's not much judgment."

"Not much?" Victor lifts a hand to his heart in mock offense.

"You know what I mean," Erin huffs again. "It's been surprisingly easy to remember everyone's names, too, not just their faces. Usually, my memory is sub-par at best."

"That's because your wolf is helping," Victor explains. "A lot of it is tied back to instinct, wolves being able to smell which Pack they belong to and stuff like that—a survival adaptation after the split. So, we tend to remember the names of Pack mates more easily."

"Ah," Erin proclaims. "I ... I wish I could stay here with you. At night."

"You know can, Star."

Erin whispers, "And you know why I can't."

Victor bites his tongue. Natalie and John. Erin doesn't want to leave them, especially knowing that he won't be living in Texas forever. Eventually, he'll come back up to New York to live with the rest of the Pack. To live with him. They haven't spoken anymore about when that will happen, but Victor is sure that it will.

So, if Erin wants to spend a few more weeks with his parents, indulging in movie nights and fast food runs, so be it.

"Little Wolf." Erin turns around so his back is to the house and leans in close to whisper, "Some of the older members are still looking at me funny. You said you spoke to them about overlooking the curse."

Victor's heart stutters as Erin's sudden aggression from last week comes to mind. If anyone heard about that ... No, they were quiet when they came home. But the surge of frustration coming off him that night was intense. He wouldn't blame them for thinking it was a side effect of the Goddess's curse. Hell, he's had the same thought. He doesn't know why Hëna would curse them—he's just as confused as Erin is, maybe even more.

He's tried to find excuses, tried to come up with reasoning, if only to ease Erin's mind about the whole thing. They still haven't found anything to dispel what he's grown up knowing. What the elders taught him.

What history has written.

And then there's his memories of that cold March night. Fire licks along walls, curtains engulfed in flame as blood stains the basket his favorite bear sleeps in.

He knows firsthand how suddenly people can change.

Quick anger is always the first sign. Which is why they've been practicing, training with Ben for a couple of hours every day, after he finishes landscaping, to get Erin used to shifting. Used to feeling human alongside his wolf. Yet the worry lingers. What if he can't teach Erin how to control his urges in time, and he hurts someone? Then where would he be? His mate would never forgive himself. Never forgive *him*. Stella always said how dangerous their kind could be without a strong foundation, without a strong Alpha to keep them in line. And he knows she's right; it's the same thing Alaric would have said.

Add into the mix a wolf who has lain dormant for two decades, and who his birth parents were ...

"I did speak to everyone." Victor pushes the thought away and shrugs. "Maybe you had dirt on your face."

"Obviously, I have dirt on my face. I'm working near it all day." Erin rolls his eyes and leans back. He points to the holes he's been digging along the back fence to match the front yard. "This is something else, though. It's like there's a ghost on my shoulder and they keep staring at it with looks of pity and ... anger. It's because of Stacy and Gray, isn't it?"

Victor hums. Damn it. So much for that talk with everyone about being discreet. What would Stella do right now? Reassure Erin that the nerves are messing with his head and let the conversation fizzle out. Yes, don't bring up the curse again, or how of course the older wolves would see the face of murderers in the structure of Erin's jawline and the color of his scent. That's what Stella would do. Move on. The past can't change. He glances at Erin and sees his brows furrowed in contemplation while his index finger picks at the cuticle of his thumb.

Fuck it. Yes, the past can't change, the dead can't come back to life, but that doesn't mean it didn't exist either. He knows whether he says it out loud or not, Erin has already thought it. He's not stupid. He probably knew from the second he was introduced to the Pack.

"Maybe they are just reminiscing ... they might be seeing your parents in you," Victor suggests softly. "I haven't said anything about it, but wolves aren't dumb. Or forgetful."

Erin's index finger freezes where it's hooked under some skin. Victor watches closely as his shoulders tense and his face contorts into bitterness, then discomfort, before settling on indifference. He counts to twelve before Erin physically relaxes, his face stretching out into a calmer, more comfortable look of contentment.

"Maybe," Erin replies absentmindedly. He raises himself onto his toes and gives Victor a peck on the cheek. "I need to get some stuff from the shed and get back to work. See you later for dinner?"

"Yeah," Victor nods, "be careful." He waits for Erin to round the side of the house before he sprints inside looking for Stella.

Has she noticed anyone expressing concern over Erin's integration into the Pack? But, if she has, why not tell him straight away? Better yet, why has no one brought up their agitation about Erin's resemblance to Stacy and Gray to *him*? Do they think he doesn't know about his birth parents and is trying to spare him pain and regret? Or are they worried that if he knows the truth, he'll try and take power from Victor? Maybe they are scared to bring it up to him since, because Erin is his mate, they worry he'll dismiss the concern straight away.

No way. His family wouldn't think like that. Besides, that's not the way Packs work. He and Erin are a team. Erin was born to lead just as much as Victor was. It's in their blood—his blood especially.

"Victor!"

Victor skids to a stop in front of the healing room. Every question he had for Stella leaves instantly when he sees her washing her hands at one of the sinks. They're red and raw like she's been rubbing them under hot water for a while.

"Stella, are you ok?" He rushes inside, eyes flitting about quickly, checking for any signs of a cut or bruise.

"Oh, no I'm fine," Stella laughs lightly. "I had a bit of a headache, is all. I think Healer Haven is attending to one of the little cubs. There was a scuffle with a chocolate bar and some board games." She shakes her head and sighs like she's physically ridding the absurd information from her head.

"Oh, ok. That's good. Wait, no, not good, obviously ... but you're ok and Healer Haven is with the others, so I'm sure they'll be ok." Victor rubs his hands against his thighs nervously. He can still feel some leftover warmth from where Erin's fingers were tapping.

Stella is looking at him like he's shifted halfway and grown an extra head for good measure. "What the hell is going on with you? I call you in here because you're running down the hallway like a madman, spreading your scent all over the place—which reeks of fear, by the way—then you start rambling and backtracking. Alphas don't ramble and backtrack when they talk, Victor. And they don't stink of fear."

Victor sits on one of the empty leather couches, guilt evident on his face. "Yes. Sorry."

"Why don't you tell me what's going on so I can help you fix it. Hm?" Stella sighs and sits beside him. The creaking of the material matches the spike in his heart. He flinches. There's no use lying. Stella always sees through his lies. Ever since he was a kid, nothing has gotten past her vibrant green eyes. More often than not, she knew what he was feeling before he did. Victor nibbles on his cheek, raising his hands in exasperation. "I'm scared."

"Scared?" Stella shrieks in disbelief. "You're the Alpha of one of the oldest and strongest Packs in America! What have you got to be scared about?"

"Everything!" Victor growls. "I'm scared that if I try and talk with Erin about the breakdown he had last week, he might think I'm trying to control him. Plus, maybe I was too rash in introducing him to the Pack. There is so much history between us, so much resting on our shoulders. What if some of the older members find it hard to accept Erin so suddenly?"

Victor rests his head on his hands, fingers pulling at the hair. He doesn't mention specifically why they would find it hard to accept Erin.

Stella looks like she's been having a hard time lately, and he knows she's been staying up late and waking up early due to insomnia. He's seen her in those twilight hours, deep bags under her eyes, lips chapped and raw from pulling at the dry skin, and hair hastily pinned in a bun atop her head. He doesn't want to pile more stress and grief onto her plate by reminding her of the people who killed her husband and brother. Who forced a burden onto her so suddenly.

The curse, his lineage. Both are valid reasons. Both make his head swim with anxiety and his stomach heave with anger. Why them? *Why them*?

He can only imagine what those thoughts would do to his aunt.

"Well, hmm." Stella taps her lips. "What about inviting him to one of the training sessions? You can hold one for tomorrow morning if you don't want to wait until next week," she suggests.

Victor raises his head, eyes narrowed inquisitively at his aunt. "I have been training with Erin."

"Not properly, Honey." She rises from her seat, one hand on her hip while the other points around the room. "It would be in wolf form, out in one of the big paddocks. This way, Erin can get his mind off whatever it is that's been bothering him, what's been causing disconnect between his human self and his wolf. The rest of the Pack can see how strong he is. It'll show them that he'll be a great addition to our lives, and hopefully balance out some of his hormones." She turns back to face Victor triumphantly, her dull green eyes now sparkling brighter than the stars.

She thinks the problem is Erin's wolf, or lack thereof, to be precise. The dots haven't even formed in her mind that Erin could be a Bellmore. Does she not recognize him? Or is she sparing him the pain that would rise if it were mentioned, the way he's been doing for her?

"Do you think it would work?" Victor questions slowly. He can't hold back the scent of fear that sneaks out with his voice.

"Oh, Honey." Stella kneels in front of Victor and places one hand on his shoulder. "As I said, perhaps it's as simple as Erin having pent-up energy, after all, his wolf has been dormant for so long. Think about it, most wolves have shifted by the time they are learning to speak, so they deal with all these hormonal instincts over the course of a few years, their human mind balancing at the same rate as their wolf instincts. Then there's your mate being thrust into this world with no previous knowledge. He doesn't know the customs. The way of our life. It's a lot for one to take in all at once. It doesn't help he's The White Wolf, there's more aggression than normal with the curse and all."

Erin does know the customs, or at least, knew them once. Victor doesn't correct her, instead focusing his attention on her other point. His aunt is right, as she often is. Humans go to the gym all the time to help regulate their hormones and balance their minds. It makes sense, even with the extra training and Erin still working around the ranch, it wouldn't be enough. Like with the extra food, he needs extra physical stimulation, too. As a wolf.

"Natalie and John know that Erin is a werewolf too, so convincing them to take tomorrow morning off should be easy enough." Victor nods more confidently now. His eyes brighten. "A training session with the whole Pack. Erin will love it."

Stella places a hand on his cheek and hums in agreement as she smiles, lips twitching slightly. "Show him what it means to be a part of the Lovelace Pack."

THIRTY-FOUR

"**A**re you going to tell me why I'm up at the ass-crack of dawn on a Tuesday instead of at home, in my pjs, eating my dad's homemade pancakes?"

Victor snorts as they walk hand in hand toward the far paddock, the one closest to the forest. Erin can see most of the Pack already there, stretching and warming up. Even a few little kids are running around.

A real family affair.

"You wouldn't be at home eating pancakes, Star. You'd be on your phone in bed, waiting until the last second to get up and drive here for work."

"Oh, yes!" Erin raises his brows. "Thank you for the clarification. Let me repeat myself then." He clears his throat. "Are you going to tell me why—"

"We normally like to start the week off with some old-fashioned sparring to get the blood pumping," Victor interrupts. "I thought—well, Stella thought, it'd be fun if you joined us this time."

"Of course she did." Erin hums, smiling when two kids start arguing over what their parents are scribbling on a piece of paper. "How have we not seen you doing this?"

Ben walks past them with a light cane basket. One of the fathers grins gleefully, dropping his folded piece of paper into it. Erin gasps, smile faltering as he realizes what it was that the kids were arguing over.

"Are people placing bets?"

"Normally, we have these on a Sunday, when the 'human landscapers' aren't around. Other training during the week was kept to the training room, human forms only, or deep in the forest. Toned down on the howling, of course." Victor reaches into one of the pockets of his jersey shorts and unfolds a small piece of paper with numerous names listed down one column and numbers down another. There's a red check next to Erin's name and another check next to the number five hundred. "And obviously, there are bets placed. Wouldn't be a training session without it."

"You're betting five hundred dollars that I'll win?" Erin snatches the paper and folds it quickly before stuffing it into the back pocket of his jersey shorts. "Practicing to shift *into* a wolf is one thing, but this?" He waves his hands around. "Are you insane? I've never trained *as a wolf* before, let alone done any kind of official boxing!"

"I am aware." Victor's face is impassive as he takes a step closer, and Erin's breath hitches. Victor reaches his hand into the back pocket of his shorts. There's a slight squeeze, Victor digging the pads of his fingertips into Erin's ass before he lifts the paper between them. He's holding it between his index finger and middle finger like it's a delicate flower. With intense eyes still on Erin, Victor finally drops the façade and smirks with a wink. Like some sort of evil villain. "Which is why I bet five hundred dollars that you would lose."

Erin's mouth drops open in silent outrage. Victor taps the paper quickly against his lips, his eyebrows quirking in a challenge before he walks away.

"Oh, it is on, Little Wolf!" Erin runs after him, ready to start fighting right away, when Stella steps into the center of the paddock holding a dark basket different from the one Ben was walking around with.

"PACK!" she howls into the morning's crisp air. Her voice is clear and commanding, but somehow still light and airy as it rides the wind. The voice of an Alpha. It makes Erin shiver. Yet when her eyes land on him, he leans in close to Victor and lifts his head, sending an unbothered gaze toward her. Victor wraps his arm around Erin's waist, pressing a quick kiss to his forehead before howling along with the rest of the Pack.

There have been no more threats since his identity as The White Wolf was revealed last week, but that doesn't mean he's forgotten. He knows this game Stella's playing is still in session. He just hasn't been able to figure out what her next move is going to be. He's trying not to lose sleep over it, but ...

He dares a glance to his left and sees Ben leaning against the fence post with crossed arms. Beatrice is sitting on top of the fence next to him, her legs swinging excitedly in the air. Smiling. They both look casual and happy as they wait to hear what their mother has to say, but Erin can see the tightness around Ben's eyes, and the way Beatrice's knuckles are spotted red and white from gripping the wooden beam like her life depends on it.

He figured it was only Ben who was wary of Stella, but whatever he knows, his sister must know, too. At least some of it. Erin doesn't peg Ben as the type of guy to endanger his little sister, which means Beatrice either found out what Ben knows herself or chanced upon something else entirely. Does she not believe that The Goddess would turn on their kind, too? Or does she just know that her mother is a lying, hateful bitch?

Whatever the case, it must be serious for her to be slipping. He's been here for six weeks now and has only spoken to her once, despite the numerous times he's ventured into the house. It's like she's hardly here. The one time he did see her in town, she was with others—wolves, he now knows. The girl with short brown hair and deep brown eyes, and an identical looking tall lumbering man sat with her at one of the small white iron tables next to Sandy's bakery.

She looked so happy then, so carefree like the young adult that she is, which he checked with Victor about, slightly put off that he's only roughly three months older than his younger cousin. This is the first time she's shown any kind of anxiety about anything.

Shit. He takes a deep breath to settle his racing heart and faces Stella again.

She's up to something today, and it's got them nervous.

He needs to figure it out before someone—he, or worse, Victor—gets hurt.

"I know we've had to tone down our traditional throwdowns due to … obstacles." Stella's smile is sickly sweet, like a hyena's. Erin crosses his arms and huffs as thunderous 'boos' sound around him. Stella holds her arms out in front of her and nods her head. "Yes, yes. But that is neither here nor there. Let us put it behind us and get ready to fight, shall we? Today we needn't hold back at all. Howl as loudly, growl as dangerously, and fight as deadly as the strong wolves you are!" Stella reaches into the basket and pulls out two names simultaneously.

"Why aren't you the one giving that speech? You're the Alpha." Erin leans over to Victor, whispering, as Stella's dry lips stretch into a genuine grin. Pain splashes behind his eyes, a migraine forming. He intuitively knows whose name is on one of the papers she just pulled. There goes another point for this Fate and Instinct guiding them bullshit.

"Stella likes to act as referee." Victor shrugs one shoulder. "I've never had a problem with it. I prefer to fight anyways. So, it's a win-win."

"Our first two fighters will be none other than our glorious Alpha and his mate, Victor and Erin!" Stella points toward them before applauding and stepping out of the paddock. Erin sends a silent curse toward the moon. He was hoping to watch for the first few rounds and spend some time taking in the surroundings to try and find anything suspicious.

"Woohoo!" Victor jogs into the center of the paddock, ripping his white shirt over his head as he does and flexing his muscles. He spins with his arms raised as everyone howls in support. When he stops, he's facing Erin with a cheeky grin plastered across his features. He places one hand on his hip while the other beckons him forward.

'Come hither,' his eyes and fingers seem to say.

"Wow." Erin rolls his eyes, chuckling at the theatrics. "You're such a drama queen."

"Oh, come on, Star, it's all fun and games." Victor pulls Erin into a hug, the crowd screaming louder at the pre-match display of affection.

Erin wraps his arms around Victor's warm neck and squeezes. He lifts himself on his tippytoes and lets his hot breath blow across Victor's earlobe, before whispering into his ear, "I'm going to whoop your ass, Little Wolf. Don't forget, I remember all my drills."

Victor shivers, his hands digging into the dip of Erin's lower back. He turns his head and noses Erin's hair, inhaling deeply. "Go ahead and try, my Star. We have no swords here."

"Don't we?" Erin steps away with a raised brow, eyes flicking to his mate's crotch before meeting his eyes again. "Be careful, I would hate it if anything ... broke." Satisfaction licks his spine when Victor gulps nervously. He removes his shirt as Ben walks over with a bright red button held securely in his grip.

"Ok, we all know the rules. Hand-to-hand combat in human form for a minimum of five minutes. After that, either competitor can shift into their wolf. There will be no cheap shots and no fatal wounding." Ben looks from Victor to Erin. "Teeth and claws are to be controlled. Understood?"

Erin tenses his legs, taking a boxing stance. "Understood."

Victor rolls his shoulder blades and tilts his head from side to side. "Understood."

Ben nods and raises his hand with the button in the air, stepping back as he speaks, "Ready ... set ..."

BEEP.

Victor moves first. He crouches down to swipe Erin's legs out from under him. Erin lets him do it and sticks his arms out to catch himself. Putting his weight on them, he kicks at Victor, who raises an arm to block, letting the momentum from the kick push him into a roll. He stands a few feet away from Erin with a smirk on his face. His breathing is rapid; the adrenaline pumping through his veins keeps him moving.

Erin stands and snickers. He may not know how to fight as a wolf, or even know any proper boxing techniques, but the muscle memory of countless sword drills comes back easily. Like riding a bike. So, at least for the next four minutes, he knows how to defend himself as a human against a wolf.

The two circle each other, gauging the next move. Erin doesn't wait. He runs toward Victor and leaps, hooking his leg over his shoulder to push him to the ground. However, Victor stands firm. He crouches, digging his heels into the dirt, and wraps his arms around Erin's waist. He swings them, pinning Erin to the ground.

"Muscle memory, Star?" Victor asks breathlessly. His eyes are bright and full of drive.

Erin laughs, the sound coming from deep within his gut. "Yeah." He squirms in an attempt to free himself from Victor's hold. He lowers his voice and smiles coyly, "I can't wait to see the look on your face when I win."

"Oh?" Victor's eyes darken, and Erin uses the distraction to pinch his side—hard—and twist. He hears Victor grunt as he flips them. He sends a flying kiss before hopping back to the edge of the paddock. Victor is stronger. He's trained more in proper technique and has more experience, his muscle mass greater. If Erin has any chance of winning, it'll be when they are wolves. Their strength will be evenly matched then, instinct and sharp canines fueling their desire to win.

Ben raises his open palm into the air. Five minutes have passed already. Wasting no time, Erin shifts, his shorts shredding in the air around them as he lets out a challenging howl. It's much easier this time to shift. Looks like his practicing has paid off. Victor's eyes widen in pride, and he raises his head in delight as howling rings around them, the Pack spurring the fight along.

He ignores the ones who shuffle back, mouths pressed firmly together.

He misses the way Beatrice jumps down from the fence and rushes to Ben, wide-eyed and panicked.

He sneezes at the smell of rotten roses on the breeze.

Red.

Red.

Red.

Victor hunches over like he's about to shift when a whooshing sound fills the air. Erin feels a pinch on the left, high in his front leg. It's familiar, the pain that burns along his veins, and the way his muscles spasm as he loses his balance.

Later.

The way Victor pales, his eyes widening to try and hold all the pain, rage, and fear within them unsuccessfully. The way his bellow breaks through the world around them like a thunderclap.

Erin looks down to see what caused Victor's wrath. There's a stick with deep purple and red feathers attached to it protruding from his left shoulder, right above the muscle leading to his front leg. No, it's not a stick. Sticks don't have nocks on the end of them.

An arrow.

Ah. Once again ...

He feels all the strength in his leg get zapped toward the arrow, causing it to finally buckle underneath him. He clenches his eyes shut, expecting his head to hit the ground hard when he feels something soft instead. Squinting, he sees a blurry Victor above him. Wrinkles are gouged deep between his brows, and his jaw is clenched so tight Erin worries he'll break his teeth.

Later.

"Erin! Erin!" Victor gently kneels on the dry grass, placing Erin's head on his thighs. One of his hands is hovering over Erin's front leg, near his shoulder, while the other rubs along his nose. "Star, you need to stay in wolf form until Healer Haven gets the arrow out. Everything's going to be ok, trust me. Trust me. You're going to be ok. Trust me. Trust me. You're fine. It's fine."

His heart hardens as his eyes close. Anger overrides the pain briefly. He's a wolf. He's a wolf... It's not meant to be like this. He's meant to be stronger. Wiser. And someone shot him. Someone dared shoot him! He's The White Wolf, mate to an Alpha, leader of one of the original four Packs of America. He's a Prince! He's been blessed by the Moon Goddess herself, and someone had the fucking gall to stick a poisoned arrow through him!

The air rushes around him, his coarse fur swishing in time with the flurry of movement around him. He tried to growl, but a whine seeps past his lips instead as his head falls more heavily onto Victor's lap, his fingers clenching the fur around his neck protectively. Angrily. Fearfully. The blue jeweled Pack ring burns like cold fire.

Later.

Later.

He needs to reassure him. Tell him it'll be ok. That what happened before won't happen again. It's not that serious a wound, even though it hurts like a motherfucker. Even though it hurts worse now than it did last time. Oh, She must have dulled the pain back then. Her magic couldn't save him, but it could protect him.

He wants Natalie. And John.

He misses his parents.

There's a loud, high-pitched ringing in his ears that's grating against the pounding migraine, stronger now than it was before the sparring started. Slowly, he manages to squint his eyes open once more and glance down at his shoulder. He can't see much from his position, but the purple and black blood oozing down his leg and chest is striking as it stains his white coat. His paw is twitching, but he can't feel it. He knows he's still on the ground, the subtle smell of sweetness from the earth filling his nostrils underneath Victor's overpowering scent. His mate is trying to calm him.

It's helping a bit, but not enough. His own scent is rushing out into the air around him, trying to soothe Victor. He presses his nose into the dirt. His nostrils burn. His smell is disappearing.

Later.

Later.

We'll talk about it all *later*.

"Fuck, it's wolfsbane," Victor growls, nose pinched tight. He tightens his grip on the hair around Erin's neck, causing him to release a loud whine. Victor gasps, quickly releasing his grip. "Sorry. I'm sorry, Star. I didn't mean to pull that hard," he murmurs into Erin's ear.

Erin raises his head to lick Victor's hands. He latches onto the red string between them. 'Don't be sad,' he says down the bond. Victor wipes his eyes and smiles. It's small, the upturn of his lips not meeting his eyes at all, but it's a smile all the same. He heard him.

It gives him all the strength he needs.

He follows Victor's eyes as they are drawn to the arrow. He finds a strange fascination in the way it trembles in the breeze, jutting out of his skin, before he diverts his attention to what's happening around the paddock. Some of the men and women have shifted and run off into the woods, while the ones remaining are running back toward the house with children wrapped in their arms close to their chests. He realizes the ringing in his ears is the sound of their crying and screaming.

Beatrice is among those heading back to the house. Her arms are full as she carries a shifted cub and a human toddler, her red hair swinging behind her back like a flag. Little Red—Rachel—jogs beside her, tiny legs taking three steps for Beatrice's every one to keep pace. Beatrice isn't screaming like everyone else or looking around in a panic, a futile attempt to see where the arrow came from. Her stride is quick but calm, and her face is impassive but firm.

Like she knows without a doubt no more arrows will rain down upon them.

Later.

Later.

Later.

Erin's heart slows to a snail's beat. Suspicion squeezes it tightly. He looks to where Ben was last and sees him take his dark navy top off. His eyes are the darkest Erin's ever seen, like a dangerous forest filled with monsters so powerful, so angry, they don't bother to lurk in the shadows of trees. Instead, they rear their heads right at the front, for all to see and feel. Erin worries for a second that they might never show bright happiness and love again.

Like before. Like what happened to the eyes of the Pack befo—

"Why isn't Healer Haven here yet!" Ben yells, taking command while Victor is waiting, frozen in memory beside Erin. "Group B, follow me to meet with Group A in the forest. Group C, keep taking the cubs inside and lock all the windows and doors. Alert the other Packs too—the ones who have already arrived and reside in the forest, and the ones yet to show—that there's been an attack. And somebody get Alpha Harkin on the line. Everyone is to be on HIGH FUCKING ALERT!" He looks at Erin and clenches his fists before shifting and running into the forest, the image so familiar it nearly makes his mind split. His memory taking him back back back.

Stella drops beside Victor, deep howls still echoing around them. She reaches her hand out to delicately probe the skin around the wound. A flash of heat rushes throughout his body like electricity. He can't catch the whimper in time before it rips out of his mouth, his head rising slightly to try and snap at her reddened fingers.

"Stella!" Victor frowns at her disapprovingly as she retracts her hand quickly with a surprised gasp. Erin's lips pull back in a vicious snarl, and he sends a heated glare at her.

"Shh, it's ok." Victor touches Erin's lips, pressing down on them to get them to relax. "She didn't mean to hurt you. She thought she was helping."

"Oh my. What on earth happened?" Stella's eyes flit from Victor to Erin before landing on the arrow. Her eyes gleam, and she gasps again, covering her mouth with both hands. She recognizes the arrow. The toast he had for breakfast curdles in his stomach, acid climbing steadily up his throat. He doesn't think it's the poison this time.

"What? What do you know?" Victor's head snaps to her again, eyes guarded. "SPEAK!"

"It's the Treelark Pack," she speaks evenly as she slowly lowers her hands from her mouth. "These are the same arrows they used when they helped those traitors massacre us."

"What the hell are you talking about?" Victor asks, irritation dripping from his words like the venom dripping from Erin's wound.

Stella exhales in exasperation. "During the rebellion, the Treelark Pack arrived as reinforcements for the Bellmores and used these arrows." She flicks the feather on the arrow with one of her sharpened red nails, causing a pang to travel through Erin. "They don't believe in the legends, ignoring what the scriptures say, and instead worship the Moon Goddess, seeing you two as blessings meant to bring prosperity and hope, not curses come to destroy us all in vengeance."

They sound smart. Erin would love to have a word with them on these beliefs. Maybe whatever evidence they have would be enough to convince Victor ... and he would love to swat that fake sympathy off Stella's face.

"They likely staged this attack in a wishful attempt to get the reincarnation cycle to start again so you two could be reborn into their Pack, since they're one of the original four, too." She grabs hold of both Victor's hands, yanking them off Erin. "It's a power grab," she warns.

How would taking out Erin be a power grab for Victor? They aren't mated yet. It's not official. They aren't marked. They haven't renewed their vows. Unless she knows. She knows Erin is the true heir—Stacy and Gray's son.

And if she knows, so do her allies.

"What the fuck … There's no guarantee that we would be born again so soon, let alone into their Pack," Victor stammers, trying to make sense of Stella's explanation.

'Don't listen to her,' Erin says to Victor. He doesn't hear, eyes spilling tears as they stay locked on Stella. No. No no no *no*. It doesn't matter if he understands her warning, her explanation of why Erin has been attacked or not. He still believes her. Erin doesn't even know if his words went through. It feels like his head has been stuffed with cotton and thrown into the ocean. The thread between them is dimming with each breath he takes. Every time he blinks, it gets harder to open his eyes again.

Later.

Later.

Later.

There's plenty of time, later, for us to find the truth, Star.

Healer Haven arrives and all but pushes Stella out of the way so she can look at the wound. The paddock is empty now except for them. Erin yelps in pain when she probes the skin around the wound. Victor flinches and grabs fistfuls of Erin's fur again, like he was the one who felt the pain. Maybe he did.

"It didn't hit an artery, but we still need to act fast. The second I pull the arrow out, you need to shift back." Healer Haven grabs Erin's snout, forcing him to fix his gaze on her eyes. Her touch is gentle, though she's gazing at him with that goddamned *same* mixed look of pity and anger. But there's something underneath it, something warm and affectionate he can't name. As he stares into her small, beady eyes, he feels the same familiar feeling from the first time they met warm his gut. Her thumb rubs against his snout.

Trust.

He trusts her. He doesn't know why, but maybe it's something all Pack healers possess. Or maybe it's something more. Something that involves that look in her eyes or the trace of power under her scent. Whatever it is, though, now's not the time to figure it out.

"You have the strength to do this," she whispers firmly.

Erin nods and forces himself to relax. The tense muscles in his thigh unclench from where they were bundled around the arrow. It hurts. It hurts so incredibly bad. Healer Haven gives no warning besides gently lowering his nose back onto Victor's lap before she reaches over and quickly pulls the arrow out.

Instinct takes over, and he shifts back automatically. The poison from the arrow and the act of getting stabbed punched his body all over again, causing him to curl into a ball as bile is expelled from his mouth, dripping down his chin. He doesn't have the strength to scream. Or care about his appearance. Or keep his eyes open. Or breathe.

It hurts.

It's always later.

Victor immediately drags him close as Healer Haven drapes a blanket over him. It's one of Victor's blankets from his bed, his layered leather and sandalwood scent engulfing Erin in a bear hug. That must be why Healer Haven took so long; she went to get something that would help keep him tethered to this world. Victor presses his body against Erin, his usually warm skin cold. He hates how it still feels good against his clammy skin.

He whines desperately as black spots swim across his eyes. Something cold was poured over his shoulder; it drips slowly down his chest. He shivers as Healer Haven presses something over the wound. Gauze, he thinks. It's rough. The pressure eases some of the pain momentarily.

The world is blurry.

When he looks at Victor, he sees fat tears rolling down his face as he looks somewhere to his left. Erin follows his line of sight and sees Stella's lips moving. He tries to focus on listening, but his body doesn't cooperate. The pain is too loud.

Closer.

Protect.

The conversation must be over as Victor picks him up bridal style and hurries toward the house. He blinks slowly, his eyes moving from Victor's face to Healer Haven's legs right behind them before moving further to gaze at Stella.

She doesn't hide the sardonic smirk that pulls her chapped lips across her wrinkly face. He's never thought of her as old—fifty isn't old by any means—but standing in the middle of the paddock now, he can't help but let the word flit across his brain.

Her hair is thin, the shade more like a yellow-orange, pale against the sun rising behind her, rather than its usual bright red as it hangs loosely around her dull face, deep eye bags staining her skin near black. The colorful yoga pants and loose top she's wearing also make her usual, toned, hourglass figure look frumpy and saggy. Her long black nails he's known to always be perfectly manicured into almond points are chipped and broken into different lengths as if she's been biting them. Even the skin around her cuticles is torn and worn away. Red. Raw.

He's the one who's dying, who's been poisoned, yet she's the one who looks like a heinous witch on death's doorstep instead of the vibrant, beautiful werewolf he first met.

He looks away from her harsh green eyes, turning his head into Victor's chest. It rumbles, and he glances blearily at his lips in an attempt to make out the words. He realizes he didn't have to as Victor snarls, the words so clear and loud they could be heard from the highest peak of a mountain.

Not again. Not again. *Please.*

"PREPARE THE PACK!" The command echoes through the bond in his mind.

Notagainnotagainnotagainnotagainnononononono

"This means war."

Then, when finally, later comes ...

They're both dead.

THIRTY-FIVE

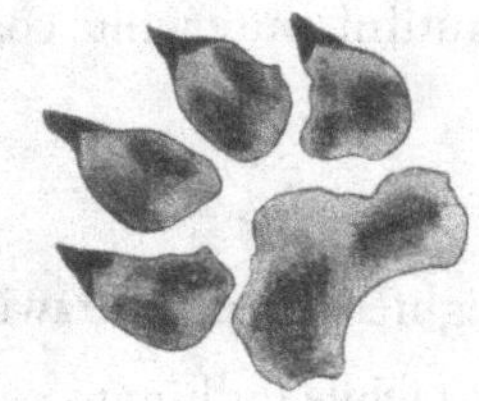

Victor waits patiently for Natalie and John to arrive. It doesn't take long.

He gently places Erin's hand on the bed and stands from the seat next to it when he hears them running up the stairs. Walking over to the balcony, the double doors swing open easily, letting a crisp morning breeze in. The green curtain dances with the new wind. He lets the thin material be. Erin's always been fascinated with the balcony, so hopefully, this will make him feel better while he sleeps.

Natalie flings the bedroom door open, John right behind her. She's beside Erin before the door has a chance to swing closed. They both have their pajamas on still—matching blue, gray, and white pinned shorts and tops. Natalie's usual long braid down her back and painted bandana are nowhere to be seen. Instead, her black hair is loose, tangled and limp, as if it too has spent all its energy worrying for Erin.

It's startling how different they look.

John takes a seat on the bed by Erin's feet. His hair is mussed, more white peeking through than black, and the gray collar of his shirt is upturned. "How did this happen?" he demands, voice grim and quiet. His eyes are burning like vengeful stars.

Victor turns his head toward the balcony and squeezes his eyes shut. The moment replays behind his lids like an old movie projector. The arrow whooshes through the air and collides into Erin's front leg, right below his shoulder. The flesh collapses inward as the arrowhead digs a hole. Blood starts oozing out instantaneously, staining the beautiful, pure white coat red and dripping onto the ground.

And his eyes.

Victor clenches his hands tighter, his nails drawing blood on his palms as he remembers Erin's eyes. It took a while for him to realize he had been injured, for the pain to travel up his leg, into his brain, and reflect in his eyes. One second, Victor was gazing intently into golden spheres of bright joy, and a few seconds later, all he could see was confusion.

That's what hurt the most.

Again.

It was the exact same.

There was nothing he could do. Even this time being so much *closer*, no heightened werewolf ability could have helped him protect Erin at that moment. Trade the white fur for steel armor, and once again, it was all his fault.

It wasn't seeing the pain and anger well in his eyes, nor feeling his clammy, pale skin after he was able to shift back. It was how his eyes gripped tightly to confusion through it all. He didn't care that he had been injured—poisoned—and was dying. He wasn't in pain because he was reliving a heartbreaking injury.

No, as Victor held him close and looked into his eyes as they slowly blinked in and out of consciousness, he knew that Erin was angry and in pain because he couldn't figure out who, out of everyone in the Pack, had betrayed him.

Victor felt the same way.

Healer Haven strides into the room carrying a basket filled with medical equipment from the healer room, forcing Victor to pause the movie of memories and open his eyes.

"Natalie and John Storm. I'm Dr. Haven." She holds her hand out for each of them to shake.

John rises from the bed and shakes her hand. "Yes, we met last time when my son fell over the bobcat."

"Is he out of the woods?" Natalie rises from beside the bed, glancing at Healer Haven's hand. She doesn't try to wipe the tears from her eyes as she walks around the doctor to the other side of the bed, sitting on the stool Victor abandoned earlier. Healer Haven lowers her hand quickly and faces Natalie. Her face is impassive as always, Natalie's stunt having no effect on her.

"No, but he is strong—one of the strongest cubs I've seen. One I attribute to his lineage and bloodline."

Natalie and John stiffen and exchange tense glances.

Victor suppresses a snort.

Healer Haven sighs. "Relax, I do not know what you know or don't know, and to be quite honest, I do not care. My priority is to this boy and his safety." She walks around the bed next to Natalie, placing the basket on the bedside table. Her hands move deftly as she begins connecting the IV to Erin's arm. "Regardless, I know this boy, and I know that he would not keep his existence from you. Plus, no human simply loves wolfsbane. Your car reeked of it. I knew for the smell to have seeped into his skin to this extent, it would have been something forced on him. I know you were simply trying to protect him, and it looks like it has paid off."

"The arrow that pierced Erin's thigh was laced with wolfsbane. Dr. Haven said Erin's constant exposure, though subtle and often indirect, means he built up a slight immunity to it. She was able to wash out the wound and flush his system before it killed him." Victor takes a step forward to stand at the foot of the bed, glancing at Erin. The blanket is pulled to his waist, his arms resting beside him, the left one bent slightly as his shoulder is wrapped in bandages that go around his chest. A sad smile twists his lips cruelly as he remembers how Healer Haven moved earlier while working. She got to work the second Erin's back hit the mattress in the healing room, knowing exactly how to clean the wound, wash all the wolfsbane out, and stitch the skin.

It was different from before.

They are prepared now.

Beatrice had stood outside the room, watching the commotion with narrowed green eyes while on the phone to Natalie and John. Ben was checking the borders and contacting Alphas. Following trails. Moving. Acting.

Watching.

Searching.

Waiting.

And all Victor could do was stand, his hand shaking as it clenched tightly around Erin's fingers. It was only when Erin was brought safely into his room, his wound firmly wrapped in a clean bandage and blankets nested around his hips, that Victor allowed himself to breathe.

"Well, Erin being The White Wolf helps immensely," Healer Haven contributes as she checks Erin's vitals and wound for infection once more. When she's done, she walks to stand next to Victor at the foot of the bed and gazes at Erin. For the first time since he's known her, Victor sees something shine behind her eyes. "It was all him. I did nothing spectacular. His strength and endurance pulled him through this ordeal." She smiles sadly, like she's remembering something bittersweet.

Oh. Victor jolts at the realization. Healer Haven would have been the one to help Stacy give birth. She knew—since Erin first arrived. She knew who he was. She was the first to hold him. To hear his heartbeat. To clean his eyes and help his lungs take in air.

Why had she not said anything? He realizes now that no one did. Growing up, there was never mention of Stacy being pregnant, let alone giving birth. They avoided the topic, often referring to the traitors as simply that—traitors. She who shall not be named. Those who gave in to the Goddess's darkness. Had Stella asked them not to say anything? Did she think that Stacy went so far as to murder her own son? But she didn't, or if she had tried, she failed.

Wait, was Healer Haven the one who resc—

"Well then." Healer Haven pats Erin's shins twice before bowing her head to his parents. She turns to Victor, baring her neck before bowing, too. "Alpha."

Victor nods as she leaves the room, waiting for the door to shut softly behind her before turning to face his guests. "Natalie, John, I promise you I'll find the Treelark bastard who did this and deal with him swiftly."

"Treelark?" Natalie rises slowly from the bed, confusion painted on her face, like she's trying to remember the name of an old movie.

Victor nods. "That's right. They are the California Pack."

"There's more?" John probes lightly. He doesn't know?

"Yeah. One in each state. However, before that, we were four. The Treelarks were one of them. They are old blood. Which is why my aunt believes the people who attacked Erin were from that Pack. Not only did the arrow bear their trademark, they've always had some ... issues with how my Pack runs our business. Erin will be safe here in the meantime, and you guys are more than welcome to come and go as you please to see him."

"HA!" Natalie barks. She crosses her arms and uncrosses them as she shakes her head. Victor tilts his head at her show of annoyance. He looks to John for answers, only to see him clutching the blanket draped over Erin's legs with a tight frown.

He's found the culprit, Erin is being looked after, and they have just been given free rein to meander around his temporary Pack house. No perceived human has been given that much grace. Is that not enough?

Natalie stomps over to Victor and points a finger in his face. "We kept him safe for nearly twenty-two years, and the minute he meets you he starts getting hurt left, right, and center!" she yells, her voice dripping with bitter malice. "It's like a curse! You, this place, they're all cursed."

Victor feels his blood freeze at her words. There it is. Irrefutable evidence. Ironic, now that Erin isn't awake to hear it, to face the truth he so desperately wanted to be a lie. He chides himself for ever thinking, ever *wishing,* that it could be true. Victor bows his head to hide the sour twist he knows his features are morphing into.

Curse. That's right. She's right. He's cursed. Erin's cursed. Because of *Her.* Because of *Him.* Their eternal Goddess did this to them. He wants to ask Her. He wants to know what they did to deserve this treatment. Did they not give enough the first time? Were their prayers too loud? Not loud enough? Why them? Why now? Was it Kazamir? Was it another Pack? Did they do something? Why do they have to suffer this goddammed fucking curse if someone else betrayed Her? If she's seeking revenge for someone else's actions? What happened after they died, after the war ended? Why did she turn on them? Why did she bring them back, then let them be separated once more?

Victor raises his head and juts his chin out. Her eyes widen slightly, a glimmer flashing across them too quick for him to catch and hold.

John stands from his seat, his eyes fixed on him.

It doesn't matter, does it?

Goddesses may be eternal, and curses may never die. But every curse can be broken. She taught him that, all those years ago in that dark, decrepit dungeon.

Victor parts his lips, ready to defend his bond with Erin, when Ben walks into the room. He doesn't spare anyone a glance, just walks right next to Victor and turns his back so no one can see what he's saying.

"We scanned the perimeter and five miles past it in all directions," he whispers, voice calm but firm, trace amounts of anger still lacing underneath. "There was no one. No print in the soil, no scent on the air. Nothing."

Victor spares Natalie and John one more seething glance before he crosses his arms and walks out onto the balcony. The breeze helps to cool his racing head. "Check again," he commands.

"Tsk." Ben comes to stand beside him, one hand on the railing as he turns sideways to face Victor. "Vic, it doesn't make sense. The Treelarks aren't meant to arrive until the day of the Council Meeting, and this isn't like their past M.Os. The intel we've received—"

"Check. It. Again," Victor growls between clenched teeth. His jaw hurts; it keeps twitching. He's clenching the railing so hard the wood creaks and bends. He doesn't care who was meant to arrive when, or what they did in the past. Someone hurt his mate, and they have hard evidence saying it was a Treelark wolf.

Stella said it herself, and when has she lied?

"They could've sent in a false statement saying they were going to arrive late and instead arrive early to plan this attack. If they have been watching, they would have intel about Erin being my mate. Or even seen him during the training session, or any of the other times he was shifted and running over the past week. Maybe they've been here even before Erin showed up. I don't know. I don't care. I just want them found and held responsible. Now."

Victor fixes his gaze on Erin through gaps in the dancing curtain, his parents huddled around him protectively. Resolve rolls around his belly for a heartbeat before he claws it up and speaks it out for the whole universe to hear. "I won't stand here in a state of confusion, nor will I let silence fester through the Pack. Tell everyone to get ready and send out notices to the other Packs. If no one is found, then the whole Treelark Pack is to blame. No one hurts me or my own and gets away with it."

Not again.

Ben slowly closes his eyes before turning to face the forest. His fingers clench the rail in front of him as his scent disappears completely. Victor snarls at that. What is he trying to hide? His disagreement? *Disappointment?* Why? At what? Does he not want the ones responsible for hurting Erin to be found? This is an active threat against them. It has nothing to do with the grievances he's had about his mother lately, so why is he acting like something's been missed? Why is he making this so difficult? Why is he pushing back?

Why?

Why?

Fucking WHY?

"Yes, Alpha," Ben rumbles.

THIRTY-SIX

The war is over with Tala and Nahale's deaths. Their sacrifice put an end to it all.

That was not her plan. This was not the way her Hope was meant to achieve peace.

The humans agreed to stop killing the wolves with the death of their prince. Despite his choice to side with her wolves, his subjects still loved him. They cried for him. Wailed at the sky, his name falling from their trembling lips, not their King's.

However, King Halian's wife could not hide her despair at her husband's demise. Her cries for him were far louder than the ones screamed for her son's death. Even if her husband abused him so, her eyes turned the other way. Even if he was the one to shoot the killing arrow, her anger was pointed at them. She grieved for her husband. Her King. And begrudgingly, her heir.

Hëna had not realized the Queen was at the back of the troops, hidden behind another row of archers over the hill at a human battle camp. Her lips were ripe with fruitcake dust when asked if Ylli could take Nahale's body for burial. He deserved to be buried the wolf way, beside his mate.

The Queen bled no tears while giving her approval.

What a family affair they made war out to be.

The wolves agreed to stop killing the humans. Kazr, the older cub with the bright red locks of hair, who had fiercely guarded her, became the next Alpha. He had no blood relation to Tala's line, but he was his closest friend. They had grown up together, as had their fathers, and their fathers before. The bond ran deep.

He was the obvious choice. The strongest choice.

The choice Tala would have made.

She placed the headpiece on his head and braided his hair into the vines down his back. He refused the mark.

"The days of one Alpha are over," he said gruffly, squeezing the other headpiece worn by heirs after they are born, jaw clenching at Nahale's dried blood splattered against the blue jewel. It looks dimmer now. Will it ever shine again?

He meets with the human Queen. Demands the release of his Pack. She agrees, wanting nothing more to do with his kind. A command is laid—the only one agreed upon to make up for the death of their Alpha and Luna. Humans are to stay far away from them. She lives on one side of this world, and he, the other.

Her husband took Tala's body, letting the wolves perform their burial in the forest alongside Alaric's final resting place. Tala and Nahale share a grave—blue, white, yellow, red, and purple wildflowers tucked around their clean bodies as warm earth is thrown over them like a blanket. Whispers of gratitude are spoken into the cool night air. It makes a striking figure. A large black wolf with a smaller pale human beside him. Nestled together. Guarding each other in death. Soft smiles tug at both their lips. She places a hand on her husband's arm before he can take their souls.

"It is not fair," she whispers.

"It is life," he responds.

But what if it doesn't have to be?

Magic pours easily from her palm, twirling around her fingertips like thread. A red thread. She gazes at her husband. Brow's trembling. Eyes pleading. Tears falling.

"Please, my Star."

He licks his lips, looking away. Looking at them. He loved them, just as much as she did. Perhaps more, in fact. Closing his eyes, he raises his hands. Bright light reaches toward the graves. The air around them glows.

The wolves do not return to the night sky.

In his palm sit two souls. One white. One black. They squirm, reaching for each other. She steps to her husband and places her hands over his. Magic sweetens the air around them, pushing and pulling against her soul as it intertwines with her husband's. The thread wraps around the souls, tethering to them. Tethering them to each other. There is a warmth in her heart. In her palms.

A howl sings between them.

The wind blows gently.

The two wolves return to the night sky.

Waiting.

"What does that bind mean now, Goddess?"

She looks at the young cub, Kazr's little one. His jaw-length red hair is still just as striking, like a poppy swinging in a field during summer. And his eyes. They are as green as the dense forest around them. Curious. Watchful.

Protective.

"What is your name?" she asks, kneeling to his level. "I have been wondering."

The young wolf grins; his canines are only just growing in. "My mama calls me Bé."

"Well, Bé," she pinches his cheek, making him giggle, "it means that they will find each other, always. In every life cycle. And they will protect you all. Lead you all. They have proven themselves. My fated warriors. Marked by instinct." She turns her attention briefly to gaze upon the wolves still gathered, listening, watching, waiting. "I said during their mating ceremony that they were bound, did I not? Fate and Instinct will guide them so, until this blessing is fulfilled. I give you my word, a promise on my soul, that this is true."

"Oh." He looks down with a pout. Her smile slips, eyes pinching in confusion. That was not the response she had hoped.

Lowering her head, she lifts his chin with her hand, forcing his gaze to her once more.

"Do not be jealous. They will not be the only ones bound together by the blood of wolves and fated by the history of stars. You all have one—a fated mate. Someone to complete you. A soul who even the stars cannot keep apart. So, once you choose and complete this life, search for them in the next. You will not remember them, not exactly, but you will know them all the same. By scent. By touch. By the beating of your heart."

They have already started to split, one Pack into four. This is the only way she knows to keep them from diverging completely, to ensure that they do not forget each other, do not forsake their history, their bond.

And keep hope that one day, the dream that she shared with her Hopes can come true once more.

"B-but what if I want to be with them, too, in the other lives?" Bé mutters.

Her lips widen. Oh, she has not had to wait long indeed! How beautiful her Hope was to live on in the memory of her cubs. For her cubs to want to be with them still. Her fingers tingle with magic.

Waiting.

This is a bad idea ...

But Tala would say to do it. He would raise an eyebrow, wondering what was taking her so long already.

And Nahale ... he would smile wide. Cheek's light and pink in blush as he watches. He would reassure her that there would be no harm in it.

Because there won't be.

Her Hope fought bravely. They deserved more time.

So she gave it to them.

But so did their Pack. The family that fought beside them. The family that didn't get a chance to live with them leading.

So ... should they not be given the same chance?

She looks to her husband. He sighs, a ghost of a smile crossing his lips. His words from before scream in her mind.

What was I expecting? They are your children, after all.

No.

"Our children," she mouths to him.

He nods.

She grabs Bé's small hands, and her husband places his on top. There are no scratches, no scars. He has heard of war, but he has not lived it, staying hidden beneath a fallen tree trunk. And she will make sure that he never has to have those memories. None of them will.

She will make certain of it.

She leans in close and whispers, "What if you can?"

His eyes sparkle, like a little bit of her magic has already woven in and blessed his soul before the spell has even finished being cast.

She gins, all teeth and blushing cheeks.

A tragedy that will end in freedom. A love that will bind them all. Eternally.

That is her spell.

That is her blessing.

It mixes with her husband's magic easily.

Waiting.

"How long will it last?" Bé asks, flipping his hands over and over, looking for any sign of difference. He will not find one. Not in this life. Kazr smiles gently, patting his cub on the shoulder.

"For as long as I live," she replies.

"How long will that be?"

"Well." She stands, lacing her husband's hand in hers. "Goddesses cannot die. So, I suppose ... for eternity."

THIRTY-SEVEN

Erin can't move his arm. There's a warm pressure keeping him from bending it. He peeps through his eyelashes and sees Victor's right hand resting above his knee. Blinking, his vision trails a path from Victor's hand to his sleeping face. His arm cuts off most of the left side of his face across his nose, but Erin can still see how his thin lips are parted slightly, the breath rustling the blanket after every exhale.

The corner of Erin's lips curve into a half smile at the picture. Suppressing a groan, he lifts his free arm and pokes at Victor's tense eyebrow. Victor sniffs, his thick brows flinching as he opens his eyes. They widen, his hand squeezing his knee in surprise before all the energy seems to leave him in a rush. His shoulders drop, and his face scrunches, lips trembling as he begins to cry.

Erin opens his arms, and Victor, mindful of the injured left one, crawls over him to lie on his right. He wraps his arms around Erin's shoulders, placing his right hand on Erin's neck so his fingertips can rub against his jaw and into his hair.

Erin pulls him in closer, so half his body is on top of him like a koala. He whispers, voice quiet and intimate, "Hey."

Victor smiles into Erin's skin, the cold press of his lips indistinguishable from the wet drops pooling in Erin's collarbone. "Hey."

"How long was I out?" Erin nuzzles Victor's head and squeezes his waist.

Victor sniffs, his shin rubbing slowly against Erin's leg as if it needs reminding that the body is still pumping blood. That he's still alive. With him. "Five days. It's Sunday now. Don't ask me for the time, I don't know. Just look at the sun or something."

"Hmm." Erin lifts his head off the pillow in an attempt to get Victor to raise his, too. "I can't see it, though, if you keep your face hidden."

Victor laughs, the sound wet and muffled by tears, but still causing both of their bodies to shake. "You just woke up and you're already being cheeky?"

Erin grins. "What can I say, the grind don't stop."

Victor rolls over slightly to rest his head on the pillow, his hand on Erin's jaw moving down to rest on his hip. His eyes are paler than Erin's used to and near empty, like all the light has been sucked out so that not even the shadows could remain hidden.

Victor takes in a shuddering breath. "I thought I lost you," he admits quietly.

Erin lets go of Victor's hand on his hip and cups his face. "You didn't. And you won't," he says firmly.

Victor shakes his head. "I could feel it, the moment it hit. We haven't marked each other yet, but I could still feel it. Maybe it was the memories ... the pain from before mixing in at that moment. I don't know. I tried to keep them separate. To live in this life, like we promised, but it was so familiar. The rush of anger, the fucking arrow—" Victor gulps, his eyes blinking rapidly as he looks away. Erin feels his arm throb at the memory, both memories, the nerves replaying the overlapping events.

Victor turns his head further into the pillow and squeezes his eyes shut. "Every time I closed my eyes, I saw it. It was like a nightmare I couldn't forget. My limbs would freeze, and the pain would hit all over again. Healer Haven said on Thursday that the wolfsbane was completely flushed out, but you weren't waking up. The longer you slept, the more the image would change. You'd get hit in the heart or the neck, and I couldn't reach you in time before you fell. Your fur would become completely drenched in red as the smell of blood covered you, and I—"

"Saved me," Erin interrupts him. He starts to lean forward, and Victor moves off to help him. Grabbing some pillows to put behind his back, Erin beckons Victor close to him again. They resume their position from before, but this time Erin drags Victor's head down to rest on his chest above his heart.

"You saved me," he repeats, fingers threading through Victor's thin blonde hair. "That's all you need to think about. I'm here and I'm alive." He gestures to his injury and smiles sweetly. "I can already feel it healing, so you must've acted quick if it's only been five days."

Victor huffs. "I didn't do anything. It was all Healer Haven."

"Nonsense," Erin scoffs. "You were here. I could feel your presence. Your scent enveloping me, chasing the poison way like how a wolf hunts a rabbit. That made all the difference."

Victor chuffs and shuffles closer, the two of them settling into a comfortable silence. Erin, feeling a cool breeze fly through the room, looks toward the open balcony. The green curtains are dancing between the double doors, concealing some of the outside world from view. He had a balcony in the palace, too, and the thick black curtains would often dance the same, albeit much slower. It wasn't so much the balcony that he loved, but the freedom of the view it showed him. And now, he wants nothing more than to run under the moon and stars alongside his Pack, but instead, he's holed up in bed. Healing. Trapped. Hidden from view.

A typical story that sounds achingly familiar.

Erin closes his eyes and takes a deep breath so his lungs can fill with fresh air. A familiar smell floods his senses. He sniffs the air. Once. Twice. Looks to the left. On the bedside table is a basket of fresh lilies. He taps Victor on the arm and nods his head toward the basket. "Did my parents bring those?"

Victor cast his eyes quickly to the basket before dropping his head onto Erin's chest again. "Yeah, they've been dropping by multiple times a day. They refused to let the flowers wilt."

Erin hums in contemplation. "They didn't make a fuss about moving me back home?"

Victor's lips curl. "They did, but I managed to convince them not to with Healer Haven's help. I—we needed to stay close. It was healing to both of us." Victor starts tapping his fingers against Erin's hipbone. "Natalie was pretty mad, though."

"Yeah, I bet. What'd she say?" Erin's lips, heavy with guilt, fall into a pout as he scans the room for any other changes. He finds none. There isn't a backpack full of his clothes like the last time he spent the night, or anything else that belongs to him finding a home in Victor's space. He feels a twinge of pain at the realization. He takes a deep breath in and exhales it slowly. Victor still hasn't spoken, causing Erin to tilt his head down slightly. Victor's eyes are glazed. Surely his parents wouldn't have been too harsh on him; this wasn't his fault. Or even the Pack's.

"Victor?"

"I'm sorry," Victor breathes out quickly. "All of this is my fault."

Erin's smile is unsteady. "We went through this already—"

"No," Victor cuts him off. He sighs harshly and detangles himself from Erin completely.

Erin's heartbeat quickens in worry at his mate's frustration. Thinking Victor is going to get off the bed, he reaches his hand out to grab a fistful of his shirt. Victor pauses, shame heavy in the line of his brows when he looks over his shoulder at Erin's trembling hand.

Reaching behind him, Victor turns and releases Erin's hand from his shirt. He holds it in his own, thumb moving over the back of Erin's palm. "I've been trying to believe it, that everything I grew up knowing is wrong. I've been considering the possibilities."

Erin nods, not trusting himself to speak. His body feels like lead, and he doesn't know if the throbbing sensation is coming from his shoulder injury or the worry in his heart.

"But," Victor drops his gaze, "I'm finding it hard. You say the curse is a lie, Star, but things like this keep happening."

"Litt—"

"No, listen to me, please. There is irrefutable evidence that there are wolves still out there who were—are—loyal to Stacy and Gray. They helped your mom and dad that night. But those wolves don't trust me. It may have been your parents who started that fight, but Stella said it was *my dad* who delivered the killing blow to them, before he succumbed to his injuries. Ever since, curse be damned, they have wanted me dead. That invitation now extends to you. They want this power for themselves. To kill us all, thinking it'll place them high on some recognition list The Goddess carries."

"I don't understand." Erin squeezes Victor's hand and leans off the headboard. Distant words speaking of power grabs ring in his ears. But the memory is foggy, the words clipped and staticky. "Regardless of what the truth is, I get your parents had to fight against mine to protect the Pack that night, but I thought Packs didn't get involved with other Packs' internal business."

"They don't, but this is a curse from a Goddess, Erin. When do curses ever make sense?" Victor sneers under his breath.

"What?" Erin mouths, taken aback. "Victor, you can't just make that assumption. You need proof. Physical proof!"

"What, you want me to run downstairs and grab the arrow that shot you?"

Erin flinches as Victor yanks his hands away, running stiff fingers through his hair. This isn't right. Victor was close, so close to believing in Erin's instinct that the truth of that night had been twisted. Even without proof, he was trying. So what happened?

He thinks back to the attack. He recalls the pain when he was hit and the screaming as people ran away.

Further. Look further.

Remember more. Past the pain.

Memories rise in answer.

No. This life. *Focus on this life.*

Ben runs into the forest. Healer Haven pulls out the arrow. Beatrice jogs calmly to the house with some of the cubs. Little Red. Stella—

Erin opens his eyes and pulls on Victor's hand. "How do you know all of this? Everything about what happened that night with our parents? About them having allies," he asks, panic loud in his voice.

Victor furrows his eyes in confusion. "Stella told me during my Alpha Acceptance Ceremony. Some of the other Alphas backed her up when I asked at the Countcl Meeting that year, but we didn't have time to get into much detail about it."

The unease rolls like poison throughout Erin's body. It curdles in his stomach. Knots in his heart. His lips tremble, a shaky breath of air sliding past them. The wound in his shoulder burns like ice fire.

"Vic—"

The door glides open, and Ben walks into the room. He softly shuts the door behind him and faces them with eyes clear and bright like green grass shining in the summer sun.

Oh.

Oh.

He's seen those eyes before.

"What if Stella was lying?"

THIRTY-EIGHT

"I think you were right, Erin. There is someone on drugs," Victor growls deep, eyes narrowed into slits. He lets go of Erin's hand and rises from the bed, never breaking eye contact with Ben. "They have poisoned my cousin into believing his mother is some kind of villain, which I'm quite sick of hearing about."

Erin's stomach churns.

A deep tension sparks across the room. He recalls the night Ben came over to his house, the mention of the fight between them. Did they never resolve it? He clicks his tongue against his teeth, moving to get out of bed when a flare of burning heat travels from his shoulder to his belly button. The sensation is like knives slashing his insides. His lips scrunch into a grimace, but he clenches his teeth hard to keep the sound from leaking out. The last thing he needs is Victor getting all protective and annoyed with him, blabbing about making his injury worse while he's in a highly emotional—territorial—state.

Then they really will get nowhere with this conversation.

"I'm not on drugs," Ben says calmly, like he was expecting this anger. He breaks eye contact first and glances at Erin's shoulder. He rounds the bed, grabs the stool by the bedside table, and drags it to the foot of the bed. He sits, motioning for Victor to do the same.

He saw the wince. Of course he did. Victor rolls his eyes but sits at the foot of the bed. Erin reaches over to lay a hand on his tense back before settling beside him.

Victor ignores him, his muscles tense like a predator ready to pounce on its prey.

"Oh? Then explain yourself," Victor commands using his deep Alpha voice. "And I'd better like your answer. I'm not above locking you up in a mental institution as soon as the Council Meeting is over and we are back home in New York."

Ben rests his elbows on his knees and laces his fingers together. With his head held high, he speaks, "Don't interrupt me. You need to listen till the end."

"Ben—"

"This is important!" Ben shouts, eyes flashing. His voice rings throughout the room. If Erin didn't know any better, if he were human, he would have thought Ben was the Alpha in that moment. "No interruptions."

Victor's nostrils flare, his scowl growing. Erin leans forward and grabs Victor's arm. He searches Ben's eyes and realizes, for the first time since they've met, he can see straight through them. No dark trees cover the path into his thoughts, and no dark shadows cover the warmth of his heart's beliefs.

All Erin can see in his bright green eyes is a forest of truth.

Many truths.

And, when he feels Victor's arm go lax and gazes at him out of the corner of his eye, Erin knows he sees it, too, despite wanting to. His sour face softens.

"Ok," Ben starts. "Short version, Stella has been manipulating you and lying to you this whole time. She was the one who orchestrated everything."

"Wait, where is Stella? What if she hears you talking to us?" Erin asks before Victor can say anything impulsive and rude.

Ben shakes his head. "She's out in Green Lake getting her nails done with Beatrice. They'll probably be out late afterward, shopping."

"You've roped your little sister into this play now? How far are you willing to go to make these delusions seem real?" Victor hisses.

"She came to me," Ben corrects. "I would never tell anyone anything that could put them in danger. Not after everything."

"What exactly does everything mean?" Erin twists his fingers around his thumb. Tap tap tapping them against his palm.

"Exactly that, everything." Ben nods. He starts speaking quickly as if Stella herself is prowling the halls looking for them. "She was the one who made the Treelark arrow and attacked Erin. She was also the one who was behind the coup d'état."

"Not this again," Victor grits and rolls his eyes. "What is with your insistence that the Treelark Pack are good wolves? And now you've resorted to blaming the one person who has been nothing but good to us our whole lives. Not only did she raise you, me, and Beatrice by herself, but she also managed a Pack. She kept us afloat." Anger causes his muscles to roll under his skin and seep into the air, mixing with his scent. His eyes narrow into slits at Ben. "How dare you go against your mother, especially with no proof. What a splendid son you are."

Ben doesn't seem to take any offense by Victor's jab. He simply raises a brow and speaks like a man who has already seen the other players' cards and knows he has the winning hand. "I don't need proof. I was there."

Erin's heart spikes.

"What are you talking about? We were all at the training session last Tuesday." Victor sighs and turns to Erin, hands pointing widely through the air between them as if he can get Ben to stop speaking gibberish instead.

"No," Ben clarifies. He locks his eyes on Erin now, startling him. "I was there the night Stella murdered both of your parents."

The tapping stops.

Erin curls his fingers into the sheets underneath him.

Victor is grumbling beside him about how the stress has gotten to Ben, and whatever he's fighting with Stella about isn't something he should be dragging them into.

Erin can hear him speaking, but the words are muffled when they reach his ears. The blood pumping through his veins slowly turns to ice as the dots connect.

Ben helped Erin arrange the date he had with Victor at the Botanical Gardens, no questions asked. And later, when Victor was avoiding him, Ben was the one who brought them back together.

He got Victor to the mall, basically kickstarting Erin's acceptance of his werewolf lineage.

He already seemed to know that Stella was actively threatening him, not surprised by the cruel act, but surprised by the intensity of them. Erin thought Stella had just warned the whole Pack, but what if that wasn't it?

He thinks back to how wary Ben seemed that morning, before the training session began. What if Ben's apprehension was because he knew what Stella was capable of?

Because he's seen it happen before.

Because he's lived it for the past thirty years.

Erin's heart drops to his stomach, the realization punching the air out of his gut.

Ben was born first. He had to go through this alone. Those memories ... Ben said Stella was the one trying to hurt Victor. He would know, not only because he's her son, but because he's the Beta. Besides Victor, Ben is the one who interacts with other Packs the most. He always has an eye on everyone and everything, gathering as much information as possible. Learning who is on Victor's side and who isn't. Reading old texts. Legends. All this time ... and they ... they were acting like fools, playing right into Stella's hands.

Ben's been trying to protect Victor since the moment he was born. To defend *him*, the second he set foot onto Pack land. He's done nothing but help them. Erin shakes his head, his hand reaching to press against his lips. They're trembling.

Erin knew they should've gotten Ben to help them from the very start. But Victor didn't want to. So, he didn't push the matter, thinking he could fight against Stella alone. He should've pushed harder. He should've asked for help himself.

After all, wolves are pack animals, aren't they?

Rule 101 of being in Pack: don't hunt alone.

Erin flinches when Victor stands from the bed and starts pacing. His feet are loud against the hardwood as his arms swing wildly in the air. He's still ranting about Ben's insolence, but the man in question hasn't moved. Ben's eyes are still locked on Erin. They look sad. His small smile is sad. Resigned. Like he knew this moment would come and doesn't regret a single moment.

Like he's relieved he doesn't have to hide anymore.

Oh.

Oh.

Erin's breath hitches. Victor stops his rambling. Concern takes over his body as he sits back on the bed. "Star?"

"You knew," Erin whispers. "This whole time since the very first day I arrived here with my parents. You knew who I was, what *we* were, beyond all this mess with Stella ... and you said nothing."

"Star, what are you talking about?" Victor places a gentle hand on Erin's knee, but Erin ignores him.

"How?" Erin asks, the word no louder than a mouse scurrying across carpet.

"As I said, I was there." Ben looks to the left, the memories no doubt playing behind his eyes. "I saw it all. The flames, the blood. I can still feel the scent of it strangling my nose and throat at night sometimes." He chuckles mirthlessly, his face twisting in pain. "It's funny, at first, I don't realize which memory it is. What time I'm reliving. Then the pain squeezes my heart when I see the woman who birthed me walk through the broken glass doors into the play den, claws adding to the blood already soaking the floor. She steps over my father's dead body, not flinching the slightest at his twisted neck. I remember thinking how his eyes shouldn't be able to look at me with the direction his body was facing. I was hiding in one of the baskets, a blanket draped over my head. Beatrice was in my arms. I was scared I was going to strangle her with how hard I was pressing against her lips to keep her from crying. She was so little ... just a few weeks old." His eyes close as he takes a shuddering breath. Victor grips Erin's hand strongly but doesn't interrupt, mouth sealed tight.

Tight.

Tight.

Tight.

"I learned a few years later that the whole thing was her idea because she wanted control of the Bellmore Pack, Erin's Pack, rightfully, regardless of what he presented as. And now that Victor has found his mate, that it's Erin specifically, Stella can't control him. And she won't be able to convince the others who still believe that the Moon Goddess cast a blessing, not a curse, now that you've both been reincarnated."

Erin raises his hand in question. "What do you mean? Isn't the whole legend built around the fact that the curse only happens after we meet?"

"Look around." Ben tilts his head. "I haven't seen any giant white or black wolves on a murderous killing spree, have you? The earth still spins, and werewolves still live in bliss."

"What if She's waiting?" Victor's jaw twitches, it's clenched so tight. "The curse may reach its end at the Council Meeting ... like some kind of ticking time bomb on a fucked up timer."

"If Stella told you that, then don't believe it," Ben says. "She would say anything to keep you in line. Originally, she only wanted to take over and rule as Alpha, but when Victor presented as The Black Wolf, her plan changed. She grew greedy, and history began to play on loop. She convinced Victor to ignore his instincts and never look for his mate while encouraging all the Packs of the exact opposite. She bred fear in you, Cousin, while dousing it across America."

"You speak as if she's really that powerful," Victor mutters, pressing his thumbs into the sides of his temple.

"She is," Ben replies. "Without the Bellmores and all their friends, Stella had complete control over the Pack."

"And with Victor believing in Stella wholeheartedly ..." The final dot connects to form a complete picture in Erin's brain.

Ben nods gravely. "Stella would be the one in control, always at the top. Whether she's Alpha or not. A power without magic. Greed as her crown."

Erin snarls at the irony of it, the resemblance to a King forgotten. "A very human werewolf," he whispers.

"This is a load of fucking bullshit." Victor gets off the bed, laughing hysterically. He puts his hands on his hips and turns to Erin. "Don't tell me you believe this shit."

"I mean ... it makes sense, Love."

"Unbelievable." Victor throws his hands up in the air and shakes his head.

"Victor." Erin leans forward and turns his body as much as he can without pain flaring along his shoulder. "What if he's right?"

"How can any of this be right?" Victor responds coldly. "Stella's practically an angel, and has been nothing but nice to you since you arrived. You should've seen how worried she's been for you the past five days."

Ben scoffs and crosses his arms. "Yeah, worried that he'd actually recover."

"She threatened me, Victor." Erin watches as his words tackle Victor and suspend him in place. "The first day I arrived, and the night you left that note on my car. Breaking tools and sabotaging the landscaping. You want to know how my camera broke, that day we all went to the mall? Stella hit me with her car."

"She *what*?" Victor's eyes flare. "No, Erin. I'm sure it was an acci—"

"Ask the Pack." A name pops up, matching the face of the wolf he remembers helping him that day. "Jerry. He'll tell you what he saw if you don't believe me.

She's been keeping an eye on me. At first, yeah, it was probably because I was a distraction. Someone who had a connection with you. Maybe she guessed there was more to it, like you did. Maybe that scared her, thinking that if I were a wolf and your mate that I'd end up holding more power over you than she did. Or that our 'curse' would involve her destruction, too. But I realize now that what she was most worried about was that I'd make you see the truth."

"Ok, this has got to be one massive misunderstanding." Victor pinches the bridge of his nose.

"No, my love, not this time." Erin shakes his head, licking his lips. "It's like Ben said. Everything I've sensed and seen about Stella all points to her being a terrible person. Even my mother warned me about her."

"Natalie gets no say in this!" Victor barks, arms dropping to his side as he whirls on Erin. "She was simply worried about you, and that's as far as her involvement gets to go. Especially now." He sighs, the sound harsh as it escapes past his lips. His face is all hard lines and sharp edges. Hands clenching as his anger suffocates the air around them. Erin senses it, goosebumps rising along his skin. Victor's Alpha is almost out of control.

Erin rolls his shoulder and lifts his head, nostrils flaring. "Fine, then what about after we told everyone who I was?"

Victor startles in confusion. "What does that have to do with this?"

"The first thing Stella brought up was me moving. She was trying to get under my skin and tear us apart."

"That was—"

"No," Erin interrupts Victor. "It would also explain those weird looks from the older wolves, too. Most likely, they don't just see my parents in me but are the ones who know about what Stella did that night. They were waiting to see what I would do. If I knew and was back to enact my revenge. Waiting to see if *you* knew and what *you* would do."

"That's right," Ben confirms. "We were a Pack of nearly three hundred, one of the biggest in America, very few broke off after the split. Stella gathered allies, promising to split the wealth between them, whispering about how she knew of a way to protect them from the curse, should The Black Wolf and The White Wolf ever reincarnate in their lives. Then, after she culled those whom she knew would never sway, Stella managed to convince those remaining after the battle that the Moon Goddess had corrupted Stacy and Gray, that *She* had gotten humans to whisper in their ear, and that was why they went on a murdering spree. Even though some knew she was lying, they swapped sides to protect themselves." He looked to Erin. "I've been working, slowly, trying to figure out who over the years. There are more than half of us now who are loyal to you."

"This is ridiculous," Victor mumbles, fingers clenching and unclenching. His face is pallid, but the annoyance in his voice is much stronger than it was before. "What's that nail salon called? I'm going to go get Stella and bring her here so we can settle this now."

"I don't know. Didn't ask." Ben uncrosses his arms and rises from his seat. A muscle jumps in his jaw. He grits his teeth.

He can sense Victor's anger fuming.

"Victor." Erin stands, throat tight.

"Call her," Victor demands. "You want Beatrice to be a part of this so badly, then she can come too."

"She was already part of this," Ben says slowly. "You think someone capable of killing their brother will draw the line at their children?"

Victor's eyes narrow into slits. He steps right up to Ben, their faces only inches apart. "What did you just say?"

Erin has never heard his voice as deep and threatening before. It causes tears to build in his eyes. He tries tugging on that string between them. Victor doesn't flinch, his fury boiling over all his senses, drowning Erin out completely.

"How many times do I need to say it? Stella was behind the coup. And yes, it was a coup, not a rebellion. She blamed it all on Stacy and Gray. She killed Uncle Shaun. She killed Aunt Hope. She killed Stacy and Gray. And she didn't even cry when Dad died. Hell, I'd say she was the one who killed him, too. Her own mate. She brought those wolves with her." Ben lifts impassive eyes past Victor's shoulder, disrespecting his Alpha, to look at Erin. It's like he knows he can't convince Victor that what he's saying is the truth.

Erin starts to wonder if the ghosts of these souls were to come back and confirm what happened if Victor would still deny it.

Victor trusts Ben. He's always trusted Ben.

But Stella's claws have left scars so deep that the trust between them is breaking.

And Erin can't do anything to fix it.

Victor clenches and unclenches his fists when Ben turns to glare at him. "Stella attacked first, and Uncle Shaun led the charge to defend with Alpha Gray. I was with Beatrice and Dad playing when the shouting began. He hid us in one of the blanket baskets before running out. I don't know how much time passed before he came back in, barely alive. A wolf was behind him, not from our Pack. They fought. He twisted Dad's head. I heard the snap. Then he died, too. Mom came in shortly after, her eyes were wild. I thought she was looking for us, to help us. Her nostrils flared, and I knew she knew we were there. But then she left. I focused and heard her moving downstairs, to the side of the house where your room was. I knew then what she was going to do. So, I left Beatrice in the basket, hidden. I had to believe that she wouldn't kill me, that she still had some semblance of love for us, or, at the very least, I could startle her, be a distraction until someone came. Or, I don't know, foil her plans enough that she lost her momentum. *Something.* I was almost there when I heard a crash. Looking over the railing, I saw Uncle Shaun fall through one of the downstairs windows into the house. He looked ... bad. He didn't get up."

Ben swallows hard. Victor shudders, taking a step back.

"Mom walked slowly toward him. The look on her face, Vic ... it terrified me. I had barely taken another breath when she stuck her claws into his heart. I can still hear your mom's howl ringing in my ears. And then it stopped. And I knew what had happened."

Erin's heart pulls uncomfortably in his chest. He looks at Victor and sees his brows are furrowed together. Pain screams across his face. Erin knows what memory he's listening to. It's scratching between his ears, too. Though he died first, the pain Victor felt right before reverberated through his body. He remembers thinking how he wanted to crawl into a hole, sink a knife into his heart and carve it out, never to wake again.

Ben takes a shuddering breath. "I ran into your room, grabbed you from your cot, and hid in the closet. You were screaming, and I don't know where Erin had gone. You both shared a cot at that time ... Stacy had known what you two were. I don't know how, but she was insistent. Not long after, Stella slammed the door open. I didn't want to think about what she'd do to us, to me, if she knew what I saw, so I took the initiative. I tumbled out of the closet crying for her, saying that I was scared and that I wanted my mother to protect us from the bad guys." He smiles sardonically. "I guess I am her son, after all. Manipulation must run in the blood."

"All this time you made her believe she was the one in control of you and Victor, that you were on her side," Erin realizes.

Ben nods once. "You were about three months old at the time, and I don't know how you got out, but the older I got, the more I questioned Stella's behavior. I went to Healer Haven first. She told me that Stacy had passed you off, telling her to call the most recent number on her phone, while Gray distracted Stella. She ran as far from the house as she could, hiding you, before returning to perform her duties."

Erin's heart thumps widely in his chest. Even when they were about to die, his parents did everything they could to protect him. That explains why Healer Haven has been looking at him differently, and why he trusted her so instinctively. She helped his mother give birth to him and then later saved him. She couldn't save his parents, but she saved him. She knew he was strong enough to survive.

And he did.

Maybe she too—

"THAT'S ENOUGH!" Victor turns and punches the wall next to the door. The cracks spread quickly, plaster scattering like petals on the ground. "That's enough," he growls.

Erin reaches out a hand toward Victor. The heat behind his eyes thickens.

The string between them is pulled taut.

It's going to snap.

Erin juts forward to hang onto it. Panic fills his lungs. His hands start to ache, the smell of burning flesh stinging his nostrils as the string continues to be dragged away from him. Each ping the string makes as it unthreads, snapping, feels like another arrow has wedged itself into his heart. At this rate, he'll end up tearing himself apart trying to hold on.

"Vi—"

"NO!" Victor's face coils tight. He turns, his eyes burning with hostility. "You only just became a werewolf. It's been, what, almost two weeks since you first shifted? You base your knowledge on what I've told you. Then, and now. So, when someone else who's nearly as strong as me throws pity in your face, you think they talk the truth? Typical Omega," he jeers. "If you believe Ben's story, that makes you a victim, too, huh? Gives you purpose and meaning. Gives *them* purpose. Power. HA! I shouldn't be surprised. That is what you do best. Play victim in our past life, and you do it again. You know nothing of this life or this world. So why do you think you can say anything about this Pack? You haven't been here. You haven't lost what I have! Why don't you do what all Omegas do best? I'll even say it slowly. Shut. The. Fuck. Up."

Erin's head snaps back like he's been slapped.

Silence.

Ben takes a step forward, canines out and claws extended toward Victor.

Erin raises his hand, and Ben freezes, his arm trembling as he contains his anger.

Erin moves his left leg off the bed. Then the right. He doesn't hold the wince back this time, fighting through the pain as he stands. Victor's eyes fly all over his body, the glint wavering in his eyes while his arms twitch like he wants to help but doesn't know if he should. If he can.

Erin makes the choice for him.

Closing his eyes, he casts one more focused glance at the thinned red fiber clenched between his fingers and around his wrists in his mind's eye. It's barely connected anymore; a small gust of wind would be strong enough to break it completely.

He drops it.

Opening his eyes, he shuffles around the bed, back straight in front of Victor. He knows Victor's livid, his muscles rumbling under his skin, begging to be set free. To shift. Erin feels the same. He lets his scent rain down around them. Strong. Hurt.

Enraged.

Victor gulps, the ferocity and pure malice of his scent likely strangling his neck. Satisfaction coils in his gut at the thought.

"I don't give a fuck about instinct. About mates and fate. Stars and blood be *fucking* dammed, Victor. If you ever—EVER—speak to me like that again, we're done. For good." He drags all the emotion from inside his heart and spits it into his words. "I will beg the Moon Goddess to take this gift away and follow her husband into the stars."

He doesn't look back when leaving the room, Ben close behind him.

THIRTY-NINE

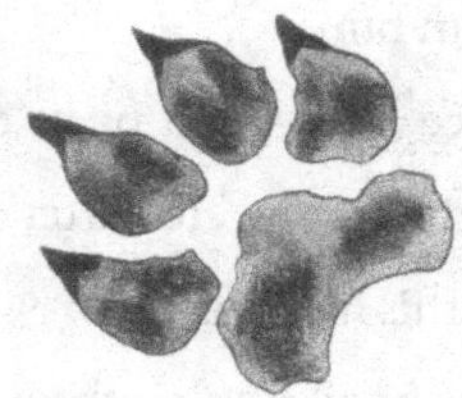

F UCK!

Victor takes off through the forest. He didn't bother stripping or following any of the lockdown protocol; torn clothes littered the ground behind him as he weaved through the dense trees. It's his protocol anyway. Let someone say something. Let someone try and stop him. He's Alpha. He's the one in charge. This is *his* Pack. *HIS.* Not Ben's or Erin's or Stel—

Rage overrides his instinct like molten lava, and he runs. He doesn't think about where he's going or what he's going to do when he gets there. Thoughts run as fast as his legs, but he can't latch onto any of them. He doesn't want to. They sting, cutting him and making him bleed. His heart thumps, loud and erratic, freeing itself from his ribcage and scaling up his throat.

The dripping blood only fuels his hate even more.

Bulldozing into a clearing, he squints, the sun from the lake momentarily blinding him. He looks to the ground, blinking away black spots. There's a shape denting the grass, bluebells crushed like something heavy had rolled around. The wind brushes against his fur, the scent of rain dull on its trail. Oh. He looks to the sky—not a dark cloud in sight. Which means …

Snout lowered to the ground, Victor presses into the grass. Erin's scent still lingers, seeped into the ground almost like Mother Nature had taken a piece of him for herself.

He growls.

Yet another thing taken from him.

Erin would probably rejoice knowing a piece of him is left in this spot. So sentimental. The spot where they connected after so long. Where they agreed to trust each other and focus on this life, this time.

Victor shakes his head, a low howl ripping through his throat. Erin's his mate. His Omega. They've known each other longer, much longer.

But what?

One word from Ben and suddenly Erin forgets all that.

Takes *his* side.

Ben's probably standing in his living room now, one of Erin's blankets wrapped around his legs, teaching him about how to run a Pack.

No way.

That's not fair.

That's not right!

That's his job.

Erin's his Omega.

Making decisions for the Pack isn't even Erin's job—it's Victor's. Stella always said Victor is the one who needs to be strong and make the decisions. No matter what anyone says. Ben needs to stop filling Erin's mind with useless thoughts.

They need to stay in line.

They need to stick to instinct.

That will keep them safe.

That will keep the Pack from falling apart and traitors from rising again.

Victor trots to the edge of the lake, looking at his reflection in the water. His black coat sucks all the light from the air while his blue eyes nearly blend in with the surface, making him look like a dark, hollow being.

This place was full of light when Erin was in it. Now, it's nothing but dull and ugly.

The color of the bluebells is irritating, the grass is prickling his skin, and the wind is too loud in his ears.

The whole world is too *loud*.

Slowly, Victor lowers his head. The water is cold on his lips. He can feel the chill over his closed eyes. The shift of sound, once his ears are covered. His crown. His shoulders. One step forward and he's submerged. The thoughts are muffled by the water around him. Slower, now. Easier to tear apart. To make sense of.

What if it's too late? What if Ben has already turned Erin into a traitor like him? What if the Pack sees it and tells Victor to turn Erin over to the elders? He'll be killed. So will Ben. What will he tell B?

'Oh, hey, sorry I had to jail your brother because he turned on everyone and converted the love of my soul into a traitor too, and together the two of them tried to kill your mom.'

The pressure in his head boils over, too tight to stay under any more. He shifts, swimming quickly to the surface. With a gasp, he gulps air into his lungs and floats on top of the water.

His mind replays the last couple of hours over and over again, like a looped home movie, without his consent. He had sensed a raging storm in Erin after he yelled at him, and knew down to the marrow in his bones he was only standing in the eye of that hurricane because Erin was letting him.

He groans loudly, the sound turning into a bellow as he clenches his hair between his fingers and wades out of the water.

Even hurt and angered, his mate refused to hurt him.

Victor wasn't that kind.

"FUCK!"

Tears fall; hot, wet drops splatter onto his chest as he wails. His knees give way, and he flops onto the ground. Horror stomps over his heart, his soul. The string tying him to Erin fills his mind's eye. It's tattered—the frayed edges look as if they were pulled too tight and couldn't withstand the pressure. Only a small piece still connects to the other end. To Erin.

But he's not there.

His presence is gone.

The light extinguished.

Erin turned his back on Victor.

Every time he sniffles, iron rushes in. Erin's blood. He tried. He tried so hard to keep hold. To stand strong. And what did Victor do? He stabbed Erin over and over again.

He may as well have pushed the knife into his own heart instead.

How could he let them leave like that? They are alone. Regardless if they spoke true or not, there is still a very real threat out there. And the two most important people in his life are without backup.

Victor rises to his knees. But that's ok. Because they didn't speak the truth. Ben was *lying*. So, even if they have gone back to Erin's house, the Treelark Pack doesn't know where that is.

Erin will be safe.

There's no way any of what Ben said is possible. Maybe there was a chemical spill, a pipe burst from the landscaping, and it's made everyone crazy. Why else would Erin be so quick to believe Ben's delusions? He hardly even knows Stella!

She can be intense at times, but that's what all mothers are like. She does it because she loves and worries for them. It's only natural for her to want the best. She's been through a lot, so she tries to protect them. Ben knows that first-hand. For him to create this wild story ... is he jealous? He hasn't found his mate, so he's trying to separate Victor from Erin out of spite.

Erin will be safe.

A unique feeling overcomes him. Blood pumps fast through his limbs, adrenaline swimming through them and making him shake. But he doesn't feel warm, and he doesn't start sweating. Instead, he feels cold like the grass he's been lying in is snow, and the blood in his veins is ice in the shape of canine teeth.

Stella.

He jumps to his feet, wipes his eyes, and shifts, sprinting faster than he ever has back to the house. Stella will know how to fix this. She knows everything. She's always known how to fix his problems. This one should be easy. In a couple of hours, everything will be the way it should be—Ben making jokes and trying to get him to do paperwork or make decisions for the Council Meeting instead of goofing around, and Erin wrapped secure in his strong arms, bright golden eyes laughing, laughing, laughing.

Happy.

Stella will make them happy again. And then the Council Meeting will happen on the fifteenth, the Lovelace Pack will be recognized as a strong, responsible pack again, and everything will be back in its proper place.

Yes.

Ok.

Erin will be *safe*.

Deep breathe. Slow down. Look through the cars.

Stella should be back with Beatrice by now and ... yes, there. Her car is parked back in the paddock. The engine smells cold. She's been back for a while. Perfect, he won't be jumping her as soon as she gets home.

He runs around the front and, using one of the wisteria trees by the door as a springboard, leaps onto his balcony, shifting in mid-air. He rushes to the closet and quickly gets dressed. All the while pointedly ignoring Erin's flowers on the bedside table and the way his heart yearns to roll around in the bedsheets that are covered in that wild scent he loves.

Sulking and whimpering won't solve anything. If he's to save Erin, he needs to tell Stella that they've all gone crazy.

Yes.

Erin will be safe.

Victor flings open the door and dashes down the stairs. Following Stella's scent leads him to the office. He slows down as he reaches the barn door, eyes wide and mouth parted, hand on the cold metal handle to slide the door ope—

"To the death of Erin Bellmore!"

Victor stops dead in his tracks. Electricity burns his fingers.

That was Matt Harkin's voice.

Raucous laughter follows his words. Multiple types. Multiple voices. Multiple *wolves.*

He flattens himself next to the wood and pulls his scent in with a frown. Stella's laugh is among those coming from behind the door, but it's not the smooth, high-pitched giggle he's used to hearing from her. It's deeper, layered.

It makes his skin crawl.

He must be getting sick. Perhaps he swam in the cold water at the lake for longer than he thought, or the stress and hurt are catching up to him. That's why he's shivering. That's why he feels faint. Werewolves have superior immune systems; they rarely get sick. But it does happen. Even to him—The Black Wolf. His eyes are blurring. More tears? Is this light-headedness?

Sniffing the air, he listens carefully. Has it always been this hard to breathe? Laced with Stella's and Matt's scent and beating hearts are Alpha Ross Cooper from Kansas, Alpha Lee Foster from Iowa, and Alpha Christian Reed from Washington. Have their hearts always been this loud? Why are they meeting this late at night? No one told him about this. Four Alphas still in current command, two of them being from the original four Packs, and an ex-Alpha meeting in secret roughly three weeks before the official Council Meeting. On *his* property.

He heard wrong.

He is getting sick.

Shit.

Matt must have said 'to the breath of Erin Bellmore' as in like thank the Moon Goddess that he's alive after an assassination attempt. Yes, of course. And that's why they've all met together, to give input into who tried to kill him and organize a lunch or something.

Although Victor's heart is beating erratically, stuttering in haste, he forces it to slow down, to remember how to beat. He hears Ben's voice in his head telling him to focus. He hates that it works.

"To the death of Erin Bellmore!" Stella repeats. Even though it sounds like cotton is stuffing Victor's ears, her voice rings clear. It sounds Happy. Excited. In control.

Just like it always has.

Goddess Fucking *shit*.

FORTY

"To the death of Erin Bellmore!" everyone cheers, glasses clinking together.

"May The White Wolf bitch toss and turn forever in Death's eerie bedchamber," Ross snickers, his pale green eyes glinting under the thick rim of his glasses.

"Ha!" Christian chugs all his whiskey before slamming the glass down onto one of the side tables, one leg crossed over so that his ankle rests on his bare knee. "That bitch will be lucky if Death even takes him," he says, running thick fingers through his coarse black hair.

"Now, now, gentlemen." Stella steps forward from where she was leaning against the wooden table, arms spreading out on the back of the brown leather sofa where the men sit. She peers down at them. "We mustn't get too hasty. Erin isn't dead yet, unfortunately. It looks like those humans unwittingly gave him the perfect out."

"I hear he's healing quickly, too," Lee hints, walking around and refilling everyone's glasses. His small, brown eyes focus on the task, his hand not pouring the liquid sitting softly on the other wrist. "We might have used the wrong dosage, the constant exposure to wolfsbane his whole life could have caused him to build an immunity instead of weakening him like we thought."

"Doesn't matter." Stella rolls her eyes. A pressed daisy sticks out of the coat pocket in Lee's suit. The white petals and yellow pollen center stand out against his deep brown skin. She pats it, nodding her head in thanks when he hands her a glass filled with amber liquid before moving to stand behind one of the red armchairs they turned. "Victor refused to let Erin stay anywhere but his room. I swear that child is getting harder and harder to control by the day."

"I told you we should've popped them the night you saw your nephew run out of the house," Christian says, looking sidelong at her. His hands form a gun, and he shoots an imaginary bullet into the air. "When was that? Two weeks ago? Would've been plenty of time to spin a story and take control before the meeting."

"You know," Ross drawls. "It does make one wonder why you waited till then to alert us of his status, Stella. One look that day, and it was obvious." Using one finger, he readjusts his glasses along his nose, while swirling the whiskey around his glass. Gaze probing.

"Ross has a point, Ms. Stella," Lee pipes, sitting in the chair under her. Stella presses her lips together to stop from snarling at his nasally voice; it's always made her skin shiver. Especially when he thinks he's spouting reason. "I mean, Stacy was your Luna. Your own brother was her husband's Beta. Surely you would've recognized the boy?"

"Don't blame the lady, Lee," Matt scolds from beside the bay window. Whatever it was that had captured his attention must have vanished as he spins back to face them, one tanned hand in the pocket of his black linen shorts, while the other sips from the whiskey rolling around the singular, massive ice cube. "There was only one werewolf who smelled like the ocean in New York, and that was our dearly beloved Stacy, Goddess curse her soul. But I arrived here first. I can attest that the boy smelled nothing like rain or the ocean until he first shifted, gentleman." His nose scrunches in disgust as he remembers the smell. "Honestly, before he stepped out of the house that day he smelled like a burnt, damp forest or something."

"Yuck, don't remind me." Christian sticks his tongue out in disgust, his lips smacking like he's trying to rid the taste from his mouth once more. "Here I thought I would come over early to say hi and eat some of Michal's pastries, and instead, I had to spend all day swallowing that."

"Well, shit, fellas," Stella scoffs, thinking back to the night she saw Erin and Victor run out into the forest. "Forgive me for not knowing something *none of us* knew or even considered. I'm not a damned mind reader." Many curse words ran through her head that night. She knew that Storm boy was up to something; he was bad luck from the second he set foot into this house, spreading around that poisonous stench. Drawing Victor's attention away from the important matters. From her destiny.

She was careful with the porch door, making sure it clicked softly behind her. There was no need to wake the whole Pack. They would question where Victor went instantly, and no doubt, smelling Erin's strong scent would give away what he is. Who he is. Who *they* are.

FUCK!

Remembering brings the anger back stronger. Her fingers itch, claws threatening to spear through the glass in her hand. She gulps the rest of her whiskey, the burn sharp down her throat. Broken glass is easier to wipe off a silk dress than alcohol. And this is mahogany red—a limited-edition color. It's her favorite. She'd never be able to buy it again, but it would give her another reason to hate Erin.

Smiling, her heart settles slightly at the thought. Everything she had worked so hard for might not be ruined. Like Matt said, there was only one werewolf in New York who smelled like the ocean. Stacy. That subtle scent of salty breeze she picked up that night had to come from Erin. Making him that bitch's son, undoubtedly. It rattled her more than she would ever admit, causing her to act like cornered prey. Her hands trembled as she ran them through tangled hair, her strides uneven as she made her way into the pantry. Mind racing, she didn't bother with a glass, grabbing a 1982 bottle of red and yanking the cork off. The liquid was rich against her tongue. Sweet. It calmed her racing thoughts. Half the bottle was gulped greedily down her throat before she took a deep breath.

Not her finest moment. But, alas, she had missed it. And now she was tired of musing on all the 'how' and 'for this long' questions. The past is in the past. She thought he had died that night. Not that she ever found a body, but what newborn baby can survive alone in the wilderness? That mistake was her fault. She'll take the blame for not being thorough and checking afterward. But she also had her beautiful newborn to look after, and a Pack to run afterward. And with Ben clinging to her legs like a goddamned monkey, what choice did she have? Her heartstrings did pull at his loud wailing. Even now ...

"I admit. I thought he looked familiar as a human, yes. Knowing now, I can see the resemblance even more. It's the eyes. The color is different, but the shape, those are Stacy's eyes. And his face. I know you all see Gray's face, too. He's the spitting image of his father. But hindsight is a powerful thing," Stella admitted, waving her arm through the air. Well, half admitted. Honesty was how one kept followers appeased. If she were honest with them, they would be honest with her, but they didn't need to know that the first time she saw Erin she had denied the possibility. She didn't want to see it, so she didn't. A trick of the light. She can twist that to her favor. It'll be a nice exercise. Child's play, really.

"I was told he died that night, as I said to you all afterward. And then we all spent the year after keeping an eye and ear out for rogue cubs. How was I to know that his wolf had gone dormant? It's not a normal occurrence." She uses a chipped nail to turn Lee's head away from her. "Cast your judgmental and cunning eyes aside to the big picture. It's time for the new plan."

Four pairs of glinting eyes swivel to her, all with matching wicked twists to their lips. Attention diverted. See? Easy. The truth was of no matter. Who he is, how he got here. That's all inconsequential. She's given too much up to back down now.

"You conjured one already?" Ross marvels, one sharp blond brow raised. Christian whistles slowly.

Stella nods with a grin. After the small, slightly panic-fuelled pity party passed, she had stood in the kitchen that night thinking. With the bottle of wine within reach beside her, she leaned both arms against the countertop, elbows locked, and head lowered. There had been two questions she needed answered if she was to gain control again.

What changed to cause Erin to shift, and without guidance?

How was she going to kill him now?

Clicking her tongue against her teeth, she had grabbed the wine bottle, gulping deeply until it was finished. Her mind ran back through every moment from the past month. Erin had no clue he was a werewolf. And she made sure he didn't catch a whiff of Victor's desire for him, or Victor of Erin's. Her threats had him spooked, the way his eyes would flash in fear as that putrid scent oozed off him. He would all but piss his pants, trembling like a newborn cub, every time she drove past while he worked on the garden, her eyes like dark daggers just waiting to be unsheathed. Especially after that 'accidental' love-tap into his hip. She had prayed to the Goddess after so long that one of the thin glass pieces of his camera lens would poke him in the eyes.

Alas, she can't have everything.

Even now, her heart races, glee bubbling at the memory as the male Alphas surround her, sipping on whiskey. Waiting to hear her perfect plan. She knew how to work a crowd. Another thing she had over her nephew; so easily manipulated. So ready to ignore his instinct! It hadn't taken much for Victor to be convinced that Erin wasn't his mate, that he was just a stupid human. They were separated for a while, and it had been slowly killing Victor. Everyone was talking about how worried they were that he would be unfit to rule. It was splendid. Everything had been going according to plan.

His power was wasted on him.

She taps her nails against the back of the leather sofa. She went with a deep, warm red this time, grateful Beatrice asked her out today. After raking her nails down the countertop that dreadful night, the deep grooves had split most of the polish. She had tried to fix them. File them down and give them a fresh coat. But then whittling an arrow and dipping it into wolfsbane fucked them up once more. Best leave it to the professionals at that stage.

Stella prowls around the room, cheek sucked in between her teeth. Pondering. Waiting.

Watching.

Watching.

Watching.

"Oh, come on, Stel," Matt pleads, rubbing at the stubble on his sharp jaw. "Don't leave us in suspense!"

Ah.

Perfect.

She smirks, the plan swirling like dark shadows in her mind. "Erin needs to die during the Council Meeting so we can use the curse to our advantage. We can say that Fate and Instinct guided them together, pawns of The Goddess, only after so long because she knew we would all be together. It's the perfect place for mass chaos and destruction. And, the boys are older. Stronger men, now, than when they were mere cubs. But, for that to work, we need as many people as possible to see Victor lose control. In our defense, he tragically dies—"

"We might not have to kill him at all," Christian interrupts. He finishes his drink before standing, facing Stella. With his summer business suit, dark skin, and emerald eyes, he reminds her of a mischievous fairy. Except these fae don't play pranks with mushrooms and blunt sticks. They use wolfsbane and silver daggers. "To lose a mate is excruciating, and with him being The Black Wolf and all, his bond with Erin might just kill him. It is supposedly stronger than average. Maybe that's what the Goddesses' curse means?"

"The rage of a wolf whose lost his mate ... huh. That's one perspective," Ross hums, turning to Stella. He flicks his glasses farther up his nose. "Didn't your mate die during the coup?"

Pain flares hot white in her chest. A cheeky smile, two deep dimples on happy display, flash across her mind. Morning dew lingers on the tip of her nose. She licks her lips, pressing them tightly together, and swallows it down. Sniffing, the image is blinked away.

"We weren't that close." She waves her hand through the air in dismissal, face neutral once more. "Anyway, it's different with Erin and Victor, so you might be onto something, Christian. However, we can't put all our eggs in one basket, so no gambling this time, men. Especially now that we are tangoing with Goddess magic. That can be the failsafe, but we move forward with the intention of murdering Erin and Victor during the Council Meeting. We'll be hailed as saviours of all werewolf kind and, with this nasty fucking curse gone and out of the picture, we will have nothing to fear, becoming the supreme leaders of all Packs across this great country we call home."

At least until those bastards are reincarnated in another few eons.

"Cheers!" they all shout, downing their drinks once more.

The thought sours her stomach. If only she were the one chosen. Cursed or blessed, the power she would have held. The kingdom she could have built with the ability to reincarnate. If it were her, she'd leave her notes, her plans, to remember in case the magic tried to stifle her mind. She doesn't know how it works, but those boys don't seem any wiser either. A great power wasted on tragic, lovesick fools.

"Now we just have to make sure there isn't a repeat of the coup d'état, where the Pack fights back and either of the boys is accidentally left alive," Matt laughs. He sounds like a dying hyena.

Stella forces a smile at him. Arrogant prick. Does he think it was easy to turn all those Alphas against Gray Bellmore? And the rest of the wolves against goody-two-shoes, apple-of-the-Pack's-eye Stacy? That bitch could do no wrong, and everyone thought Gray was a Godsend. Their romance was spoken about like a fairy tale love story. It had taken her *years* of planning and side-stepping to organize that coup. To play into the human she had so stupidly befriended and twist the fear they all grew up with, that any second two wolves could rip it all from them, everything they've built.

And making sure no one spilled the beans to the Council or other Packs she knew wouldn't side with her, all while pregnant? Then, only being three weeks post-partum when the planned night came around, and still succeeding tremendously, despite this current setback?

She spent so much money on makeup to cover the bags under her eyes from stress.

Yet these men stand here and act like all she did was swipe a credit card, and people magically died, giving them power.

Lee walks around again, filling everyone's glasses. She holds her glass over the back of the sofa for him, mindful to curve her lips into a bright smile and not a snarl. And it was women who were the ones forced to stay home and clean. Typical men. Stupid.

"Your son better not get in the way, Stella," Lee stresses. "He's a loyal Beta. He'll do all he can to protect both Victor and his whore mate."

Stella narrows her eyes and clenches the glass in her hand so hard tiny cracks can be heard. Silk be damned. She'll give the top to Beatrice, who can use it while painting. Still, she would prefer not to pick glass out of her fingers tonight. Beatrice paid for the manicures today; what a waste of her money it would be.

With delicate poise, she places the glass on the small round table in front of the sofa. Fear waits in the dark corners of the room. Quiet. Poisonous. It grows rapidly with each Alpha's scent at the slowness of her movements. Both feet planted firmly on the carpet, she clasps her hands over her knees and smiles like a snake.

At.

Each.

Of.

Them.

An image flashes. A young boy, climbing a new gazebo. His bright green eyes blaze just like his father's. A smile splits his face, one front tooth missing. Laughter *squeals* in her ears.

"Ben isn't to be touched. I'll make sure he, and others, don't get in our way. Understood?"

Glasses raise toward her.

"Yes, Alpha," they all sing

FORTY-ONE

"I can take you somewhere else if you want?" Ben turns off the truck's engine, twisting in his seat to look at Erin. This is the first time either of them has spoken since leaving the ranch. "Layla's apartment? Or Fletch's?"

"Fletch?" Erin teases.

Ben shrugs. "He's into cars, I'm into cars. We bonded."

"Of course," Erin chuckles. "Silly me." He takes a deep breath, eyes on the muted green door separating him from his childhood home. So many memories were made behind those walls with his parents and his friends. So many decisions his parents made to keep him safe. To keep him alive. And all it took was a whiff of spiced leather and fresh sandalwood for him to throw it away. The guilt rolls in his stomach like lead; the sting is worse than the residual pain burning his shoulder.

"Are you going to tell them?" Ben asks. "Your friends?"

It's Erin's turn to shrug now. He's been thinking about it ever since they had that fight so long ago. They're family—his Pack before he knew what that meant. They tell each other everything. He wants them to know about this side of his life. About his new family. About the pain and the struggle, but also about the happiness. How there aren't emotions known to humans that can describe the connection he feels to the Lovelace Pack. He wants to try ... but lying to them has gotten so easy lately.

"They'll be in danger if they know," Erin exhales. The decision was made for him. He didn't get a say in the matter. "Not with Stella alive."

Ben hums, tapping his fingers on the steering wheel. "What about your parents? Have you said anything to them?"

"Have you?" He raises a brow.

"Not my place." Ben seems like he wants to say something, his lower lip pulled between his teeth. An old habit. Erin smirks to himself. Everything seems so obvious now.

"Thank you, Ben." Erin smiles at him. "For everything. For now, and before."

Ben stops tapping, surprise lining his face before a small grin appears. His cheeks tinge pink as he laughs. "You don't need to thank me ... Prince Nahale."

Erin laughs. It feels surreal hearing that name spoken by someone other than his mate. From someone who looked much younger when he used to call him. "Of course I do. You've done a great job here by yourself for this long. This was never your burden to carry. I'm sorry it took me so long to get here." He pats Ben on the shoulder. Pride fills the air around them.

"Not your fault. This was always going to be my job." Ben nods, swallowing thickly. His eyes tighten, a serious look painting his face darkly. "And I think you should tell them. Your friends. They were your Pack before we were. Stella won't be around forever. But you—they—will be."

"You sound so sure," Erin says, eyebrow raised.

"I am." Ben pulls the keys from the ignition. "We've dealt with worse. And this time we have more knowledge, resources, and skills." Now it's his turn to place a comforting hand on Erin's shoulder, a small grin lifting his face. "And you don't need to tell your parents anything. Not if you don't want to. Whatever you say or don't say, I'll back you up."

"Well then." Erin nods. "I'm starving. Let's go eat, hm?" Carefully, he opens the car door and steps down, Ben right behind him. The smell of roasted potatoes and fried beef gets stronger the closer they get to the front door. It makes his stomach rumble. Loudly. When was the last time he ate? Has Victor eaten? Is he still in his room? Did he punch the wall again? Hopefully he didn't hurt himself. What will his parents say that he's arrived here with Ben and not Victor?

The door flings open before Erin can reach the handle. Natalie stands on the other side, hair pulled into a messy bun, and summer pajamas wrinkled, her oversized shirt falling off one shoulder. Dark bags line under her shining blue eyes. She must not be sleeping well. A glance behind her into the living room proves that. Sofa pillows are thrown on the floor, and a blanket hangs half off the couch, the navy writing journal she writes in flopped where she must have been sitting, pen still rolling across the carpet.

"John!" she calls over her shoulder before pulling him into a hug, holding his head into the crook of her neck and shoulder as the steps thunder with the weight of someone running down them.

That was all it took.

Erin crumbles.

The tears fall fast as he wraps his arms tightly around his mother. She whispers into his ear, soothing noises telling him everything will be okay. It will all be okay. A hand on his back guides him inside, still wrapped in his mother's arms, and the door closes softly behind them. Erin distantly hears Ben speaking lowly with someone before the hand on his back starts rubbing circles across his shoulder blades. Baked cookies and rock music. John.

"What's wrong, cub?" Natalie pulls back. She's frowning, pain sparkling clearly between her wet lashes. The guilt returns, this time snaking along his limbs. Erin shakes his head, wiping the tears from his eyes.

"Erin woke up a couple of hours ago. Sorry we didn't call. There were some urgent situations within the Pack that arose. We all thought it best for Erin to come back home to finish his recovery. He needs peace and quiet, and right now the house is a bit chaotic."

"And Victor?" John asks. "Will he be coming over later? That whole scent and needing to be close thing?" Suspicion lines his voice. He walks to the table, grabbing some tissues and passing them around. He looks weathered, too, with more gray sprinkling his hair than Erin remembers him having before.

"Victor is dealing with the Pack." Ben nods, voice impartial. Like a businessman reading off the notes for the meetings of the day. "He'll come over as soon as he finishes. But he sent me here in the meantime to watch over Erin. I'll keep him safe."

"Of course. You're in safe hands. That's a relief." Natalie smiles, patting Ben on the bicep before turning her attention back to Erin. He sees it, the truth in her eyes. She doesn't buy their excuse. She knows something's gone wrong. That there's another reason why Ben's here and not Victor. Of course she knows. How could she not? She's the one who—

A loud noise growls behind them. Ben clears his throat and smiles, head tilted. His neck starts to stain pink. "Oh. Sorry ... the food smells so good."

"Well! There might be something to these werewolves yet!" John claps him on the back with a smirk. "Let's go eat. Especially you, Erin. You need food to help heal. Supernatural creature or human, that fact won't ever change."

"I'm not too hungry." A lie. Partially. The food smells delicious, but just the thought of moving his jaw around food to swallow makes nausea twirl his head. His stomach growls for a different reason now. Who knew crying and having a mental breakdown could eat away an appetite? He steps out of his parents' arms, nodding to the stairs. "I think I'll just go sleep."

Natalie frowns. "You've been sleeping for days. Your father's right. Your body needs proper food."

"Mom—"

"Dr. Haven gave him some pretty strong medicine," Ben interrupts. "She said some side effects may include drowsiness or loss of appetite. It shouldn't last for long, but it's best for Erin to listen to his body. To his wolf. We can try some crackers or bread in half an hour if he still feels like he can't eat."

Natalie's mouth drops open, ready to say more, when John puts a hand on her back. "Come on, Nat, let's not question these werewolf things." He turns to Ben. "You, on the other hand, have no excuse. Let's chow down."

Ben nods rapidly while John and Natalie start shuffling into the kitchen. She spares one more glance at Erin before John guides her around the corner. Ben follows, and Erin mouths a silent 'thank you' to him. Leaning heavily on the handrail, he climbs the stairs. With every step, the pain in his heart grows. It started as a dull ache, the initial shock and adrenaline from his fight with Victor at the ranch fading in the car ride over. Then, seeing his mother, it rushed forward, like he was stabbed with that wolfsbane coated arrow all over again. Perhaps he should have sat down to eat with them. Perhaps he should have told them what happened. Maybe they could have helped.

Helped how?

What can she do now? Sever the bond? Take away his pain? The bond's pretty much gone now. Victor did that all on his own. And the pain …

No.

It was Erin's choice to let the string go.

He walked away.

After everything. He left first. So now, he needs to deal with the repercussions of that, no matter how painful.

And if he had said all that to his parents … they would have killed Victor. He knows that much to be true. No matter who he is.

By the time he opens his bedroom door, silent tears fall from his eyes. His arm is on fire, the wound pulsating as it tries to heal. He ignores it and stands in front of his photo wall next to the door. His eyes are drawn automatically to the newest photo of him and Victor placed in the middle.

It was late afternoon when he took the photo, the setting sun casting both their faces in light. Looking at the wide grin splitting Victor's lips and causing his eyes to squint, Erin thinks once again that their faces would've looked bright and happy even without the sun's golden rays spraying across them.

He's been trying so hard to forget about Victor since leaving the ranch. Letting go of the string so he could pick up the broken pieces of the jar and stuff his emotions back inside was one of the hardest things he's had to do. Looking at Victor in the photo now, the way his arms are relaxed where they wrap around Erin's waist, the feeling of longing rushes to the surface.

Like the touch of a ghost, Erin can feel strong arms circle his waist and a warm chest lean into his back. He whimpers, the tears falling faster now. He closes his eyes.

A knock on the door makes him flinch. Clearing his throat, he swats at the wet stains on his cheeks. "Come in," he calls.

Natalie pokes her head through. She smiles ruefully. "Your dad and I are going to head out. Mrs. Heights two blocks over has had a bit of a scuffle. And being that old and having no family, we figured it's best for us to go and make sure she's ok and doesn't need to be taken to the hospital. Plus, her porch rail will need to be fixed if she ever wants to step into her house again."

Erin nods.

Natalie searches his face. "You'll be ok here on your own?"

"Ben's here."

"Ben is here," Natalie repeats with a sigh. "Ok then, cub. I don't know how late we'll be. But text me if you need anything. Rest."

Erin takes a shuddering breath and clears his throat again, smiling slightly as he turns away from the photo wall and sits on the edge of the bed. "I will. Bye," he calls, voice cracking. There's shuffling in the hallway, and a second later, Ben walks into his room, a plate of food in his hands.

"Looks yum."

If Ben takes notice of the trembling in his voice, he doesn't comment on it.

"It is. Your dad's a great cook." Ben places the plate on the desk and sits down. They hear the front door close behind them. The lock echoes around the empty halls. "Want a bite?"

"No." Erin chuckles, the sound tiring and void of any humour. He watches Ben eat, grateful for the company as he flops back onto his mattress. It smells like him—rain in a forest. He wishes it smelled like Victor instead. His mattress was softer, too. "This must be hard for you, going against V—" Erin gulps as his name sticks its claws into his throat, refusing to leave. Thinking it is different to saying it.

"Yeah, it is. There's this pain in my stomach, like I'm being stabbed continuously. Over and over," Ben admits. His gaze drifts to the photo wall, and he smiles softly. "But I don't feel guilty because I know what I'm doing is right. You shouldn't feel guilty, either."

"I don't." Erin looks down and intertwines his fingers. "Not at what I said to him, at least." It's the truth. He doesn't feel regret or guilt for walking out on Victor. What was said about him was wrong, and he won't let people speak to him that way. But ... "What if some of it's true though?" he mumbles.

The chair squeals as Ben twists so he's facing Erin. "What do you mean?" he asks, voice tense.

"I mean ..." Erin's index fingers start picking at the nail on his thumb. He can hear a strident laugh dancing around in his head as chipped black nails dig into his skin. "I know it's not true. We were babies at the time, and the people who died that night didn't die because of us. But it's true that so many people have died since we were born. And even then ... even before. How can that be a blessing? Maybe some of it is our fault ... maybe we really are cursed. If we had never met—"

"Wolves would have died anyway. Stella would have found a way, whether the Goddess intervened or not. Same with Kazamir. And the King."

The tears are falling much faster now, blurring Ben's figure when Erin looks at him. It's getting harder to breathe, and his chest is starting to ache. There's a tense pressure on his neck and shoulders, weighing him down. He's scared. The laugh in his head becomes shrill as it splits into a barrage of voices.

'Your wolf should've stayed dormant forever, stupid Omega.'

'You should've died alongside your worthless parents.'

'If only you had killed the heir as soon as you saw him. What a sorry excuse for a Prince.'

'I chose wrong. This is how you spread hope? I pity those who come after you.'

Erin's heart burns in his chest. His breathing increases to try and keep up with the fast pace. He can hear Ben's calm voice, but it's muffled like the soundwaves are trying to cut through water that's been frozen over with ice.

"Back then, the humans had better weapons equipped to wipe us out. That's the truth. And then there's Kazamir." Ben snarls, his scent seeping out softly, like he's mindful not to dose his Alpha's mate in his scent but still trying to offer reassurance. "He was always going to betray us. Loyalty was a gene the Goddess didn't weave into his blood. You gave us more time. You gave us hope. You saved us. Afterward ... yeah, it was rough, and I didn't expect things to get so convoluted over time. But they did. That's the price of survival. As for my mother, she would've attacked regardless. Your birth was just an excuse, a moment where leadership was weak. Or so she thought."

Erin rises, pulling his knees to his chest and bowing his head until it reaches them. He pushes the palms of his hands over his ears like that will get rid of Stella and Victor's voice in his head. Or his father from before. And Her. It's loud. It's so, so loud. And dark. He can't see the string tying him to Victor anymore.

Where is it?

Why did he drop it?

Has Victor yanked it back?

No.

He wants it again.

He wants it again.

He wants it again!

It doesn't matter whether Stella knew who The White Wolf and The Black Wolf were or not. It doesn't matter if Ben sounds convinced all this would have happened regardless. It was only after he was born that Victor's parents died. They were protecting the Pack, yes, but on orders from Gray. Erin's father ordered them to fight Stella's men. He ordered Victor's dad to fight against his sister. Ben and Beatrice had to walk on eggshells their whole life, wondering if their mother was going to attack them again or try to kill their pseudo-brother.

The ringing in his ears becomes louder like someone is scream-laughing directly into them. His mind is overheating as multiple thoughts trample through his head. He can't focus on any of them. He misses Victor. He wishes he had known his birth parents. He wants Natalie and John to come back. Why does Stella hate him? What happened to the tree where they met? Was that destroyed, too, like everything else he touches? Who started the legend of the curse? Who took the freedom from their tragedy, twisting their blessing into a curse? Was it one from Kazamir's line? Was it a Bellmore? That would mean—

It's all his fault.

It'sallhisfaultit'sallhisfaultit'sallhisfault—

Familiar arms wrap around his waist, and a head is lowered over his as his favorite scent wafts up his nostrils.

Silence.

The voices are all pushed back. Only silence remains as his body automatically relaxes.

But Erin's mind fights it.

He screams at his instinct, causing his muscles to tense once more. Clenching his hands, he pushes against the chest in front of him, trying to leave the protective hug. "No, no. Leave! Don't look at me," he sobs as tears and snot mix on his upper lip.

Victor leans back to grab Erin's wrists, forcing him to stop struggling and to look at him. The last rays of the setting sun peek through the blinds, casting Victor in warm light and making his eyes shine like flashlights in the night as they focus solely on Erin.

"I'm sorry, Star."

Erin sniffs as he stares at Victor between his legs. He looks worn out and tired. His skin is pale, and his hair is disheveled, the ends damp. His dark green shirt is soaked through. Did he run all the way here? The smell of sweat isn't that strong though ...

"Why are you wet?" Erin blurts. He looks around the room and sees a large white backpack tossed by the door. His fingers twitch, unclenching slightly, but he doesn't pull them out of Victor's grip. "Where's Ben?" He feels slightly guilty at the amount of accusation in his tone.

"He left to make sure Stella doesn't notice I'm gone yet," Victor says breathlessly. "And I'm wet because I went for a swim in the lake."

"Oh." Erin raises his eyebrows as more tears fall from his eyes. "But why would it matter if Stella knows you're gone? Haven't you spoken to her?"

"No, I haven't." Victor shuffles closer.

"Why?" Erin's lips tremble when he licks them. They're salty. He wants Victor to kiss the sting from them.

"Because you and Ben were right. Stella has been manipulating me all this time." Victor's hands travel down Erin's arms, settling in the crook of his elbows. Erin lets his arms lower, his knees pushing open more on instinct so Victor can get even closer.

"Oh?" He sniffs, brows twitching. "And why would you believe the words of a stupid Omega who knows nothing about what it means to be a werewolf?"

Guilt and pain scar Victor's face at Erin's words. He places his head onto Erin's shoulder and nuzzles his neck. "Because you're my mate," Victor speaks, his voice wobbly.

Erin scoffs, staring ahead at the closed bedroom door to the right. "You didn't seem to care about that earlier," he grumbles.

Victor raises his head into Erin's line of sight, forcing them to lock eyes. Tears are clinging to his eyelashes that fall like rain every time he blinks. "Erin. I am so sorry," he sobs as he squeezes Erin's wrists. "I was frustrated and confused. That isn't an excuse! I know I've fucked up. I just lost control and ... when you've been told something for your whole life and suddenly it's all a lie, it can be very confronting. Especially knowing—" He releases one of Erin's wrists to cup his face, wiping some of the tears off his cheeks with his thumb. "Especially knowing I allowed it to happen for so long. The guilt turned to anger because I didn't want to accept accountability. And then I was ashamed. As Tala, I would have seen it right away, but I, as Victor, didn't. Then I berated you for seeing it before me. Berated Ben. I regretted the words as soon as they left my mouth. You aren't stupid or dumb. You are the smartest, most adaptable, and handsome person I've ever met. And you being an Omega in this life is a blessing I thank the Goddess for each day."

Erin takes a deep breath when Victor leans forward to rest their foreheads together. "I am so lucky to have found you again and been blessed with you as my mate."

"But what if it's my fault?" Erin admits quietly.

"What?" Victor leans back slightly to look at Erin in confusion. "How would my outburst be your fault? I didn't mean to make it sound like—"

"No." Erin shakes his head. "No, I mean everything else. After I was born, Stella attacked and your parents died. And even now, it was only after meeting me that your family was destroyed. And before. I was a Prince. A human Prince. I made your Pack weak, gave the King a reason to attack more strongly. He wanted you all dead, but he wanted to rip my happiness from me more. That's why he made me go to the river that day and stand there, watching. Hearing the choking. *I* poisoned Alaric."

"Erin, you listen to me because I'm only going to say this once," Victor says, voice firm. He cups both of Erin's cheeks. His hands are warm. Gentle. Just like they've always been. "My whole life I dreaded meeting my mate because I was told everyone I loved would die if I ever did. There was a void in my heart, in my soul that no one could ever fill." He threads his fingertips slowly through Erin's hair. "We are not cursed. Our love is a blessing. The greatest blessing the Moon Goddess could have ever given me is meeting you. I hate myself for ever thinking otherwise, and that's a regret I shall have to carry for eternity. You didn't destroy my family, you enriched it. You saved me. Then, and now. The Pack wouldn't have accepted you if they didn't think the same, and my father would have accepted you, too, had he been given time to truly speak with you. I know it. So how is that not good?"

Erin lifts his hands to hold onto Victor's wrists, and Victor's voice softens. "I don't blame you for the coup, and I know no one else does either. Okay?"

Erin closes his eyes and sees the torn, bloodied rope. Oh, it's come back. He hesitates, his heart still heavy with dread.

Can ... can it even be fixed?

A laugh bubbles from his stomach.

Does that even matter?

He's going to try anyway.

Erin smiles in relief as his mind clears. Determination thaws the cold panic in his veins. They can save the Lovelace/Bellmore/Storm Pack, whatever they want to call themselves. They can save all the wolves from Stella. They can clear up this belief eating away within all the Packs. The Moon Goddess is someone to be revered. She fought alongside them. She helped them. She didn't need to. She didn't need to wed them, to bless them with the chance at having a family. To stand with them at the end. He didn't either. And yet they did.

Even now. She's still helping them.

So why doubt her?

Carefully, in his mind's eye, Erin lowers onto his knees in front of the torn red string. He leans forward, picks it up, and ties each snapped piece into a knot until the thread is completely connected again. It still looks battered. It looks frail. But he can see it. His grip is firm as he holds it tight. It'll strengthen in time. It'll grow, as they grow. And he won't drop it again.

Never again.

He opens his eyes when he hears a gasp. Victor has his own eyes closed, a flush painting his cheeks red. His chest is rising and falling slowly as he takes deep breaths. Victor snaps his eyes open when Erin places his left hand on his cheek.

"You pull a stunt like this again, and I'll slap you with this bond binding us until you're black and blue. You hear me, stupid Little Wolf?"

Victor laughs, and suddenly, the world is bright again. He presses his lips to Erin's softly. "Yes, Star. Whatever you wish. Always."

Erin kisses Victor back, his breath stutters when Victor's heavy-lidded eyes darken as desire burns deep. One of Victor's hands moves to Erin's waist, while the other one squeezes his neck. Erin slides his hand over Victor's cheek, his eyes following along. First, he traces both of Victor's thick blonde eyebrows with the tips of his fingers before skimming down his nose. Victor lets out a deep chuckle when Erin pokes the tip.

The laugh encourages him. He uses his finger to trace Victor's lips. Despite being thin, they are still incredibly soft with a prominent cupid bow. He shivers when Victor flicks his tongue out to swipe at Erin's fingers.

The world stops as Erin's eyes close to slits. It's silent, both in the room and outside. The only sound in Erin's ears is his beating heart and heavy breathing. The space between them is filled with their scents. Rain and leather and sandalwood. Spice and forest and moss. Erin doesn't know where his starts and Victor's begins.

Victor squeezes his waist again before leaning forward. Erin meets him halfway, tilting his head to the side as their lips connect. The kiss is gentle, a simple press of their lips, moving together. Slowly. Memorizing the shape of each other. Victor moves up, kissing Erin's cheek. The bridge of his nose. His eyelid. The space between his brows.

His breath fans across Erin's face. The presence of him is all-consuming. Familiar. Safe.

Mine.

Mine.

MineMineMineMine.

"I don't want to wait."

Victor stops his gentle worship. His eyes are wide, his gulp audible. Erin cups Victor's neck, pressing his fingers into the spot right in the middle. Grabbing Victor's hand, he presses it on his neck where Erin's mark used to sit. He wants to see it there once more. He needs to see it. To know that this feeling between them—the hope placed on their shoulders—is real.

He wants proof that nothing can separate them again.

Understanding crosses Victor's eyes, and he softens. "We spoke about this, Star," he whispers.

"Then why do you sound like you're in pain?" Erin digs his fingers deeper into Victor's neck. "Hm?"

"Because you know I want you. Want this," Victor says, voice tight. "But there are too many variables. Too many complications. Like your parents and now Ben—"

"So take out the variables. Take out the complications." Erin rests his forehead on Victor's. Breathing him in deeply, he lowers his voice. "We both know my parents would be ecstatic. We can deal with those repercussions. It'll just be a ... slightly uncomfortable conversation. I know we were never meant to remember the time from before, but we all do. If our love was stronger than the Goddesses' magic, we should tell them that. As for Ben, he just wants to protect us. He has been protecting us. This will give him the confirmation that everything he's done was right." Erin presses a chaste kiss to Victor's nose. "Tell him you remember. You'll get to see how adorable he looks when he blushes."

"That's my cousin, Star," Victor chuckles. He regards Erin, watches him with vulnerable eyes. The silence stretches between them. Erin's heart spikes. His scent leaks, uncertainty curling at the edges. He pushed. He knows he pushed, and ... maybe not at the right time. But he needs this. *They* need this. He can feel it in his bones, in his soul.

It's fate.

It's instinct.

It's blood.

"If we are to hold a chance at beating Stella, we need to be honest. Not just with ourselves, but with everyone, Victor," Erin whispers, face solemn.

Victor breathes deep. "Okay." He smiles wide. The same blinding smile he wore that first day they met at the ranch. Back then, Erin thought he had fallen and was looking at the sun. His heart warms, his lips mimicking the smile shown to him.

"Okay?" Erin wraps his arms around Victor's neck, his legs tightening around his waist as Victor stands, lifting Erin off the bed completely.

"Yes, okay." Victor smirks. "I told you, whatever you want, you'll get. I'm not about to let you get mad at me again." He lowers Erin onto the middle of the bed, his hands wrapping under Erin's knees that are clinging to his waist.

"Smart wolf," Erin laughs. "Happy Omega, happy life, right?"

"Something like that," Victor smirks. His teeth nip his ear before licking at the sweat gland right underneath. Erin moans deep in his throat. "And I would love to see the look on Stella's face when she realizes we've officially mated."

Erin shivers, biting his lip. One of these days, he's going to figure out how to lower his voice like Victor does. That deep timber prods at the hot coal in his stomach, causing the flames to spark wildly. It's not fair for him to be the only one affected.

"I still want a wedding," Erin pants. It's getting harder to concentrate. Victor has moved to his neck, gently kissing every inch of skin.

"Of course, Star. Whatever you want."

"And a studio, for my photos. A big one." Erin lifts his hips as Victor runs his hands from his thighs to his ass. His fingers are soft when they press into his skin. It turns him on even more than if he were to squeeze harshly.

"Yes, my love. I'll get the best architect to build you one. And if not, I'll buy whichever building you desire." Victor keeps trailing his kisses over Erin's jaw as his fingers hover, moving to the waistband of Erin's sweats, the heel of his palm kneading his dick straining against his underwear.

"And kids. I want kids." Erin sees the exact moment Victor registers his words. He sits back on his haunches, hands still, fingers clenched tightly on the waistband of Erin's sweats that are now halfway down his thighs. His eyes are closed. Erin knows who he's thinking of. "Do you want kids, Victor? When this is all over? Because I do. With you. I want the chance to try again."

Victor nods, face scrunched tightly in pain as thin tears spill down his cheeks, breaking Erin's heart into a million pieces. "I worry." The corners of his lips twitch, his voice no louder than a pin dropping onto carpet. "I want ... but ... Stella. If I were to die, you'd be in so much pain. I don't know if you'd survive it. If a child could, all alone. We both know what it's like to live without parents."

"They would never be alone, Love." Erin sits forward, legs falling to rest on the mattress on either side of Victor. He places both hands on Victor's cheeks. "They would have Pack. And I am not weak. If you were to die, I would live on after you, if only out of spite, so I could hate you for leaving me in this world all alone."

They never spoke about it. About him. About the life the Goddess blessed them with the opportunity to create, regardless of the outcome. He wasn't a wolf then, not truly. The Goddess's magic changed much, but he couldn't shift. They didn't know if he would've been able to—

But Pack came first. And the moment was gone. Never knowing and forced to live on with only his memory. But still. He was theirs. He was something they created in their minds, their souls.

Now they sit in the same spot. The same stakes. But like Ben said, they know more now. They're prepared now. This time, they will win. Erin will get everything he wants. And right now, he wants more.

"That doesn't mean I'm giving you permission to die." He rests his forehead against Victor's, their noses touching, smile soft in tease. Lowering his hands to Victor's shoulders, he leans forward to kiss him. His lips are cool, the salt from his tears mixing into the kiss.

Victor kisses him back gently, mouth opening to give Erin the access he wants. "I won't," he puffs between kisses. Their tongues meet, sliding together. It's like a dance. Like the first time Tala bent and kissed Nahale. Slow, but sure. Soft, but eager. Nahale had seen it coming from miles away, dropping hints all day that he wanted to be kissed. The brush of his fingers through his long, thin hair, rubbing at the shell of Tala's ear as he passed it. Leaning closer than normal when speaking. Baring his neck as he swiped at sweat pooling on his collarbone. Finally, Tala had gotten the hint. His lips trembled then, nerves portraying his cool façade of Wolf Heir, like they tremble now. "I promise I won't."

Erin's filled with warmth deep in his stomach, and he smiles against Victor's mouth. How wonderful. They've kissed so many times before. They've mated, they've had sex, they've done it all so many times before. Yet now ...

It feels like the first time all over again.

It takes the form of words. They grow and grow, surging from deep in Erin's gut. Each time Victor tilts his head, deepening the kiss. Each time Erin runs his hands over Victor's arms, his chest. His heart thumps loudly, keeping pace with the beat of his mate's heart he can feel underneath the palm of his hand. It might explode.

What a story that would be.

A heart exploding because it couldn't contain three little words any longer. They've said it countless times before, in so many different ways. But this time. But now—

"I love you," Erin whispers against Victor's lips. "I love you." He wraps his arms back around Victor's neck, pushing forward, gripping the back of his shirt. Victor takes the hint, twisting sideways as he falls onto his back. His eyes have dilated, the black pupil almost completely covering his moonlike iris. Erin finishes the job Victor started before, tossing his pants to the side and straddling his hips. "I love you."

Victor runs his hands from Erin's knees to his hips as he pushes against Erin's lips harder, sucking on his lower lip, like he's trying to force everything he has into him. Grabbing the bottom of Erin's shirt, he lifts it to his neck, mindful of his shoulder. They separate briefly. Victor's eyes are darker than the deepest part of the ocean when he tosses the fabric on the floor beside them.

Erin knows his eyes are just as dark, like pools of molten gold.

"Say it again," Victor pleads, already lifting his shirt over his head while Erin begins to unlace the string of his shorts, pulling them down. "Say it again, Star."

"I love you." Erin grinds against Victor, the material between them soaked through already, before claiming his lips once more. "I love you, Victor Lovelace. Alpha. *My Alpha.*"

"I love you, too, Erin Storm-Bellmore." Victor smiles widely, hips bucking. His hands fall to Erin's thighs. "You're the most beautiful thing I've ever laid eyes on."

Erin's breath hitches. He smiles wide and leans back, staring at Victor before tilting his head to the side. He presses his right hand against Victor's lips.

"Suck," he commands.

Victor does.

Eyes lidded, gaze unflinching, he kisses his knuckles, the joints on his middle finger. His ring finger. Then he takes Erin's fingers into his warm mouth. Deep. Holding on gently with his teeth as his tongue swivels, coating. Preparing. Erin licks his lips at the sight, his other hand caressing Victor's chest, drawing circles against the hair there. Then, he removes his fingers, thumb swiping at the spit pooling in the corners of Victor's lips as he rises on his knees.

Slowly, he reaches back. Two fingers swirl at his entrance before pushing in. The stretch is easy; he's used to the sensation. Muscles relaxing, arms tense with anticipation for what's to come. Victor will have no issue fitting. He pumps himself a couple of times, rocking back and forth on his fingers, never breaking eye contact with the man below. Victor parts his lips, a wolfish smirk forming as he tugs at Erin's balls a few times, in tandem with his thrusts, his other hand lifting to rub against Erin's hip. Erin stutters, losing his rhythm as his eyes close and head drops back between his shoulder blades.

Cheeky bastard.

Curling his fingers, up, up, there. He moans low in his throat, loud, the way he knows Victor adores. It works. Victor's top teeth capture his bottom lip, a muscle jumping as he clenches his jaw. He growls, his grip on Erin's hip squeezing once before his hand is moving backward, backward, backward.

Erin presses his weight down as he's filled, stretched ever farther until his dick is grazing Victor's, still trapped beneath the thin material of his underwear.

Victor lifts onto his forearm, nuzzling his nose against Erin's throat. His cheek. His ear.

"Knowing I have an eternity to do this with you sets my soul on fire. You are my Star, and I'm but the Little Wolf trapped on the ground watching you shine," he declares, voice but a purring whisper. He nibbles Erin's ear. "That watched you *explode*."

Something stirs deep in Erin's stomach. It's simultaneously hot and cold. It's something instinctual. He gives in.

Throwing his weight forward onto Victor's chest, Erin growls, body flinching inward and legs trembling as he comes. Breathing heavily, he gazes at Victor through half-lidded eyes.

Victor runs a hand over his chest, over Erin's cum, before lifting his hand to his lips and sucking. Erin's stomach flops inside out. With Victor's help, the last piece of material separating them is ripped off. Erin pushes Victor back down onto the mattress.

"Now it's my time to watch you bask in my shine," Erin breathes.

Victor's deep rumble soon turns into a sharp exhale as Erin teases him, his ass moving to rub his dick. Hands trail all over his body, touching, wandering, probing anywhere they can. His hips. His thighs. His spine, vertebra to vertebra. His stomach and nipples. Anywhere Victor can touch and embrace without breaching the control Erin has claimed in this moment.

Smirking, Erin teases Victor a few more times. He waits until the blush staining Victor's sharp cheekbones has traveled down his neck, and his eyes are hardly open. Leaning forward, he takes Victor's bottom lip into his mouth so he stops biting on it, licking it gently. That was all he needed. Victor grunts, his brows pinching, hips bucking, and fingers flinching across Erin's back as hot liquid pours across his lower back and down his thighs.

He hasn't even finished shaking before Erin is shifting and lowering himself down, Victor's dick still hot and twitching inside of him. They move together, languid in their movements. Exploring the pleasure that drags with every slow push and pull. Erin rises all the way up before dropping down just as slow, Victor meeting him there. Gently pulling his ass cheeks to the side so that his dick has more room to move. So that the shallow thrusts can become deeper. Harder. Rougher. So that he can hit that spot Erin loves each time.

Erin's hands rest on Victor's chest, feeling the weight of his heart beating below the surface. Beating for him. For their future. His breath fans across Victor's face, mingling with his. Brushing a few loose strands out of his eyes, they don't break eye contact. Not when the pressure builds. Not when they moan loudly. Not when they arch their backs, trying to get a close as possible. Not when more moisture slicks down his legs or when Victor grows inside, stretching him wider than he thought possible. He winces at the pain. He laughs at the pleasure. Victor fills him completely, making sure there's no way for anything to leak out. Making sure it *takes*.

Canines sharpen, necks bared as noses nuzzle. They bite.

Only when they break, when the pressure explodes, do they each close their eyes. Soft panting breaks the silence filling the room. Victor shuffles, mindful of Erin, and leans to the side. His stomach is warm, Victor releasing inside him, and Erin between them.

It burns.

It's pleasure.

It's something no one can ever take away from him. From them.

Something they will never forget.

Ever.

FORTY-TWO

They soon forgot.

Years pass, and Hëna's fears are strained as the Pack, already split, begins breaking apart into smaller ones. They claim new land as territory. Different languages and cultures are spoken. They stay in contact, a small victory she breathes in relief for. These rituals and meetings are held every twelve and ten moon cycles.

Every twelve and eight moon cycles.

Every six years.

Every three.

She does not listen to them fight over rules and regulations. She does not watch as the young cubs bond and wed. It is too painful. It is too similar to what once was, yet isn't now.

The humans branch out, too, taking control over more land. The great stone palace is forgotten over time, spiders webbing the corners as the forest reclaims what once was its own. The stone breaks. Walls crumble. The dry material stolen and reused. New countries and languages are formed. More stone trails, firmer and darker in color than before, connect these places. Concrete, it is called.

Her life is forgotten, her husband and brother, too, as magic is forgone for science—technology. It fills the air. The striking smell is pungent wherever she turns.

Through it all, she watches her wolves stay hidden. They blend in. Build their own empires and make their own money. They are an adaptable species. She cannot help but be proud of them. Even if their instincts slowly diminish, if their wolf forms grow smaller and ranks are born, presenting as a smell woven into their instinct.

Alpha.

Beta.

Omega.

Another genetic mutation.

She prayed for many nights from her palace courtyard that this one would continue aiding in their survival.

For they have survived. Not how she had wanted, how her Hope had deemed ... but they are an adaptable species.

She still walks among them, occasionally. Watching. Waiting.

Waiting.

Waiting.

Wait—

Wailing. A small cub. Her eyes flick down.

Ylli walks out and stands behind her. His hand presses onto her shoulder, squeezing. His eyes glimmer.

Her heart *pounds*.

"Name him, Shaun. Quick," a beautiful wolf pleads. A healer rushes around them, small, beady eyes calm as they flick over machines attached to the new mother.

"A boy." Laughter mixes with tears. "You delivered me a boy, Hope."

Her magic *howls*—

"Stop being so dramatic, Shaun, and name the cub. Before your sister and the others get here. Quick, Quick!" Hope holds her new cub against her breasts. Her breathing is shallow. Her skin is pallid, hardly distinguishable from her tangled blonde hair. But her blue eyes shine bright, still. Like twin moons.

Like the eyes of the small, pink, cub she holds tight.

The healer hands scissors to Shaun, a small smile curving her lips.

Tears fall fast. Wet laughter rings out again.

The cord attaching the cub to his mother is cut.

"Victor," Shaun cries, leaning to press a kiss on the top of his mate's head before pressing their foreheads together. One of his hands presses gently on the cub's head. "His name is Victor Lovelace."

Oh.

Oh.

Hope smiles.

Fate and Instinct laugh.

FORTY-THREE

Erin blinks against the light shining through his blinds. He forgot to close them. Again. He's going to make it Victor's job in the future.

Groaning, he slowly turns to face his mate, pins and needles shooting from his lower back. He readjusts Victor's arm around his middle so it lies lower, the warmth of his hand acting as a heating pack on his spine.

Victor's big hands touched every inch of exposed skin all night, making Erin feel like he was a sculpture being moulded by a God. He remembers Victor's cool tongue licking the sweat from his skin and the pinch of his teeth as they nibbled on his Adam's apple. It was fast and hard, all those spots inside him pressed and probed at. They definitely let their desire crawl out more than once during the night. What young man wouldn't leave his inhibitions at the door when his lover kept begging, "Faster, rougher, deep—yes, *there ...*"

Erin hides his face in Victor's arm, the heat of his skin doing nothing to help the blush blooming across his face. He screamed some real embarrassing things last night and yet ...

He lifts, gazing at the man beside him, at all the red love bites across his broad chest and neck. It was still vulnerable. Intimate. Like Erin was finally, truly, getting to see the real Victor—not the reincarnation of Tala or Alpha of the Lovelace Pack. Just Victor.

Erin smiles to himself, placing his palm flat on Victor's chest, feeling the rise and fall as he breathes. The steady beat of his heart is soothing like a lullaby. Hopefully Victor was able to see him for who he is now, too.

Sighing, he hooks a leg over Victor's waist so as much of their skin is touching as possible, snaking his hand to cover the new dark mark covering Victor's neck between indents of teeth. A shadow image of the one he feels still burning his neck between the back of his ear and shoulder. If Stella says anything to try and come between them again—

"Such a strong killing instinct coming from you so early in the morning, Star." Victor trails one hand over Erin's back, massaging the muscles, while the other glides through his short hair. "Feeling protective, are we?"

"Maybe," Erin says with a grin, his face pressed into Victor's collarbone.

Since they mated, his instincts have been stronger. They say an Alpha's mark will help to stabilize an Omega, so maybe that's what happened. With his wolf lying dormant for so long, and storming out all at once, he's been all over the place. A raging ball of hormones and long-forgotten memories playing 'pick me, pick me! Look here I am, do what I say!'.

Victor's mark helped to reel in all his wolf needs and calm him. It bridged the gap between his self as Erin Storm, the human, and Erin Bellmore, the wolf. And it reinforced their bond; the red string now tying them together no longer looks frayed and held together by knots. It sparkles in his mind as if it's been reinforced by steel. Simple biology. Or werewolf biology, he supposes.

"I don't want to let you go," he sighs.

"You just can't get enough of me, huh?" Victor's deep, rough voice murmurs into Erin's ear before kissing it. Erin hears the laugh hidden beneath and swats at Victor's chest playfully. Victor barks a laugh, pressing sweet kisses to Erin's forehead. "I don't want to let you go either," he admits.

"Then don't." Erin smiles, all canines like a wolf, and moves so he lies completely over his mate, his arms wrapping around his neck. Victor runs his palms down Erin's back, all the way from the top of his spine to the bottom of his ass. Erin feels the tingle under his skin electrify when Victor presses gentle kisses to his neck and shoulders.

His breath hitches, a high-pitched noise somewhere between a whimper and a moan running past his lips when Victor uses one hand to squeeze his ass, his fingers lowering to tease his rim, while the other hand lightly runs his fingernails across the back of his neck. He taps Erin's mark, outlining the white wolf. The teeth marks. Over and over and over again.

"I thought the bond marks would have shown like last time, and these we would have had to get tattooed again," Erin hums low in his throat. His body tingles. Heat boils in his lower stomach.

"Don't question the magic, Erin." Victor hardens underneath him. "I'm more than grateful all I had to do was bite you and give you my seed to regain my mark, instead of sitting through that painful needlepoint work again."

"Noted." Erin laughs. All he has to do is apply a little bit of pressure, and Victor's finger—

He digs his fingers into Victor's hair, pulling hard. Victor growls.

"We haven't showered yet, Little Wolf. And I need to pee."

"You peed last night," Victor smirks, his breath scorching against Erin's collarbone. He bends his leg up slightly, causing the leg Erin has around his waist to hitch up even further. "I knotted you last night, many times. What kind of mate would I be if I didn't check on you?"

Erin squirms as Victor starts sucking on his collarbone. He bites the bone and rolls the skin between his teeth before letting it go to lick at it. Heat punches him in the gut as Victor makes his way over his shoulder and toward his neck. His mark. It cools into disappointment when Victor changes course again, heading back to the front of Erin's neck.

"I don't think it heals that quickly," Erin pouts. He begins rocking his hips, small, subtle movements that let him slide his dick against Victor's. It's rough, with dried cum sticking to both their stomachs and chest. He knows most of it's his, but Victor's smell is strong in the air too. He preens. Of course it is.

"Even more reason why I should check. Hm?" Victor presses three fingers into Erin's ass, causing him to arch his back. His face digs further into Victor's neck.

"There," he pants as Victor works him. Curling his fingers and scratching that itch he feels deep inside. It's slow, like last night. Victor actually doing what he said he was going to do and clean him out. Slick drips between his cheeks, down his balls. It moves along their shafts, adding welcome pleasure to the sensation. Victor moves underneath him, too, aiding in grinding pressure against their dicks. Erin's hands move to cup Victor's head, his fingers playing with the lobes of his ears.

"Kiss me," Victor demands. Erin does.

It's all tongue and lips, neither focusing too much on what their mouths are doing between heavy gasps. But it doesn't matter. They're together. They're touching, hardly a gap between their bodies. Electricity jumps between them, in them, around them. The air is drenched in their love. Victor's grip tightens on the back of Erin's neck. His fingers pump faster. Erin's hips match his speed. Victor twitches underneath him and grunts, biting Erin's lips before warmth plops onto the space between them. It pushes Erin over the edge, too.

"There," Victor pants, lips twitching into a smile against Erin's. He takes his fingers out, wiping them against Erin's ass. "All out."

"Don't spread your cum on my ass," Erin laughs.

"You weren't complaining when I spread it on other places last night." Victor peppers kisses on Erin's cheek. Erin laughs, detangling himself.

"What happens in the sheets stays in the sheets. I was a different man then." Erin wades to the bathroom, conscious of Victor's bright eyes on him. "Come on, now I really need to pee. As much as I love being a pillow princess, we have a long day ahead of us. Let's wash up."

"A what? What's a pillow princess?"

"Look, I'm not going to say I told you so," Ben grunts as he dumps a pile of folders on the table. He grabs a piece of buttered toast, taking a large bite. "But I told you so."

"Whatever." Victor stuffs his mouth with more eggs from his seat at the table. "You could've been a bit more understanding when telling us what happened that night."

Ben leans his hands on the back of one of the chairs. "I thought I did pretty well, you know, considering I had to tell you that the woman who birthed me and raised you is actually a murderous psychopath."

Erin rises from his seat with a chuckle. After showering, they headed downstairs to eat. His parents had already left for work, making no mention of Victor being here or his crying breakdown from the night before in the note they left. He's grateful for that. Serious conversations should never be had on an empty stomach. Which is why Victor whipped up some bacon, eggs, and toast while Erin brewed the coffee. It settled something in his heart, watching Victor move around his family's kitchen wearing his shorts and old band-tee. His scent is all over Victor now, and not just because he used his shampoo and conditioner. Briefly, he wonders if this is how Victor felt watching Erin move around the ranch, around his bedroom.

It's a nice feeling.

It's a possessive feeling.

He doesn't know how he's going to hide it from Stella.

He glances at the clock.

The plan is already taking root in his mind; it's something he's been thinking about since Victor first introduced him to the Pack. Without all the evidence, though, he couldn't find a way to put it into motion. For every play he made, he thought up a counter Stella would use. The game of chess in his mind was a loop he didn't know how to get out of.

Until he came out of the shower, and Victor said he'd called Ben over to help them. Finally.

Now they sat at the table, game faces on. When Ben strode through the front door, he kicked off his boots and jacket. He wasn't wearing a business suit, but his drawn brows and smug frown sure made his white t-shirt and black shorts feel like one.

"This is everything I could find out about who started the curse and about what transpired the night of the coup d'état."

"Does it mention anything about a timeframe for the curse?" Victor asks.

"That's the thing." Ben takes a seat, leaning his elbows forward on the table. "Nothing I've ever found said what would happen once you guys got back together."

"Just that chaos and destruction would rain down on all of wolf kind." Victor crosses his arms over his chest, lips pulled to the side in thought. "No shape or hint about what that means? Seriously?"

"It sounds to me like a rant session between friends that got overheard and spread. For a very long while." Erin places a cup of coffee in front of Ben. "How did you find that all out, by the way? I know you said you started asking questions after what you saw the night of the coup, but Stella doesn't seem like the type to just let people ask questions."

Victor hums in agreement while Ben whispers a 'thank you' to Erin. "She doesn't keep any records or drop her guard, does she?"

"No, she doesn't. I realized something was wrong when Stella started telling people Gray was the one who had killed Uncle Shaun. I had seen with my own eyes that she was the one who did it. If Uncle Shaun really had turned and gone over to Alpha Gray's side, then why lie about who killed him? She could've said she had, out of self-defense or something, and then garnered more sympathy. It just didn't add up. So, I started paying more attention to Stella, seeing who she met with and watching how she spoke to us."

"The Council Meetings," Victor says with dawning realization. Ben had taken a page out of Stella's book.

Ben nods, taking a sip of coffee. "Ask the right questions and you get the right answers. It took longer than I would care to admit, but once I learned the truth myself about what happened that night, my memories returned." He taps the side of his head. "I don't know if it was the shock or betrayal, but I didn't question it, after all, Godd—"

"Goddesses don't die. And neither, too, do their spells," Erin finishes for him. "What about the records back at your house in New York? How did you get them here so fast? I thought it would've taken you ages to read through them all."

"I've read most of them already, but I sent Beatrice back up to get them all. In chunks so as not to alert Mom." Ben shrugs. "I had a feeling this summer was going to be different as soon as I saw you at that party two months ago."

"That's where she's been running off to all the time?" Victor shrieks.

Erin flicks Victor on the arm. "I told you we should have asked him sooner!"

Victor sucks his teeth, snatching Erin's hand and placing it in his lap, while Ben nods.

"Anyway, these were more for you, as evidence in case you didn't believe me. The things I remembered didn't add up with the lies I was hearing, the lies Stella was using to push and manipulate Victor. With all the proof I needed being in my mind, I was able to figure out Stella's motive that night fairly quickly."

"That's why you got super weird when the Treelark Pack said they were going to arrive late," Victor says, realization dawning as his eyes widen. "And why you never questioned me when I first thought Erin was my mate. You recognized him. You knew who the humans were that Healer Haven had called."

"Yeah, I did." Ben moves his coffee to the side and starts separating the folders on the table. "Which is also why I was so worried about what the Treelark's arriving late meant. I thought Stella had somehow gained more control. I thought she might have figured out who Erin was and had started attacking the other Packs already or something. The Treelark Pack is one of the few that have stood against Stella from the start. Alpha Adam was best friends with Gray. He never believed that Gray would have given into the Goddess's darkness, which makes him her biggest threat."

"Is that all he never believed in?" Erin asks. He leans forward on the table, eyes racking over the files. Memorizing. The clock on the wall ticks by. Victor's pinched brows slowly drop as his lips part.

"No way ..." Victor mutters.

Ben winks. "As smart as ever, Prince."

"You're saying that there are others? More wolves who reincarnated?" Victor whispers.

"Yeah. I don't know how many, but I do know that while the blessing The Goddess Hëna gave you two is slightly different, more powerful, and stronger, you weren't the only ones she gave it to. I don't know how many exactly or how they got picked—"

"Wait, I'm confused." Erin holds up a hand, frowning. "So why do so many wolves fear and hate her then?"

"Because Stella is a manipulative bitch, that's why." Victor looks to Ben, clear hatred lining his darkened eyes. "She used the fear of the legend to spread it, solidify it. No wolf would dare speak out against the majority, nor risk saying they came from a time forgotten without any solid proof. If they weren't locked up for being crazy, they'd be shunned or hunted, hated for getting a second chance. And after seeing what Stella is capable of ... wait, is she reincarnated, too?"

"No."

"Well, that's one small victory."

"I still don't get it," Erin insists, turning his eyes to Ben. "Why did no one stand up? You're wolves. You know how to fight."

"We were waiting for you."

Chills scream along Erin's neck. He turns to Victor, finding the same look in his eyes. Pain. Regret. Longing.

"I'm sorry we took so long," he replies.

Ben smiles. "Don't sweat it. You're here now, and we're all itching to fight. You weren't the only one whose wolf was trapped in a cage. Though ours were more figuratively speaking than yours was literal."

"Stella's been in the lead this whole game." Erin drops his head into his hand. "How do we get ahead? Do you know who she has on her side right now? There are, what, fifty-two Packs in America, right? She can't have all those wolves under her control ... can she?"

"It's a possibility." Victor places a hand on Erin's shoulder, kneading it gently. He looks to Ben. "Honestly, the reason I figured out everything you said was the truth was because I overheard Stella in the office. She was with Alphas Harkin, Cooper, Foster, and Reed. They were excited about killing Erin and me." Erin squeezes his hand on his shoulder. "So she has at least those Packs loyal to her. None of them seemed to think any differently about the curse either, and they didn't look relatively familiar to me."

"Yeah, those are the main Packs that are loyal to her. They have been since before the coup, and helped her stage it, too. They're under the assumption that they'll have extended power in their regions once she becomes supreme bitch ruler." Ben taps one of the piles. "I've put together a list of everyone who was friends with the Bellmores and those who I know believe the Moon Goddess to be in the blessing delivery service. Some have gone along with Stella throughout the years, but a good majority have kept her at arm's length. Especially once Victor presented as The Black Wolf. I think they thought if they simply held out long enough, Victor would take over, and Stella would be forced to the sidelines. Good or bad, he was the lesser of two evils."

"Because she sat back quietly the last time a blood relative got in the way," Erin mutters.

"Yes, well." Ben smiles ruefully. "These Packs we should speak to first. No one really knows the whole story. I never told them what I saw. They only know bits and pieces. Assumptions. Rumours. Their own memories from before." He shrugs. "If it's you two asking, they may well fight alongside us."

Erin crosses his arms on the table and leans forward. "It must've been hard ... sneaking around the house and putting up an act in front of her. Especially once the memories came back."

Ben exhales, resignation dark in his eyes. "It was at first. She reminded me so much of Uncle Kazamir ... but Vic was right, Stella has been a great mother to us. But at what cost? I lost my father in that war, and you two lost both of your parents. If she hadn't been power hungry, none of us would've had to lose anything. And you would've mated much sooner." He tilts his head, smirking as he points to their bond marks.

"Jealous?" Victor rubs his fingers against Erin's mark.

Ben barks a laugh. "No. I've been far too busy staging a secret coup against my mother to bother myself with finding my mate."

"Like mother, like son," Erin teases. Grabbing one of the folders, he begins to rifle through it. The detail is incredible, down to each person's middle name and their BMI. Ben wasted no effort in gathering intel.

"Same could be said for you." Ben looks at them—*really* looks at them. Something swims in his eyes. Pity? Regret? Pride? "I'm lucky I still have memories of them, albeit fuzzy. You guys, and B, too, can't recall anything. But you remind me of them. You both do."

"None of that matters right now," Erin says, looking up at Victor. He's looking out the small window above the kitchen sink. Eyes distant. Lost in memory. "We need to focus on what we can do to keep those of us still alive safe. We can have a sleepover trip down memory lane afterward."

"There's something you need to know, first, Ben," Victor says, voice firm. He looks back at his cousin. Ben sits straight in his seat, the command clear. Even Erin heard it, his muscles tensing in response. It wasn't strong, but the Alpha coloring his voice was there. Simmering. Not commanding but ... asking for attention. He inhales deeply. "Last night, when I overheard Stella speaking, she acted like losing Uncle Andrew was inconsequential. Brushing it off like someone does to a fruit fly over watermelon in the summer. But she commanded the others to leave you and B alone."

"Well." Ben's lips purse, eyes shuttering as they draw close together. He crosses his arms over his chest. "Maybe her heart does still beat." He sighs. "That doesn't change the course of action we need to take."

"I know, I—" Victor reaches over, placing a hand on Ben's shoulder. "You're my cousin. My Beta. I wanted you to know. She's a monster, but she did care for us. Or you, at least. Which means you aren't stone-hearted either. Ok? I know that, and I'm sorry for how I acted yesterday."

"I'm just doing my job." Ben nods with a small grin. Victor frowns, about to say something, when Ben grabs his hand off his shoulder, holding it tight. His eyes are the clearest shade of green Erin's ever seen them. "Truthfully, Cousin. This is my job, and I want to do it. I ... I wasn't old enough last time. Not just during the coup d'état, but before. I was too young, left behind to hide in the trees with the other cubs. I heard your howl. I knew what it meant. My father took over after, but the Pack still split. The humans, too. He did what he could, but I could see it in his eyes—the pain and guilt. He thought he failed you, both of you. That's why he refused the mark. So when She blessed me, too, it gave me the chance to protect you. I ran with it. The coup happening only solidified my determination. I need to help. I want to help. I'm your Beta. Your Pack. So let me do this."

Victor searches Ben's eyes. Waiting. Watching. He must find what he was looking for because he nods, squeezing Ben's hand with a smile. "Ok."

"Ok." Ben grins, and for the first time, Erin sees the youth in his face. He looks like any other 30-year-old free of stress and enjoying life with a good job and a proud family. Not someone run-down with stress pulling on their shoulders.

"So," Victor thrums the table with his fingers, "the Council Meeting is in just over two weeks, and Stella's support is much bigger than ours. She has a plan to kill Erin that night. I don't know how, probably should have stayed to hear that part." He sighs and grabs one of the folders on the table, rifling through it. "But she's banking on me losing control in front of everyone to prove that the curse is real. Then she'll kill me in 'tragic defense'."

"Curse is fulfilled, the strongest wolves dead, and complete command of nearly all Packs across America goes to her." Erin looks at the folders strewn across the table. He thinks of everything he's learned about Stella while working on the ranch and everything he's been told about how werewolf packs operate. All the lessons his father forced him to sit through in the palace about war strategy.

Victor huffs. "Cliché move if you ask me, which will also never happen. I'd never let Erin die before me."

Erin's eyes gleam. The plan might work. They could win this if everyone works together. Which means he does need to tell—

Meow.

The pairs of eyes swivel to the hallway. Mr. Wolf is perched on the railing of the steps. He's looking at them. Blinking slow.

"You hungry, Mr. Wolf?" Erin asks, rising from his chair. "Want a treat?"

Mr. Wolf jumps to the back of the couch. His head cocks low, focusing back onto the front door. His long black tail swishes behind him.

Meowwww.

"Does he want to go out?" Ben asks, leaning back on the chair's hind legs to watch. "I thought he knew how to get in and out of the house himself?"

Erin nods. "He does." And if he's not hungry, then that means only one thing. A glance at the clock proves him right. Shit, he didn't realize how much time had passed. Victor doesn't know yet.

The front door opens, and car keys are thrown into the ceramic bowl on the glass table by the door as Crocs are kicked off.

"Ding dong!"

Three sets of eyes flick to the two humans entering the house, shuffling toward them. Sharp brown eyes instantly fall over open documents.

"Don't tell me you guys adopted a kid already! I thought I was going to be the nanny?" Fletcher teases. He plops four plastic bags of Chinese food onto the kitchen counter while Layla sets down a case of apple cider.

"Sorry we took so long," she puffs, placing her hands above the thin jacket she has tied around her hips. "We were going to make some cheesy mice for lunch, but someone," she glances pointedly to Fletcher, "had to burn the rice. So, Chen's honey chicken and rice it is. I also got some mongolia beef, spring rolls, and whatever number 24 and 13 said," she beams, shrugging one shoulder.

"Cheesy mice?" Ben asks.

"A Storm delicacy." Erin stands, heading to grab some bowls. "Rice, ground beef, shredded cheese, and the consumer's preferred choice of condiment. We had it all the time growing up."

"Oh." Ben doesn't look convinced, but stands and helps to clear the table while Victor moves, resting his hip against the counter beside Erin.

"What are your friends doing here, Star?"

"I invited them for an early lunch." Erin looks at him, passing him the bowls from the shelf. "I told you not to eat so many eggs for breakfast."

"Let me rephrase." Victor clears his throat. "Why are your friends here while we are discussing Pack politics?" He raises his brow.

"Because they are Pack."

"Erin—"

"Victor." Erin cups his jaw. "They are my Pack. I need you to trust me on this. If this is going to work, I need everyone on my side. Everyone. Pack stands together, thick and thin. Fate and Instinct want us to play this game with Stella? Then sure, I'll play. But with *my* rules."

"You're going to tell them," he says. It's not a question but a realization. One he doesn't get a say in.

Erin nods and grabs some cutlery. "I was going to tell you. I'm sorry I forgot. But you wouldn't have changed my mind anyway. Now, what do you want to eat?"

"A pile of wolfsbane?" he mutters. Erin narrows his eyes at him. "Come on, Star. We both know this conversation is not going to go well. I shouldn't be here for it!"

"And why not? You're my mate."

"You mean your proof."

"Proof?" Erin's brows raise in shock. "Don't forget, Alpha, I'm a wolf this time around. I'm all the proof I need. I want your support … just in case my friends decide to kill me first and ask questions later."

"What are you two whispering about?" Layla calls from the table, beer in hand. They're all sitting, curious eyes pinned to where he stands half hidden with Victor beside the fridge, bowls and metal chopsticks in hand. Well, Fletcher and Layla are squinting curiously. Ben's looking down, beer on the table in front of him clenched between his palms, face wan like he actually did swallow a pile of wolfsbane.

"Nothing of importance." Erin nudges his brows at Victor over his shoulder. A silent, 'You want to fuck me later? Then help me convince my friends that I'm not a terrible person who's been lying to them all their lives.'

Victor trudges behind Erin, plopping down in one of the two spare seats at the table.

"So, how've you guys been?" Erin asks. "It's been ages." He forces a smile while passing out the bowls. Fletcher wastes no time in piling his high with MSG goodness.

"Dude, summer's almost over, and I haven't seen you at the pool once!" he whines. "You'll forget how to swim at this rate."

"Doubtful," Layla mutters, crunching on a spring roll.

Erin chuckles, "Sorry, Fletch. I've been a bit busy working on the ranch—"

"And getting fevers apparently." Layla fixes him with a cold stare. Erin's smile falters. "Yeah, your mom told us. I called her after hour twenty-seven on the ghost train."

"Look—"

"No, you look here." She points her chopstick at him. "After everything that bitch has done to you, all the sabotage and hitting you with her car for fucks sake, Erin, you still insisted on getting heatstroke working at her ranch? And for what? For him?" Her chopsticks swing between Ben and Victor. "You start dating, blow up at us, which you apologized for, thank you, but I'm still waiting for a proper explanation to that conversation about what is happening next when summer is over. I didn't want to push it, knowing it was a sore spot for you, and you made it sound like something big was happening. I could tell you need me and Fletcher to just be there to support you, but we couldn't even do that. You went kind of MIA after that, shot responses, vague excuses as to why you couldn't come hang. I know your parents, they aren't that strict with you helping them with the business. And I know you haven't been out taking any photos either, because your camera lens is still in the shopping bag!"

Erin's gaze flicks to the bag on the counter. He completely forgot ...

"No job is worth dying over, Erin. Not even if it's because someone else is in trouble and needs your help. Especially not if you love them."

"Wow, okay." Victor places the beer he was nursing onto the table. The bubbles swim angrily. "First, there's no need to push Erin into deciding anything right now. We plan to be together for a very long time. Second, how much do you know about what my aunt has been doing?"

Layla narrows her eyes, but Fletcher beats her to the punch.

"What do you know?" he asks, chin up and brow raised. His eyes aren't smiling. "Erin's gone all funny since you showed up. Now I want to know why."

Victor scoffs, leaning back in the chair. "I asked first."

"And I asked second, who cares? I've known Erin longer. Which makes you not knowing that *of course* we'd know something laughable."

Victor's nose twitches. "Well, I'm his mate. That outranks everything."

Fletcher pulls back, hand raising and mouth dropping to banter more when they suddenly snap shut. His hand drops, and his eyes widen, flying to Erin. They move to a spot in the juncture of his neck.

Oh shit.

Erin shrinks in his seat just a bit.

Fletcher's brows twist in deep, deep betrayal, and he gulps.

Double shit.

"Mate? What the fuck does that mean?" Layla asks. Her eyes widen. She, too, seems to remember a crazy conversation held halfway through summer about how the hot newcomer to town was high on drugs because he kept spouting nonsense about being a werewolf. About sharp teeth elongating like a wild animal.

"Erin ... why did you get a matching wolf, moon, and star tattoo with Victor?" she asks.

The realization that maybe ... maybe that man wasn't high on drugs hangs unsaid in the air.

Ben clears his throat. Erin snaps his eyes to him. He sees the push in those green eyes. Subtly was never going to work here; shock was always a part of the equation.

It's now or never.

"So, remember those wolf dreams?" Erin squeaks.

FORTY-FOUR

Stella wakes early Sunday morning, the sun just starting to peek over the treetops, and heads down to the kitchen for some coffee. It's been a week since Erin left the ranch to recuperate at home.

Stella didn't question his insistence. She remembers the anger puffing Victor's bottom lip when he told her Erin wanted to rest at home, saying it was 'too loud for him here' and some other sorry excuse of 'him being a new wolf and still not used to all the sounds.'

The glee she felt at that moment made her fingers shake.

Poor baby Erin, too overwhelmed even with Victor's scent that close by?

Of course, Victor had mistaken her reaction as fear toward Erin's safety and worry for him that his mate would be apart from the Pack. She played her part, reminding her idiot nephew that Erin sleeping in his bed only at night, and still coming over during the day, is vastly different from staying away twenty-four-seven.

Victor then proceeded to reassure her that he wouldn't let anything bad happen to Erin, so she needn't worry.

What a joke.

She walks to the sink and stares at Natalie and John working. One of Erin's friends, the one who came by last time, has been here helping. What was his name? Fluffy? Fred? Flicker? While she's been overjoyed not having to smell Erin's sweet scent of rain—an annoying constant reminder of his status as an obstacle in her way—his not working at the ranch means Victor isn't at the ranch either. Within the past week, Victor has only come home twice. He practically lives at the Storm house now! It's making it hard to keep him in line.

Ugh. She juts her hips forward to lean against the sink, tapping her nails on the mug in her hands. This won't do. Victor hasn't been acting any differently around her, still pouting to her those two times he did come back, tears fresh on his waterline. He said that Erin's not been acting like himself. He's 'temperamental' but getting better every day, the wound no longer needing the massive bandages around his shoulder—unfortunately—but not fast enough for his liking, thankfully. Even with his immunity, the dose must have been strong enough to do some lasting damage to his nervous system, affecting his hormones and brain chemistry. He is still a new wolf, after all. She'll take the win of crippling him, even as small as it is. That's fine. It'll do no good to convince Victor to have Erin come back to the ranch. It's better that the Bellmore child stay away so his presence doesn't influence others.

Or scare them.

Not yet.

Stella's tapping increases when a crack echoes around the room. Her lips pinch. She takes a step back from the sink, holds her mug in her left hand, and curls the fingers of her right hand into her palm. The nail on her middle finger is broken, a split running from one side to the other.

"Fuck!" Stella yanks her lips into a snarl and slams her mug on the counter, coffee spilling and staining the white marble. She pushes her nail into her mouth, hooks her teeth under it, and yanks it off. She'll have to go get another manicure with Beatrice now. Poor girl. She spoils her mother, and this is how she gets repaid.

And with all that traveling she's been doing, too, back and forth to the house. How studious she is in her studies. She must have really liked that backwater university.

Stella sighs, rubbing her forehead, trying to beat the headache before it knocks. Ever since Erin arrived, her hormones have been all over the place! She's running herself ragged. Her nails are breaking, her hair is thinning, the color losing its shine, and she keeps waking up with dark circles under her eyes.

Stress. It's the stress.

Not to mention how long it took for the itchiness and swelling to go down after dipping the fake Treelark arrow in wolfsbane. Her hands were red for days afterward. No amount of lotion or medicine could help with the pain. Thankfully, she's such a great actress, and those other foolish Alphas didn't notice anything was amiss.

He truly is a fucking curse.

"If I were The White Wolf, I wouldn't be having these problems," she mutters with a snarl. The rubbing didn't help; she can feel another headache starting to pound behind her eyes. It travels quickly under her nose and cheekbone.

Great.

Placing her palms on the counter, Stella inhales deeply. She imagines all the stress being bundled in her stomach and exhales it quickly. *Patience.* These things take time. Power isn't given, it's taken. She thinks of all the gains she's had over the past twenty-one years—the successful coup d'état, raising Victor to have unwavering faith and trust in her, gathering allies with the other dominant Packs, and shooting Erin with a fake Treelark arrow. Crippling the everyone's hope that the curse could be avoided.

Stella purses her lips into a smirk as she picks up the coffee mug and continues drinking it, heading outside to sit on the porch. John spots her and waves with a joyful grin, the young man beside him in the green baseball cap doing the same. Fletcher! That's his name. She stretches her chapped lips, ignoring the opening of thin cuts, and grins back.

"Puny idiot," she gripes as the metallic twang of blood from the chapped cuts on her lips runs onto her tongue. "Your son will be ash on the wind soon, and here you are waving to the one who's going to burn him alive."

That's why she'll always be better than those two, magic curse or not. Who does the Moon Goddess think she is? Clearly not someone who's good at her job. Erin and Victor are weak because they were given power. And they haven't used a lick of it! She's strong because she worked hard to take it. And she will take it. Beatrice will look splendid with a crown over her growing red locks, the spitting image of how she looked when she was her age.

Stella's eyes narrow when Natalie runs over to John, concern rippling across her face. It's scrunched tightly, like she's trying to hold tears back in her blue eyes. There's hair falling out of the long braid down her back, and her usually straight red bandana is askew. Stella buries her scoff in her coffee mug. So professional.

She continues watching as Natalie speaks quickly into the phone by her cheek, a loud gust of wind ruffling the loose hair over her face, stopping Stella from reading her lips or hearing her voice properly. Then, she's thrusting the phone into her husband's hands. John nods along, Fletcher standing by with concern pinching his shoulders. No matter, she is the superior breed. Setting the mug onto the ceramic table beside her, Stella pulls her hair behind her ears, face the perfect image of blissful nonchalance. Her ears twitch as she listens in. Focus. Drown it all out except for—

"He j-j-just l-left!"

Sobbing. It's loud with a lot of sniffling and hiccups, like the person is having a hard time breathing. Erin? Is it that slut's voice wailing through the phone?

"We fou—I don—I don't know … w-why …"

Stella leans forward in surprise. Yes. That's Erin's voice, she's sure of it. But why is he crying? She sniffs the air for Victor's scent but doesn't find it. Delightful. Butterflies flap their tiny wings in her stomach. Something must have happened between them. Did they have a fight? Oh! She forces the smile off her face and steps to the edge of the porch. She can't make out much more of Erin's words over his sputtering cries. Stacy was an ugly crier, too. How disgusting. She rolls her eyes, stalking toward them. That family really has no decorum.

"Ok, Erin, I need you to calm down, Son. I can't understand you." John moves the phone away from his mouth, hand covering the speaker as he looks to Fletcher. "Call Layla and send her over to the house, now," he whispers. "You go too."

"Oh my, is everything all right?" Stella layers as much intrigue and motherly concern as possible into her voice, eyes trailing after Fletcher as he scurries past her, head down and eyes pinched tightly.

Natalie flinches. "Oh, yes, Ms. Lovelace. Everything's fine. Erin's just feeling a bit unwell." She lowers her voice and beckons Stella closer. "I think he and Victor got into a nasty fight ... you know, young love with big future decisions and all that. It must have finally boiled over."

Stella gasps, her hands flying to her mouth to hide her grin. "Oh no! That's terrible. I'll go check to see if Victor has returned home yet." Pressing her lips together tightly, she runs back into the house, grabbing her mug as she goes. The second the door is closed behind her, she opens her mouth and laughs. It's throaty and loud like a wolf who found a dead deer just sitting in the snow, ripe for the taking. The force of it causes her to bend over.

"Maybe the Moon Goddess does give out blessings!" she shrieks with delight. "My patience has paid off, and I didn't even need to lift a finger!" Placing the mug in the sink, she leans her hands against the counter. Though this does slightly complicate things. The time to strike must remain the same—it needs to be public. How can she get Erin to arrive at the meeting now if he and Victor aren't together? Wasn't there some kind of agreement in place beforehand?

Keys jingle in the door, and she rushes toward it, smothering the air with the scent of her concern. "Victor? You're home early. I figured you would stay at Erin's house all day."

Victor lifts his head when he enters, despair and hatred radiating off him in strong waves. His eyes are bloodshot as tears fall silently out of them, and his body is trembling like one push will either send him toppling over or jumpstart him into battle. He's fighting his instinct as Alpha, as a mate. Fingers clenched tight and jaw twitching.

Oh, they did fight.

"Honey, what happened?" Stella rushes toward him, pulling him into a tight embrace. She feels him tense under her arms before he squeezes her back.

"You were right. My instinct was wrong about Erin. He doesn't want to move to New York," he grits through clenched teeth into her shoulder. "He said if moving into the Lovelace Pack and starting a life with me here, now, is what it means to be mates, then he doesn't want to do it. He put his life and family here over me."

"Oh, my dear boy." Stella makes her voice lower, so it sounds dejected as she runs her hands up and down Victor's back. His voice sounds like he's swallowed gravel. Has he been screaming? At Erin? Glee runs through her as joy sings in her veins. She clears her throat of them. "This is why I told you to forget about him. I knew he was trouble."

Mentioning New York the other night was the right thing to do. It's been eating their relationship apart slowly. Of course it has. She's used to playing the long game. She recalls how confident he looked after being reintroduced as Victor's mate. He thought he could outmaneuver her in this game? He hasn't even been able to grasp the rules.

"People like Erin are selfish cowards, dear, they don't spare a second glance at those who love them." She pulls away, looking into Victor's sad eyes. "It isn't common for mates to reject each other, but ... it can happen. I suppose with Erin's wolf lying dormant for so long, its instincts have been dulled. Or the constant exposure to wolfsbane all his life has damaged his wolf's soul, even if he is The White Wolf, making him more human than wolf in the end. He just couldn't grasp our instinct."

She brushes some of Victor's unkept hair off his forehead, her eyes narrowing when her fingertips become greasy. Sweat? Victor was holding his bike keys when he walked through the door, which means he drove back from Erin's house. He shouldn't be sweating this immensely, even with Texan weather. Her eyes roam over him, latching onto the massive band-aid covering his neck.

"What's this?" She brushes it with her fingertips, flinching when Victor pulls back suddenly.

"A-a scratch." He looks away from her, hand covering his neck. Fear spikes the air. "Erin scratched me when he fought. I grabbed a bandage before I left. It was pretty deep, and I didn't want you or the others to worry before it healed over. I didn't want it—" Victor gulps, looking away from her to the floor.

Stella arches a brow. Stay calm. Smile. "Didn't want it to what, honey?"

Victor sighs, and it's like all the anger at Erin dissipates. And what replaces it ... He looks to her, eyes wide in ...fear?

"I didn't want it to be seen as a sign that The Moon Goddess's curse was starting. That this meant Erin would go on a rampage and kill us all."

A lie. Telling by how worn the edges of the band-aid are, it's not new. Which means only one thing. It's not a scratch. At least ... not just a scratch.

"Victor. Did you mate with Erin?"

Silence follows her words. Victor gulps, the air thicker now with pain and rejection. That could explain the excessive amount of sweat. His *bonded* mate rejected him. Wounded him. His body is physically fighting itself. That's what the fear is truly about. If he doesn't do something about removing the bond, then he may very well drive himself to death. Before the Council Meeting.

FUCKING SHIT!

These stupid, *stupid*, idiots.

"Vict—"

"No!" he shouts, hands clenched tightly at his side. He turns to her, tears falling freely down his cheeks. "No, we didn't bond, and that's the whole point. When I was there, I asked Erin to bond with me and brought up how it might be better to come home, to here, since the smell of Pack was stronger and Healer Haven had better equipment, but he got mad. We had a bit of a scuffle, which led to him half-shifting and scratching me. That's all. I'm fine. I'm strong. I won't let this be the thing that kills us all, I promise."

Stella gasps, fury in her eyes, but Victor raises his hands, taking a step toward her. "It was an accident!" he rushes out. "I hardly felt it at all. It was just bleeding a ton, but because there was residual wolfsbane still in his system, it transferred to me, and the wound is just taking longer to heal. They only had old bandages lying around, and I didn't want to stay there any longer. I swear, Aunt Stella, please don't tell Ben!" His shoulders droop, all the fight falling out of him now that he has told her the truth. How easy it is to wrangle it out of him. Like morning yoga.

"We've been fighting on and off for the past week, and today ... that was it. We—he made the decision."

Well, that cuts down planning in half. With how broken Victor already is, watching Erin die in front of him will push him over easily. Like a leaf in the wind. It's the one and only good thing that came from Stacy giving birth to the bastard boy.

"Come on, let's get you cleaned up, and we can think of a way to persuade Erin together, hm?" Stella drapes her hands around Victor's back and leads him upstairs. He walks in front of her, his steps slow as though he could falter at any moment. "I won't let this be the end for you two. Don't worry. Okay? He just needs time. This is a lot for one person to handle. He's so strong for having lasted this long, even after being attacked like that. And you are, too, for keeping the conversation going and trying to bring him back to safety. He hurt you, which is something an Omega must never do toward their Alpha, but look at you!" She kisses the side of his head as they reach the fourth floor. "I've had wolves on the hunt looking into the legend of the curse, seeing if there is any way to break it. They haven't found anything ... but I won't let all that hard work go to waste now. I mean, look at you! Standing firm and being understanding in Erin's lack of knowledge. I think that you two might just overcome this nasty curse yet!"

Victor sniffles, lips pushed together tightly. She clicks her tongue, keeping one hand on his back as they near his bedroom door. "I'll tell you what, let me talk to him. I'll take care of everything, leave it all to me. Ok? Give him some of my magical aunt wisdom." She pinches Victor's cheek, smiling at how he tries, and fails, to hide his grin.

"Ok," he whispers. "Thank you, Aunt Stella. I really wouldn't be able to run this Pack without you beside me."

She beams, a wide, genuine smile that pulls her lips wide and crinkles her eyes. "What's Pack for, if not this?"

Oh, how she wants to shift and run through the forest, barking ecstatically. What would Matt say? He'd probably buy that dress she'd been eyeing. Yes! How wonderful this turn of events has been. Her reign is truly about to begin. Hopefully, everyone's ready. And if not ... well, they've got all this land now.

What's a few more dead bodies?

FORTY-FIVE

"So, I've been thinking," Fletcher says, brown eyes squinting under the rim of his baseball cap.

"Oh, do you need some Panadol?"

Fletcher pokes his tongue in his cheek, resting his palms on the long stick he found. His eyes squint. "You've gotten mean since becoming a man of the moon."

"I wasn't bitten and turned." Erin rolls his eyes.

"So you admit to always being mean then?"

Erin sighs. "What were you thinking about?" He leans against the side of the shed and flicks through his camera roll. There are so many gaps between projects, with some of them not even having a before picture. The bright flower hedges along the new fence, the sealer they painted on it fading nicely to a deep charcoal, look like they sprouted out of thin air. And the structure he was most looking forward to capturing ...

He supposes that's what happens when he takes time off to deal with murderous aunts and exploding truth bombs.

"Well, I've been thinking, should I just move in? At least until next week?" Fletcher rests his chin on his hands, his body swaying as he moves the stick around.

Erin stills. His eyes flick to the house, ears focusing on each timber creak. Wolves are early risers. Including *her*.

"What's happening next week?" Erin adjusts his red cowboy hat, swiping at the sweat already gathering on his forehead, before motioning for them to start walking. Fletcher's eyes blow wide, lips parting as he follows.

"You know, school stuff. Athlete things. Big muscles and raging pre-school frat parties. All that. Your dad makes the *best* hangover soup. If I sleepover, there'll be no need for me to drive every day to get it." Fletcher laughs, tapping his friend's shins with the stick.

Erin smiles. He hears the message between the lines, and he's grateful for it. For them.

He's a wolf freshly mated, freshly bonded, and now forced to stay away.

He needs them—his Pack—now more than ever. It's only been three days since he last saw Victor, and already it feels like he's being shot by a blue-tipped arrow every second that passes and he isn't beside him. It's torture, one so different from before. The pain he felt, knowing he only had to wait until the sun rose to be back by Victor's side on the ranch, was *nothing* compared to this.

He can't see Victor at all. Can't touch him. Can't smell him. Can't speak to him.

And he's so *fucking* close.

His parents have been helping where they can, but it's not enough. He needs more. He needs his siblings. *His* Pack.

Fletcher's been helping around the ranch, coming back after for dinner. And Layla is always swinging by when she doesn't have a shift at the café to keep him company. The night always ends with him asking them to stay over, and they've agreed. Every time. Of course they have.

Stretched out on the couch, in his bed, at the dinner table, and in the backyard. Erin takes comfort in their presence, in their scent and casual touch. They drag him out of the house to train at the gym, his shoulder so close to being fully healed, and bake waffles with him afterward in the kitchen. They've been keeping him grounded and sane in a time when all he wanted to do was rip his skin off and jump into a raging inferno.

And it's only been three days.

Three.

Fucking.

Days.

"What do you think?" Fletcher leans against the fence, turning to face Erin. "And, warning, I may have already told Lay, and she may already be packing a bag. She even called dibs on sleeping on your bed with you, which I thought was rude. She's smaller and fits on the couch much better."

"Of course she did." Erin laughs at the pout pulling Fletcher's lips. "Don't worry, we can all squeeze in my bed, I'm sure we'll fit. So long as you don't fart and stink up my room, I'll make it work."

"Ah. Your optimism is delusional, my friend. Is that why it took you so long to tell us you were part howl?"

"A fact I'm regretting now." A lie. Erin lets his camera drop between his neck and smacks Fletcher across the chest. "How long until these jokes stop?"

"Until we're dead and buried, wolfman," Fletcher smirks. "That's my revenge."

Erin clicks his teeth and sighs. "I thought being called a lying, fake friend was your revenge."

"Hey, those were Layla's words, not mine."

"You're right, yours were more colorful."

"A rainbow just for you, sharp teeth." Fletcher blows him a kiss. Erin groans, his head dropping to the side onto his shoulder.

"You know why I didn't tell y'all," he mumbles.

"Yeah." Fletcher smiles softly, moving to adjust his cap. The smell of freshly mowed grass spikes through the air. It calms Erin. "Yeah. I know."

Erin bites his lips.

It was hard to tell them the truth last week. Though he had made up his mind, the fear still clung to his heart. Its grip was strong. Even now, his mind drags him back to that moment, replaying the yelling. From Layla. From Fletcher. From him. The rage and non-stop crying. The pain tearing his throat red.

Red.

Red.

Red.

Ben and Victor had to take over. They explained it all.

By the end of it, Layla was sitting with her shoulders dropped, long blond hair falling like a curtain to cover her face. Her pink lips trembled uncontrollably. Fletcher stood behind his chair, gripping the wood tightly. He was the quietest he'd ever been, mouth shut so tight his jaw was turning white.

Erin was worried that they wouldn't believe it all.

He was petrified that they would.

The thought plagues him still. He'll wake, fear tense as it sits on his chest, wondering how long until one of them jumps at him, screaming, 'Joke! The van is on its way to take you to the loony bin.'

It hasn't happened, but—

"You worry too much, Erin." Fletcher bumps his shoulder against his side. Erin sways dramatically, chuckling. "We trust you. Trust us, too, yeah?"

That's right.

Eventually, they had turned to him, scooping him into their arms. Like before. Like when they were kids, once again having sleepovers inside the pillow forts in the living room.

"Yeah." Erin leans on the fence, elbows on the top rail. "Also, are you sure you're ok to help? Won't you get into trouble having your friend cover all your shifts at the pool?"

"Nah, so long as I don't miss my swim meets, I'm good." Fletcher waves a hand through the air. "Bros before hoes and all that."

Erin barks a laugh when a creak sounds behind him. He turns his head. The back door is swinging closed as Stella slinks off the porch, heading his way. There's a sad smile on her face. Pity glitters in her eyes as her red hair blows freely in the dry wind. He sniffs the air; strawberries fill the space between them, concern dripping off each one.

Damn, she really is a great actor.

"Well, that's my cue." Fletcher gulps and starts walking backward, saluting Erin. "I'll be waiting for your parents by the shed."

Erin nods. Ok. His heart thumps loudly in his chest. Leaning off the fence, he fiddles with the camera hanging around his neck.

Showtime.

"Erin, it's been a while, hun. How're you holding up? Your shoulder looks better!" Stella tilts her head, voice thick with worry. It makes Erin sick. His stomach starts to roll, those breakfast burritos his dad made hitting the back of his throat. He gulps, forcing the nerves back down, and plasters a grateful smile on his face.

"Yeah, it is. I'm doing all right, thanks for asking. And thanks for letting my friend help out my parents in my place. I know it was kind of last minute, and to have a human stranger milling around so close to the Council Meeting would've been tough."

"Oh, anytime. We're fam—" Her lips are still holding the word 'family' in their grasp, he can practically see it, as she raises a guilty hand to her mouth.

"He told you then," Erin mumbles, voice clenched. He titters, looking down to avoid seeing the disappointed look pass over her face, feet shuffling in the long grass. It's been growing fast since they sprayed it. He'll need to mow it before they leave on Friday.

"Yes." Stella moves to Erin's side, laying a hand on his shoulder. He hears more than sees her nod, lips clicking against her teeth as she sucks in a breath. "Terribly unpleasant for the both of you. You must be in so much pain."

Erin's face coils, his brows aching from how tightly they are twisting. "How ... how is Victor doing?"

Stella's glossed lips twitch. "He's been attending to his duties quite well," she says, pleased. "Most of the preparations for the Council Meeting have been completed already, which is great since it's next week," she laughs, taking her hand off Erin's shoulder. His eyes dart to her fingers. They're not as red as Ben said they would be, but if he squints, he can see the residual still there, hidden underneath a fresh coat of black polish. "The work of being the best real estate agents in New York never ends."

There it is.

"That's good. I'm glad he's doing ok." Erin looks out toward the forest. "New York seems ... like a lot."

"It can be," Stella hums. "I've seen many humans and wolves fail in that city. It's not for everyone. Especially the weak hearted."

Ouch.

He recalls Victor's snarling words.

'It's like the ranch is a chessboard, and we're all Stella's pawns being maneuvered around as she wishes.'

Well, it's a good thing he's never cared much for chess anyway.

He preferred Clue.

"Yes ... I figured. That's why I said I didn't want to bond with him." Erin turns to Stella, eyes watering with fresh tears. "I hope you know I meant no harm. I just don't want to fail and have that reflect poorly on the Pack. And with this curse hanging over our heads ... Ms. Stella, please believe me. I don't want to kill anyone."

"Oh, Erin!"

"Victor explained a bit about it to me, and it's too much pressure!" He tightens his throat, forcing his voice to come out in a strangled whisper. "If the only thing I can do with my cursed life is to stay away, then I'd rather fight Fate and Instinct on that. New York wouldn't work for me anyway, so I'd much rather focus on staying here. Far, far, *far* away."

"How kind of you, hun!" Stella pats his shoulder, the one he injured. The small bandage covering the wound juts out over his neck, covering something else, too. Her calculating eyes rake over it before she turns to look at the house, tracking each window as if she can see through the curtains to the people inside. Her mind working on how best to control them all. "Victor is a very focused individual, though I worry as he retires to his room straight after his duties are completed. It's almost like he's Rapunzel, or Juliet! Oh, you know, from that play—working and then locking himself away in his tower on the fourth floor. Except this time, there's no knight or Romeo waiting to climb into his bedchamber. Yes, getting back home to the hustle and bustle of social life will do him good. Maybe he'll meet a nice Omega back home. One not bound by curses. My friend has such lovely kids who are of age. They'd much such beautiful babies together."

Erin's skin prickles as her gaze slides onto him once more. He feels her scent start to waft around them, Stella trying to command obedience. Erin keeps a strong hold of his own scent, letting Stella believe he's allowing her to dominate the conversation. Let her think her threats are still working, audacious as they are.

"You're right." Erin turns his head to Stella, facing her head-on. His voice is firm and resigned when he speaks. "Life isn't a fairy tale, and reality is a bitch. I learned that quite young. Perks of being human."

Stella's eyes sparkle in triumph at Erin's response. She finally takes a step back, shoulders relaxing as her hands clasp together in front of her. "Oh, how I wish life were a fairy tale," she laughs. The sound is light and high-pitched, like she has no care in the world. "How exciting that would be!"

Erin bites his tongue and says nothing. He pulls at the collar of his jumpsuit so air can drift down his chest. Thanks to what Victor calls 'bites of my love', Erin is forced to wear the long jumpsuit properly instead of tied around his waist.

"Yes, well, I should go." Erin raises his camera slightly. "I need to finish taking progress photos before my parents get here and we keep working. The deadline is fast approaching."

"That it is, hun," Stella hums. "Ah, but before you go ..." Her eyes narrow to slits, the green all but disappearing. Erin hesitates, sweat trickling down his neck at the contemplative look glinting across her eyes.

"You should still come to the Council Meeting." Her smile is warm and radiant like the sun. "I seem to recall Victor mentioned something a few weeks ago about you taking photos for him during the event? Rouge wolves aren't normally welcomed to this event, but you can be an exception. I can introduce you to the members of the Texas Pack, too. You've briefly met Alpha Matt Harkin already, right? Yes, of course you have. That man is always lurking around, a nosy gambler he is!" She laughs, waving her hand in the air between them as she leans off the fence. "It'll be good to speak to him and learn how his Pack functions. Especially since you are staying here and not coming with us to New York."

"Oh, I don't know ..." Erin scratches the back of his head.

"Aw, come on." Stella reaches and clutches both of Erin's hands in her own. "You won't be alone. Plus, word has already spread to other Packs about The Black Wolf finding his mate. So, naturally, everyone is ... curious, would be the polite word. It'll be good to show your face to everyone. Let them see that you and Victor are still fighting this curse, albeit not together anymore."

Of course. How silly of him. Naturally, everyone wants to know all about him. Erin closes his eyes to hide his eye roll. Now that he knows Stella's true intentions, her theatrics are so repulsive.

"And," Stella pulls Erin's hands toward her, causing him to bend down, "since you and Victor will be separating, it'll spare the need for a statement to be released later," she whispers. Erin twitches his fingers in Stella's hold and looks down in shame.

"It's not normal for mates to reject each other. Other Packs may see that as a sign of weakness. It could reflect badly on Victor and this Pack later if rumours are left to fester about why you two split. Best face the music and get the story straight right away." Stella lets go of one of Erin's hands to gently grab his chin and lift his head. "Think about him, hm?"

Erin thinks of Victor being humiliated and tears well in his eyes. Real ones. He sniffs, plastering a sad smile onto his face. "Ok." He squeezes Stella's hand. "Thank you. I didn't realize the repercussions. This is all still so new to me. I know Victor is your nephew, but you've always treated him like a son. And ... even though I've hurt him, you're still being so nice to me. Thank you, Ms. Lovelace."

"Of course." Stella pats his cheek. "You'll always have a home here, should you ever change your mind. Love takes time, right? Like you said, this is all so new to you. No one can expect you to get it right straight away."

Erin wipes his eyes and nods. Stella grins, patting his cheek once more before all but skipping back inside the house. Once the door has swung shut and Erin hears her soft humming travelling deeper into the house, he lets loose. The sneeze makes his whole body shake. "Ow." He rubs his shoulder, another sneeze racking his body. That one he felt in his throat.

"Ugh." The sweet aroma of champagne and strawberries makes his nose twitch uncomfortably. He turns back to face the forest, flapping his hands in the air to help the wind dissipate the stench. Does she ever hold back?

He rubs his nose before pressing down on the corners of his lips to stop them from smirking. That was far more fun than he thought it was going to be.

"Wow, that looks amazing, Erin!" Natalie says, proud grin on her face as she strolls toward him. There's a black wooden box held loosely in her hands. John is beside her, one hand gripping the handle of a cane picnic basket while the other is pressed to his wife's back. The setting sun beams behind them, casting their shadows far on the freshly mowed grass.

Erin looks up from where he's standing in the newly built gazebo, fluffing some emerald-colored pillows. "Wait! Freeze!" He holds a hand out to them, waiting until they stop walking to bend over the stone table and grab his camera, and snaps a few shots of them. Checking to make sure the resolution is ok, he smiles. "Ok, you can move now."

"To see the world from your eyes, Goldy," John chuckles, ruffling his hair as he walks past.

"It's not that different than what you see, Dad," Erin replies, sitting.

"Oh? That so?" John quips. He places the picnic basket on the table and looks around, a low whistle blowing past his lips. "One of our best yet, Love."

Erin has to agree.

"No, I don't think so," Natalie whispers. She's looking at Erin, not the gazebo, with tears in her eyes. Her hair is out, her red bandana keeping her long black locks out of her face as she walks up the steps. Erin reaches out to hug her around the box she's holding.

"Are you trying to say that I'm your best project, Mom?"

Natalie only laughs in response before finally taking a moment to take in her surroundings. Her eyes roam slowly around each pillar and flower petal. The structure itself is quite big, the circular gazebo being able to seat at least fifteen people without them bumping knees on the built-in benches, even with the giant stone rock placed in the center as a table. It was made with cut evergreen trees from the forest on the ranch, the wood stained to match the charcoal fence. The loose jagged rocks he took a tumble on were laid on top of uprooted soil to act as stepping stones leading to the entrance steps, while the rest were either joined around it to create two flower-filled pots on either side of the entrance or placed on the other side of the yard where the stone fire pit is going to be. The plan is to finish that tomorrow and then spend Friday morning mowing the lawn, packing their supplies, and doing any other small miscellaneous tasks that need to be completed. Like final photos.

"Has Fletcher left already?" Erin asks, his index finger rubs over his thumb.

"Yeah, he's picking up Layla for moving day," John says, placing the picnic basket on the middle table.

"What?" Erin looks between his parents. "You knew!"

"I don't know what you're on about, Son." John waves the air. "Tell him, Wife."

"My husband's right, Erin." Natalie nods, finally placing the wooden box on the table next to the picnic basket. She straightens it carefully before running a hand over the smooth top and sitting. "I will not comment on the matter any further."

Erin shakes his head with a smirk, letting the matter drop.

He loves these people in his life so fucking much.

Sitting next to his mother, he taps his fingers excitedly on the lid of the box. He's never seen anything like it before, but familiarity knocks behind his eyes. There's a deep blue jewel pressed in the middle with wave designs engraved all around. An ancient smell clings to the box. It must have come from the office ... and yet ... he doesn't remember seeing it the day he raided the house with Victor.

"What's this?"

"Oh, a present for you." John steps back from the table and circles his arms around Natalie's shoulders. "For helping us with this project."

Erin quirks a brow and opens the box. His breath leaves his lungs all at once, the escape so quick there's not even a sound. Inside the box is blue velvet, two glass ornaments resting delicately on top. One is a white wolf with an eye made of a blue quartz jewel and a black wolf with an eye made of a golden quartz jewel intertwined from the neck up, while the other is a white stained glass crescent moon wrapped tightly around a ring of stars, like a hug.

"The wolves are from us, and the moon is from Stacy and Gray," Natalie says softly. She holds on to John's hands where they rest by her collarbone. "They wanted to have something custom-made for you, an heirloom you could pass on."

Erin jolts, realizing why the jewel looked familiar on the lid. It's the same as Victor's ring; the symbol representing their Pack. From *his* headpiece—it wasn't lost. The wave designs on the lid must've been carved by Stacy. He hovers his trembling hand over the two objects, words stuck in his throat. His emotions are like a wild hurricane spinning out of control in the space between his heart and head.

"We thought you could hang them up here as suncatchers or take them with you wherever you decide to go. A piece of home to always remember," John says, his voice soft. Calm. Firm, in command, but welcoming and loving all the same. It makes Erin feel safe, like no matter what happens, these people who raised him won't abandon him.

Ignoring the tears blurring his vision, he reaches over, pulling his parents into a bone-crushing hug. He can't think of any words available in the English language that would adequately express his feelings toward them. So, he says the closest thing to it, "I love you both. Thank you. For everything. Then ... and now. Both times. All times."

"We love you, too, Erin," Natalie whispers into his ear. "I only wish I could have done more. This life you have now, how I hoped it wouldn't be stained with so much pain."

"You did more than enough. Trust me." Erin squeezes them for a couple more seconds, letting their warm scent of love seep into his skin before pulling back. His eyes flash gold. "The Moon Goddess has a plan, remember? We must never doubt her. She's always watching. I'd hate to piss her off now, so close to the finish line."

John barks a laugh. Natalie swivels, swatting him on the arm. "Now," she pats Erin's cheek, causing him to sniffle and laugh. "Shall we eat?"

"Mm," Erin agrees with a small smile.

While they start fussing around the table, pulling out food and drinks, Erin grabs the box and takes a seat by the gazebo entrance. He places the box beside him. The beautiful ornaments sparkle in the midday sun, causing designs to dance in the air and along the wood around him.

He twists, gazing around at the whole ranch. Being situated in the corner of the backyard, close to the fence line, anyone sitting inside can see the enriching forest from all angles, as well as the newly renovated house. His mother chose the colors well, opting for mocha browns and light grays to contrast the dark-stained wood of the gazebo and surrounding fence. Paired with the deep green of the forest beyond, the place feels like a hidden gathering spot in a magical fairyland.

A land far, far away from werewolf politics and murderous aunts.

Snorting, he glances at the little paper flower descriptions sticking out of the stone pots guarding the gazebo entrance. He has a suspicion Victor was the one who told Natalie to plant the snapdragons and lilies, simply because they are some of Erin's favorites. They were meant to be wisteria, a mirror image of the flowers growing along the front of the house. His heart swells regardless; even though their landscaping design changed, it still looks splendid. And thankfully, his dad was still able to plant the wisteria toward the back of the gazebo.

The wind shifts, and he sniffs the clean air. Oakmoss is thick around them. The smell of Pack. What will it look like once everything is grown? A tall wisteria tree, its purple flowers hanging over the gazebo like an umbrella, while multi-colored snapdragons shield the front, filling the air with an enticing aroma. His fingers tingle. What a photo that would be.

And how loud. So many bees and insects.

As his shoulders shake with silent giggles when he thinks about all the critters that will be attracted to the ranch now, something shimmies under his veins. His power. It burns. It gives him strength.

It's a power filled with love. With hope. With promise.

It's a power they forged. They carved it into the moon, burned it into the stars. They bound it between them, string soaked in each other's blood.

Looking out at everything he's accomplished with his Pack, while thinking of everything he has yet to succeed in, he finally understands why She did it. All of it. From Nahale, to him—Erin. She let them stay together. All of them. And gave them a way to keep the Pack protected and prosperous. Always.

And maybe—he selfishly hopes, at least—She was just trying to let them try again.

Erin takes a deep breath. Longing howls through him. He almost swears he can hear an answering howl in reply.

Patience. Soon they can be together, wholly and properly.

Erin eyes his new gifts one more time before closing the wooden box.

FORTY-SIX

"Oh, please stay for dinner," Stella pleads to Natalie on the front porch while John and Erin pack any remaining tools into the truck parked in the driveway. They were able to stick to the schedule, and after two long months, Storm Landscaping's contract has come to an end. By the time the moon rises, not even their scents will remain.

At least for the next week.

"Thank you for the offer, but we have a tradition we stick to," Erin says, politely declining the invitation before his mother could say anything. "After finishing projects, no matter how small, we have a family feast. Roasted vegetables and various meats. Soda and beer. That kind of thing."

Besides, who's to say she won't try and poison him with food next?

"Oh, all right. I would hate to get in the way of your family," Stella says. She plasters an innocent look on her face and holds her hand over the porch steps toward Natalie. Erin turns, lifting an eyebrow as Natalie puts on a gentle smile and walks up the steps. Stella has to retract her arm and take a step back to avoid Natalie running into her.

Natalie grips Stella's hand in a firm shake. Erin smirks at Stella's wince.

"It's been such a pleasure working on your ranch these past two months," his mother grits. "Please call us should you need any future landscaping done."

Stella hums, her lips pushing together into a tight smile. "The pleasure has been all mine. The finished project looks amazing! If you knew your way around New York, mayb—"

"We do," John says. He holds out his hand for his wife to take, guiding her down the steps and toward the truck. "Quite well, in fact."

"Well then." Stalls pats her thighs as Ben walks out of the house, a thick envelope held loose between his fingers. "Ah, right on time." Stella snatches the envelope from Ben and opens it, her eyes skimming over the green bills inside. "All of the agreed upon payment is inside. Please let me know if you ever need anything else."

Erin grabs the envelope. He keeps his eyes fixed on Stella as he speaks, "Don't worry, we have no intention of moving anytime soon, so we won't be needing your real estate services."

"Shame." Stella's lips widen into a perfect grin. Her eyes sparkle like royal emeralds.

Erin licks his lips, chewing the inside of his mouth to stop from snarling. He glances at Ben, nodding once before turning. He can smell Victor on the balcony as he walks to the car, his moon-blue stare burning holes through his clothes.

His bond mark *sings*.

Erin climbs in the car without looking back. He can't let his desire get in the way now, no matter how intense it burns his insides. They are so close to the finish line.

The curtains have begun to draw back.

The orchestra has tuned its instruments.

Final call for seats has been rung.

The funeral procession is ready to march.

Stella may have started this war. She may have set her twisted terms and rules, thinking no one could figure her out.

But she underestimated Erin's love of boardgames. He figured her out. And with *his* Pack, *his* mate, his *Alpha*, they'll be overriding those rules.

They'll be the ones to end this, and it won't be like last time.

Because it's not revenge Erin has been whispering to, who he's been forming plans with to make Stella pay for what she's done. For what she's taken from him by playing cards with Fate and Instinct. For letting her greed shine brighter than her wolf.

No.

He held the cold hands of justice.

And justice gripped back.

FORTY-SEVEN

Erin parks his car in the paddock beside the house. His limbs feel heavy in his lap as he gazes at the setting sun peeking through the forest trees. The Council Meeting doesn't officially start until the sun is fully set, meaning he's early. Yet, there are already tons of cars here, reminding him instantly of how cramped the lots got at Danny's Warehouse. And just like then, the air is humid.

But unlike then, he doesn't have to wait the five-minute walk to the front door to see the most beautiful pair of eyes.

Pride swells within him as he gets out of his car, eyes trailing over Victor's body. He walks from the fence to wait by the hood of Erin's car, wearing black chino pants with a deep blue silk top, the sleeves rolled to his elbows, and black suede shoes. His hair is gelled back, the side part much more prominent now that his bangs aren't flopping whichever way they want.

Victor grabs Erin by the waist and pulls him into the shadow of a Ford truck. Erin hardly manages to take a breath before Victor is stealing it, his hands roaming Erin's body. He then places one firmly on his lower back, pushing into his spine, while the other rests gently on his neck, the heel of his hand tilting Erin's chin up.

Erin wraps his arms desperately around Victor's neck, mouth just as frantic. He pulls them even closer, parting his lips and whimpering when Victor's scent darkens around them. Victor smirks, his tongue steadfast as it swirls inside, just the way Erin likes it. His knees tremble, the threat of them buckling real as Victor keeps hold of him. Erin tugs at the hair on Victor's nape, a sharp pull that has him gasping and leaning back. But not far; his face is only inches away. Hot breath fans against his cheek.

"Sorry," Victor mutters, voice rough. He clears it. "I … you … I thought I was going to die these past two weeks," he breathes heavily, words lost to the dense air around them as it's gulped down. The desire is strong in his voice, the lust bright in his scent. Erin chuckles, resting his head against Victor's collarbone. He moves the shirt slightly to place a sweet kiss there, a simple press of his lips on tan skin; the rough patch of the bandage on Victor's neck scrapes along his fingers.

"Yeah, let's never do that again. Even if it was the only way to keep our scents off each other and Stella in the dark." Erin steps out of Victor's arms and looks at his reflection in the car window. His dark blue dress shirt is wrinkle free, as are his black chino pants. And Victor was mindful to keep his hands out of his carefully styled hair. But … he presses his fingers against his lips. "I look like I just had a make-out session with someone," he mumbles.

"You did," Victor replies sarcastically. He doesn't seem to mind the state of his lips, instead focusing on flattening the creases out of his shirt collar Erin had been gripping onto.

"This isn't the image I want the other Packs to have of me." He pouts over his shoulder at Victor before opening the car door and reaching over the center console to grab his camera.

"Maybe it's the one I want them to have," Victor says with a wicked grin over the door.

"You—"

"I want them to see that you belong to me," Victor interrupts. His eyes are bright as he watches Erin, grabbing his hands to play with his knuckles. "You're my mate. My partner. Mine, in every shape and form. In this life, and the next. I am not going to lose you."

Erin feels his irritation subside as power surges within him. It starts from his heart and spreads quickly throughout his body. The blessing. Love. He can hear what Victor isn't saying. He wants Stella to see them together as a united front, that she hasn't won yet. That she never will.

"I know." Erin tightens his grip on Victor's hands, placing a kiss on his knuckles. When he looks into Victor's pale blue eyes again, he knows his hazel ones are reflecting the same image. "Now, let's do this."

Victor smirks as they walk side-by-side through the cramped paddock to the front fence. "The Packs that have already arrived are Harkin, Cooper, Foster, and Reed," he whispers into Erin's ear. "They started officially arriving a couple hours after lunch."

Stella's team. He glances toward the house; Ben's following Stella as she flitters around the yard. She hasn't seemed to notice them yet, too preoccupied with welcoming every individual from her allies' Packs, but Ben does. They lock eyes briefly, Erin's warm hazel on his deep green.

'Get ready,' they seem to be screaming at him.

Erin gives a subtle nod as he and Victor take their positions at the front gate. He drapes his camera over his neck before reaching out, fiddling with the Pack ring on Victor's finger. The cool press of the jewel is refreshing against his clammy hands.

"Oh, almost forgot," Victor mumbles. "We won't be needing these anymore."

"Wha—" Erin turns just as Victor yanks the bandage off his neck, stuffing it into his pocket. He grins, doing the same to the soft white material on his neck.

"There. Much better."

Erin shakes his head with a grin.

It doesn't take long after that for the sound of tires to reach his ears. He takes a deep breath, focusing on Victor's presence beside him and the steady beat of his heart. He has just enough time to squeeze Victor's hand as tightly as he can before werewolves are filing out of cars. Many wolves, out of many cars. He plasters a grin on his face and raises his voice to a soft, pleasing tone as he welcomes them all with Victor.

As his mate.

Fuck you, Stella.

Most people compliment him on the landscaping design, having heard through the grapevine that his family was the one to undertake such a harrowing project. Erin's smile twitches—word in werewolf society spreads just as fast as a wolf can run, it seems. But the awe and genuine happiness on their faces make any uncomfortable jitters in his stomach turn to pride. He feels giddy with it.

Until the fear starts to show.

"Look, they've bonded!"

"I thought they'd rejected each other?"

"Then what are those marks? They look so different. Ancient-like ..."

"Hmm, I think I remember seeing them somewhere before ... in a dream?"

"It must be the curse. Fate and Instinct ... they couldn't resist."

"So it's starting? Will chaos erupt tonight?"

"Stella said it wasn't going to happen, that she had a plan, that Erin was fighting it ..."

"He must not be that strong after all."

"But ... it's been months. Surely if something was going to happen it would've already, right?"

"Are you saying ... the curse may not be re—"

"Mama? Are we all going to die tonight?"

Erin's stomach churns, jaw clenching. Just a few more hours. Just a few more hours ...

Once the last of the sun's rays dip under the horizon, leaving only the moon torching the sky, the Council Meeting officially begins. Alphas and their mates, Betas, and other honorary members of the Packs from all across America parade into the backyard. Women wear long dresses and high heels, while the men have fashionably dressed suits. Handbags, headpieces, jewelery. Erin scoffs. And Victor had said prom attire? Yeah right. This is more like a wedding.

Or a funeral.

He gulps.

There are more pillows and chairs set around the backyard with a massive table stretching from the house all the way to the fence. One corner is piled high with clean plates and cutlery, while the rest of the table is filled with a variety of food and drinks. There are also punch bowls filled with juice and glasses of champagne, beer, and wine.

Erin remembers Victor describing how revolutionary it was when Council Meetings started hosting buffet-style feasts instead of the sit-down ones. The ability for wolves to wander around as they ate meant more mingling, ultimately leading to healthier Pack relations. He sees it now, the air of ease between these wolves who haven't seen each other in four years.

"I'm going to get us some food," Victor says. Erin nods, watching him go before wandering over to the fire pit. Thankfully, there are two seats left. He smiles at the wolves already there, young men and women he remembers greeting at the gate. They're from the Treelark Pack. They wave, smiling back at him when a stench wafts from behind him. His lips clamp shut.

The timing of this woman.

Now that he has more time to look at her, Erin realizes how out of place Stella looks under the moonlight. She's wearing denim-colored heels with a dark forest green dress, the color making her eyes look like they'll pop out of her skull instead of deepening and enriching them like it's done for Ben. She's had her hair cut too; the loose curls that stop right at her chin look like dry slinkies that have stuck together after being hacked with a saw.

She stares at him, her face harbouring no emotion on its pale, wrinkled surface before a grin splits it in half. She raises her thin eyebrows high at the same time she lifts her glass of champagne toward Erin, miming taking a photo with her other hand. Psycho. She must not have seen his mark. He smiles back, lifting his camera just as Victor walks to his side, taking the remaining seat by the fire, two plates filled to the brim with food in his hands.

"You're going to make yourself sick." Erin grabs the plates from Victor, his nervous smile turning into a genuine grin.

"Eh. I need the fuel if I want to make it through the night, and so do you." Victor carefully sets a napkin on each of their laps before taking his plate from Erin and digging in.

"I don't know if I can stomach eating anything right now," he mutters with a shake of his head before sparing a glance at the moon. It's a half-moon, the dark sky hugging one whole side of her light. What rays do shine float around like a protective halo, while the stars sparkle in their guard uniforms around it.

He can taste the suspense on the wind and hear anticipation rolling under the skin of those around him. They might not know, not all of them, but they can feel it. Smell it.

It's been a long game, but tonight it ends.

Soon the moon will be at the highest point in the sky.

"Mother, Father," he whispers. "Please protect us. *Please.*"

Victor squeezes his knee.

Hopefully, all hell doesn't break loose.

FORTY-EIGHT

Packs separate.

There's no call, no bugle horn ring. Just instinct, guiding the wolves apart as the moon howls above them. The Alphas stand side by side close to the fire pit, their Betas standing slightly behind and to the right of them. Their mates are on the left. The rest of the wolves form clusters behind their respective Packs.

Erin weaves back through the crowd to stand beside Victor, successfully dropping his camera off inside the house, just as Stella glides to the fire pit. She steps atop the empty stone benches and faces them all. The fire crackling in front of her sends glowing red and black shadows dancing across her face, like a witch stirring her cauldron.

"Thank you all for coming tonight. It's been a long time. Twenty-two years, in fact!" She grins as laughter floats through the air, waiting for it to die down before looking toward Erin and Victor. "So much has happened within these past few months alone, as I'm sure all of you have heard, let alone four years!" More laughter. Louder sneers.

Erin keeps his face indifferent, despite the growing agitation swimming under his skin and the eyes he feels racking all over him. Letting Stella goad him into reacting now would be pointless. Victor grabs hold of his hand, threading their fingers tightly. Cool metal slips over his finger.

It's time.

"First, I—"

"Sorry, Stella," Victor interrupts with a smile. "I know we agreed that you would start this meeting since you have more experience, but there's so much I would like to say that I can't wait. My skin is just buzzing with excitement."

Stella's smile falters slightly, her gaze flicks to the mark along his neck, and her eye twitches, but she manages to keep the mask in place. "Of course, Victor. Don't be nervous. We're all friends here." She presses one hand to her heart and bows her head as Victor steps beside her, Erin right beside him. Shoulder-to-shoulder.

He grins when Stella lifts her head and sees him. Her smile falls completely when she notices their hands. The matching mark bright along his neck. And the glittering jewel on Erin's ring finger. Murmurs run throughout the yard at the break of tradition. The first rule Victor taught him about Council Meetings is that Alphas lead the meetings, and while mates are permitted to attend, they never address the other Alphas directly.

Good thing they've broken plenty of rules before. They're practically pros at it now.

He raises his chin, flicking an eyebrow at her.

What is it people say in these situations? Ah, right.

'Check. Mate,' he mouths at her. Her lip curls upward as she attempts to hold back her growl.

Victor raises his free hand, and silence descends over the yard. "I know there are still so many of you who doubt me. This is my first time holding a Council Meeting since becoming Alpha, so I understand." He places his hand to his heart. "That is something I thank you for. Allowing this meeting to happen a year later than it normally does, so that I could have enough time to prepare, is something I am eternally grateful for. I wanted to host a perfect Council Meeting for you all. To prove that my Pack was ready to hold this responsibility once more."

His voice booms across the ranch; there's an air of command around him. In his firm voice. His straight back, head held high. Erin sees respect when he looks into the eyes of the other Alphas and everyone else present, even those on Stella's side. They all sense his power and strength, and not out of fear. No, they bow down to it. They respect it. *Revere* it.

He is The Black Wolf, the Alpha of the Lovelace Pack. A man hungry for justice.

"Which is why I want to remind you all that now is not the time for doubt or fear." Victor looks across the yard, his voice somehow getting even louder. "Now is the time for strength and unity, not just in the Lovelace Pack but with all Packs. Just like there was before the Lovelace Pack coup d'état."

A nervous laugh wobbles past Stella's lips. Erin glances at her over his shoulder. Her eyes swivel around the ranch in suspicion, watching how every single person reacts to Victor's words. Seeing if any of them are starting to believe him. Waiting for them to betray her. Her anxiety makes him feel almost bad at what's going to happen next.

He faces forward once more, squeezing Victor's hand, eyes narrowed.

Almost.

"Twenty-one years ago, on a cold March night, you were all manipulated and subdued into believing that Stacy and Gray Bellmore started a rebellion, leading to half of my Pack being killed, including my parents. But," Victor points toward his aunt, "that was a blatant lie spread by my aunt, previous Alpha of the Lovelace Pack, Stella Lovelace."

"Now—" Stella takes a step forward, but Ben grabs her wrist, holding her in place. She looks at him, surprise morphing her lips. "Wh—" She tugs her arms. Ben doesn't budge. "Let me go. What are you doing here? Where is your sister?"

"Safe," Ben rumbles into her ear. "Far from *you*."

"As you all have heard by now, Erin is my mate, The White Wolf." Victor raises his hand laced with Erin's into the air, the Pack ring glinting enchantingly in the moonlight. "And he is also Stacy and Gray's son. Stella was the one who orchestrated the attack that night. She thought that if she got rid of the Bellmores, she would have control over the whole Pack and, ultimately, in the end, control over all of you, too. What she didn't account for was Erin and me being *blessed* by the Moon Goddess. Not cursed. We found each other again, not out of some twisted vengeance spelled from our patron mother, but out of Her *wish* for us to try again. To have the opportunity of a second chance. One without chaos and destruction ruling our lives."

Victor ignores Stella's noises of protest from behind and continues to march through his speech. "We learned the truth. A truth I know some of you hear, standing before me, know too. *Remember*. Like I do." His voice is rumbling now. It takes on a growling edge as anger sharpens his words before piercing the hearts of those around him. He yanks the collar of his shirt down to show the black mate mark surrounded by a ring of teeth indents on full display. Gasps ring out around them as people finally take notice, *really* take notice. Erin bares his neck to the side, revealing his matching mark. Recognition glimmers in the eyes of some of the wolves around them.

Ah, Ben really was telling the truth. A part of him didn't believe it, didn't dare hope ...

Erin's heart thumps all the way to his stomach.

Good.

They offer even more reason to end this twisted fucking farce.

These wolves, they are his Pack. Whether they wear Bellmore blue or not. So he's going to protect them as such. He wants to see Victor's vision for this ranch come to life. He wants to come back every three years, capturing with his camera the growth of the wisteria by the gazebo. Watching as little cubs run around, laughing. Exultant. *Safe*.

"I know which of you have decided to side with Stella, and I know which of you were good friends of the Bellmores. I don't stand beside you now as The Black Wolf, or as Alpha Victor of the Lovelace Pack. I stand before you as a wolf who had his life ripped to shreds by greed and envy. Multiple times." Victor turns his head toward Erin and smiles. "A wolf who has finally found those shreds and tied them back together." He takes a moment to look directly into the eyes of each person standing in front of him, eyes gleaming brighter than the moon above them. "We don't have to fight, but I will if I must. I won't let my life be taken from me again, nor the lives of the people I was born to protect. The people I want to protect."

Erin holds his breath. The Alphas on Stella's side of this war all ooze various degrees of rage, while Alpha Harkin stands, red linen pants and matching top near identical to the fury that has puffed out his cheeks like a blowfish. He glances at the other Alphas and sees them looking between their Betas and mates.

Erin's eyes narrow. A finger pushes thin frames up a straight nose, toward sharp blonde brows. Long, dark fingers flex and lips twitch. A hand tap tap taps against a bluebell snug in a coat pocket. Her allies are hesitating, not making direct eye contact.

Except for Alpha Adam of the Treelark Pack. He's looking directly at Erin, a bittersweet smile on his face. Erin looks at his wife, Evelyn, he remembers from the records, only to see the same remorseful look adorning her face.

Oh.

He gulps down the tears threatening to spill and bows his head at them. When he looks up again, Alpha Adam has taken a step forward.

"Alpha Victor is right," Adam says, voice steady as he addresses the crowd. "I was good friends with Gray and his mate, Stacy. They always believed that peace triumphed over violence. That there was more to this world, one not built on bricks of fear and secrets. I believed in their words. In their vision. I *implore* you, wolves, Pack, look at the truth. Why do we sit here and believe that the Goddess who made us would then later betray us? For what reason would She seek revenge? The legend is incomplete." He glances at Victor and Erin. His brown eyes look wiser than he ever remembers Hëna's looking. "They told me, once, about some friend—"

"NO MORE!"

Erin spins just as Ben is tossed to the side. He breaks through the fence, the grass and dirt kicked up where he slides. Erin's heart pounds in his throat. Ben doesn't get up. Scraps of cloth rain down as Stella's dark brown fur glints red in the moonlight. Like it's been coated in blood.

She lunges toward Erin.

"NO! Victor roars, pulling on Erin's arm in an attempt to get him to jump off the bench and out of Stella's line of sight. He doesn't budge. His mind recalls the past—all the memories from training late at night with Victor and Ben before they were forced to separate, Fletcher promising Donny he'd personally train his kids so they could try out for Green Lake's junior swim team if he let them borrow the old cotton warehouse for a few days. The hours of pumping weights and shifting back and forth while fighting ignite a fire deep in his muscles. His mind goes back farther, to a time when another war waged. The sweat that clung to his skin under his armor until his arms and legs felt like lead from swinging around a steel sword and holding up those ridiculously large metal shields.

No.

He didn't run then, so there's no way in hell he's running now.

Erin tugs his arm from Victor and digs his heels into the bench, pushing all his strength into his calves and thighs. When Stella is close enough that he can see the droplets of spit rolling down her canines, he jumps in the air and shifts, raking his claws deep across her back.

She howls in outrage, narrowly avoiding falling into the fire pit. The other Alphas have scurried away. Some of them stand snarling, their shoulders tense and claws elongated in a half shift, while others have already given in to their desire. Wolves snarl, and metal glints harshly in the moonlight. Daggers. Knuckle rings. Weapons, drawn and gripped tight. They came ready to fight. Ready to defend.

But no one moves yet.

Their eyes are all alert as they flick between Stella and Erin, waiting for the signal to attack. It's like they can sense it, that this fight is between the Alphas that started it all. Between heir and usurper.

Erin climbs back onto the bench and, lifting his head high toward the moon, lets out a howl. He pushes out everything he's been feeling over the past few months—all the anger, regret, guilt, and heartache, but also the joy, comfort, delight, and love. The sound resonates, and others join his song.

More than he thought.

More than he had dared to hope.

Had She known so many of them still believed in her magic? Her love?

Is She proud of their strength? Their resolve?

Does Her heart break, knowing they all must fight again?

Erin knows it must. She has always cared for them all so deeply. Which is why he will try to end this fight quickly with as minimal bloodshed as possible.

Stella is the threat. Not the other wolves.

Cut off the serpent's head, and the body falls dead.

When he looks back at Stella, he sees her staggering as she tries to keep herself standing on all fours. Her lips are pulled back in a snarl along her snout so aggressively that her eyes are barely visible. What Erin can see of them, however, is filled with two swirling hurricanes of dark fury.

'You must be confused.' Erin stomps his front paw on the stone bench and peers down at Stella in pride, forcing his thoughts toward her through the Pack bond. She flinches. He grins. Victor and Ben taught him. Since they are of the same Pack, they can all communicate. Just find the string of stars binding them. It has come in handy, for sure. But the taste of Stella's smell in his mouth is not one he wants to hold onto for long. He'll need a whole bottle of mouthwash to rinse the sweet decay from his teeth.

He's not the weak little baby he was before, nor is he a fragile, naive human prince wearing the fake skin of a wolf.

He's The White Wolf, mate to the Alpha of the Lovelace Pack. He's the son of the kindest werewolves, Stacy and Gray Bellmore. He's a Prince blessed by The Moon Goddess.

He will take back his throne and crown. His Pack. His mate.

Tonight.

'My turn, Stella.'

FORTY-NINE

"I bet you're wondering how all this is possible." Victor steps off the bench and stands in front of Erin. He crosses his arms, a smug grin prowling across his face. "What, did you *really* believe that Erin rejected me? Wait, no, did you really believe that I'd *let* Erin reject me?" He scoffs. "And here I thought you were meant to be this mad genius, Aunt. Always three steps ahead."

Erin growls softly, nudging Victor's back with his snout. They're here to stop her from taking over, not poke and prod her into going on a full rampage. Fists are forming and jaws are clenching, canines splitting lips, as the wolves around them try to stay civil. The air reeks of battle. It's drenched in that sour smell. If this is what it smelled like back then, when the wolves fought the humans, who he knows were even more prideful and bloodthirsty than now, it's a miracle any of them could keep the food in their stomach.

Erin licks his lips, stomach rolling. He wants this to end with as little bloodshed as possible. Stella was the conspirator. The others were lambs, twisted into believing they were wolves, and followed along. He's willing to spare them.

If they listen and aren't provoked.

He nudges Victor again.

Victor doesn't take the hint. Resentment falls off him in waves, like a faucet that's been blocked for so long and is now finally unclogged. He uncrosses his arms and takes a step toward Stella, his voice is deep when he sneers, "Wow, Stella, you think you're the greatest actress alive, huh. I mean, what did you expect? After living with you for so long, it's only natural that we'd pick up some tips and tricks."

Stella growls, the tone lifting at the end as if in question.

"Oh, right." Victor motions toward Ben, who's being helped up by Adam. His shirt sleeve is torn from his elbow to his wrist, the pale green dress shirt turning a deep yellow as blood seeps into the material. Adam lifts Ben's arm up and back, a pop reaching Erin's ears at the same time a grimace scars Ben's lips.

Erin whines low in is throat. Of course, it's always the innocent who bleed and break first.

Victor's nose wrinkles when he sees the blood, his voice darkening even more. "Ben's known all along. Ever since he saw you dig your claws into my father's heart and blame it on Alpha Gray afterward. He's known since the age of eight. EIGHT, STELLA! HE WAS EIGHT WHEN HE WATCHED HIS MOTHER BECOME A MURDERER!"

Gaps sound in the air. Looking around, he sees mixed emotions in people's eyes. Most of the younger ones are watching Stella closely, their eyes wide with shock as they wait to see what she does next. But the older ones, the ones who knew what the Lovelace Pack was before the coup d'état, are glaring at Stella with narrowed eyes full of scorn and disgust.

Whispered howls rise in pitch behind him as wolves shuffle. Alpha Lee Foster's normal brown skin has paled, his lips pulled tight in revulsion. Erin doesn't know if it's reality that has finally sunk in for him, or if it's the truth that the curse doesn't exist that has changed his mind. Either way, his Pack stands beside others now, sharp teeth and claws trained on the Harkin Pack. As does the Cooper

Pack. Alpha Ross has his fist clenched around Alpha Christian's hand, who is holding—

A gun.

Shit.

Shit shit *shit*.

The thought didn't even cross his mind that werewolves would bring a gun to a wolf fight. Just like before. Just like last time.

He didn't want this to be a bloodbath. Why must history repeat itself?

A gun. A blue-tipped arrow.

He shakes his head.

Focus on the present.

Right now, without a doubt, everyone in his Pack is willing to fight with him. Ben had reassured him multiple times throughout the week that Victor had talked to each wolf under the age of twenty-five about Stella. They were all made to hear her misconduct and lies, and choose for themselves. Erin trusted Ben's words; he trusted that his Pack would side with them. Even though he knows Stella, knows how good she is with her words. How she gets even better in front of an audience. He went into this night knowing that, should Stella refuse to go down without a fight, some wolves could be swayed back to her side.

But ... they could also be swayed to *their* side.

Whatever remaining worry in his heart slides away. His spirit stands proud, skin rippling as newfound strength floods his system. His eyes shine gold.

"Come on, Aunt Stella," Victor jeers. "This fight is outnumbered. There are representatives from fifty-two Packs here tonight. You only have two of them left on your side." Victor points at the Harkin and Reed Packs now foolishly clustered in between the back fence and the middle of the yard, the Treelark Pack snarling like guards in front of them. "You remember when you taught me how to do additions and subtractions? Can you do the math now?" He swishes his hand to where the Lovelace Pack, as well as the rest of Victor and Erin's allies, have prowled forward.

Stella flinches and growls menacingly, her eyes widening in understanding as the numbers sink in. She snaps at Victor, her canine teeth clanking together like a glass plate that's been smashed on the floor. Erin jumps off the bench and prowls toward her. He's much bigger than she is, his head at least two feet taller than hers. He looks down at her with pleading eyes.

'You're surrounded,' he says to her through the bond. 'We weren't sitting around and twiddling our thumbs this whole time. It wasn't hard getting the Packs allied with you to switch to our side. And though some here tonight still remain undecided, don't you think they'll fight if provoked? Do you think they'll choose you?' He gestures to the yard with his head, at the Packs that remain undecided, now standing close to the back porch. 'Look around! In what world would any wolf let you be the supreme ruler? That right never belonged to you.'

'That's how it once was!' Stella's calculating eyes flick over all the Packs, pupils dilating until hardly any of the green is left. Without warning, she shifts, hands held out. Goosebumps sprinkle across her nude skin, but she pays it no mind.

"Listen to me, please," she pleads. "I am doing this for us. We know the tale, the stories of how we used to be one before the split, with one Alpha to rule us all. There are texts, there is proof! We were strong then. We fought hard and won the battle against the humans. We can have that strength again. I can lead us forward on that path! My blood is of his blood—the Alpha of the one Pack from after the battle. He protected the Packs' most precious treasure during the fight, the one the old King of the humans tried to take away. I-I-I have seen the clues, I can find that treasure for us. We can share it! But the Moon Goddess ruined it all. She turned on us and created that damned curse—"

"No," Erin speaks. He's shifted back, standing nude. Victor grabs a discarded suit jacket from the ground and takes a step, but Erin stops him. He is wolf now. This is how wolves live. So, as such, he will address their kind as one of them.

"You don't know what you are talking—"

"I do," Erin interrupts Stella, voice firm. He takes a deep breath, arms held loose at his side and head high. Like a prince. Like a wolf. "I do know, more than anyone, what I speak of. You are right. There was once one Pack, with one Alpha to rule them all. Alpha Alaric, and then ... Tala." He shakes his head. "You are not from that blood, Stella, but the blood that came after."

"See! Then—"

"We did not defeat the humans. The wolves were strong, and they fought hard in that battle. The legends are steeped in truth. But ... but humans are selfish and cunning. They have no honor. They lie and trick. Some of your blood even fell for their lies, and, even with the Moon Goddess and her husband's help, the wolves lost. Both sides lost. The battle—" Erin sighs, turning from Stella to face the crowd.

Those crying already know. He hates that he's making them relive those moments.

"I know all this because I was there. What you call a curse was a blessing. To me," he looks over his shoulder at Victor, "and to my mate. That is something I am forever, eternally, grateful for."

Victor steps forward, lacing his hands with Erin's.

"Time has changed, and our kind has evolved. And honestly, I think we're better off for it. There is no treasure. That which you speak of—what was being protected that day—was me. Human prince turned half wolf. Kazr of your blood was protecting me as I lay dying on the battlefield. He then did what he could afterward, freeing the trapped wolves my father had in the dungeons and keeping our kind hidden for as long as he could. He passed on the title to his son, and that son to his, and so on and so on, the blessing not being forgotten. But with the split ... well ... I guess wolves learned to adapt. Human greed had spread, and the wolves ate it up to survive." Erin turns back to Stella. "There is no curse. There is no great power or treasure. You are not Alpha. You are simply a murderer, and I won't stand for that in *my* Pack. Your history has been built on a lie, an old bitch session from hateful wolves eons ago. Just like you."

"You've lost, Stella," Erin snarls.

"LIKE HELL I HAVE!"

She shifts back, her fur standing as straight as a rod along her back. Hardening her eyes, she pounces. Erin has just enough time to push Victor off the bench, sending a prayer to the Goddess that he lands safely, and shifts. Stella wraps her paws around his neck and pushes him back, her teeth aiming for his jugular. He brings his own paws around Stella's back, letting her push him onto the hard ground. He winces as the scalding fire pit stings his ear on the way down. With Stella's sharp, yellow teeth mere inches from ripping his throat out, he uses the momentum to raise his feet and kick her off.

Erin's wish didn't come true.

Guilt claws at his insides. He has failed Her.

Once more, their Mother Moon Goddess will have to watch her children fight in a bloodbath.

All hell breaks loose.

How many graves will they dig this time?

FIFTY

The sound of ripping clothes fills the air as wolves start shifting. The ground shakes as they run at each other without holding back, their full speed and strength let loose like starving dogs from a cage. Erin's attention is pulled from the snarling and barking when Victor appears beside him, his cold, wet nose pushing at his side. He licks his burned ear.

'Ok?' Victor asks down the bond, his voice soft with worry.

Erin rolls over and stands, shaking out his sore muscles. His front leg might be fractured, but besides that ... He turns and nuzzles Victor's throat.

'Yeah, hardly a scratch.' He'll heal quickly. Victor's rounded eyes trail down to his red paws. 'Stella's blood, from her back,' Erin clarifies. Victor huffs out a shuddering breath and nods before turning to face his enraged aunt. She's being pinned down by a shifted Ben; the only difference between their deep brown coats and green eyes is the splotches of red blood clumping in her fur.

Erin hears wood breaking and snaps his head toward the gazebo. He lets out a huff of relief when he sees that it stands still. It was the wooden fence behind it that had been snapped in half from a wolf falling on it. And that's not all.

Grass has been upturned all over the yard, the fences broken like they were at the start of summer. Stone is broken. Flowers are torn. Food is all over the grass, staining the back of the house. There's even a gap missing from the porch, the glass from the window behind it scattered across the dark wood.

The metallic stench of blood dances in the air. Wolves are getting injured. Broken bones are snapping and healing. Canines are clamping on arms, shredding skin and muscle. Wolves fight roughly, from the house to the forest.

No arrows rain down on them.

Noses break.

No swords are plunged into stomachs.

Fur is engulfed in flame, a hose yanked from the spiral beside the house to douse the fire.

No wolf is dying in a pool of blistering poison.

Wolves are shifting and howling and snarling and *crying*—

Erin doesn't want anyone to die. He only wanted them to be punished. To be locked away. He didn't think it'd escalate like this. He didn't think the wolves would be even more ferocious than before, so willing to turn on each other.

Even if it is to protect.

Even if they are trying to ensure a future where Her Hope can come true.

This is not the way.

She would not want them fighting this way.

Erin's blood pumps.

All this death, all this blood and chaos and destruction ... It's all because of Stella.

Erin growls low in his throat. Victor licks his snout, eyes hard. He sees what Erin does. Feels the same pain and anger. Placing his front two paws on the stone bench, Victor lifts his head into the sky, letting out a commanding howl.

Finish it.

Now.

Wolves howl around him in response.

Leaving them to it, trusting his Pack and allies to hold their own, Erin turns his attention to Stella. She's fighting her son, their tails rigid and legs tense as they circle each other. Ben pounces, pinning Stella, but she dodges and twists to the side, causing Ben to land half on top of her and half on the ground. Her jaw breaks open, wasting no time in sinking her teeth into his shoulder. So close to his jugular. Ben howls, a high-pitched welp that bleeds red.

Red.

Red.

Red.

Victor runs toward her the second she pushes Ben off and tackles her to the ground. They roll around, nipping and clawing at each other's flesh. Erin jumps and digs his claws into her back, right above her pre-existing wound.

Stella lets out a bone-curdling howl as she rises onto her hunches. Erin holds on, letting gravity pull his claws down her back and through her injury before he lets go. He uses her like a springboard, pushing her away from him and landing beside Victor.

'Stand down, Stella,' Victor commands. He takes a step toward her, blood dripping from his teeth. The breeze dances around them, carrying Victor's Alpha command with it. Erin realizes it then, as the fighting around them dies down, leaving hurt whimpers as the only sound to fight for dominance against Victor's words on the breeze. The wolves may have branched off and formed new Packs, electing their own families as Alphas. But the genes are still there. The bond, the loyalty, the *instinct* to the one Alpha still exists.

The old bond can still be heard howling.

'I don't want to kill you, Aunt. But I will if I must.'

Stella shifts and staggers in the middle of the field. Her hair is bloody and loose as it falls around her face and into her irrational eyes. "Kill me? HA! Please, you could never kill me. You are WEAK. PATHETIC! And I ... I refuse to live in a rotten cell for the rest of my life, and I sure as hell won't be giving any of you the satisfaction of *taking* what's mine," she grits, jaw clenched and throat tight.

Something dangerous and frenzied glints in her eyes as she spits the words into the air. It's not determination or strength of will. She knows she has lost and has given up.

Pride.

Confidence.

A true wolf's bane.

So much pride wafts from her shattered form as she laughs manically. The sound is toneless, more aligned with quick breathing and a snarky grin. It's nothing at all like the windchimes Erin heard the first day he arrived here.

Stella raises a hand in the air, the moonlight raining down around her lovingly. A final caress by the Goddess to her lost child.

A final spell blessed.

It makes no difference.

Not even Hëna's light can brighten Stella's dead soul anymore. And Stella doesn't seem to gather any comfort from the divine Mother's goodbye.

"I. AM. STELLA!" The shrill scream flies through the air, the trees seeming to bend around the noise in an attempt to avoid it. The claws on her right hand elongate, and she stabs them into her heart. Her eyes flick to her children. Ben has shifted back and is holding a weeping Beatrice in his arms. When did she get here? She was meant to be staying with Fletcher and Layla in town at the arcade, with the other kids—a way to keep them out of sight. To ensure that, should the worst-case scenario take place, and they all died, wolf kind would live on. Properly. With someone who knew the truth. The modern version of a hollowed tree truck hidden in the forest.

She must have run back to check. To help them fight. Damn that blood running through her veins. They can never sit back silently. Always so willing to fight, to protect those they love …

Ben's face is passive. His eyes are pained. Just like his mother's.

As the pain begins to swell within her dark green eyes, the last of her control finally slipping away, Stella digs her claws deeper into her chest before dragging them down to her belly button.

No hesitation.

No flinch.

No one dares to move as the sound of flesh tearing and bones breaking fills the air like thunder. Stella makes no noise as she falls. No pained yell or trembling lips whimper for help.

Even in death, she was as confident as a Queen.

Erin looks toward Victor. He feels a weight unhook from deep within his heart and lift off his shoulders, dispersing in the moonlit sky.

It's over.

It's over.

It's over ...

FIFTY-ONE

Erin sits in the gazebo with a black canvas bag beside him, waiting for the sun to rise. He was hoping that soaking up the first rays of the sun would help his skin appear less dull. The vitamin D has to be stronger at sunrise, right? Untainted by pollution and all that.

Regardless of whether the old wives' tale helps rid the dark circles from under his eyes or not, it's warm. Erin leans back against the cold wood and grabs a pillow to clutch in his lap, closing his eyes. The night was long. He tried to sleep afterward; they all did. But not even Victor's comforting presence wrapped tightly around his back—his silk sheets pulled all the way up to his nose so the husky scent of sandalwood and leather engulfed him—could relax him fully.

There were no dreams.

There was nothing.

And that hurt more than anything.

After Stella stabbed herself, the Harkin Pack was subdued quickly. Christian Reed and his Pack gave no struggle, either. It was like Stella's claws hadn't just stabbed her heart, but the hearts of all those around her also, draining them of energy. A curse, finally broken.

Matt Harkin was the worst of them, brown eyes bulging out of his face as he pranced around, howling, trying to blame the Goddess for Stella's demise. His Pack ring glinted on his finger, and Erin had to look away. The red color was so similar to Stella's hair. To her blood. To the red strawberries that were always brought to mind with her scent.

Red.

Red.

Red.

Victor suggested everyone retire for the night, let the Lovelace Pack grieve the death of one of their own, and reconvene the next night—after a proper burial—to hold an actual Council Meeting. The other Alphas agreed. Everyone was tired and overwhelmed, and healers needed time to help the wounded enough for proper conversations to be held between Packs. The children would be returning soon, and parents needed to think of how they were going to explain everything to them.

Especially the curse.

In some twisted game, the curse *was* real. Chaos did rain down upon them after Erin and Victor met, brought together from two opposite sides of the country. It just wasn't their blood that filled a grave.

Fate and Instinct. What mischievous spirits they are.

Luckily, Stella was the only casualty, but the Packs that rebelled alongside her still need to be punished for their crimes. Dread heaves in his gut thinking about having to discuss those punishments. For the first time, he thanks King Halian's insistence that he sit in on all those meetings. His experience gained then will come in handy now.

Especially when Victor and him tell the rest of the Pack in Bellmore what has happened.

Sharp pain stabs behind his eyes. It travels along his cheek and across his nose. He frowns, groaning softly as he lets go of the pillow in his lap to rub at his temples. And then there's the part where he'll be required to answer questions about his past life ...

"You haven't slept yet, have you?"

Erin flinches, his eyes flying to the large, lumberjack of a man standing at the entrance to the gazebo. It's a testament to his parents' skills that not one of the steps creaked when Alpha Adam Treelark climbed them.

Erin exhales, a single chuckle passing by his torn lip. "Is it obvious?"

Adam laughs, the sound deep and warm as he takes a seat beside Erin. "No, your dad used to be the same way. Gray could never fall asleep the night before a Council Meeting. How did he put it again?" His head tilts as his brain tries to recall a conversation from long ago. "If the mind is awake—"

"Then so too shall be the eyes," Erin finishes with a rueful smile. He takes a deep breath and clutches the pillow tighter, pulling it farther up his chest. Like a shield for his heart. "My adoptive mother used to say that when I was little and couldn't sleep. Now I know where she got it from."

"Hmm." Adam smiles sadly as he looks out at the yard. "I'm sorry about the property. I hear your family spent near two months on the landscaping."

"Eh, it's ok." Erin shrugs. "It's not as bad as I thought."

Thankfully, the house wasn't damaged. Landscaping, he can easily fix. Wiping food away and repainting wood? That's easy. But completely renovating a wooden house when all Erin had planned for the last week of summer break was cuddling Victor in his soft bed, lying nude in the grass under sparkling stars, and throwing midnight parties with his friends?

That wouldn't have been a headache, but an everlasting migraine.

Erin glances toward the cracks crisscrossing like spider webs near the fire pit in the adjacent corner of the yard. "Besides, I think the ranch has character now. It was lacking in ..."

"Chaos?" Adam supplies. Erin nods, laughing alongside him as Adam drapes an arm over the back of the gazebo. "Well, you may look like your father, but you certainly have your mother's spirit, that's for sure. I don't know where you got those golden eyes from, however."

Erin grins and looks down. He remembers the dream he had of the two wolves, one with ocean blue eyes and one with steel-colored eyes. If he weren't Prince Nahale, reincarnated, what color eyes would he have now? Maybe one blue eye and one gray eye. Heterochromia, like Mr. Wolf. He smirks. That would have been a look for sure. Victor would have loved it.

"How's your arm? I saw you take quite a tumble at the start." Adam leans forward on the bench and places a gentle hand on Erin's shoulder, patting it twice.

"Good." Erin nods. "It healed quickly." He notes Adam doesn't have a scratch on him. Experience as a wolf, perhaps? Has he fought in battle before? Erin tilts his head to the side, mind trying to remember what it is the Treelark Pack does for a living. Arms dealership? Military men? *Politics*? It was something—

"You were very brave last night," Adam whispers, voice soft. His brown eyes seem old, much older than Erin knows him to be. It settles something in his heart, like a comforting hug he didn't know he needed but was expecting. "Now let's do it all again." Adam stands. "I'll see you later tonight, Erin Bellmore of the Lovelace Pack. I'd love to chat with you more, but it seems someone else is in need of your presence." At Erin's confused look, Adam points to his phone on the table. The screen glows, a photo of three human shadows, two of them holding peace signs in the air, lights the space around them.

Erin's heart flutters in anticipation.

"Yes, of course." Erin stands as well, holding out his hand. Adam grins as his large, rough hand wraps around Erin's, shaking it once before walking casually toward the forest. Erin watches him until his figure disappears behind the trees, the smell of pine needles trailing after him.

Was he brave? Telling everyone the truth ... was it the right thing? Guilt eats him, still. There's a possibility it would have come out eventually, but it also might not have. He only spoke of him and Victor, but this secret belongs to so many other wolves, too. He knows this is not the outcome She had wanted ... but ... she created this world for them to live freely, did she not? So, doesn't that mean letting them choose?

His phone rings again.

Right. At least his friends' questions will provide good diplomatic answering practice.

Grabbing his phone, he holds it out in front of him and presses accept. The screen flashes, and he has only moments to breathe in the silence one last time before the call officially connects.

"ARE YOU ALIVE?"

Erin flinches, eyes blinking rapidly at Fletcher's scream. "Yes, I am alive. We're all alive. I texted you last night."

"Good," he sighs dramatically. He's sitting at his desk in his room. "Just making sure Stella hadn't stolen your phone or anything."

"God, she wouldn't go that far to trick us anymore, not if everyone was dead." Layla rolls her eyes before hesitating. The glow from the lamp behind the couch casts an eerie shadow across half her face. "Would she?"

"You didn't meet the bitch, Lay." Fletcher shivers. "Like a parasite," he whispers.

Erin laughs under his breath, half listening as his friends debate Stella's evil tactics. It's good to hear their voices. His body relaxes, tension from his shoulders he didn't realize was still bundled tight finally releases.

"Oh, where are your parents?" Layla asks around the glass straw in her mouth, drawing him out of his thoughts. "I thought they would have been with us last night, ya know, in case any of the other wolves decided to branch off and stage an assassination attempt."

"They wouldn't do that." Erin looks to the side, one eye twitching. At least he thinks they wouldn't do that. "Mom and Dad have gone to see a movie tonight with some old friends. Liri, I think her name was, and her husband. I don't remember his name."

"Ah, lucky!" Layla brings her leg up onto the couch, her chin resting on her knees. "We should go to the movies before summer is up."

"Tsk, tsk." Fletcher flicks a finger in front of the screen. "Foolish human thou is! Why, the wolves have-est a home movie theatre with our names embroidered on the plush leather seats! We shall convene there for movie gathering hither-to!"

"Oh my God," Erin snorts. "The seats aren't embroidered. And that's not how you use hither-to."

"Wait! The ranch!" Layla puts her iced coffee down quickly, practically bouncing out of her seat with how fast her legs are shaking. "Does that mean us three can use the ranch after y'all leave? I mean, it'll be empty, but the plants will need watering. Right, Erin?"

"She has a point." Fletcher points toward her, posh Shakespearean accent forgotten.

"I'll ask Victor, but I'm sure he'll say yes."

As if summoned, a laugh flows toward him.

"Stop, it's overflowing!"

Erin turns to the house and catches sight of Victor and Ben laughing through the open kitchen window. He locks eyes with Ben and raises his hand in a wave. Ben waves back before turning to Victor. Erin focuses his attention back on the screen.

"Is that him?" Layla asks, her voice drops. "Is he ok? And Ben?"

Erin nods, not trusting his voice to speak until he gulps, licking his lips a few times. He texted them before getting into bed last night that the Council Meeting was going to re-happen the following evening and that Stella had died, but she was the only one. For once, neither of them replied. He was thankful for that, for letting him simply exist in the shock of the events beside those of his kind.

He sighs. "I should get going now. Lots to do today. I'll call you guys later for a proper in-person debrief?"

"A hundred percent." Layla nods.

"I've booked you in, friend." Fletcher salutes.

He loves these people in his life so fucking much.

Erin laughs, waving as they say their final goodbyes. As much as he would love to talk with them all day long, he does need to focus on today, on what his life will look like now. University is starting back up soon; an email sits drafted on his laptop to the school board.

He's been too scared to press send. To get Victor's opinion. To discuss the option his heart has already decided on.

No matter how much he knows it's going to *ache*.

He resumes his watch of the morning sun, chewing on his bottom lip. Things are changing now … for better or for worse. But at least they are alive to help this time.

Small victories, no?

"Good morning, Star." Victor places a steaming cup of coffee into Erin's hands and dips his head forward, landing a wet kiss on his cheek. The sun is almost fully over the horizon when Victor slides next to him. "Goddess, look at those freckles. I could kiss each one of them."

Erin laughs. "Good morning, Little Wolf." He takes a sip of coffee. The sweet liquid instantly boosts his energy, giving life to his tired muscles as it travels down to his stomach. "Are many people awake yet?"

Victor shakes his head and places his arm around Erin's shoulders. "Just us, or at least we're the only ones acting like it. Honestly, I doubt anyone got much sleep last night. As for those in the woods … who knows what they're up to. I can smell Alpha Adam, though. What did he want?"

"Nothing much." Erin leans into Victor's side, breathing in his scent. "Just talked about my parents a bit, and then he said we did well last night. I think he wanted to say more, but Layla and Fletcher called me."

"We'll have plenty of time tonight to talk to everyone. About everything," Victor reassures him, rubbing his hand up and down his arm.

Erin nods. "How's B?"

"I think ... it was a long time coming, according to Ben." Victor sighs heavily, his head dropping down to rest on top of Erin's. "The burial service today will be tough, though. Despite it all—"

"There was good. I know. Those parts of her can't be erased. I would never ask them to be either." Erin holds his mug in one hand so the other can cup Victor's cheek. Despite all her wrongdoings, Stella was still a good person at one point in her life. And she was Pack. Honor and tradition alone demand them offer others a chance to say goodbye. Especially the kids.

"Greed is still a poison deadly to humans," Erin utters. "And werewolves are half human, no matter how some may try to hide it. No matter how she created us to be." Instinct is instinct. A scary thing indeed. You can't fight against it nor resist it, no matter how hard you may try.

"Humans were born from us, which means we're the root of it all. Is that what you're saying?"

"Your words," Erin says with a shrug.

"Well, right you are." Victor leans over Erin to place his empty mug on the stone table in front of them. When he turns back, there's a mischievous twist to his lips. Erin raises his brows in question, holding the mug to his lips to hide his responding smirk.

"When I talked to the other Packs in an attempt to get them to ally with us during our fake break-up, I was quite surprised to hear that you had such a diplomatic side to you." Victor turns in his seat so one leg is resting on the bench as he faces Erin. He places his hand on Erin's knee, running it along his thigh repeatedly.

"Well, I was a Prince back in the day." Erin places his mug onto the table, eyes glinting darkly. Victor bursts out in laughter, the deep timber ringing like music to Erin's ears. A possessive need to keep that music to himself causes his breath to hitch and his heart to double in speed. He places a hand on Victor's neck and drags him down until their lips crash together.

Victor parts his lips instantly to slip his tongue into Erin's mouth. Shuffling, he grabs Erin's hips to pull him into his lap and wraps his arms around Erin's middle. Protective. Safe. The kiss is nothing hot. It's not steamy nor causes heat to rush anywhere but to his beating heart. It's firm and real.

Real.

Real.

Real.

"This is real," Erin whispers, pulling back. He threads his fingers through the hair along Victor's neck. Eyes wide and searching. Needing to make sure that this whole thing hasn't been a dream. "You've found me."

"This is real, Star. I've found you." Victor smiles. He places a hand over Erin's heart. "I can hear you, I can see you, I can smell you. And you can do all that to me, too. I'm here. We're alive. We're going to be ok."

"Yeah." Erin takes a deep breath, swallowing the wave threatening to pull him over. "Yeah." He chuckles softly. "Sorry ... I just ... I need you to know that I live my life *because* of you, not *for* you," he articulates each word. Slowly. Making sure Victor hears each one. The sun turns his hazel eyes into intense golden arrows, fixed exclusively on his mate.

"I know, I'm the same." Victor nods his head and cups Erin's face. "We do this because we want to. I chose you, before the stars bound us and fate tied our blood. Before anyone else got involved. It's you and me. My Prince. My Human. My Wolf. My Mate. Always."

Love.

Erin has never felt so loved before.

Tension disintegrates from his bones. Worry he's been carrying with him since he first walked into Donny's Warehouse and saw those twin moon-filled eyes latch onto him.

"Good." Erin smiles, tracing a finger under Victor's eyes. "Good." Quickly, he bends over to pick up the bag, presenting it to Victor. "For you."

With a frown, Victor reaches inside the bag and pulls out a thick black book. Fingers trail over the pressed leather cover. A black wolf, standing on a rock with its head tipped back in a silent howl. His mouth drops open in a silent gasp as he flips through it.

"I told you back in June that I'd get you something proper for your birthday," Erin says as Victor flicks through the photo album, lips slightly parted in awe as he gazes upon candid photos Erin's taken of his Pack over the past two months.

"I didn't mean ... That was such a hectic day, and I completely forgot," Victor whispers. He looks at Erin with wide eyes. "Holy shit, this is the best birthday present I've ever received."

"Really?" Erin chuckles. He takes the photo album out of Victor's hand and places it beside them, along with the empty bag, before leaning forward once more. Their chests are flush together, his voice low as he whispers against Victor's lips. "That's too bad because I have a few more gifts prepared."

"Oh?" Victor nips at Erin's lips. Erin kisses him back quickly before standing and rounding the table. He holds his hands out over it, fingers wiggling in the air expectantly. Victor tilts his head slightly, picking the pillow Erin dropped off the floor before standing in front of him. He grips Erin's hands tightly.

"My Little Wolf, my love. I promise you, in the presence of Hëna, Mother Goddess of the Moon and her eternal husband, Ylli, God of the Stars, to wait for you."

Victor's hands squeeze Erin's, his lips pulling inward. As his thumb traces circles over Erin's palm. He recognizes the words. It's not exactly the same, and it's definitely no grand ceremony. But ... who does big weddings nowadays, anyway? He spares a glance at the sky, eyes catching on the setting moon and glimmering stars.

Watching.

Waiting.

That's all the audience they'll ever need.

Erin continues, "With my nose now as strong as yours, and my vision sharper, my heart is still just as strong, if not stronger. No matter how lonely. No matter how long it takes. I'll wait for you. I'll love you. And should I find you first, which I technically did,"—Victor laughs—"I'll chase your paw prints in the earth. I'll run to your light. For you are the one I choose to bind to. My love is eternal, just like the stars in the sky."

Erin smiles, waiting as Victor takes a deep breath.

"My Star, I promise you, in the presence of Hëna, our Mother Goddess of the Moon and her eternal husband, Ylli, God of the Stars, to find you. To love you. Even if you look different. Even if you smell different. I'll find you. I'll remember you. I'll love you. Always." He reaches forward, hand lingering on Erin's cheek, thumb brushing underneath his eye. Just as before. "For you are the one I choose to bind to. My love is eternal, just like the moon in the sky. And should I be born human in our next life, well," Victor's eyes grin, "then maybe we can talk swapping roles."

Erin chokes, happy tears welling in his eyes. "I, Erin Storm-Bell-more-Lovelace-whoever the fuck," he giggles as Victor laughs, wiping the tears from Erin's cheeks, "proclaim this vow of love as eternal and true. My heart knows this sworn oath to be true, so I speak it from my lips as such."

"And I, Victor Lovelace, Alpha of the New York Pack, proclaim this vow of love eternal and true. I engrave it on my soul and speak it from my lips," Victor declares, voice soft.

"You may now kiss the bride," Erin says, voice deep in mockery of someone else's voice.

Victor smirks, leaning forward across the table to claim Erin's lips. It's gentle, soft. It's spiced leather and rain in a forest. It's early morning coffee and maple syrup drenched pancakes. It's mint and Nutella. And strawberry ice cream and blooming flowers.

It sets fireworks off in his stomach.

"You said there were a few gifts?" Victor asks against Erin's lips. "I don't know how you'll beat this, but what's the other one?"

"Ah." Erin rounds the table so he's standing in front of Victor. "I spoke with Healer Haven beforehand. I wanted to check."

"Check what?"

Erin lifts his head, standing on his tippy toes just slightly so Victor doesn't have to bend his head as he whispers, "Time to get started on those promises we made in our vows, Little Wolf."

FIFTY-TWO

Laughter fills the air around her, and she turns away from the giant mansion.

Ylli stands—her shawl thrown over his shoulder so she does not dirty it—beside a wolf with striking gray eyes. Grins beam on both their faces as they watch another wolf, Shaun, she remembers his name as, try to wrangle a couple of young cubs. One has blonde hair that glints in the sunlight as he makes use of his fast legs, having just learned how to balance on two of them instead of the four he learned first. His pale ocean eyes are set firm in concentration. The other is older by a few years; his red hair is easily seen through the purple flowers as he tries to climb the newly built gazebo. It's so similar to his father's and mother's that she caught a glimpse of, before they left.

Hëna smirks. It truly is beautiful, the gazebo. Her old friend pulled through to help bend and twist the vines of wisteria around it. The vines just like—

"I want you to name him."

A gust of wind blows around them, ruffling her long braid down her back. Her old friend's eldest daughter always likes to make her chilling entrance known when the seasons change. Tightening her arm around her new friend's arm, she turns back around.

"How do you know it's going to be a boy, Stacy? Does being a werewolf offer you secret magical powers or something?"

Stacy laughs. The sound of the forest reverberates around them as wisteria fills the air, mixing in with the scent of the ocean. Her new friend has an arm raised to keep the giant white sunhat on her head, lest the breeze yanks it off, and her freshly washed long brown hair blows all around them. She would have thought making sure the deep blue sundress she wears doesn't fly up would be the more pressing matter.

Alas, her new friend never cared for things such as that. Her instinct is much like the wolves of old.

And she supposes the bump riding low on her stomach would help with keeping the dress in place.

"Come on." Her new friend turns her head slightly. Ocean eyes close in a beautiful smile. "Name him, please?"

Waiting.

A shutter clicks from behind them.

Found?

EPILOGUE

ONE YEAR LATER

"Where to, sir?"

Erin closes the door to the taxi and leans forward so the driver can hear him. "Bluenight Road, Bellmore. Just drive to the end of the road."

The driver nods, and Erin sits back in the seat comfortably. He's been in New York for five hours, and already the lively atmosphere is becoming background noise. Slowly, his migraine subsides as he gets closer.

Closer.

Closer.

He pulls out his headphones, ready to listen to some music Victor sent him, when his phone buzzes. With a grin, he connects the Bluetooth and accepts the video call.

"Erin!" Natalie's cheerful, paint-splattered face appears on the screen. "How'd the interview go?"

"Good. They loved my portfolio," Erin says. "One of them even asked how I got so close to wolves without being afraid."

Natalie giggles, one brow raised. "And what'd you say to that?"

"I told them that I must've been a wolf in a past life, and the animals could smell it on me. They knew I was one of them." Erin grins playfully.

His mother's giggles turn into full hoots of laughter, causing Erin to chuckle as well. He can hear shuffling in the background, and soon, John is pulling the camera away from Natalie's face so he can be seen too.

"Oh, the wolf of the hour!" John's voice booms loudly, bouncing from empty wall to empty wall. "Look at our son, interviewing at a famous photography company in New York."

"Thanks, Dad." Erin smiles softly. He sees Mr. Wolf slink past in the background. Already made himself at home, it seems. That cat could be dropped on Mars, and he'd have a new kitty litter spot found in ten minutes. "How's the move going?"

"Good, good." John nods his head confidently. "Your mom and I are just applying the finishing touches on some of the walls, then we're going to start bringing in some furniture."

"Oh, make sure you thank Victor for us again, Erin," Natalie pipes up. "It was so nice of him to let us move in here and change the design the way we wanted."

"I will. I think the place needed some warmth anyway," Erin says. "Get rid of all the bad juju and all that." His eyes soften around the edges as he recalls their excitement when Victor said they could officially move into the ranch at the start of summer. No one will be using it for the next three years, and, with Erin preparing for his move to Bellmore, Natalie and John could do with a more open, relaxed space. Especially with the business.

Erin knows Victor was being genuine; he really does care about Erin's parents like they're his own. But he could also hear another unspoken reason Victor wanted Natalie and John to move into the ranch—the whole thing reeked of Stella. Everything from the dull color scheme to the posh furniture screamed her name. Rustic farmhouse is meant to be *homey*, not whatever Stella had done.

It was a bit sad to see her final touches erased. Before round two of the Council Meeting that late summer night last year, Victor and Ben had spent all day chopping wood. They waited until dusk and made a wooden pier in the middle of the forest. Then, when the first rays of the moon touched her skin, Beatrice stepped forward and burned Stella. She was insistent that it be her, not Victor, as Alpha. Her words sounded more like a plea than a demand to his ears. He thought that's how Victor heard it, too, and why he allowed her to break tradition and let the match go herself.

Closure through an act of destruction. Like mother, like daughter.

He thought she might cry, that Ben or Victor would let a few drops fall from their clenched jaws. But they didn't.

No one did.

He didn't think too much about why afterward, seeing the clenched fists and teeth biting down on lips for hours later, he left it on an assumption that the Pack thought Stella didn't deserve people to cry for her. A final act of respect for their fellow wolf. Their packmate. Everything she got was through her own power; she brought it on herself. Whether that be her rich and glorious life, or her sacrificial death, thinking she could make herself a martyr. She caused all of it.

The sky cried, though.

The moon bright as she wept tears, a blanket of stars bright around her in comfort.

Layla and Fletcher didn't mention it again either. After the debrief two days later, their attention turned toward the status of the ranch instead. Erin was grateful for it, to be honest. He didn't know how many times he could keep reliving those moments; it was starting to take a toll.

But Layla had taken Erin's promise that Victor would let them use the ranch to heart after all. And once she starts creating, her deadlines are strict. So, during their final year at college, she, Fletcher, and Erin spent most of their time on the ranch. Beatrice joined them also, once her transfer to Green Lake was approved. It was nice, easing a part of him to have a wolf from his pack so close. But it hurt too, the blood was so similar, the resemblance striking in the right lighting, only for it not to be *him*.

Those were the days when they all cuddled together on the couch, eating ice cream and watching sad movies.

The days when he went to bed wrapped in Victor's old clothes, the green curtains dancing in the breeze from the open balcony window, and howled.

Some days will always be better than others, and the ranch was quiet when they needed to study, the vast scenery providing wondrous backdrops and focus points for Erin and Layla's photography projects, and Fletcher took the gym room in perfect stride.

Erin drew the line at adding a pool, though, at least until his parents finished moving in and making the house theirs. Which was going to be a while, since they only said they would officially move in after Erin graduated. Something about moving things around and uprooting the trees causing bad chi flow ... whatever that meant.

Now, along with the renovated front and backyard, there's a proper 'parking lot' set-up in the paddock next to the house, as well as the picturesque rock structure Natalie had first envisioned leading toward a nice trail into the woods. No sabotaged trees or broken cameras in sight.

If Erin made sure all the new designs were tailored to hold future Council Meetings, a dream whispered between swaying tree branches, warm fences, and cold lake water, speaking in the back of his mind, no one picked up on it.

"And the shed!" John wags his finger at the camera, dragging Erin out of his memories. Ah, yes, the shed. That was a hard secret to keep from his parents. After Natalie and John agreed to take over ownership of the ranch, Victor sent enough money for Erin to organize a proper work shed in one of the neighbouring paddocks. It's still bright red, but there's now insulation, ceiling fans, storage compartments, sinks, a fridge, and multiple worktables. The perfect structure for any landscaper.

"Yeah, I'll remember to tell him you said thanks," Erin chuckles. "He'll be asking me all about it anyway."

"We're nearing the edge of the road, sir," the taxi driver says, guilt evident in his voice at interrupting Erin's conversation. Erin looks out the window and sees how the busy streets and dirty sidewalks have now given way to lush green trees and a kept dirt trail.

"Ok, thank you." He catches the driver's eye in the rear-view mirror and smiles appreciatively before turning his attention back to his phone. "I'm almost home, so I have to go now. Say hi to Mr. Wolf for me. Once I've settled in, I'll come get him."

"Oh, he'll love all the attention up there, that's for sure, Son," John snorts, saluting the camera.

"Be safe, Erin. We love you!" Natalie blows a kiss to the camera before waving.

It's now or never.

"Mom."

Natalie comes back into frame, taking the phone from her husband. Worry creases her forehead. "What is it, cub?"

"I picked out a name," Erin says carefully.

Remember.

It's time.

No more secrets.

Know that it all worked out.

Natalie is silent as she walks outside, the sound of the door closing behind her loud between them. She looks confused. Shocked. A hand rakes through the ends of her long locks, no braid in sight. A blue shawl sits over her shoulders and on her head, keeping the hair out of her eyes. They squint, then widen. Like bright moons in a star-filled sky. Her throat bobs. Realization hits her so hard she plops onto the grass.

"What was the name?" she asks softly.

Erin grins, all teeth and blushing cheeks.

"Näyli."

Natalie's lips pull down as they tremble. She nods.

Erin opens his mouth to say more when the car stops.

"This is the end of the road. You sure you have the right place, kid?" the driver asks cautiously, eyes flicking across the scene through his windshield.

"I've got to go, Mom. Talk to you later. There should be a package arriving soon. Open it straight away. Okay?" He waits for her to nod one last time before hanging up.

"Kid? You hear me? I don't want no cops knocking on my door later."

"Sorry, don't worry." Erin reaches into his wallet and hands over the money for the ride. "My house isn't far from here. You won't be held accountable for my murder or anything."

The driver barks out a laugh as he counts the money. "All right, whatever you say, kid."

Erin hops out of the car and grabs his duffel bag from the trunk before he starts strolling through the trees. He waits until the taxicab is halfway down the road, the distance too far for any human eye to see, and sprints. His duffel bag is slapping against his thigh painfully, but he doesn't care because right through the trees and in the clearing is—

Victor.

Erin's breath hitches as he gazes toward Victor. He's sitting in the white wooden gazebo Storm Landscaping fixed so many years ago, the top of his mating mark peeking over the collar of his white t-shirt as he fondly watches a group of little kids play tag between the surrounding forest trees and the lush green grass.

No sea of red blood.

No field of deadly wolfsbane.

No thunderous storm lights the sky above.

Just the dark blue Victorian mansion, standing proudly with windowsills and balconies full of flowers, looking exactly as it did in the photo Erin found last year, before he knew what it meant. Even the wisteria tree inside the gazebo looks the same, albeit more weathered, as moss-covered vines wrap snugly around the white pillars.

But it's still hanging on. Strong. Just like they are. Erin readjusts the strap of his duffel bag and walks forward. Between finishing his final year in college and Victor dealing with Stella's abrupt departure, they hardly had enough time to themselves. For a whole year, minus Christmas, Thanksgiving, and a weekend getaway here and there, all they could do was send text messages and schedule video calls like any other long-distance relationship.

Neither of them admitted it, but being physically separated for that long was torture. They thought two weeks was bad? It didn't hold a candle to a whole year.

But Erin was right to make the call that anytime they met in person, it was Victor who had to come down to Texas. Looking at the sight in front of him now, he knows deep in his soul that had he come up here, there was no way he would've had the strength to leave again.

And now, his mate sits just ten feet in front of him. His smell waves at him on the breeze. His skin glows in the light of the afternoon summer sun.

Erin beams, his skin itching with excitement when he hesitates. This was the last place his parents were alive. He was born here. He had a life mapped out for him here. Looking back toward the mansion, his smile falters. There are no signs of the coup d'état anywhere in the wood. Nothing to remind any of them what took place here.

Except for him.

Looking out to the forest, he thinks back to where his mother stood with *Her*. What were they talking about? Which room in this vast property was going to be his? Stacy must have known about it all. That's why … that's why—

A feeling wells in his chest. He can't contain it anymore. As he lets the wind pick up his scent and carry it, he looks back toward Victor, toward the ghosts he knows he'll feel around every corner of the house once he finally sets foot inside.

He whispers, "I'm home. Everyone … I'm finally home."

Victor's nose twitches, eyes squinting and ears twitching before he swivels on the gazebo bench and locks eyes with Erin.

Oh, how he's missed those orbs of moonlight.

He runs into the gazebo, duffle bag plopping uncaringly onto the floor, the purple petals lying scattered over the baby blue benches and pillows billowing at the disturbance. Victor has a wide smile on his face as his arms open, ready to welcome Erin into his lap.

"Nice ring," Victor says with a smirk as his arms squeeze tightly around Erin's waist. He feels Victor inhale deeply, his nose nuzzling his mark as he desperately tries to get as much of Erin's scent deep into his lungs, into his soul, as physically possible.

Erin laughs, resting his cheek against Victor's jaw and mimicking the action. He lifts his left hand off Victor's back to wiggle the antique blue ring sitting on his index finger and the thin, silver moonstone ring on his ring finger.

"Thanks," Erin can't tell if the dancing rainbows on the wisteria tree trunk are from his rings glinting or the two glass wolf ornaments hanging in the middle of the gazebo. "Family heirloom."

Found.

Natalie places the phone down onto the grass beside her, face tilted back. John walks behind her, rubbing her shoulders. It causes her shawl to fall off her head, and her husband takes the chance to place something over her head.

A soothing star, nestled between thin silver, finds home on her forehead and between her brows.

"Näyli. What a wonderful name," she mutters. "Like a strong storm."

"Indeed, Light. I'll get us some tea," John says. He kisses the top of her head before heading inside. She hums, watching him go.

They knew.

When did the memories return?

They were never meant to remember. That wasn't the plan ...

Erin's shift. That must have been it. And the others ... Ben. He definitely knows. Those curious eyes watching, glimmering, as he blushed and smiled just like she remembered. Oh, how he has grown, though. A fine young wolf. She had never intended him to have that burden. Never intended her blessing to twist into a curse. She couldn't intervene, not again. Not as before.

Now ...

Do more wolves remember, too? How many? Is it going to ruin this—

No.

This time is different. And it's not up to her to decide, anyway. She cast her magic, placed her bets on her Hope, and they pulled through. They evolved. They won. They are alive.

Finally.

Finally.

Finally!

She laughs. Truly laughs. The sound comes from deep in her stomach, a feeling she hasn't experienced since she first created this world. These souls. These wolves. Since she first saw them sitting underneath that tree with her old friend.

"Now that's a sound I haven't heard in a while."

She grins. Impeccable timing, as always. "I laugh all the time, Liridoña."

"Come now, old friend, let's not start lying now, hm?" Liri takes a seat in the grass, whisking her head so her long golden hair falls back over her shoulder. She holds out a steaming mug of tea to her, a small box clasped underneath her arm. "Here, Ylli gave these to me."

"Thank you." She takes one of the mugs, blowing over the rim before sipping. Delicious. "What's the box for?"

Liri shrugs. "I found it on the doorstep. It's addressed to you."

Oh? She takes the box, instantly recognizing her son's handwriting. This must be the package he spoke of.

"Husband! Come out here and open this with me! We have a gift from Erin!"

"So soon?" Ylli drags a chair from the porch to where they sit in the grass, a cup of tea held between his fingers. She waits for him to sit before breaking the seal and opening the latch.

Her breath stills. Her husband hums, the sound similar to a small laugh.

"Oh my," Liri says from over her shoulder. "Well, would you look at that. It seems your dream came true, my friend."

Hëna lifts the thin silver necklace out of the box, a sigil welded out of metal hanging in the center, right above where one's collarbone would be. The crown of a king, with a bare tree running through the center of it, purple wolfsbane growing along the roots. An artifact from his people. An identifier of his status as Prince of the humans.

A reminder that they have not forgotten.

That they will never forget.

"Yes," she chokes out a laugh. "Yes, it seems it has."

She remembers Kazr taking the artifact from Nahale before the burial. Victor must have found it. Or Ben? She laughs through her nose. Brazen cubs, the whole *Pack* of them.

How nice, this thing she called instinct. To weave into the wolves, to watch it spread amongst the humans. It shrunk. It grew. It twisted and danced along to Fate's unforgiving beat, but still. They did not give up. They heard it. They clawed through the game set upon them and made new rules. Ones they will sing back to her under the light of their ancestors in the sky.

They will not forget her.

They will be free.

For Goddesses do not die, and neither will their blessings.

"Magic well cast, Wife."

"Indeed, it was, Husband."

A tragedy that ended in freedom.

How beautiful a love bond that is.

"So," Liri exhales, looking around the ranch. "It's a nice place you got here. No cobwebs and broken statues. And oh, look! Curtains not layered with dust!"

"Ha-ha." Hëna rolls her eyes, carefully placing the promise back into the box and passing it up to her husband. "I haven't lived like that in eons, so stop teasing me. I'm very emotional right now. At peace. Don't stir it up with your low jabs."

"I know. That's why I'm here." Liri winks, bumping her shoulder into her friends before taking a sip of her tea.

Hëna watches her, the way her friend's lips tighten at the corners, and not from holding back a smile. The way there are deep bags underneath her eyes, subtle on her deeply tanned skin, but there all the same. Her hair, her flared jeans, and flowing lace top ... even the sandals she kicked off before sitting down, they are as perfect and free-spirited as Mother Nature always is. But a pain and sadness cling to her. Like a thin summer blanket. She can smell it. Her magic shrinks against it.

"Do you need my help, old friend?" she asks softly, brows pinched. "What ever became of that problem you had ... your son? Time?"

"I—" Liridoña smiles sadly, the cup of tea forgotten on the ground beside her. She leans back on her arms, legs straight in front of her, and tilts her head toward the sun. She sighs. "I have chosen a warrior. A ... few warriors." She looks sidelong at her friend. "Thought I should take a page out of your book. Meddle. Pack. All that crap."

"Liri—"

"It's fine. He's fine." Liri sits straight, pulling Hëna's hands toward her. "Trust me, because I trust them. And I'm here for you now. To celebrate your win! Your cubs did it!"

Hëna sighs. "I'm letting this go for now, because I trust you." She squeezes her friend's hand. "But you must promise me that you will come to me if you need help. I will do what I can. Like how you helped me, all that time ago."

"Obvi—"

BEEP BEEP BEEEEEEEEEP BEEP BEEP BEEEEEEEEP.

"Oops." Liri scrambles, taking a brown phone out of her back pocket. A frown pulls at her lips when she reads the message there. "It's my husband. I'm needed back home. We'll have to schedule a rain check. Maybe back at your palace, if this place isn't finished yet?"

Hëna nods, standing with her friend. She hugs her tightly. "You guys are always welcome at any of my homes."

"I know. The same goes for you." Liri kisses her friend on the cheek in parting. "Oh, but now that I've said it, I can't wait to see how your old palace looks, now that you're back to your usual self, glowing and radiant. Don't forget that my home exists, and your brother's, too."

"I know, I know," Hëna laughs. "This is a favor to my cub. Once it's done, I'll be back up there. Besides, I was meaning to call my brother and see what has been keeping him too busy to help me here."

"You didn't want his help!"

"I didn't want his meddling," she clarifies. "We'll talk more later. Go, go. Don't want your beloved waiting." She waves to her friend, who walks backward to the house, blowing kisses. Her husband chuckles at her antics. And she—

"Liri!" Hëna calls, hesitant. Her friend stops, halfway up the back porch, and turns to her. This world worked out. She learned a lot. She ... maybe ...

She looks to Him. His eyes are dark, gleaming like a night sky.

Ready for new stars.

New constellations.

New Gods.

"Leave the door open on your way out."

Content Warning

This novel contains the use of explicit language, explicit sexual relations, and on-page death and suicide.

If you do not wish to read these scenes, they can be skipped, and the story still makes sense. Below are the chapters they take place in and the specific page numbers they fall onto. Reader discretion is advised.

<u>**Sexual Relations**</u>
Chapter Twenty-Eight.
Pages 283 – 288
Chapter Forty-One.
Pages 427 – 429
Chapter Forty-Three.
Pages 435 – 436

<u>**Death**</u>
Chapter Twenty-Six.
Pages 261 – 265

<u>**On-Page Suicide**</u>
Chapter Fifty.
Page 498 – 499

Acknowledgements

First—thank you, reader. This book wouldn't be possible without your support, your willingness to pick up this book and give it a chance. I know she's hefty. I know it may be daunting. But what is fantasy if not the willingness to travel to a new world and learn all it has to offer? I didn't want to give you something half-assed, and still, I feel like there is so much more of this story I could have told ... but, alas, that is the nature of summer, is it not? A quick moment in time—a blimp of existence—and then we move on.

Originally, this story was written for an online publishing firm, and I didn't get much say in the tropes and genres. Gay romance and wolf shifter stories were popular, so that is what I catered toward. But there were so many rules and regulations to follow, and these weren't just reader expectations.

So, when the opportunity presented itself to take this story off that platform, flesh it out, and self-publish it, I jumped. Back then, I felt like there was so much more to tell of Victor and Erin's story, which the near 90,000 added words can attest to.

I wanted to show a story where any kind of love was possible, that love itself was eternal, and that hope can be found in something as simple as a *laugh*. The drama didn't come from the boys being gay—that was never the point. Love doesn't have a specific color or race attached to it—it simply is. I wanted to show how truth can get twisted over time, how anyone can be greedy, and feel sad. Rage.

Happiness. *Hope*. I wanted to show how sweet relationships can be, how loyal family is—both blood and found.

All in all, I wanted to allow y'all space to witness how beautiful emotions can be. How fun life can look—and remind you that we are all human, at the end of the day. Even if we look a bit different.

I hope the magic in this story reminded you of that. That it offered you the escape you needed, and that you took some solace in the love I tried so hard to weave between the lines. Hope, Self-discovery, Love—these are all things that fuel our human instinct. Don't forget it. I don't want to say I intended to teach people to be kind or accepting, aha, I'm not trying to preach anything, but I just wanted to sprinkle a little bit of understanding.

Of magic.

That said, everyone loves a *bit* of drama, don't they?

To my editor, and bestest of friends in the whole wide world, Chloe Higgins. Thank you so, so, so, so much. I don't have enough words to actually describe how much you've helped me. This story quite literally wouldn't exist without you. None of the drafts would. All the marketing tips and tricks, dealing with my podcasts and insecurity breakdowns at 11 pm after a full day of writing—this book is credited to you as much as it is to me. You have been so incredibly understanding through this journey. I hope for our friendship and work relationship to continue for a very long time, like Liri and Hëna, so that one day I can call you 'old friend' and tease you about having a messy house with kids running amuck.

To Peter's Book Club, Jenny and Liridoña. You guys are the reason I started taking writing more seriously again and, honestly, the reason I didn't give up in this publishing career. I was lost, stagnant, waiting for other people. But you guys told me, 'Why wait? Do it now.' So, I did. I fell in love with reading even more by talking about books with you, and picked up books across so many more genres that I hadn't touched in so long. I thought I could get by simply editing other people's stories, staying in my lane, and letting all the old stories (both those already drafted and those which were only thoughts) become lost to time. But you two convinced me that wasn't my truth. You helped me see that I was basically gaslighting myself. So, thank you. Half of these characters wouldn't have been born if not for you, especially our favorite Goddess. Thank you, Liri! Let's show some love for all the beautiful Albanian names you introduced me to. And thank you for reminding me what true friendship looks like.

To my beta readers, Lili and Jason, and those who read the OG version of this novel, your insight and perspectives as readers were incredibly insightful. I knew there was a lot that I needed to fix during editing, but having that validation and confirmation that I was on the right track made all the difference in my completing this book on time. All the feedback helped so much in honing the techniques I wanted to use in this book and in delivering the message that I wanted to express. And it was a massive ego boost that you all liked it, even with so much re-writing that needed to be done still. I mean, nearly 34K words from what you all read in draft one to draft two? Insane. That's a whole new book and plotline ahaha. But you all saw the vision and encouraged me. You saw the potential, and for that encouragement, I shall be eternally grateful.

To my dear mother, Angela. The interior design was better than I could have imagined. All the love and thank you's you've heard me say already. I won't eat up words here because everything that needs to be spoken has already been said. You know me most in this world, whether you think so or not. That is true. Mothers know best, after all, ahaha. And if not, if there are words left unspoken, well then, whisper them to the moon and I'll ask the stars to send my reply. But thank you again. I love you!

To Mr. Mason—my best friend, my son, my brother, my loyal wolf in an anxiety dog skin. I know you can't read, but let me use this space to talk about you. Your barking and insistence to sit on my lap while I was working in bed has not been forgotten. Not even the time you moved and hit delete on the whole document. But I know how hard a dog's life can be—especially one who is 12 years old—so thank you for being my electric blanket in winter while I was editing draft two and making social media content. Mr. Miles, too, wanting to come in and out of my room while I was working, was not a distraction at all; it was a forced break filled with annoyance and made me so incredibly irate that I was able to write Stella's chapters easily. You two are shits, but I love you. I hope for you to always find joy and freedom howling at the moon and running through the stars (but not yet, boys, we still have plenty of time left here).

And lastly—to my pack. R.I.P.bb. If I write any thanks, I'll cry. I'm getting teary even now thinking about how much I love you three to bits. But please, just know your support and love and honesty are what made me want to write so much friendship into this story. I wanted to try and showcase what a healthy platonic love between humans looks like. I hope I did that ok. I hope I was able to proudly show you all off. You three—Emma, Chloe, Lilijana—are the three things I will never stay humble about. I *fucking* love you biddies, and I am so *fucking* proud of you. Look at us. We fucking did it! If meeting you used up all my luck in this life, then so be it. But I believe that everything happens for a reason. We were meant to be friends, until the moon falls from the sky and the stars wither and die.

About the author

Stories are everywhere in this world, timeless constructs that help society develop and grow. So, it's about time we listened, don't you think?

Anisa Worthington is a fantasy and contemporary fiction author. She writes stories that are inherently about magic and love, weaving one or, often, both elements into her stories. Because that's what she believes storytelling is. Magic. Ever since she was young, she's had this unwavering belief. She credits Rick Riordan, Shakespeare, and the many musicals her mother would play on repeat for this belief, too.

From growing up in Texas, USA, to settling in Sydney, NSW, reading, analysing, and imagining stories has been a constant in Anisa's life. If she isn't sitting beside her dog with her nose buried in a book—either reading or providing an editing service—she's listening to music and daydreaming about future fantastical adventure stories.